THE HEMLOCK QUEEN

By Hannah Whitten

THE NIGHTSHADE CROWN

The Foxglove King

The Hemlock Queen

THE WILDERWOOD

For the Wolf

For the Throne

THE HEMLOCK QUEEN

The Nightshade Crown: Book Two

HANNAH WHITTEN

orbit

orbitbooks.net

Cover design by Lisa Marie Pompilio
Cover illustration by Mike Heath | Magnus Creative
Cover background image by Shutterstock

Map by Charis Loke

Orbit
Hachette Book Group
1290 Avenue of the Americas
New York, NY 10104
orbitbooks.net

First Edition: April 2024
Simultaneously published in Great Britain by Orbit

Orbit is an imprint of Hachette Book Group.
The Orbit name and logo are registered trademarks of Little, Brown Book Group Limited.

Library of Congress Cataloging-in-Publication Data
Names: Whitten, Hannah, author.
Title: The hemlock queen / Hannah Whitten.
Description: First edition. | New York : Orbit, 2024. | Series: The nightshade crown ; book 2
Identifiers: LCCN 2023036442 | ISBN 9780316435291 (hardcover) |
ISBN 9780316435499 (ebook)
Subjects: LCGFT: Fantasy fiction. | Novels.
Classification: LCC PS3623.H5864 H46 2024 | DDC 813/.6—dc23/eng/20230816
LC record available at https://lccn.loc.gov/2023036442

ISBNs: 9780316435291 (hardcover), 9780316577120 (BarnesAndNoble.com signed edition), 9780316435499 (ebook)

Printed in the United States of America

LSC-C

Printing 1, 2023

Let this be a reminder that you are wholly your own.

LA VIE ET LE JOUR
APO
CALDIEN
BURNT ISLES
RATHARC
GOLDEN MOUNT
Kettleburgh

MAP BY CHARIS LOKE

Time present and time past
Are both perhaps present in time future,
And time future contained in time past.
If all time is eternally present,
All time is unredeemable.

—T. S. Eliot, "Burnt Norton"

The young man said he found the Fount,
For which he had long sought.
He found it on the Golden Mount,
And all his questions brought.

He asked about the sun and he asked about the sea,
He asked about wind, moon, and fire,
The earth beneath his knees.

The Fount answered his questions
So he moved on to requests,
His reason was eternal life,
Endless, with no need to rest.

The Fount said that it wouldn't work, It said there was no way,
Not while he was human
And a human he would stay.

So he brought his friends and lovers,
He sailed them to the Mount,
And they drank the soul of everything
Out of the gleaming Fount.

—Auverrani tavern song, outlawed in 400 BGF,
when the Church was established on the
mainland and the pantheon officially
recognized as divine

THE HEMLOCK QUEEN

Chapter One

Everything is everything. All powers move together and come from the same source.

–A prophecy of Elan Adabbo, Kadmaran monk. Deemed unnecessary for cataloging when sent for consideration to the Priest Exalted.

There were many things Lore didn't feel like doing today. Getting up early. Choking down breakfast. Her head felt like it was inhabited by a thousand tiny men with hammers, courtesy of the wine she'd downed before bed to make sure she didn't dream. The combination of ache and dry, sour mouth made even the most delicate pastries taste like something from a refuse pile. Getting dressed also wasn't high up on her list of things she wanted to do, and she'd let Juliette, her lady's maid, stuff her into a pale-peach gown that really did nothing for her coloring just because she didn't have the energy to fight about it. That was typical for her, these days. Not having the energy to fight about things.

But out of all that, entering the catacombs was still number one on her list of things she absolutely, positively did *not* want to do.

"Are you ready?" Bastian stared into the newly opened well, his dark brows slashed low over his eyes. The gleam of the rising sun made them a lighter brown, rich and whiskey-colored. A slight golden phosphorescence swirled around his fingers, light gathered from the air, faint enough that it might be imagined.

Lore knew it wasn't.

The Presque Mort ringing the well couldn't see the Spiritum, since they couldn't channel it. Still, they eyed the Sainted King with a layering of trepidation and awe that didn't mix quite right.

For all that he was the herald of their god's return, in power if not in flesh, the Presque Mort still didn't seem to care much for Bastian Arceneaux.

"No," Lore answered, even though she knew it wouldn't make a difference. No, she wasn't ready to go back down into the dark. No, she wasn't ready to try to lay all those corpses to rest, the victims of the Mortem that Anton had pulled out of her and sent to kill entire villages overnight.

But they were *her* victims. Her responsibility.

And even as she told herself that the very last thing she wanted to do was channel Mortem, her fingers still itched for it.

Bastian glanced at her as if he'd heard the thought. Both of them. But when he turned away from the well and reached up to cup her cheek, he only addressed the first. "It wasn't your fault, Lore," he murmured, an endless repetition he'd kept up for the three weeks since his father had died. His coronation wasn't until the day after tomorrow, but he held himself like a King already. "It was Anton, not you."

But Anton wouldn't have been able to do it without her. Lore's ability to channel the magic leaking from the body of the Buried Goddess, interred beneath the Citadel, had made all his plans possible. Power he'd waited for, watching her grow up, watching her inch closer and closer to a destiny she couldn't escape before bringing her here and snaring Bastian, too.

Her fault. All of it.

But Lore didn't argue. This wasn't something that could be left undone.

He gave her a worried look, lips drawn to a line. "You don't have to do this. I can probably figure out a way—"

"No." She shook her head. "No. I'm here. I'm doing it."

Bastian searched her face, his hand still on her cheek. He touched her so casually, heedless of whoever might be watching. Lore was still getting used to that. She was so accustomed to being something secret.

Finally, he nodded.

As if waiting for the signal, the Presque Mort who'd volunteered to accompany them stepped forward. Only one of them had, though this trip underground would have official Priest Exalted dispensation. The remainders of the holy order still weren't keen on entering the catacombs.

The Priest Exalted stood behind the open well, still dressed in black Presque Mort clothes instead of the white robe of his station. The Bleeding God's Heart pendant hung around his neck, though, winking in the afternoon light.

He met Lore's eyes for a heartbeat, one blue, the other hidden behind black leather. Then he looked away.

Bastian ignored the Priest Exalted entirely. But when Lore's gaze tracked from Gabe back to him, he gave her a small, sorrow-tinged smile, as if the other man's indifference hurt him, too.

"We'll be fine," Bastian murmured, low enough for only the two of them to hear. "We'll be fine."

The Presque Mort who would be accompanying them into the catacombs was named Jerault, and Lore was fairly certain the only reason he'd volunteered was because he and Bastian used to be lovers and the monk still held a candle for him. Apparently, Gabe was one of the only monks who took that particular vow so seriously. When Bastian laughingly told her of his and Jerault's history last night over dinner, she'd felt the mortifying sting of tears, though she'd hidden it in her wine.

Jerault was handsome, maybe a year younger than Lore, with golden hair and gray eyes that narrowed slightly with the observance of how close the King and his deathwitch stood. When Bastian turned to the well, Jerault let out something close to a longing sigh.

It was almost funny, the way everyone was so convinced she and Bastian were sleeping together.

On the other side of the well, Gabe kept his silence, his mouth a thin line beneath the shadow of his eye patch. Lore expected him to say something, or at least to force his face into an expression that wasn't blank with the barest seasoning of disapproval. But he did nothing.

He'd raged at the idea of her going down there with Bastian, once. It'd bothered him enough to go to Anton, to betray everything, and now he acted like he didn't care at all.

She cared, though. It'd be so much easier if she didn't.

Bastian mounted the spiral stairs first, climbing down the side of the well, the bright white of his shirt fading the farther he went. He held no torch, but he flicked his lighter when he was halfway down, the glimmer of flame touching a cigarette in his mouth. Of course Bastian would smoke while they went to lay an army of screaming corpses to rest.

Gods, Lore hoped they didn't scream this time. Her head couldn't take it this morning.

She went next, and Jerault followed behind, all of them silent. When Lore was nearly to the bottom, she looked up.

Gabe had moved, finally. He leaned over the well, his tattooed hands braced against the sides, staring down at them. He was too far for her to see his expression, but maybe it had softened, a little, shown his signature Gabe-flavored worry. She'd take anything, at this point.

If it wasn't there, she didn't want to see. Lore finished the climb into the well without looking up again.

The catacombs pressed in from all sides, oppressive darkness, and Lore stood close to Bastian as she fashioned a torch from the supplies left on the packed-dirt floor, her hands trembling. "Why didn't you bring one of these?"

Bastian shrugged, taking the half-finished torch from her and completing the job. "Seemed wasteful." He handed it back. "There's nothing to be afraid of, Lore. We are the most powerful things down here."

She snorted. "The Buried Goddess might beg to differ."

"She's dead, which makes me confident I could win an argument with Her."

Lore gave him a weak smile and leaned in toward his body, just a bit, pulled into his gravity. He kissed her forehead, quick and quiet, fleeting enough to be imagined in the dark.

"Everything will be fine," he murmured, a now-familiar repetition, his lips still close enough to brush her skin. "I promise I will keep you safe."

The refrain had grown constant in the last few weeks. Bastian's charge that he would keep her safe, keep her close, do whatever he had to do. And she would let him. Lore was too tired and cast adrift in this new life to do anything else.

Torch in hand, Bastian led the way into the tunnels. When Lore blinked, her internal map of the catacombs fell into place, but she didn't think they'd need it. The night they'd come down here and found the rooms of corpses—the night Gabe betrayed them—was burned deep into both of their memories.

Jerault cleared his throat. "Is there… ah, should we be worried about…"

"There's no one down here," Lore said.

The Presque Mort's relieved exhale was powerful enough to stir her hair. He was walking very close behind her, like he was afraid of being left in the dark. Lore couldn't find it in herself to be annoyed.

"And if there was someone down here, that's what we have you for." Bastian glanced at the monk with a flirtatious smile. "I'm confident you could protect us from just about anything, Jerault. I recall your stamina."

Jerault made a noise like he'd swallowed a mouthful of wine the wrong way. Lore rolled her eyes. Bastian ashed his cigarette with a pleased smirk.

They walked quickly, none of them wanting to stay down here longer than was absolutely necessary. The flame of Bastian's torch flickered on the pockmarked stone, and when they reached a fork in the path, it briefly illuminated the words carved into the wall.

Divinity is never destroyed. It is only echoed.

Lore scowled at it as they passed.

It didn't take long to reach the vault that held the young, healthy bodies from the villages. Her sense of Mortem, simmering just beneath her consciousness, rose up like a black tide, nearly overwhelming.

She closed her eyes and imagined a forest. A small grove of uniform trees, a sacred place, keeping her safe, keeping her contained.

It helped, a little. Not as much as it used to.

"No screaming." Bastian turned from the wall to Lore, brow arched, the flickering torchlight gilding his hair. "That's something."

Jerault shivered. "I thought you were exaggerating that part."

"I exaggerate absolutely nothing ever, Jerault."

The lock Anton had made with manipulated Mortem was gone. Lore pressed her hand against the stone, just to be sure, but all she felt was the Mortem inherent to the rock. "It'll open easily."

Bastian nodded, all business now, no more teasing the blushing monk. "We should come up with a plan, probably," he said, stepping up by her side, like he didn't want her to be the first one inside the vault.

"The plan is: I go in there and give them back some death." Now that they were here, Lore wanted this over with. Get in, channel, get out. "Honestly, I probably could've done it myself. You didn't have to come."

"I would never let you do this by yourself."

"Thus why I didn't argue." She said it fondly. She didn't want to be down here alone; he knew that. "Seemed like a waste of time."

"A wise woman," Bastian replied.

Lore pushed the stone door open.

The room beyond was dark. Bastian found the fuse hanging from the ceiling, like he had before, and lit it from his torch. Light slowly traveled around the room, illuminating the chamber.

The blessedly silent corpses were on their plinths. Lore didn't know if someone had come down here and rearranged them, or if they'd cleaned themselves up, walking away from the door after Lore closed it that night, settling back on their slabs like sleepwalkers returning to bed. Each body had their hands folded over their chests, hiding the eclipse scars on their palms, mirrors of the scar she and Bastian shared.

Her fingers closed instinctually.

Lore was prepared to hold her breath, tithe her heartbeat, do everything she was used to doing to drop into that space where life and death were tangible things to be manipulated. But this time was different. Her heart tithed its beat, still, but it was easy, a simple pause before picking back up again. It felt more like an afterthought, her body going along with a remembered ritual even though there was no real need.

That should concern her, probably. The floodgates of her power had been opened, and any dams she'd built against it were long since worn away.

One moment, she saw all the dim colors of the vault, and the next, everything had faded to black and white. Knots of Mortem hovered over the chest of every corpse, inverted stars.

She looked over her shoulder, to where Bastian stood, and nearly had to pull herself back out of channeling-space again. He was so bright he hurt to look at, every inch of his body flushed in white light.

Lore recovered quickly, turning back to the task at hand. Mortem hung a bit denser over the closest corpse—the woman she'd raised that first time, the one who'd triggered the wave of rising bodies, chanting *they've awakened*, ponderously climbing off their slabs.

Might as well start with her this time, too.

"Do you need me to leave?" Bastian asked. When Spiritum had been new in him, it had canceled out her own power. It didn't do that anymore. Whatever had happened the night of the eclipse had changed her, made her something he couldn't snuff out.

With a shake of her head, Lore stepped up to the corpse, not wanting that particular conversation to linger. The men followed, ringing the plinth like mourners at a funeral.

Breathe in, breathe out.

Her fingers twitched as she gathered in Mortem, enough to craft a death for every corpse in the room. She pulled it from the walls, the stone, from the dry-packed dirt where nothing could grow, and from the knot hanging in the air over the dead chest of the woman on the slab. It braided around her fingers, weaving like a cat.

It didn't feel terrible, like it used to. It felt almost...natural, now. The side effects were the same, the sludged pulse and tingling fingers, but they didn't hurt. Didn't feel uncomfortable, even. They just were.

Mortem filtered through her body, turning to her will, and slowly, slowly, Lore began to push it back out—

A muffled scream. Jerault's.

The corpse's hand shot up, clamped around Jerault's throat. Black-edged nails dug in, laced with creeping rot now that Mortem came close, drawing crescents of blood as the Presque Mort's feet shuffled ineffectually on the floor. The corpse's face was implacable, blank eyes still staring upward, like the hand acted of its own accord.

A fail-safe. Something built into that thick knot of Mortem above the body, making it act in defense if someone tried to nullify the army once awakened.

In Lore's black-and-white vision, she saw the spark of Spiritum in Jerault begin to dim. Long strands of white light stretched like the slow-motion collapse of a star, the ends turning dark as life alchemized into death, the inherent Mortem in Jerault blooming out of his fading life.

Another blaze next to her—Bastian, rushing toward them. All the while, the corpse's hand squeezed tighter, tighter.

Lore's fingers stayed over the corpse, pushing out the Mortem she'd channeled in, faster now, hoping that it'd loosen the iron grip. But it was too slow; Jerault would be dead before she could lay the corpse to rest. Bastian's hands streaked into her vision, trailing light, scrabbling at the corpse's hand as it closed inexorably on Jerault's neck. She heard the snap of bone, one of the corpse's fingers broken.

With the hand not channeling Mortem, Lore seized the Spiritum spinning out of Jerault. She channeled the bright light of it through herself, running congruent to the dark of Mortem, turning both to her will. Then she thrust the Spiritum back toward Jerault.

It was difficult work, this bifurcation, channeling death and life at once. Lore fed light into Jerault, keeping it burning, and death back into the corpse. The light coalesced in Jerault's center, churning over itself, shining in defiance of the death that wanted to take over.

"Help?" she said quietly, her black-and-white vision turning to Bastian. He'd snapped another of the corpse's fingers, the dry skin and bone dangling down the back of its gripping hand, but the strength left in the remaining three was still enough to choke Jerault.

Bastian let go of the corpse and held out his hands. Lore released her grip on Spiritum, letting the threads of it naturally go to Bastian, drawn by his light. It channeled through him like poured water, flowing through his body before going back to Jerault, strengthened by its proximity to the Sainted King.

A wide smile turned up Bastian's mouth.

The hovering Mortem drifted down to the dead woman's chest, tendrils reaching to Lore and then to the body like pieces of a broken spiderweb. The knots held tight, but Lore picked them apart with twitches of her fingers as she took them in and channeled them out, she and the corpse the center of a ragged constellation.

When it was done, the woman on the slab actually looked at peace.

Lore lurched backward, breathing hard. Her body was a mess of contradictions—her blood pulling through her veins like it was half-frozen, but faster than it should be; her lungs hauling in too much air as her limbs tingled with pins and needles.

She'd channeled them both. Mortem and Spiritum, at the same time.

Gods, and she'd thought she had a headache before.

Bastian held Jerault up by the shoulders, examining his throat. Bloody marks from the corpse's nails scored his skin, and broken blood vessels already bloomed to nasty bruises, but other than that, he wasn't worse for wear. He looked stricken, though, and when Bastian released him with a clap on his back, the Presque Mort gazed at Lore like he was seeing a dream and a nightmare at once.

Lore didn't know whether to smile back or scowl, so she just stared at him blankly.

Satisfied that Jerault would live, Bastian turned toward Lore. "Let me see—"

"No, I'm fine." She whirled toward the door, hurried out of it as quickly as she could without running. "I'm fine."

In the dark stone corridor outside, Lore leaned back against the wall, her head tipped up, her breathing labored. The discomfort of Mortem channeling was a familiar annoyance by now, but the intense dichotomy of coming down from Mortem and Spiritum together felt like every stitch that held her together was rapidly fraying.

It was almost...exhilarating.

Her heart thudded in her chest, pumping great gouts of cold blood. Her lungs held so much air, but her throat felt too dry to let it all in and out as it should.

"Fuck," Lore muttered, rubbing at her chest.

A glimmer in the corner of her vision. Something in the shadows, deeper in the tunnel.

Lore turned.

It was too dim to see any kind of detail. Just the vague shape of a person. But that was all Lore needed.

She leaned against the stone wall, trying to make her body re-regulate after so much magic, staring at her mother.

The Night Priestess stared back. Her hand rose, just slightly, the half-reach of someone who knew whatever they strove for was impossible to grasp.

Then she turned and disappeared into the dark.

Chapter Two

The art of dreamwalking is more about concentration than magic, though magic is necessary. While dreaming was thought to be under the jurisdiction of Lereal, the most important factor is that both parties–the dreamer and the dreamwalker–are able to use magic from the same source. Therefore, strong Mortem channelers are often able to achieve dreamwalking. One can only assume that right after the Godsfall, when elemental magic was still in the world, those who could channel any sort of power could also walk in each other's dreams.

–*Mortem and Non-Death Applications*, page 113, by Antoinette Harleone

You *saved* him."

It was the third time in an hour Bastian had said the words, in a voice of shock and awe, shaking his head with a smile on his face. The first time had been shortly after they sat down to a private dinner laid out in the solar, the second time had been over the soup course, and now he said it again as the remains of dessert—which Lore had only picked at, her stomach still unsettled—were tidied by silent servants. Each time, she'd only given him a tight smile in return and shot conspicuous looks at the people around them, hoping he would take the hint that she didn't necessarily want this bit of news all over the Citadel.

But Bastian was oblivious, so this time, she spoke up. "He probably would've been fine if you'd kept breaking fingers."

"No, he wouldn't," Bastian scoffed. "He was being strangled, Lore, and you stopped it. You channeled Mortem and Spiritum together to stop it. That's *incredible*."

The servants had kept their faces impassive up to this point, but now their eyes slid toward one another, slightly widened. Lore slumped in her seat.

"How did you do it?" Bastian asked, pouring himself more wine. Lore pushed forward her own glass, and he refilled it nearly to the top. "Do you remember specifics? What it felt like?"

He asked like someone who wanted to re-create an experiment. If he'd had pen and paper handy, he'd probably be taking notes. Lore slid farther down in her chair and took a too-large gulp of her wine, eyeing the servants. She didn't want to get too far into details when anything she said would be woven into rumor before the sun had fully set.

"I didn't really do it on purpose," she said. "I just... acted. It was instinctual."

That seemed to please him, oddly. In the greenery-crowded windows, the sun was well on its way to setting, the light thick and golden as honey. "So it came naturally," he said, sitting back. "You didn't have to... to *do* anything special, to channel them both together. It just felt right."

Right wasn't exactly the way she'd put it, but Lore wasn't interested in making this an argument. That would mean they'd have to discuss it longer. She took another un-lady-like swallow and set down her glass. "I'd really rather not talk about it anymore, Bastian."

He set down his own, drained to the dregs. "Lore..."

"No." She waved a negating hand. "Please choose a different topic of conversation, Your Majesty."

Her use of his title seemed to knock him out of whatever spiral he'd found himself in. The sun finally slid behind the curve of the earth, and as the golden glow changed to soft twilight, Bastian sighed, rubbing a hand over his face. "All right," he said quietly. "I'm sorry. I don't know, I just felt like I should..." He trailed off. "What would you rather discuss?"

Gabe. She wanted to discuss Gabe, wanted to ask Bastian what he'd thought of his stoicism as they climbed down into the catacombs today, if he'd managed to have any real conversations with their former friend since raising him to Priest Exalted. She knew they met together. He was a key leader of the Church, and one of Bastian's official advisers. All of her own conversations with Gabe had been during sessions to keep up her mental forest, and he'd carefully avoided speaking of anything else. It felt like talking to a statue.

But she wouldn't talk about Gabe, not now, when rumors were being spun out of the air by everyone within hearing distance. It was too raw a wound, still. It needed a bandage in mixed company.

Instead Lore took up her fork and picked a little more at her nearly untouched dessert—fruit and cream and some kind of flaky pastry. "Horse," she said finally. "I know you were going to make a party of laying him to rest—"

"The florist is on standby. For *Claude*."

She gave him a weak smile. "But would it be all right to leave him for a bit? He isn't hurting anyone." And she liked visiting him, sometimes. It was a nice reminder that she could do things that weren't awful, that Mortem was a tool that could be turned to good occasionally.

"That's perfectly fine with me," Bastian said. "I'm rather fond of him, repulsive as he is." He'd finished all of his dessert, so he reached across with his fork and took some of hers. She smacked at his hand halfheartedly, smearing cream across his thumb, but he just licked it off. "Maybe we can rent him out for parties," he continued around a strawberry. "That'd be one way to raise money for the next citizen payment. Maybe it'd make the treasurers hate me less."

"As long as you're making payments to commoners, they're going to hate you." Lore finished off the rest of the dessert before he could steal more.

"The glamorous life of a monarch." Bastian rose from his chair. "Speaking of, I have meetings."

"At night?"

"Church meetings."

The momentary lightness she'd felt crashed back down around her again, the subject she'd been avoiding finding them anyway.

Maybe Gabe and Bastian were both better at this than she was. Maybe they could put all the mess of a month ago behind them for the greater good.

Lore had never been very interested in the greater good.

Bastian came around the table and kissed her on the forehead. It was new for him, this sweetness. The easy intimacy that had risen between them before had never been the delicate kind, but lately, it seemed he wanted it to grow in that direction. There was almost a tentativeness to it, as if he expected to be rebuffed. But she never did. Sweetness was as foreign to her as it was to him, and she craved it.

Though she always thought of Gabe, every time.

"Don't wait up," he said. "I'll be late."

Then he was gone, and the servants came over silently to clear the rest of the dishes. Lore watched the sky through the window, honey and lavender and encroaching indigo. No moon tonight.

Lore tried not to drink herself to sleep. Most nights, she was successful. But the threat of dreams always hung around her head, knocking at her temples, and when they were loud, an extra glass or two was the only way she knew to drown them out.

Dreaming was dangerous. Dreaming had made her a weapon. And though Anton wasn't here to manipulate her anymore, Lore still didn't *like* dreaming. She wanted her head blank and her mind empty when she lay down, wanted to have no thoughts at all until she woke up in the morning.

So when she closed her eyes, she was not at all pleased to find herself *here*.

It was obviously a dream. Lore was in her forest, the one Gabe had taught her to grow around her mind, with its uniform trees that looked too perfect to be real. Smoke twisted through the sky, billowing into the air from some nearby fire.

One she was setting herself, apparently. Lore watched her hand, through no directive of her own, reach out with a lit torch, touch it to a tree. She stepped back, a silent passenger in her own head, and watched the trees catch, joining the blazing inferno of the others, trapping her in a ring of fire.

She lifted her face and screamed.

Then, with a wrenching feeling like tearing off a bandage, Lore woke up, sweat-sheened and gasping.

Her consciousness came back to her body slowly as she panted into the dark, twitching her fingers, her toes, small tests to ensure she was awake.

The dream felt like nonsense to her. That was good. At least, she thought it was. It certainly didn't feel like the dreams she'd had when Anton was pulling at her power, and that was good enough.

Catacombs, her mind whispered.

Lore scowled into the dark. Some vestige of that dream must still cling to her, even though she couldn't remember it having anything to do with the catacombs. Dream-logic, detritus caught in the current of her thoughts like trash in a storm drain.

She pressed the heels of her hands against her eyes, pulled them away only once she'd pressed so hard she saw stars.

Back in the southeast turret, her bed had no canopy, and her bed linens had been a shade of mustard-yellow that even she knew was years out of fashion. Here, in one of the many spare bedrooms in Bastian's palatial apartment, the canopy floating above her in the breeze through the open window was the same gauzy fabric as the deep-summer gowns in her closet, ghost-white and billowing.

Even with the window open, the air in the room was stifling. Summer in Auverraine was ridiculously warm and humid, hot as boiled piss both at midnight and midday, and this year was shaping up to be worse than most.

A bottle of wine sat in a bucket of melted ice on her nightstand, half drunk already. Lore stared at it for a moment, weighing whether or not the dry mouth and pounding head in the morning would be worth the hope of dreamless sleep.

She decided it wasn't, but still pulled the bottle out of the ice to press the cool glass against her forehead. The dream had banished any hope of a restful night, and if she went back to sleep, she'd probably dream some more. Still, she'd rather her inevitable morning headache be due to sleeplessness than alcohol. She'd been down that road before, when an indulgence flirted with becoming a dependence, and the Citadel was too treacherous a place for that.

With a sigh, Lore got out of bed. Stretched. Found the silk dressing gown she'd left wadded on the floor and shrugged into it, not bothering to tie it closed. She'd grown fairly adept at avoiding stray courtiers on these frequent night wanderings, and it was a fair bet that anyone she ran into would be more scandalously dressed than she was. While the older courtiers were drawing in on themselves, wary and angered by Bastian's new measures, the younger set seemed to welcome the advent of a new royal paradigm. She wondered how long that would last once the tax increases started.

Her throat hurt. She should find a glass of water, probably. She could call a servant to fetch one for her, but she was loath to wake them up. Of course, this thought led to the notion that she could go ask Bastian for a glass of water, since he would know where to find one in his own apartments. Surely he was back from his meeting with Gabe by now.

But the last thing she needed was to wander half clothed into Bastian's rooms in the middle of the night.

The attraction between them was obvious. The want was there. But this situation was already fucked through all seven days without adding *actual* fucking to the equation.

She snorted, remembering having a similar thought weeks ago, when she felt caught between Gabe and Bastian, drawn to them both. The feeling hadn't abated.

And she'd thought things were complicated *then*.

Sulfur smell, ember snap; she struck the match in her hand and saw it spark. Lore put flame to wick and shook it out, throwing the spent match back in the basket meant for the purpose, then picked up the candle and crept out of her room.

Outside her door was a hall with one side open to the main room of Bastian's quarters: the marble-and-gold solar where she'd had tea with Alie weeks ago. A wide staircase in the middle of the hall led to the floor of the solar, lined with lush green ferns. Three spare bedrooms made up the second floor, and a smaller spiral staircase at the end of the open corridor led to Bastian's rooms above, taking up the entire third story.

Lore stared at the spiral stairs for a moment, lip between her teeth. Then she shook her head and started for the main door.

When she moved in, Bastian had gotten rid of the peacocks—thank all the gods—and so, other than the soft patter of water from the fountain in the room's center, the solar was silent and still. Plants stood clustered by the windows, casting jagged shadows across the iron-striped floor.

She scuffed her slippered foot along one of the iron bars. They were thinner here, slivers of metal in the tile rather than the thick pieces on the Citadel's ground floor, but they served the same purpose. Reminders of holy authority, holy responsibility. An Arceneaux King was charged with keeping Mortem contained and the Buried Goddess... well, buried. And here Bastian was, harboring a deathwitch as he sat on the throne, Apollius's chosen ruling at last.

If anything was proof that the gods were all dead—or at least past caring—it was that. Anton had been so adamant that Apollius wanted Lore gone once she'd fulfilled her purpose, so sure that Bastian's power was the sign of His return. But there was no sign of Apollius, and Lore was still here, and the world hadn't ended yet.

She stalked out into the hallways of the northwest turret.

The windows were sparser, here, framing the moonless sky, the stars shining brighter for its absence. Lore wandered with no destination in mind, changing direction anytime she heard voices.

Eventually, her wandering brought her down to the main floor of the Citadel. She'd grown more familiar with its warren-like corridors, the openings leading into opulent rooms filled with statuary or fountains or art. The steady motion of her footsteps dulled her mind, her vision narrowed to the floor in front of her. This felt more restful than sleep. At least she didn't have to worry about dreaming.

The floor in front of her changed, became the threshold of the Citadel door.

Lore looked up. There were supposed to be guards here, but she saw no one—they'd abandoned their posts for more pleasurable pursuits, probably.

She pushed open the door.

Outside, the muggy air lay over the grass in whirls of fog. The lack of a moon turned everything to fuzzy-edged shadows, amorphous, easy for the mind to turn to monsters.

Lore stopped beside a topiary, turned her face starward. The night wrapped around her like a blanket.

Rose thorns picked at the silk of her dressing gown as Lore wandered through the gardens. The dressing gown was Bastian's, really; his initials were embroidered across the chest. He'd given it to her the night after the ritual, when he'd brought her to his apartments, cold and bloody and numb with shock.

I will take care of you, she remembered him saying. His hands still glowed golden, his eyes almost the same, his voice with more resonance than it should have. *You're mine.*

At least, she thought that's what he'd said. Her memories were fuzzy. She recalled that he'd looked different when she woke up the next day, as the sun was fading down to dusk. Tired, eyes dark. When she'd come to him, stepping silently to his side as he stood by the window, he'd wrapped his arms around her in silence.

The wrought-iron fence guarding the Presque Mort's stone garden loomed from the mist. Lore didn't pause to wonder if she should enter. She just did, some instinct pulling her forward.

Stone flowers, stone leaves. In the far corner, a greenhouse, one she'd never ventured into.

Lore wandered forward, toward the well.

She stopped when she saw the person standing in front of it.

"Daughter," her mother said quietly, her voice carrying through the fog.

Chapter Three

The past comes back, endlessly. Nothing is set in stone until we are dead.

–Amita Giro, Kirythean poet

Lore's feet felt frozen to the ground. Everything in her ran hot and cold, the urge to run and the urge to stay still tugging at her equally so her muscles tensed but would not move.

Her mother was haggard. In the dim starlight, she could see the circles beneath her hazel eyes, the tired lines bracketing her face. She looked like she hadn't slept any more than Lore had, lately.

When the Night Priestess stepped forward, Lore moved back, keeping the distance the same between them. Her mother sighed.

"Why are you here?" Lore's voice came out rough; she really should've found a glass of water. "What do you want?"

Eyes that matched her own stared her down. "I don't..." Her mother trailed off, her lips pressing into a line. She looked away, as if she'd find the words she lacked somewhere in the garden.

"You *lost*," Lore hissed. "Don't you get that? Whatever doomsday prophecy you and Anton and the others believed in, it was a lie. I'm alive, and the world hasn't ended."

"Endings take their time," her mother murmured, still not looking at her.

Lore swallowed, hard.

The Night Priestess kept her distance, not coming any closer. With a sigh, she made eye contact again, though it seemed to pain her. "You think you know why I'm here. You don't."

"Shut up." Lore shook her head, clenched her fists at her sides. The ridges of her scar rubbed together painfully. "It's over. You won't convince me to *die*."

"I'm not trying to," her mother said. "I came here to stop you."

Lore's mouth was already open, ready for a poisonous retort. She snapped it closed, teeth ringing together. She'd had the dream, woken up, started wandering. The voice in her head, whispering *catacombs*, the one she'd thought was her own subconscious picking through the events of the day…

"You felt the call," the Night Priestess murmured. "We felt it go out. Things are coalescing, Lore. Time is short. You have to go." The last word seemed forced out, as if her throat had tried to close around it. "You have to run."

A sharp breath of humid, flower-tinged air; it almost felt too thick to breathe. "What are you playing at?" Lore wrapped Bastian's robe more tightly around herself despite the heat. "Three weeks ago you wanted me to die, and now you want me to run? You think that will cover up the fact that you're wrong, that your whole religion is based on lies? There's no apocalypse coming, *Night Priestess*—"

"Lilia," her mother whispered.

"And even if there was—" But the name barreled into her, crumpled Lore's words together like a carriage crash.

"I'd never ask you to call me Mother," the Night Priestess said. Her eyes closed. "Not after… but my name is Lilia."

None of the Night Sisters used names. They all called one another Sister, their individuality folded up and hidden in the vastness of their mission. How long had it been since this woman used her name?

Lore didn't know what to say. Sweat pricked at the back of her neck, even as a cold, seeping chill wound its way all down her spine.

"If you run, there might be a chance," her mother—Lilia—continued. "The powers are sharpened by closeness, and now that you're here, the others will begin to awaken. If you go, you can be saved. You can all be saved."

"So you don't want me dead," Lore said, her lips numb. "But you still want me gone. Away and alone." A short noise burst from her throat, something she couldn't categorize into any specific emotion. "You can't stand the thought of me having anything."

A tear squeezed itself out of Lilia's still-closed eyes. "I deserve your anger," she said, her voice measured and even. "And I don't deserve your trust. But Lore, I promise, everything I have done has been for good reasons."

"But those reasons were never me," Lore replied. "Maybe you thought they were good, but I'm your *daughter.* Were they good enough to kill me?"

"I saved you."

"You abandoned me." She could have yelled it. She meant to. But when the words left Lore's mouth, they were simple and matter-of-fact. "I was a child, and you sent me away, all alone to a world you knew I had little chance of surviving. So was that really saving me, or just making sure your hands were kept clean?" Lore stepped forward like a predator, fog curling around her, all the night's dark at her heels. "You would have killed me three weeks ago, for a god who you don't know exists. And now that it seems you were wrong, you change your mind?" Another step forward. Lilia took a tiny, cringing one back. "Tell me it was for the greater good. I dare you."

"Hello?"

The voice came from behind the well, the part of the garden backed up against the walls of the Church.

Gabe.

Both of them froze. The Night Priestess looked terrified; Bastian had never filed the paperwork that made the Buried Watch an official part of the Church again. They still, officially, didn't exist, and if Gabe found one of them in the stone garden, it was not likely to go well.

"Don't tell him," her mother whispered, the mist making her movements ghostlike as she turned back to the open well and mounted the stairs. There was no other invective, no other plea. Just a mother to a daughter.

And damn her, even after everything she'd just said, Lore knew she wouldn't.

Lilia stopped halfway sunk into the dark and looked up at Lore. "If you change your mind," she said, "I'll help you. Drop a rose into the well."

Then she was gone.

Gabe stalked into Lore's view a heartbeat later, mist swirling around him like the hem of a cloak. He held a gas-flame lantern in one tattooed hand, swinging reckless light around the quiet garden, bouncing off his pendant. The well was still open, and he frowned at it, not even noticing Lore yet. "I was certain we closed that." There was a tired edge to his voice; Lore wondered if he'd slept at all.

She also wondered if she should bolt. Slip backward into the fog, hope her pale dressing gown camouflaged her as she made her way to the gate, into the Citadel, to her bed in Bastian's apartment. The place she hadn't really chosen, but had ended up, Gabe's actions forcing a decision she wasn't yet sure how to make. Didn't *want* to make.

The lantern light swung again as Gabe looked up from the well, splashing yellow glow across Lore's face. It was bright, and she cringed away, the movement sending curls of fog around her face.

"Lore?"

Shit.

She'd wanted to have a real conversation with Gabe for so long, wanted to ask him how he was doing, wanted to rage at him, wanted to hold him. But now she didn't know what to do. They just stared at each other across the stone flowers.

"I..." Gabe trailed off, rubbed a hand beneath his eye patch. "Why are you here?"

It sounded both plaintive and accusatory at once. Lore drew herself up, glowering. "Couldn't sleep. Took a walk."

His one eye glanced at the embroidery across her chest, his jaw ticking like he could read it clearly in the dim light. "Long way to walk, from the Sainted King's quarters."

He had no right to sound like that. As if *she* were the one who'd somehow betrayed *him*. Whatever spark had once been between them was long since snuffed out, smothered by what he'd done. Lore wasn't one to trust easily, and when it was gone, it was gone.

Yet here she was. Still caring. Still wishing they could find their way to friendship again, even if they could never have anything else. She wanted one piece of him, at least.

"I needed some fresh air," she responded, and didn't match his vitriol.

Gabe noticed. He deflated, shoulders sinking, his head turning away so all she saw was the shadow of his patch. When he spoke next, it was low, earnest. "Has he been good to you?"

Of course he wanted to talk about Bastian. But it was a genuine question, so she gave it a genuine answer. "Very good." She still felt the phantom breath of his kiss on her forehead, that sweetness she didn't feel equipped to accept or show. "It's not like that with us, though. Not really."

He looked up, brow arched over his blue eye. "But you want it to be."

Not a question. Just a statement. Lore gave a slight shake of her head, but it wasn't a negation. It was an attempt to heal the look on Gabe's face, to glaze it over and make this easier. She didn't want to hurt either of them, and that seemed impossible to hold, a knife that was all blade and no hilt.

Gabe straightened, physically shaking off the conversation and steering it elsewhere. "Is anyone else here with you? I thought I heard two voices."

"No," she said before she could think about it too hard. "Just me. Talking to myself."

"New habit?"

"Have to pass the days somehow." She gave him a wobbly smile. "I'm better company than most courtiers."

"Never thought you'd be good at all that," Gabe said. "Rubbing elbows with the elite."

"You're one of those elite, Mort."

"And look at us now, skulking around in the dark." Still a joke, but with a sharp end to it, offered gingerly.

He scratched at his chin, the reddish-gold stubble growing in there, angled his eye at the ground. "Alie said you were doing well," he said. "When I asked her last. But I'm glad to hear it from you."

"Alie's helped." Her friend's direction during official state functions was a lifesaver, and that was not an understatement. Lore's strange, precarious position in the Citadel meant that no one really knew how to treat her at things like balls and dinners, of which there had been far too many since Bastian became King, and of which there would be many more after his official coronation. He hadn't hosted any, but the invitations inevitably came. He didn't turn them down, not even from the courtiers that treated them both with suspicion, and Lore sometimes with outright disdain. Alie's calming presence at Lore's side had diffused many a situation that could've ended with wine to the face, or a fist if the mood hit.

They lapsed into silence again.

"You know I'm sorry, right?" Gabe finally said, whisper-low. "I don't... I don't know that what I did was *wrong*..." His eye darted to the corner of the stone garden, the shadows of the greenhouse lurking there by the overgrown walls. "But I'm sorry it hurt you, Lore. I was just trying to do the best I could."

"We all were."

Tell me it's for the greater good. She didn't forgive him, but she wanted to, and the want came so much easier for Gabe than it did for her mother. Lore knew that wasn't fair. She couldn't change it.

Gabe nodded. Then he turned, headed back in the direction he'd come, the lantern swinging in his hand. Briefly, she considered calling after him, but the conversation had come to a natural close, and she didn't know how to pry it open again.

Lore stood alone in the garden, a million stars staring down at her. First her mother, then Gabe. Already everything felt surreal, her thoughts as churning as the fog. The night had often seemed like a time outside of reality, when things were more ethereal and less concrete.

What a time for awkward conversations.

Dew soaked her hem, dragging it along the ground as Lore let herself out of the stone garden, wound her way through rosebushes and topiaries, pushed open the Citadel door. A soft trek back up through the mazes of wealth to Bastian's apartment, to her own bed.

Something in her was unsettled. Some pull that hadn't been answered.

Catacombs, the back of her mind whispered again, but Lore was already falling asleep. This time, it was dreamless.

CHAPTER FOUR

Does it matter if he hasn't married her? The boy treats her as his Queen. It's as if he doesn't understand what we've done for him. Though things did not go as planned, he has still been installed in the position we desired.

The situation can be remedied, if the girl is taken care of.

–Correspondence from Count Alphonse Levett to Duke Alan Lavigne, while the former was on house arrest following the eclipse ritual. Intercepted and presented to Bastian Arceneaux, the Sainted King. Reports say he smiled.

Time to wake up, dearest."

The words might've been gentle, but the way Bastian pulled the covers off the bed decidedly was not. Lore curled up on her side with her arms over her face to block out the light. "Why?"

"Because it's another delightful summer day in the Court of the Citadel." Bastian put a delicate mug of coffee on the table with an audible *clink*. He waved his hand over the steam, wafting it toward her face as if the smell would entice her from her mattress. "And because we have to go to the farmlands today. Or did you forget?"

She *had* forgotten, what with the chaos of yesterday. But the reminder of a royal appointment out on the very edges of Dellaire—in the farmlands that she'd had a hand in destroying—did not make her any more eager to wake up. Quite the opposite, in fact. Lore pulled her pillow over her head. "Why do *I* have to go?"

Her words were muffled by goose down, but the plaintive wheedle in her voice was clear. So was Bastian's sigh. "Because you are my deathwitch, Lore. The highest office in the court."

"An office you made up."

"And made the highest." The mattress bent as he sat. "Staying near me is also best for your safety. But I won't rehash that conversation."

"If I never have another conversation about staying close to you, it will be too soon." Still under her pillow, Lore scrunched her eyes shut. "We don't even know if I can get as far as the farmlands."

The Mortem strung all through her, the magic that had never let her leave Dellaire, seemed to have loosened its hold somewhat ever since the ritual. Not that she'd tested it—she hadn't left the Citadel since then—but she could feel it. Something about holding both Spiritum and Mortem had made the chains of one loosen, opened up the world for her. She supposed she should be grateful for that.

"Seems as good a day as any to find out," Bastian said. "If you don't drink that coffee, I'm going to. You have thirty seconds."

Reluctantly, she pulled her pillow off her head.

Bastian looked just as stunningly beautiful as he always did. His dark hair curled around his collar, the golden circlet studded with rubies across his brow, bisecting the well-healed scar slashing from his forehead to the outside corner of his right eye.

He hadn't used Spiritum to soften it, to make it heal as less than brutal.

He arched a brow at her when she sat up, her coffee cup held teasingly close to his own mouth. She held out her hand, and he surrendered the bone china. "You look like you need it. When did you go to bed, ten minutes before sunrise?"

Lore blew across the top of the coffee before taking a sip. "I went to bed right after dinner, thank you. I just didn't sleep particularly well. Bad dreams."

His teasingly arched brow slashed low instead, suddenly serious. "You're dreaming again?"

Burning trees, screaming sky. She'd dreamed, all right, but it hadn't been the same. More like a memory than a dream at all.

Lore set the coffee aside, stood up to rummage through her closet. "Yes, but not anything important. Not like before." Lore swallowed hard as she dug through gowns. In summer, the courtiers of the Citadel dressed in things that either showed as much skin as possible, or touched skin as little as they could. Lore went for the second option, gauzy tentlike gowns that floated around her like a cloud.

But Bastian wasn't swayed. "I thought he was supposed to be teaching you to guard your mind."

He. They hardly ever said Gabe's name to each other, as if he were a haunting. "He is."

"Not well, apparently. I'll have to talk to—"

"No, Bastian." Lore whipped around, a gown she'd barely looked at clutched to her chest. Deep, bloody red, not really appropriate for summer. "This isn't about him, it's about me."

Her fear. Her shame. Her selfishness.

You are the seed of the apocalypse, her mother had said in the dark of the eclipse. *Endings take time*, she'd said by the well last night.

Bastian sighed, tipping back his head. When he came toward her, it was careful. Warm hands on her shoulders, placed light before settling firm.

She didn't look up, staring at her bare feet on the plush carpet.

"You have to let it go, Lore," he murmured.

But she never would. The dreams with the smoke twisting over the sky weren't the only ones she was afraid of—the regular nightmares were just as bad. Where she saw the child in the vaults with his black eyes, mouth unhinged and spilling whispers. Where she saw obsidian walls closing around her, and she couldn't scream no matter how hard she tried.

"The power is *yours*," Bastian said fiercely, almost like he was trying to convince himself as well as her. "You control it. No one else."

Lore kneaded the red dress in her hands to soothe the itch in her fingers. She could still feel Mortem in inanimate things, if she tried, reaching past the bounds of the forest she'd grown in her mind. It was almost soothing. "I know," she murmured. "I know the power is mine."

And though it wasn't the complete thought, she left it there, because the rest of what she felt about her magic wasn't easily put into words. She didn't want to admit she was afraid. Didn't want to tell him that sometimes her entire mind turned toward the terror that maybe Anton was right. Maybe the more she used her power, the more like Nyxara she would become.

Lore didn't believe that. Refused to. And yet.

"Maybe I should stay here today," she said. "There's no reason for me to go with you to the farmlands, is there?"

His hands on her shoulders tightened, just a bit, before falling to the dress she held. "The reason," he said, "is because I want you to."

"Not quite good enough."

"Lore." There were so many ways he said her name. Teasing, imploring, longing. But this was imperious. Almost like the beginning of an order.

That made her bristle. But there was no real time or energy to fight for the sake of fighting. Who she'd been before would have done it, but she wasn't that person now.

She didn't really know who she was now.

So Lore nodded.

Bastian pulled the dress away from her, lip curling. "But you aren't wearing *this*." He stepped around her to the disaster she'd made of the closet. "I'll choose your gown, since you've demonstrated time and again your taste runs toward questionable, and call up Juliette to do something about your hair."

An hour and many muttered curses from Juliette later, they were on the road.

When August was the Sainted King, he was rarely seen outside the Citadel. Business that needed attending beyond the walls was delegated to other nobles or bloodcoats, with precious little oversight of either. On the rare occasions that August went out among the rabble, it was in a fully covered carriage guarded by a phalanx of guards. Most citizens of Dellaire didn't know what their former King had looked like beyond the oil paintings in the South Sanctuary, which Lore thought were a bit more generous than they should be.

In this, as in all things, Bastian was different. He often rode out to view the many construction projects he'd begun to improve Dellaire, and never hid in a carriage to do so. His coronation tomorrow was open to everyone, commoner and noble alike, and held in the South Sanctuary rather than the North. The captain of the guard—Curly Mustache, her old nemesis who'd aided in her capture after raising Horse, and whose name she'd never bothered to learn—was nearly apoplectic at the perceived security risk. But Bastian was adamant that the citizens of Auverraine should know their King.

And no one could argue that it wasn't a good idea, that

Auverraine wouldn't benefit from building more trust between King and subject. News had spread quickly that there was a new Arceneaux on the throne, and reports from the Burnt Isles said that there were more sightings of Kirythean warships on open waters than usual. Now was decidedly not the time for upheaval within their borders, as the signs of imminent war increased without.

Lore hadn't even known there was a complete military outpost on the Isles until recently. Apparently, the burned-out archipelago was useful for more than just a prison.

The open carriage lurched over the cobblestones, and Lore grabbed the side with a soft curse. Mortem was a slow spiral of darkness in her middle, tempered with the gold of Spiritum. It was calming, to feel them there, but her nerves were still on a fast trigger.

"Carriages make me nauseous, too," Alie murmured. She looked straight ahead with the concentration of someone sighting in a gunshot. "I have to keep my eyes on the road ahead or I feel like my whole stomach is going to come out my mouth."

"You didn't have to come," Lore said as they hit a pothole. The streets were brittle from the amount of Mortem the Presque Mort had channeled into the rock, back when leaks were more common. Fixing them was one more item on Bastian's list. "I promise, I'll be fine. We can have them take you back—"

"We're already almost out of the city." Alie tossed Lore a quick smile, then hurriedly looked forward again. "And I didn't have anything else to do. Bastian made me an adviser; I thought it was best to come along. He stays in need of advising."

Another lurch made Lore clutch the side of the carriage harder. "True."

The edge of the city drew nearer. Up ahead, on a black charger brushed to high sheen, Bastian halted, turned to look at Lore. The anxiety churning her stomach was reflected on his face.

Part of her wished he would come back here and ride with them, just in case things went sideways and the magic didn't let her leave. He'd been confident it wouldn't be a problem, and she'd tried to borrow some of that confidence, but now she felt it slipping through her fingers, and she couldn't find a handhold.

Bastian turned on his horse, rode past the border of the city. Moments later, the wheels of the carriage rolled over the boundary line that marked Dellaire's edge.

Nothing happened.

For the first time in her entire life, she was outside of Dellaire.

Bastian's horse wheeled around. He grinned, big and bright, and Lore returned it. Mortem and Spiritum thrummed a minor harmony in her marrow, the thing that was supposed to kill her setting her free instead.

The King turned his charger, cantered back to the front of the procession. The Presque Mort fell in around him. Bastian had taken to keeping the monks as bodyguards rather than the bloodcoats. There were only a few of them left—those who'd been with Malcolm on the night of the ritual, who hadn't been part of Anton's scheme—and while no one's loyalty was a guaranteed thing, they were easier to trust than anyone else at this point. Malcolm himself rode closest to the King.

Gabe wasn't here.

I don't know that what I did was wrong, he'd said last night, wreathed in fog and lantern glow. The fact that he even presented it with a dusting of doubt was an improvement, she guessed. Stupid of her to want more.

Alie reached over and patted her leg, oblivious to the monumental shift in Lore's paradigm and mistaking her discomfort as something to do with the pockmarked road. "I hate to be the bearer of bad news, but the bumps will only get worse from here. Nothing outside of Dellaire has gotten much maintenance lately. Not even the high roads."

The high roads, paths that stretched between countries and connected the continent. Lore had known this was one of them—one that led directly into Kirythea, she thought, though it'd been a while since she spent time with a map—but now, with the newfound realization that Mortem no longer tied her to Dellaire, the knowledge was gilded. "He'll fix it."

"Maybe," Alie said. "Though I'd think creating an easier inroad for Kirythea shouldn't be a high priority."

That dimmed Lore's giddiness, just a bit. Her own life was such a mess, sometimes it was easy to forget about how the rest of the world was, too.

Alie's chin firmed, dark-green eyes fixed straight ahead. "My father always complained bitterly about the roads. I hope that when the time is right, Bastian uses *his* money to repave them, specifically."

Lore gnawed on her lip, unsure whether her friend wanted silence or something comforting. Lord Severin Bellegarde was on house arrest at one of his estates. Alie, who'd been completely in the dark about her father's affairs, had elected to stay in court rather than accompany him. Good thing, too—Bastian had all but abolished his father's former advisory board, and Alie had stepped in to fill Bellegarde's shoes. Lots of shoes, in fact. As far as Lore knew, Bastian's current council consisted of Alie, Malcolm, and herself, with Gabe representing the Church when necessary. Lore was mostly there by technicality, since gods knew no one should be taking advice from *her*.

August had kept a far larger council, and the fact that Bastian didn't was yet another point of contention. But with a handful of nobles on house arrest, and more having left the court for their own holdings in protest of Bastian's policies, it all held steady for now.

"Think we can get Bastian to take your father's wine stores, too?" Lore said. "Doesn't seem fair for him to stay in seclusion and drink. Sounds more like a vacation than a sentence."

Her attempt at lightness fell heavy. Alie gave her a level, worried look. "There are better ways to make sure you don't dream, Lore. Bastian told me you've been drinking too much."

Damn man.

"It's nothing to be ashamed of," Alie said quickly, her lace-gloved hand resting on Lore's arm. "You've been through so much, and things have changed so quickly—"

"Don't." Lore leaned back against the finely upholstered carriage cushion. "Don't make me being a lush into some sort of martyrdom."

"Then don't make it into a joke." Alie's hand lifted; she faced the front again, jaw set. "Sooner or later, Lore, you're going to have to deal with what happened. All *three* of you will."

"I'll deal with it when they do," Lore grumbled.

Alie sighed. They rode in bumpy silence for a handful of heartbeats. The countryside rolled by, humidity a shimmering veil of silver over the impossible green. Placid cows grazed behind rough-hewn fences, raised soft eyes to watch them as they passed. Lore didn't think she'd ever seen one this close before, and part of her wanted to call to the driver to stop, to see if one would let her pet them.

It *smelled* green, even, sharp and sweet at once, with the animalic tinge of livestock that somehow wasn't nearly as odious out here as it was in crowded Ward markets. Lore took a deep breath, held it in her lungs.

"I'm sorry," Lore said. She had so few friends, so little idea of how to keep them.

"Me too." Alie held out her hand; Lore took it.

When Alie spoke again, her voice came gentle against the tramp of hooves and the clatter of carriage wheels. "How is he?"

Guilt was a rock Lore had to swallow past. Hearing the care in Alie's voice when she talked about Gabe would always do that to her, apparently. Alie's gentleness reminded her of her own hard edges. "As well as he can be, I guess."

She didn't say anything about the garden last night. That was hers.

"He should be here," Alie murmured. "No matter what he thinks about Bastian, how he feels—he's the Priest Exalted, and he should be here."

Lore didn't reply.

The ruffle of crinoline broke the silence as Alie rearranged her skirts. "He made the right decision eventually, Lore."

When Gabe stood with them instead of Anton. When he saved her. *I still don't know if what I did was wrong.* Did that mean he wasn't sure if choosing them in the end was right, either?

"Just try to remember that," Alie finished softly. "Remember that he saved you, when all was said and done."

Lore twined the pale-peach ribbon of her sleeve around her finger until the tip of it purpled. "I know. These things just... they take time."

"Hopefully we have it." Alie shook her head. "Did you hear the latest report? A Kirythean contingent was spotted near the Eroccan border two days ago."

Lore's fingertip went numb. "What did Bastian say?"

Worry twisted Alie's mouth. "He said there's no use panicking until they actually cross over. And it was a small group; less than fifty. Just traveling if we're lucky, scouting if we aren't."

There had been very few times in the last couple months that Lore would count any of them as *lucky*.

"I assume they stopped in Erocca," Alie continued. "If they'd kept going, they'd be in Auverraine right now. And surely we'd know."

"Surely," Lore agreed quietly.

When the endless green of the countryside changed, it was abrupt. Gone were the lush fields and trees—well, not gone, really. Just changed.

Gray, now, instead of green. Lifeless stone, like the Presque Mort's garden, every leaf and blade frozen in rock. The procession slowed, everyone struck speechless.

Lore remembered that day of the leak, Malcolm running into the throne room as she and Gabe prepared to lie to August. How Anton let her come along. How the Mortem *surged.* Coming for her, drawing her out, another trap she'd fallen into so easily.

Gods, and she used to think she was a good spy. Good enough for poison running, maybe. The court was a completely different game.

Lore still wasn't sure who'd set that particular trap, though. Not Anton, for all that he'd used the leak to his advantage—shaped the Mortem, made it increase her power so he could use it as a weapon. But he couldn't have *made* the leak happen. She didn't think her mother and the other Night Sisters could have, either. A Mortem leak was power pouring directly from Nyxara's body, and even the most powerful channelers couldn't pull magic from the goddess Herself.

Which meant the leak had to be a coincidence, didn't it? Not a trap at all.

She couldn't quite convince herself of that.

Alie's eyes flicked from the ruined farmland to her. She didn't say anything, and Lore was grateful.

Up ahead, Bastian finally pulled his reins, bringing the black charger to a halt and raising his hand. The Presque Mort around him stopped obediently, the few bloodcoats on the fringes following suit. Behind him, Malcolm nervously patted at his own horse's neck, murmuring calming nothings in its flicking ears.

Down the road, coming in the opposite direction, a collection of small carriages made their way toward them. The farmers whose fields Lore had channeled all that Mortem into, the ones who'd lost livelihoods because of the leak.

Bastian dismounted. Then he started walking toward Lore and Alie, in the opposite direction of the approaching farmers. Even from this far away, determination blazed on his face, his jaw set and his hair curling from beneath his golden circlet.

The braided magic in Lore's center pulled tight, like someone had grabbed one end and tugged. It made her gasp, her hands closing to instinctual fists.

The Law of Opposites, making her stronger when he was near. She hadn't felt it this keenly since the night of the ritual, and part of her wondered if he was doing it on purpose, somehow. Calling to her, pulling her forward.

Bastian came level with the carriage. He didn't say anything. Didn't have to. He just held out his hand.

And here was the real reason why he'd wanted her to come today. Lore knew it in a rush, so obvious now that she couldn't believe she hadn't caught on before.

The fields needed to be healed. And maybe Bastian could do it on his own, maybe their combined magic in him was enough. She could always refuse. But she knew innately that their power would be stronger if they did it together.

Magic sang down her bones, already coiling under her skin, Spiritum and Mortem both. And though she itched to use them, to let them go, Lore squeezed her fists tighter. Fear and eagerness tugged at her, equal in strength, enough to pull her apart.

"I don't know if I can," she murmured, quiet enough for only him to hear.

"I do," he replied, his outstretched hand unwavering. "I know you can."

That boundless confidence, affirming and oppressive at once. "No, you don't. Bastian, I might have saved Jerault, but that is only one good thing. Mortem is death, I can't use it for—"

"What's life without death?" He gave her a smile, but it was a softer one than he normally used, one only a few people ever saw. "Try for me, Lore. Please."

Life and death. Two halves of one whole. Like their scars had been, a sun and a moon, before Anton made them reflections.

Lore put her hand in Bastian's.

He led her back up the dusty road, the heat of the day wavering visibly over the granite waste of the fields. Mortem and Spiritum twirled in Lore's middle. From the corner of her eye, she saw the changes in her body, subtle: veins blackening, and a shimmer of gold outlining her skin, some sort of diseased sun. The same thing was happening to Bastian, their clasped hands a nexus of opposites, strengthening each other, life and death and night and day. She could feel the ridges of his scar, perfectly matching up to her own, the souvenirs of the botched eclipse ritual.

In the distance, the carriages holding the farmers' contingent had finally caught up, the billow of rocky dust in their wake slowly dissipating, resettling on the barren road. There was a low murmur of voices, the coarse sound of horses whipping their tails to chase off flies. Nothing else.

In the distance, Lore thought she could see another dust cloud, as if a second contingent was approaching.

Malcolm's hands were clasped behind his back, his black Presque Mort clothes dulled by a fine coat of grit. His dark eyes flickered between Bastian and Lore, apprehensive. "Do you know how to do this?"

"I guess we'll find out." Lore's voice was hoarse. "What if I make it worse?"

He raised a brow. "Can't be much worse."

"Comforting." Bastian seemed on edge, now, much more so than before they turned back to the high road. His jaw was a tense line as he watched that encroaching cloud of dust get closer.

"What is that?" Lore rose on her toes to see beyond the carriages.

"Nothing." Bastian spun sharply, facing the farmers. "Wind."

The murmurs of the gathered farmers quieted. They were sun-leathered, rough-hewn, and looked at Bastian like they weren't quite sure he was real.

He nodded to them smoothly. "I appreciate your presence. I

know that my request was an odd one, that usually those who own the land you work would be meeting with me instead. But I specifically wanted to meet with you, who do the actual labor, rather than those who profit from it."

Sidelong looks from the farmers' eyes, and the stiffening of shoulders from those who were a touch more well dressed than the others—landowners, Lore assumed. Even out here, society stratified itself.

Bastian turned away and faced the stone fields. Miles of wheat and grass and trees that should be green but weren't, perfect statues producing nothing.

All because of Lore.

Her hand was still in Bastian's, a fact she didn't remember until his fingers closed lightly around hers, a bolstering pressure she couldn't quite bring herself to return.

Down the road, the dust grew closer. Began to resolve into the shapes of horses and marching men.

"We just have to feel this out," Bastian said quietly, meant only for her. He didn't sound nervous, for all that it was an admittance he had no idea how to do this. "Like you did yesterday."

"Bastian." Lore tried not to make it obvious, but her gaze kept turning to the road, to what was clearly an approaching traveling party. "There's someone coming—"

"Never mind that." His voice was low and sure. "Focus on us."

Her fingers spasmed, scars and calluses in reassuring harmony.

"I can feel them both—Mortem and Spiritum, inside and out." The corner of his lip ticked up, a slight smile. "Can you?"

She could. Inside, a twined rope of black and gold, embroidering her bones. Outside, entropy, the stasis of dead matter in rock and withered root, all the things she'd killed.

But lower, beneath all that death—a spark of life in the farmlands, still. Spiritum, the thinnest thread. So frail she was afraid she'd snap it if she reached, but there.

Lore's eyes drifted closed, and there was her forest, the trees tall and impenetrable, guarding a dangerous mind. In the blue sky beyond, smoke twisted, and the scent of charred bark filled her nose, her lungs.

"You can do this, Lore." Bastian's voice, still so quiet. "I'm here. We're here together."

That was something to cling to. Him, being here.

Bastian stepped behind her, his chest an inch away from her back. A moment, then he held his hands to either side, slow and deliberate. Feeling this out, just like he'd said. Following deep instinct.

Lore put her hands in his, her knuckles against his palms. A slow shiver worked all the way through her, knitting the two of them together, dropping them into a space that felt outside of time.

Slowly, the forest she'd grown around her mind thinned, leaves falling until there was open space, blue sky, endless horizon.

Allowing herself to feel the fullness of her power, on purpose rather than in a moment of panic, felt like finally working out a cramp in a muscle. She didn't realize she'd stepped closer to Bastian until she felt his chest flush against her spine.

"Can you touch them both?" His breath swept against her ear. "Grasp them together?"

She could. Bastian behind her was a current of light, an ember blown to flame. He illuminated her darkness but didn't obliterate it; he only deepened her shadows. She could reach out and tug at Mortem and Spiritum both, the light and the dark, make them hers, make them obey.

"I couldn't do it without you." There was something different about Bastian's voice, the timbre slightly more resonant than it should be. The words didn't really sound like him, either—he wasn't one to perform his caring, preferring action to something spoken. "None of this works without you."

Lore didn't know what to do with that, with a raw vulnerability that she craved but couldn't allow herself to touch. It sounded like something she'd heard before. All of this did, really—something that had happened before and would happen again. Lore was grounded in herself, in her body, but also *outside* of it. Both herself and someone else.

So she pulled away. Leaned almost imperceptibly forward, just enough to put some air between them. "Are you ready?"

The space she'd forced seemed to break Bastian out of a reverie. She felt him shake his head, just slightly, as if trying to dislodge something. "As ready as I'm going to be."

He sounded like himself again. As if that moment had been as unexpected for him as it was for her.

Lore pulled in a breath, held it. Her lungs went still and aching, her heart slowed, her vision grayed out. Except *graying out* wasn't the right way to phrase it, not anymore. Everything was colorless, except for Spiritum.

Before, the magic of life had appeared as a corona of white light, blazing around the edges of every living thing. But now that she held both powers on purpose, Spiritum was gold as sun rays, and she could see it even in dead things—that thin filament of life remaining in the trees, the grass. Death to life and back again, one eternally springing from the other.

"Gods," Bastian breathed out behind her. "Gods dead and dying, it's everywhere."

Her heart tithed a beat. His did, too.

Then, in tandem, their pulses picked up, drumming hard and fast, a flow of life that made her cheeks flush.

Her hands rose. His did, too, the motion sinuous and graceful, their palms still cupped together like they were trying to catch the rain. Strands of black and gold wound around their fingers and breached their skin, their bodies just continuations of each other, melded together by flesh and heart and power.

The magic channeled through them. Then it channeled back out.

Here they diverged, each breaking into their own part of this dance as naturally as if they'd done it thousands of times. The strands of Mortem diverted to Lore, flowing from Bastian and into her, and from her into the dead matter around them, encased in stone—the rocks of the road, the dry layers of topsoil, where decay hadn't yet turned into fertility. Spiritum went to Bastian, gold flowing out from him and finding each filament of life in the stone-entombed earth. Strengthening it, coaxing it to blaze, to bloom.

This wasn't like before, with Gabe, unraveling the rocky shroud she'd accidentally made around Milo that night in the alleyway. It could've been—she could've done this herself, only taking away the stone—but with Bastian, it became something more. They weren't just freeing the fields from not-death, they were infusing them with new life, making them stronger and more fertile than they'd been before.

It was beautiful. It was terrifying.

And in Lore's head, shadows were closing in. Something vast, waiting to devour her, a barrier torn down, flames in her trees and the sky filling with black smoke—

With a strangled cry, Lore tore herself out of channeling-space. Her knees hit the ground, her palms in the grass.

The grass.

She opened her eyes.

Green. Green as far as she could see, the fields restored and blooming.

Her heart felt like it was going to beat right out of her chest, the pounding all but drowning out the confused whispers of the farmers on the road.

"Lore." Bastian knelt next to her, hand on her back. "Lore, are you all right?"

But he sounded distracted. And when Lore looked up, she saw why.

The dust cloud had cleared. In its place was a contingent of maybe fifty people, a few of them on horses, most on foot. All wore silver armor covered with a deep-blue tunic, a golden circle of laurel leaves embroidered around the collar. One of the riders in front held an unfurled pennant, hanging limp in the lack of a breeze. Another laurel crown, surrounding a rearing black stallion on a cerulean field.

It may have been a while since Lore looked at a map, but she still recognized Kirythea's banner.

All of them were frozen, every Auverrani citizen holding their breath. All except Bastian, who stepped forward with his head held high as one of the Kirythean riders dismounted.

The Kirythean nodded. Bastian nodded back.

"Maxon Agripolus," he said. "I see you received my invitation."

Chapter Five

War games don't have rules. The only rule is to win.
—Heria Abraca, Kirythean general

What the fuck, Bastian?" Alie's voice bounced off the marble walls and tile floor of his apartments, echoed in the lush green leaves of the ferns. "What the *fuck*?"

No one else voiced the sentiment, but it lived in their faces. Gabe was pale beneath his eye patch. Malcolm stood with his arms crossed, staring at the floor like he couldn't quite believe the last hour had happened.

Lore couldn't either, really. After Bastian greeted the Kirythean delegation, everything became a dreamlike blur. Lore, politely nodding as Bastian introduced her. Did he call her his deathwitch, or something else? She didn't remember. Alie, her mouth a thin line, curtsying delicately while her eyes shot daggers. Malcolm, managing a quick bow and nearly tripping over a loose stone in the road while he did it.

At least Gabe hadn't been there. Lore kept repeating that to herself. Gabe hadn't been there to see the delegation sent from the man who had pulled out his eye as a child. Hadn't been there to see Bastian nod to them like friends, like equals.

She couldn't help but think that had been on purpose. Bastian, trying to spare Gabe what he could, in the same sideways, wounding way he always did.

Even now, Bastian could barely look at him. When they'd entered the room, Malcolm having gone to fetch Gabe from the Church for an impromptu council meeting they all unanimously agreed had to happen, Bastian had only glanced at him once, his mouth open, as if an apology waited behind his tongue. It never came out.

The daggers in Alie's eyes had only sharpened in the carriage ride back to the Citadel, the Kirytheans following discreetly behind, their flag rolled up and politely stowed away. To make eye contact with her was to risk a cut then; now it was close to a severing. She rounded on Bastian. "How long have you been planning this? It took at least two weeks for them to get here from Laerdas."

Two weeks. The timeline softened a tension in Lore she hadn't realized was there. Two weeks meant after August's death, meant she hadn't been fooled once again, Bastian colluding with Kirythea under her nose. At least she hadn't walked right into yet another trap.

"Almost two weeks exactly." Bastian sat in a chair by one of the ferns, running a hand down his face. He'd been so calm as he greeted the Kirytheans, so collected as he made his show of power to the gathered farmers—the people handpicked to see this happen, and even now Lore saw the brilliance in making commoners the first to know. A way to build quiet solidarity, show them that he was a King focused on everyone in Auverraine, not just his court.

But now Bastian looked exhausted. Exhausted and a bit shocked, as if he couldn't really believe what he'd done. "Kirythea was already lurking around the border," he continued, looking at his muddled reflection in the marble floor. "With armies. The news reached me the day after August died."

"And you didn't think that was information you should share?" Gabe's voice was quiet, but his one blue eye blazed like the heart of a flame. He stood against the wall near the door, as far away from Bastian as he could get, but the space between them crackled like a thunderstorm sky.

"Not when I knew it was futile." Bastian met Gabe's stare, finally. "There wasn't time to fight with you, Gabriel. Not when we both know your answer would be bloodshed."

Gabe said nothing, but his sneer was a gleam of teeth.

"I couldn't just ignore them and wait for whatever plans they were making to be sprung on us," Bastian said. "It was either meet them in combat, or invite them here. We aren't ready for all-out war."

Alie sneered, the harsh expression sitting oddly on her features. "But we're ready to play host to our greatest enemies?"

"No. We're ready to show them how powerful we are." Bastian leaned back, jaw set. "The Sainted King is the leader of the Auverrani military. I know what I'm doing. This is our best shot at trying to broker some kind of peace."

"Maybe we don't want peace," Gabe growled.

"We certainly don't want war," Bastian countered. "At least not right now. They'd flatten us, Gabe. You know it."

Alie's eyes flickered toward Gabe, standing by the door. Her mouth opened, then closed again on silence. She rubbed at her temples like a headache was knocking at her skull.

"It's all well and good to ask for trust." Deferred anger bubbled in Lore's chest, though she wasn't exactly sure what it was for. Bastian's foolhardiness, yes, but also for how he'd all but ordered her to go to the farmlands today, and how quickly she'd capitulated. It had been the right decision, in the end, but she still resented how it'd been made. Something in her resisted saying no to him. That unsettled her.

"If you want a council, you have to treat us like one," she continued. "You can't make all the decisions on your own, Bastian. We all know that doesn't work."

She didn't really mean for it to be a barb, a reminder of his father. But the wounded look that flashed across his face said it was, anyway.

Bastian leaned forward, braced his elbows on his knees. His throat ticked as he swallowed, hard, shifting his eyes between her and Gabe. For a moment, he looked like someone on the edge of confession, as if the space between his deathwitch and his Priest Exalted was the only safe place to let down his guard.

"I know," he said quietly. "But give me this one."

And what could they do now? Kick the Kirytheans out, after they'd been welcomed into the Citadel, albeit in secrecy? It was fine to talk about what Bastian *should* have done, but he hadn't, and now they had to live with it.

Alie sighed. The tension bled out of her shoulders, but not her frame—her fists were still tight. "What's the plan from here?"

"To continue showing our strength." Bastian took the golden circlet from his head and put it on the table beside him with a musical clang. It left an indention in his forehead; he rubbed at it absently. "Maxon, Caius, and their entourage will be here for a month. For that month, Lore and I will continue to use our power, make it abundantly clear that we are not to be toyed with. There's a reason I arranged for them to arrive right as we healed the fields. That kind of magic can't be taken lightly."

Lore shifted uncomfortably in her chair. Healing the fields with Bastian had been alarmingly vulnerable, achingly tender. Using it as a show of strength seemed . . . wrong, somehow.

But it wasn't a bad plan. She could admit that much. Even if it felt like Bastian was taking something sacred and fashioning it into a weapon.

That's what she worked best as, wasn't it?

"Maxon and Caius." Malcolm shook his head. "You sound quite chummy already. Who are they, anyway? Or did you just invite whoever happened to be lurking at the border?"

"Originally, I invited Emperor Jax himself—"

"Bleeding *God*," Alie muttered.

"—but he couldn't make the trip, and suggested Maxon in his stead." Bastian rubbed at the mark the circlet left on his forehead again. "He's a cousin or something. It doesn't really matter. What does matter is that he will send word back to Jax of everything he sees here, and what he sees will be a country too powerful to invade."

"As long as they don't talk to the wrong courtiers," Gabe said darkly. "As long as they don't see how many of them are angry with you. As long as they aren't smart enough to exploit it."

"I've gone easy on them," Bastian replied. "I can change that at any time. I send one marchioness the way of Anton, and they'll all fall in line."

Gabe's shoulders tightened. They stared at each other, King and Priest, a wave at the edge of breaking.

"Fine." Malcolm pushed himself off the wall, held his hands behind him in an almost-military stance. The daggers on his harness caught the falling light. "This has already progressed too far to stop now. Tell us the logistics."

"Unless you're planning to undertake all of this entirely on your own," Alie murmured. "Council be damned."

Bastian shook his head. "No, Lore was right. You're my council, I should treat you as such. This was a onetime occurrence; in the future, I'll consult at least one of you before making such a decision."

Alie glanced at Lore, her lip between her teeth, then looked away.

"The guards will stay in the Church," Bastian said. "Where the Presque Mort can keep an eye on them."

"Delightful," Malcolm muttered. "Are we putting them up in the cloisters?"

"Put them wherever you have room and can closely watch their movements. We want to keep them away from Maxon and Caius as much as possible, so we can better control what kind of information is getting back to Kirythea—we don't want the Kirythean guards hearing too many rumors we can't monitor. Maxon and Caius, we'll keep in the southeast turret. It seemed to work fine the last time we had spies in the Citadel." *The last time*, when the spies were Lore and Gabe, when they'd been led every step of the way down the path Anton and August wanted taken. Lore supposed that *did* bode well. Though Maxon and Caius were probably better spies than she and Gabe ever were.

"So we're just accepting that they're spies," she said.

"Of course they are." Bastian picked up his circlet, spun it around on one finger.

"So how do we know they aren't going to try to assassinate you, or stage a coup, or a whole host of other bad things that an enemy delegation could do from inside your stronghold?"

Bastian laughed, a hoarse bark of sound. "I truly don't think we have to worry about that. I can take care of myself, beloved."

Beloved. That was new.

Across the room, Gabe glowered.

In the window, the sun finally died, its fiery burn fading to soft lavender twilight.

Chapter Six

Your King is your lord, a shepherding partner who will lead you in the way you should go. All authority I grant him; look to him as you would to Me.
–The Book of Mortal Law, Tract 903 (green text, spoken by Apollius to Gerard Arceneaux)

She knew it was a dream because there was no scar on her palm. Her hands stretched out, white and unblemished, softly touching the deep-brown bark of the tree in front of her.

That was the first sign. The second was the colors—they were so vibrant Lore felt like she should squint, but in the dream, her eyes were used to such saturation. The green leaves were so deep an emerald that the veins in them looked nearly blue, the cloudless sky a brilliant sapphire streaked in violet.

Lore took a deep breath. There was no charred smell, no smoke, and it calmed her, somewhat. There was no tug at her chest, no water rushing over her ankles, no shadowy figure by her side. It was a dream, but it wasn't dangerous.

Not in the same way.

"It's yours."

That voice, coming from behind her...she both recognized it and didn't, somehow knew its contours though the tone and cadence were new. Still, they itched at a memory, like maybe she'd heard them recently, or something that sounded similar.

Hands came around her waist. Real-Lore, locked somewhere in the recesses of her brain, eyed the hands with apprehension, but dream-Lore leaned back, resting against a strong chest like she'd done it a thousand times before. "It's a start," she sighed, alien pain in her voice. How strange, to hear a heartache, feel it coming from your throat, and have no context for it. "And no one but us can come here?"

The arms around her waist tightened, palms flattening over her hips and pulling her closer. "No one but us."

"And the others."

"And the others," the voice agreed, with barely hidden irritation.

"Lore."

It was still dark out, but Bastian's voice reverberated through the door at her back. He must be standing close, his hand pressed to the wood, his head bowed forward. Were the door not there, he'd probably be touching her.

Lore didn't answer. She shifted her position, though, making sure her shoulders rasped over the wood of the door, so he'd know there was no way she hadn't heard him. She hadn't lit candles, her room blanketed in darkness, but he somehow knew she was awake. That shouldn't surprise her, she supposed.

"Lore, let me in. I brought dinner, I know you didn't eat." He paused. "Please."

At least he still said please. Bastian had never been a man to beg, never one to let himself be the least powerful in any situation. But to her, he said please.

Another sigh. "Do you really think the silent treatment is a good idea?"

"It seems to be working just fine," Lore muttered.

"Well, now you've gone and fucked it by not remaining silent."

She resumed her silence, pointedly.

"I just want to know why you're upset."

"The act of war, maybe?"

"I thought you agreed with me."

"I agreed that we had to make the best of it now that the Kirytheans are here," Lore snapped. "But no, I do not agree that an *act of war* was the best course to take right now, and I certainly do not agree that you should have done it without talking to me."

To the council, she meant. To all of them, not just her. But she didn't correct herself.

"You've done quite a lot of that recently," she murmured, almost too quiet to be heard through the door. "Making decisions that involve us without letting us know."

That time, she just meant her.

Bastian was silent for a moment. "It was an act to avoid an act of war, actually," he finally said. "Not an act of peace, but an act of decidedly not-war."

Lore sighed. He'd conveniently sidestepped the issue of unilateral decision making, and she could press the issue, but it was so late and the day had already been so hard. "A stupid one."

"Wouldn't it feel better to say that to my face?"

She *was* hungry. "Bleeding God," Lore muttered, and moved out of the way.

Bastian pushed the door open, framed in shadows. He didn't look good. His shirt was wrinkled, and dark circles stood out under his eyes. She'd slept in the time between the end of the impromptu council meeting and now—slept deep enough to dream—but it didn't look like he had. Though she supposed no one looked their best in the middle of the night. He held a tray in his hands, bread and soup. When she didn't reach for it, he put it on the ground next to her.

"Eat," he said, nodding toward the tray.

"Did you?"

"Not important."

"Like hell." She ripped the bread in half, held out part of it.

Bastian looked down at her, face unreadable. Then, moving slow so she could push him away if she wanted, he took the bread and sat beside her, sliding down the wall.

Lore scooted over a bit more, making room. After a moment, she reached out and grabbed the soup, dunked in her bread. She chewed while she pointedly held the bowl toward Bastian so he could do the same. They ate in silence, and when both bread and soup were gone, she picked up the mug of tea on the tray, wafting the scent of chamomile, and took a sip.

"I'm sorry I didn't tell you," he murmured.

"Weak," Lore replied, lips moving against the mug.

"The tea, or my apology?"

"Both."

"I know." He sighed, tipped his head back against the wall. One knee was pulled up, his elbow resting on it; the other stretched out long. "I had to," he continued, launching into an obviously rehearsed explanation. "Kirythea was clearly planning an invasion already, and once they heard that August was dead, you know they would have taken advantage of the unrest. We have to show them a united front."

"But did you have to show them *us*?" It was a stupid question; she felt small for asking it. Of course they needed to show Kirythea their power. Still, she hated that this one miraculous thing that was wholly their own had become a spectacle. "They didn't have to watch. Not for our first time."

The words could have been talking about things more intimate than channeling. But that felt right, somehow. Sex was mundane; magic was not.

Bastian leaned his head against the wall. "I'm sorry. But we had to heal the farmlands anyway. There are already food shortages."

"I know." The shortages had been a problem even before what happened with the fields. Kirythea bottlenecked trade routes, and when winter came and the passes to Caldien froze over, going through Empire territory or by sea was the only option.

"I just wish..." She twisted a loose thread in her nightgown, trying to find words for something wordless. "I wish there had been a different way. And I wish you'd told me what you were planning, so I would have expected a bigger audience."

"Why does the size of the audience matter?" He sounded genuinely curious.

Lore shrugged, not wanting to talk about the vulnerability, how raw it felt. Maybe channeling together only felt that way for her. Maybe it was different for Bastian, who'd never had to think of his power as something profane. Maybe she'd made all of this into more than it really was, in her fierce desire to prove that she wasn't something monstrous to be put down.

Not that Bastian would do that, even if she was. She still had that much faith in him, at least.

When it became clear she wouldn't answer, Bastian sighed. "I wanted to tell you. But if I told you, I'd have to tell Gabe. And we know how that would have gone."

Just *Gabe*, he said. Not *the council.* She and Bastian might be two halves, but whatever they made was split into thirds.

Lore tapped her thumbnail nervously against the side of her teacup and changed the subject. "Nothing happened, right?" She pressed her eyes closed; it was news she only wanted to hear in the dark. "Tonight, when I was asleep, there were no... nothing like the villages?"

A pause, one that felt like it stretched years. "Of course not." He sounded stunned. "Why would you think that? Did you dream?"

"Yes," she said quietly.

Shocked silence, but when Bastian spoke, his voice had a

dagger edge. “Remaut isn’t doing his job, then.” *Remaut* now, not *Gabe*, creating distance. “This is the second time, isn’t it? You dreamed after we channeled in the catacombs.” He looked at her, contemplative. “And you think that’s why.”

It was odd, to hear the fear she’d been secretly harboring put into such stark terms. Odder still, that he’d pick up on it so quickly, with barely any input from her. “Seems to be the logical conclusion, yes.”

“But nothing *happened*,” he said. “You channeled, you dreamed, and it was fine.”

Fine didn’t seem like the right word for it. Lore could still recall the dream voice, so familiar, those hands on her waist. And the night before, her torch against trees.

No, the dreams hadn’t killed anyone, but they didn’t feel completely benign, either.

“Maybe you don’t need to work with him anymore,” Bastian said. “He’s busy, so are you, and we can—”

“No.”

Her own vehemence surprised her almost as much as it did Bastian; he closed his mouth, his eyes narrowing.

“I still need him,” Lore said, looking straight ahead. Her jaw hinged open to elaborate, then shut. There was nothing else to add.

Next to her, Bastian shifted. The light in the window glimmered across his hair, bringing out golden highlights. “I don’t think you actually need him,” he said quietly. “But I understand wanting to.”

Lore didn’t say anything to that. She didn’t know what to say.

A moment, then Bastian sighed. “You know there’s more keeping him here than you. You know that I’m not going to ship him off to the Burnt Isles. Don’t feel like you have to pretend you need him in order to save him.” His jaw clenched, then softened. “He doesn’t deserve it.”

They echoed each other so often, Gabe and Bastian. She remembered all the times Gabe told her the then–Sun Prince didn't deserve her trust, her friendship, her compassion. But it was never a question of deserving. She couldn't fathom *not* giving them those things. Either of them.

"It's not that," Lore said. "Just because I had two dreams that didn't result in murder doesn't mean the danger has passed. Especially if we're going to channel more moving forward."

"I don't see a way around that," Bastian murmured.

"I know." Lore took another sip of her tea, and when she spoke, it was direct and matter-of-fact, all the wavering forcibly pressed out. "But I'm afraid, Bastian. Anton told us that if I keep growing in power, bad things will happen, and I know it was religious horseshit, and that we aren't beholden to the Church anymore, but I am *afraid*."

His hand settled on her thigh, light pressure. "They were lying, Lore."

She took a shaky breath.

"They wanted you dead," Bastian continued. "You dead, and me..." He trailed off. The hand not on her leg opened, turned to show his palm, the eclipse carved there. "They were trying to scare you. Scare me. Make us think that there was no way forward together, no way but the one they wanted. But there is, and we've proven it. We're here, the world is fine, and they were wrong."

Her mother in the dark garden, surrounded by slow-churning fog. *Endings take their time.*

"Still," Lore said quietly. "I want to keep working at making my barriers stronger. Keep things as contained as possible."

Bastian's lips flattened, but he nodded.

"And next time you want to invite an enemy contingent to watch, please tell me first."

He slid her a look from the corner of his eye. "Feel free to punish me as you see fit."

"I think you'd like that too much."

"My ruse is found out," he said, and he did sound slightly disappointed. He stood, stretched, reached out his hand to her on the floor. "It's still a few hours to dawn. You should rest while you can."

"I guess I'll need it," Lore said, looking forlornly at her unmade bed. "I have an appointment with Gabe in the morning, before your coronation."

Bastian's eyes flickered from her to her bed. "I could..." But he trailed off, shook his head. "Good night, Lore."

"Good night." He slipped out the door, taking the tray with him.

She knew what he'd been about to ask. He was going to ask if he could stay.

And she didn't know how she would've answered.

The walk into the Church had never gotten more comfortable. Lore always felt like an interloper there, something to be quickly cleared away, like a scuff on the marble floor or a smudge on the windows. The feeling had only magnified, for all that she was the King's deathwitch. Bastian made her safer, but the Church still held no love for her.

Lore wore a hooded cloak, pulled up to obscure her face. It was Burnt Isles hot, despite the near-dawn hour, but the confessional where she and Gabe met was in a little-used room off the South Sanctuary, and there was always the chance she might meet someone in the commoners' section of the Church who'd known her as a poison runner. By now, everyone in Dellaire knew her name, but she still tried to avoid her old life crashing into her new one. They were too oppositional to hold at once.

The Church confessionals were near the library, and the only way there was past the wall of stained-glass windows depicting the pantheon. Usually, Lore tried to walk past them as quickly as possible, but today, for reasons unknown, she lingered in front of Hestraon, the god of fire.

She'd never spent much time thinking about the elemental gods. Most people didn't. They were relics of the past, slowly dying off one by one before the Godsfall, leaking out trace bits of magic from the corpses left behind. The powers of the elemental deities were small compared with the huge, consuming magic of Nyxara and Apollius, so even when They were alive, They were overshadowed. They'd come to the mainland right before the Godsfall, rather than staying on the Golden Mount like Apollius and Nyxara. Lore wondered if that was part of the reason why They were less regarded. Familiarity breeding contempt, and all.

Lore frowned up at Hestraon. His hair was reddish, the same color as the flames of His forge, His hammer raised to beat down the metal sword on the anvil. The stained glass didn't provide much detail to His face, making it nothing but a white blur glowing with weak light.

She didn't look at Nyxara's window at all, a shapeless swirl of deep blue and black and purple. She kept her eyes on her feet, instead, on the way the light through all that darkened glass cast the shadow of a bruise on the floor.

The door to the confessional room was closed. Lore took a deep breath, calmed the nerves that always sparked to attention right before she was going to see Gabe.

Well. *Talk* to Gabe. He never let her see him during these meetings, staying hidden behind the lattice that divided priest from penitent. They could be civil during council meetings, but something about being alone together made them both skittish.

Lore pushed open the door.

The confessional room wasn't as ornate as the Sanctuary, but neither was it plain. Whitewashed ceilings soared far over her head, crossed by solid oak beams and lit by rose windows in shades of blue and red. Rows of empty pews lined either side of the room. Confession wasn't a required part of devotion to Apollius, and only a few people still held to it, so the confessional rooms remained empty. The clergy kept them up, though, on the off chance someone might want to list their sins to an anonymous ear.

At the front of the room, the confessional itself took up the entire wall. One half was covered by a dark velvet curtain, and the other half was solid wood. Inside, the wall between the two halves was a swirling metal lattice, worked like lace. The priest and the confessor could hear each other, but not see each other clearly.

Lore walked to the curtained half like one might walk to a noose, gripping the fabric and tearing it aside. Behind it, a simple stone bench and a single lit sconce on the wall. Next to it, the metal lattice, spanning the length of the booth.

He was there, sitting on the opposite side of the lattice. She could hear the faint in-and-out of his breathing, see his slow movement from the corner of her eye as he lowered himself to the matching bench on his side. If Gabe noticed her, he didn't give any indication. He never did.

The silence stayed. Lore didn't know how to break it. Things had seemed... well, not easy, when she'd seen him in the garden, but easier. The night blanketed things and blunted the sharper corners. Now, in the light, everything could cut.

But surely that night in the garden meant something.

On the other side of the lattice, Gabe sighed, long and weary. "Close your eyes."

Or maybe it didn't.

"Really?" Hoarse, and with a rueful laugh. "Really, Gabe? That's it?"

Freeing, to finally say it, this thing she'd felt ever since they started meeting in this damn confessional. To stop pretending this was fine. Stop pretending they didn't have unfinished business.

A pause, long enough that she thought he might ignore her. But then: "Were you expecting something different, my lady?"

The honorific made her fists clench. Because she *had* been, and that was stupid. Just because they could act like friends for two minutes in the middle of the night didn't mean anything had really changed. They were still the deathwitch and the Priest Exalted, two people who'd been friends, then almost more, then nothing.

But she still didn't want to give him the last word. She wanted to remind him of that night, smash the brittle cocoon of indifference he'd built. Even if it meant she'd have to lie and cover her own tracks. She'd spent these last weeks tamping down her own recklessness, choosing the easiest path to keep her new life as simple as it could be. It was a relief to let it go, if just for a moment. "What were you doing out in the stone garden, Gabe? I know you couldn't hear me from inside your cloister."

He stiffened. "If I answer that question, will you?"

"I told you why I was there."

"Right. Fresh air." He snorted, unconvinced. "Couldn't sleep the night before your big performance?"

Of course. He thought she'd known about the Kirytheans. She remembered the odd look Alie had given her—she probably thought Lore had known, too. It was wounding in a way Lore didn't know how to articulate, that lack of trust. Knowing that, at least on some level, they saw her the same way the court did. Bastian's co-conspirator.

She swallowed. "I didn't know."

"You expect me to believe that?"

"I hope you do." Her voice came out very small. "I could never lie to you, Gabe, could I? Not like you could lie to me."

That was unfair, and she knew it. He'd never lied to her directly. The falsity in their relationship had come from what Lore wanted to believe about him, even when all the evidence had constantly pointed toward his faith, his Church, his inability to let go of the doctrines that gave him purpose.

She and Gabe and Bastian could only ever have honesty, as much as they all hated it.

So in the spirit of that honesty, she said, "I'm dreaming again."

He froze on the other side of the lattice. "No deaths?"

"No." She sat down, elbows on her knees. "But still, if I'm going to be channeling, I need to keep my defenses strong. Maybe we should meet more often."

She tried not to sound eager for that.

Gabe didn't respond for a moment. Then, low: "More channeling. With *him*."

So many ways to read that tone. Fury, longing, confusion.

"I don't see a way around it," Lore answered, echoing Bastian from hours before. Lightly, almost without realizing, she traced the scar on her palm. "That was the point, right? I stayed alive, and now we both have each other's power. Seems silly not to use it. Especially not when it could stop a war." She made a noise that wasn't quite a laugh. "All that talk of apocalypses, and here we are."

Gabe didn't respond. They sat in silence.

Finally, he shifted on the bench. "We need to get this over with," he said. "The coronation is in two hours. Close your eyes."

She did and saw her forest. The scent of smoke itched in her throat.

Chapter Seven

I truly can't believe he opened the event to everyone...
it smells like a horse farm in here.

–Lady Marguerite Volier, overheard at His Royal Majesty, the Sainted King Bastian Leander Arceneaux's coronation

The session didn't take long, once she and Gabe got going. Lore imagined her forest, grew her trees, sat in the center of the grove and watched the cerulean sky. It seemed so easy, when they were doing it like this. Much harder in the middle of channeling, when she had to thin the forest enough to grasp Mortem, but not enough to let down all her guards.

Still, once she was done, it was long past her appointment with Juliette and the other lady's maids to make her presentable for the coronation. The icily beautiful woman gave her a hard look when Lore rushed through the door, her hair flattened to her head with sweat, and then told one of the other maids to let the guards know this would take longer than previously anticipated.

Even with that less-than-auspicious start, by the time Lore was seated on a gilded chair in the South Sanctuary, she couldn't deny that at least she looked good. Her gown was the lavender-pink of sunrise, with long, gauzy sleeves trimmed in golden thread that nearly swept the floor. The skirt matched, flaring out around her generous hips, and the close-fitting bodice turned the softness of her middle to an hourglass. A combination of thin paper and hot irons that made the room smell horrific had coaxed her wavy hair into defined curls. Crowning it all, a small golden circlet, similar to Bastian's, set with rubies and onyx.

She'd tried to refuse that particular accessory. But Juliette had smacked her hand away and settled it on her head in one fluid motion. "King's orders." And that was that.

Now Lore wished she'd fought a bit harder against the circlet. There'd been a rush of whispers when she was escorted in by two Presque Mort and led to her chair, and the whispers hadn't stopped. Her place was far back on the platform at the front of the sanctuary, clearly for the sole purpose of keeping her out of the crowd. Lore thought sitting in the front row with Alie would've been safer, but Bastian wouldn't be deterred, apparently. He was constantly afraid that someone might try to assassinate her.

Not afraid enough to keep from inviting the Kirytheans, though. Lore could see Maxon and Caius in the gallery, seated with some of the most elderly nobles, those least likely to question who they were—or most likely to forget they'd seen them in the first place. Today was crowded and exciting enough to hide them in the chaos, but that wouldn't work for long if Bastian wanted to keep them in the Citadel.

Lore didn't know Bastian's plan for introducing the Kirythean delegates to the rest of the court. She assumed he'd tell her that plan, but the last couple days had proven the adage about assumptions and asses, so she'd better demand an answer if she wanted one. Rumors had to be circulating already, started by the farmers who'd witnessed the arrival yesterday. Surely that's what Bastian had wanted. The real question was how much he would let the rumors grow and fester before he told the court what was really going on.

He'd probably let them go on for ages. Gods knew the rumors about Lore only became more and more ridiculous.

"And this will only make them worse," she muttered to herself, shifting in the chair.

"Pardon?" The Presque Mort behind her arched a brow. She was a pretty woman, if severe, no scarring visible. Her near-death experience must be the kind that didn't leave a physical mark.

"Nothing." Lore shifted again. This dress was damn itchy, and the crowded sanctuary did nothing to alleviate the heat. "When are we starting, again?"

"Momentarily." Satisfied that Lore was just irritating, not actually in need of anything, the Presque Mort straightened. "The Sainted King is delaying a few minutes, to allow as many as possible inside."

The sanctuary already looked full to bursting. Courtiers took up most of the pews in both the lower and upper galleries, casting sidelong glances at the aisles and along the walls, where commoners packed in tight. It made the crowd a study in opposites: plain cotton against airlike chiffon, rough-spun linen against watered silk. An obvious scale, with an obvious favorable tilt.

Lore let her eyes focus long enough to study the familiar figures a few rows back, where courtiers had left some open space for the wealthier commoners. A woman with white, weathered skin and pale hair, next to one with dark braids tipped in sea glass tied atop her head in a colorful scarf. Val. Mari. Her *real* mothers.

She didn't wave—she didn't want to risk calling more attention to herself—but Lore gave them a smile. Or tried to. It probably looked more like a grimace.

Mari beamed back, waved with no fear of attracting notice. Happy to see her, regardless of the strange circumstances. Val returned Lore's smile, but it was subdued, and worry deepened the bracketed lines around her mouth. That was Val, constantly on edge, always thinking about the countless ways something could go wrong. In this particular scenario, Lore could think of quite a few.

Lore looked away, staring at the floor instead of the crowd. She didn't want to risk seeing someone else she knew from her poison-running days. The trajectory of how she'd gone from that to this was common knowledge by now, gossip dripping from the Citadel to flood the rest of Dellaire, but she didn't want to see what her old crew thought of it on their faces. Didn't want to see the shock, the distrust, the possible revulsion for her Mortem abilities and how she'd used them.

Truth be told, Lore tried not to think of her old life much. It wasn't that she missed it, and wasn't that she *didn't*, more that her well-honed survival instinct had never left much room for reverie. Here she was, and here she'd stay, and everything in her was tuned toward making the best of it. Her life hadn't given her much opportunity to live in the past or future. She was eternally in the present moment, scratching out of it what she could.

Lore shrank back in her golden seat, turning her eyes away from the crowd completely, looking out the window instead. The stained glass depicted Apollius healing what looked like a broken arm, a rather macabre subject for an art piece, but the colors were faded enough that she could get a fairly good look at the sky outside. It was cloudy today, threatening rain.

A door next to her opened. Gabe emerged in Priest Exalted white, his eye patch gleaming like it'd been buffed for the occasion. He was close enough for her to reach out and touch, but he didn't even look at her.

A lectern was set at the front of the platform, a Compendium already open atop it; Gabe stalked over and gripped the lectern's sides in white-knuckled hands.

The crowd quieted, every eye fixed on the Priest Exalted at the front of the room. He cut an incongruous figure. Red-gold stubble on his cheeks, a missing eye, a vicious expression as he stared down into the Compendium like it had personally wronged him. Righteous anger personified.

He looked up from the Compendium, though he still gripped the lectern, his tall body bent over it like a predator protecting its meal. "Stand."

All stood.

Gabe looked back at the Compendium. When he read aloud, the words were stilted, and he crashed through them in a rush. "Apollius, Lord of Day and Life, we ask that You continue to bless us in our faithfulness and continue to guide Your chosen Kings in the ways of power."

The Book of Prayer, then. Lore hadn't spent much time with any part of the Compendium, but of the three holy books that made it up, the Book of Prayer was the one she was least familiar with. Apollius wouldn't pay attention to her prayers even if she recited them word-for-word while standing on her head.

Today, at least, the Priest Exalted didn't seem particularly convinced of them, either.

"Make them holy," Gabe continued, "and make us joyful in their leadership. For in submission there is peace, and true happiness is found in knowing how to be led." He straightened, flipping the page as he took a step back from the lectern, like he didn't want to look at that particular prayer anymore.

A door on the opposite side of the platform opened. Bastian. He wore the same cloak as he had at the only First Day service Lore had attended, bronze and deep-orange flaring out from his shoulders like the sunrise itself. That day, he'd worn a sardonic smile, a playful glitter in his eye. Now Bastian was all business, his handsome face stern, his shoulders held straight.

Behind him entered two clergymen, robed in plain white. One carried another cape—crimson and gold, the one August had worn for those long-ago morning prayers—and the other carried the crown of Auverraine on a velvet pillow, the heavy gold sun rays nearly tall enough to cover his face.

For a moment, Bastian and Gabe just stared at each other. Neither looked at Lore, but she felt caught in their crossfire anyway, the point to an invisible triangle.

Gabe broke eye contact, his throat working as he swallowed. He looked back at the Compendium, flipping pages to reach the Book of Mortal Law in the back. "According to the Book of Mortal Law, Tracts Eleven Hundred Eighty-Nine through Twelve Hundred Twenty-Five, there are three duties of an Arceneaux King. Do you know them?"

"To uphold Apollius's law in all things," Bastian said, as the white-cloaked clergymen unfastened the orange-and-bronze cape from his shoulders. "To lead the world in the direction of His holy plan. To be His emissary on the earthly plane as we wait for His return."

Outside the window, the cloud cover began to break. Slow light seeped around Lore's back, the rose window behind her catching the approach of the sun.

Some soft murmurs began in the crowd, but Gabe didn't look up from the Compendium. His jaw tightened with every word from Bastian's mouth. "And do you swear to uphold these duties as Apollius's chosen monarch?"

"I do." For the first time since he'd appeared on the platform, Bastian looked at Lore. There was a determination in his face that reminded her of the night of the eclipse, when he'd jumped through burning roses with blood on his brow.

"Read from the section I marked," he said to Gabe, his eyes still fixed on Lore. "From the stricken Tracts."

A soft gasp made its way around the room.

Gabe stared daggers at his King. When he spoke, it was breathing-low, pitched so only those on the platform could hear. "Are you sure about this?"

That made Bastian's eyes briefly flicker his direction. "Are you questioning me?"

"You're going to get yourself assassinated," Gabe hissed. "Maybe take a break between blasphemies."

A small, almost-cruel smile bent Bastian's mouth. "Are you worried about me, Remaut?"

The grind of Gabe's teeth was nearly audible. He flipped through the Compendium again, to the very back, this time. The Church library held only a few Compendiums with a record of stricken Tracts; they were illegal for anyone else to own. Lore wondered what Malcolm's reaction had been when he was asked to retrieve one for the coronation.

"Life and death are inextricable from each other," Gabe read, his voice echoing through the huge room. "Through darkness, light is brightened. Through light, shadows deepen. One may not exist without the other. They must rise together, equals once again, and never be parted."

Bastian watched Lore as Gabe's voice rang through the room. She didn't know how to arrange her face, how to look casual.

Protection, that's what this was. Declaring to everyone that her power was just as holy as his own. All her insides twisted, and heat pricked at her eyes, gratitude and embarrassment and fear streams running to a single river.

Gabe shut the Compendium. The sound seemed to echo as much as his voice had. "If you will abide by these strictures," he said, as if the interlude with the stricken Tract hadn't happened at all, "then you are the Sainted King of Auverraine, chosen by our god. Rule in His stead."

Bastian knelt; the clergyman placed the sun-rayed crown on his head. The thing had to be heavy, but he stood with ease.

And the sun fully broke through the clouds.

It wasn't a slow reveal, a natural peeling away of gloom; this was a brilliant streak of light through every window in the South

Sanctuary, slicing through the shadows like a sword point. The rose window at the back of the platform illuminated in a sudden blaze, spotlighting Bastian and his crown in a flood of color.

He stood there a moment, gazing out at the gathered citizens, his face serene. Then he turned and offered out his hand to Lore.

And even though she wanted to take it, wanted to be part of this light-filled moment, she couldn't quite bring herself to. She'd darken this, somehow. She always did.

"Please," Bastian murmured, his eyes spearing into hers, the color of molten gold.

Gabe stiffened.

Slowly, Lore rose from her chair. She grasped Bastian's warm, callused hand, let him lace his fingers through hers.

They stood there, light flowing around them, and after a heartbeat, the crowd began to cheer.

Chapter Eight

True power whispers rather than shouts.
–Malfouran proverb

I understand that a coronation ball is tradition," Lore said. "But I want to go on record as saying this is not a good idea." Despite the words, Lore twisted to look at herself in the full-length mirror, making her skirt swish around her legs. "In fact, I'd go so far as to say it's a bad one."

"What makes you say that?" Bastian lounged on one of the plush upholstered chairs in the corner of her room, one leg slung over the rose-colored velvet arm. He twisted his finger in the air. "Turn around again, we need to make sure the fit is right."

Lore scowled as she twirled, a study of contrasts. "The fact that you had stricken Tracts read in the Church, for one. Gabe was right, you're only magnifying the target on your back with that. The older nobles are mad enough at you already."

"*Gabe* and *right* in the same sentence, coming from your mouth. Never thought I'd hear that again."

She flushed, her scowl deepening. "The . . . unexpected guests, for two."

None of the maids fluttering around her seemed fazed at her wording, so maybe whatever rumors the farmers had started weren't yet in the Citadel.

"You think they're invited?"

"Are they not?"

Bastian grinned. "Of course they are. Give it another twirl, it's still not lying right at the bottom."

Lore gritted her teeth and spun again.

A ball and dinner immediately following the coronation of a new King was customary in Auverraine, but the reality of the thing hadn't struck Lore until she was hustled up to her room by the same Presque Mort who'd guarded her during the ceremony. When she got there, Juliette and a cadre of other handmaids waited with a truly gigantic white ball gown.

It was, without quarter, the finest thing Lore had ever worn. Even finer than the black gown from the eclipse ritual, before that unfortunate stab wound had soaked it in her blood. This dress was similarly simple, a tight bodice that hugged her from breast to hip before flaring out into layers of nearly translucent chiffon, only made opaque by sheer volume. Puffed sleeves of the same chiffon began just under the jut of her shoulders, leaving them bare, and gathered at her elbow. It felt like wearing her own personal cloud.

But even a perfect cloud-dress wasn't enough to distract her from the feeling that something was about to go terribly wrong at this damn ball. Even if she couldn't manage to convince Bastian.

"We have plenty of room for the unexpected guests," Bastian said, voice smooth. "And don't worry over my safety. Leave that to Remaut, if he's so inclined. I can't imagine that's truly his problem, though. He'd probably be thrilled to see me assassinated."

Juliette's lips tightened, but she pretended not to hear. Fantastic. Another rumor for the mill.

Lore narrowed her eyes at Bastian as she embarked on yet another slow twirl. "That's not true, and you know it."

Her twirl apparently brought to light some new minor imperfection, and Juliette waved a hand for her to stop. A pause, a plied needle, and the invisible problem was vanquished. Lore met Bastian's gaze in the mirror. "I know it's tradition, but a ball right now seems ill advised."

"Thankfully," Bastian said, "I'm not asking your advice. I'm the King, I want a ball, so we're having one."

Heat flushed Lore's chest. She wanted to fight with him, but knew doing so in a room full of lady's maids was as ill-advised as this fucking ball.

Juliette made another minuscule adjustment to Lore's skirt and fluffed it out, as if there wasn't a half argument between the King and his deathwitch happening over her head. "I think it's as good as it's going to get, Your Majesty."

Not exactly a ringing endorsement.

"Good." Bastian nodded, jerking his chin toward Lore's dressing table. "Hair."

Juliette bustled her over, and Lore's skirt rose around her like the foam on a wave as she sat down. "Is there a reason you're involved in me getting ready?" Lore asked as a comb was jerked through her tangles. The curls of this morning were now hopelessly flat, her hair once again just a mass of plain gold-brown waves.

She expected some pithy rejoinder, but instead the Sainted King sighed. He stood up, crossed over to where she was seated in front of the smaller mirror. Juliette waved a hand again—in a manner that seemed much gentler than when she waved at Lore—and the maids backed away, graceful as a school of fish parting for a prow.

Bastian braced himself on the back of Lore's chair, leaning over her slightly. His eyes met hers in the mirror.

"I'm sorry," he murmured.

Lore raised an eyebrow.

"I'm sorry that you're caught up in all this royalty bullshit." He looked exhausted. Maybe he wasn't sleeping like he should, nerves keeping him awake like they did her. "Balls and coronations and...and all of it. I know it's not what you wanted, but I have to keep you near me. Keep you safe."

She frowned into the mirror, suddenly stricken with the desire to reach up and cup his cheek, try to soothe away the worried lines across his brow. The flash of anger she'd felt disappeared, easy as dew in morning heat. "That's not your job, Bastian."

"It is." Matter-of-fact, no room for arguing. "And it's what you want. You can't lie to me."

Her lips closed tight. It *was* what she wanted, and she hated that. Lore had taken care of herself for twenty-four years, and her most secret longing was not having to anymore. It was a large part of why she didn't fight with him, why she let him lead. Because he knew the Citadel better than her, yes, but also because it was so nice to be taken care of.

Even if she hated herself for it, just a little.

Behind her, Bastian was lit in lavender light from the falling evening, the moon a sickle sketch above him in the window.

"So let me do it," he said, barely a whisper, so even the maids behind them couldn't hear. "Trust me, Lore."

Stepping back, he motioned for Juliette and her small army to resume their assault on Lore's hair. Bastian looked at the window as he left the room, something like relief softening the lines of his body as the world tilted toward night.

Bastian hadn't hosted a party since August died, and the enthusiasm of the guests made it clear they'd been waiting. The throne room was full of courtiers dressed in their finest, a wall-to-wall throng of silk and satin. Before, the ages of the guests at Bastian's parties trended young, but now there were courtiers of all ages dancing to the string quartet tucked behind the throne, drinking from goblets they filled at the wine fountains flowing freely in every corner of the room. The older generation of nobles had made no secret of the fact that they didn't approve of Bastian's policies, but in true Citadel fashion, they'd apparently put aside their differences to spend an evening in revelry.

So much revelry, in fact, that it seemed none of them had noticed the Kirytheans in their midst.

"Is he not going to announce them?" Alie chewed her lip behind her half-full wineglass, like she was trying to hide the movement of her mouth from the rest of the room. "He's just going to let them wander around the Citadel without telling anyone?"

"He has a plan," Lore said. "He just hasn't told me what it is yet."

Alie gave her a sharp look, the same one she'd given her in the solar after the Kirytheans first showed up. Distrust, not as well hidden this time.

"He can't keep doing that," Alie said after a moment, her voice clipped.

Lore took another gulp of her own wine, careful not to spill it on her dress.

Her dress had been the subject of many stares since she entered the room on Bastian's arm. Lore tried to ignore it, tried to make herself as unassuming as possible. Hard to do, when she was the only person dressed in white. Bastian had left her when they entered with a quick press of his lips to her hand, going to make his diplomatic rounds.

So now she was hiding in the corner with Alie, the two of them watching the Kirytheans with the rapt attention of mice on cats.

Maxon was a natural diplomat. The way he held himself reminded her of Alie, actually: open and warm, but not weak; someone you could easily approach but not talk over. He was handsome, on the shorter side but broad, with close-shorn hair that shone deep-brown in the light of the chandeliers. His face was hard-planed, sculpted, his brows dark over serious green eyes. More than one passing courtier threw him an appreciative glance, but he spoke to no one save his companion.

Caius seemed like an inverse of his fellow delegate. As tall as Gabe, almost, though built slender rather than muscled, with dark eyes and golden hair he wore in a queue at his neck. Both men were dressed in fine but nondescript clothes, things the eye glossed over in a sea of luxury. While they sat well on Maxon, they seemed odd on Caius, as if he would be much more at home in the armor and tunic he'd worn when they rode into Auverraine. Maxon seemed content to drink wine and casually watch the crowd, but Caius did so with an intent that couldn't be ignored, sharp-eyed and observant.

"That's the one you have to watch out for," Alie murmured. "He looks like he doesn't miss much."

Lore glanced at Caius, then away, afraid he would notice. "He'd almost be handsome, if it weren't for the whole definitely-an-imperial-spy thing."

Alie's lips twisted.

As if he knew they were speaking of him, Caius's eyes flickered toward the corner where she and Alie stood. His brows drew down studiously, as if memorizing their faces.

Lore gripped her wine tighter.

"Mouse!"

The crowd around them parted, letting through two women who looked entirely different than Lore remembered them. Mari wore an honest-to-gods gown, something Lore had never seen her mother do. It swept the floor, the same shimmering green as the sea glass clinking in her braids, which she'd artfully twisted atop her head. Val wore breeches and a men's white shirt, as usual, but both of them seemed new, and her boots were polished to high shine.

Val whistled, glancing around as she and Mari came to stand beside Lore and Alie. "Some party. Do you—*oof!*"

Lore threw her arms around both her mothers, mindless of crushing the white ruffles Juliette had worked to perfect. "It's so good to see you."

"You too, mouse." Mari smiled, pushing back Lore's hair. "You look beautiful."

"A beautiful cream-filled pastry," Val agreed, holding out the skirt of Lore's gown. "Something you need to tell us? You're the only one here in white."

Heat slashed through Lore's cheeks, but she was saved from answering by the chiming of a silver bell, held by a liveried servant at the front of the room. Time for dinner.

Everyone made their way to the doors. Bastian stopped by the wall, the courtiers eddying around him, waiting for Lore. He held out his elbow, and she slipped her hand into the crook of his arm. "Next time you invite my mothers to a royal event, you might want to specify a dress code for Val," Lore murmured. "If this was anything less than a coronation, she probably would've shown up with belladonna stains on her shirt."

"I think she looks lovely. And it wouldn't be the first time someone attended one of my events stained in belladonna."

"True enough."

The doors out of the ballroom opened on a long room with glass walls and a glass ceiling, lit with chandeliers hung within arbors of blooming roses. The crowd murmured appreciatively, but when Lore looked at the flowers, all she could think of was Anton.

"When are you planning to announce our guests?" she asked quietly as Bastian led her to one of two seats at the apex of the room, both crowned in more roses. The other courtiers at the table weren't anyone she recognized as friendly. In fact, the looks they shot her dripped with thinly veiled hostility.

"Tomorrow," Bastian answered, just as low. He dawdled, changing course to take her to one of the rosebushes lining the walls so they couldn't be overheard. "At First Day prayers."

"You mean you're going to make Gabe do it?"

"What? No." He shook his head. "I'll do the introductions."

"But Gabe will be there."

"He is the Priest Exalted, so yes, I assume so." But Bastian seemed uneasy about the fact. His eyes flicked downward, as if working through a difficult equation.

"And you don't see how that might be a problem?" Lore hissed. "What with their Emperor being the reason his father is dead and he has one less eye?"

He sighed. "I'll do my best to keep them away from each other. Far enough where they don't have to interact. But I can't coddle him, Lore."

"I hardly call that coddling—"

"I don't want him hurt any more than you do." And he said it so earnestly, the muscle in his arm spasming beneath her hand. "But I can't sacrifice everything to keep Gabe happy. Or whatever emotion he has in place of happiness." He snorted. "He'd be even more determined to be miserable if I tried."

Lore pressed her lips to a thin line.

Bastian turned from the roses, leading her again to their seats. Lore tried to tuck down the froth of chiffon around her ass, as much to make more room as to avoid eye contact with her tablemates.

Bastian made introductions, and she tried to keep them all straight in her head. The Viscount of Something, the Marquise and Marchioness of Or Other, even an admiral. The names slipped away, but they were enough for Lore to realize that Bastian had purposefully put them at a table with all the courtiers left in the Citadel who hated him most. Here were those who vocally despised the tax hikes, who derided the ideas of citizen payments, who thought Bastian Arceneaux was unsuited for the throne.

Fantastic.

The marchioness broke the tense silence once introductions were over, sipping broth from a delicate spoon. "Your Highness," she began, almost a simper. "Some of the other ladies and I have been wondering if summer progress is still happening this year? I understand that many of the estates typically visited are...are hosting...I mean, they're under extraordinary circumstances—"

"Like house arrest?" Bastian grinned widely and took a long drink of wine.

Her face blanched, but the marchioness kept her smile. "Precisely. However, those of us who are still loyal would so love to continue the tradition."

Gods dead and dying, this place and their traditions. They'd probably all jump off the Citadel Wall squawking like seagulls if their great-great-grandparents had done it first.

The marquise glowered at his wife, and she pretended not to see it, her fixed smile strained at the edges.

Bastian swirled his spoon in his soup without eating. Lore recognized the part he was playing. The careless layabout, the feckless Prince, the person all of these nobles were used to. She could see through the act so easily now, it surprised her how thoroughly fooled she'd been when she first met him.

"It could perhaps be arranged," he said finally, with a shrug. "There are a few estates that aren't housing traitors left. And who knows? Maybe by that point we'll have cleared a few out." He turned to Lore. "We'll discuss it."

The smile stayed, permanently affixed to her face, but the marchioness went a bit paler, her eyes flicking between the King and his deathwitch.

Lore didn't say anything. She took another sip of her wine. This was a show, she knew, just like reading that Tract at the coronation. Letting the courtiers know she was part of this new paradigm. She understood, but she truly hated it, and hated even more that the best way she could play her role was to stay silent.

"Well," said the marchioness, "I hope you find the idea to your liking, my lady. All of us used to look forward to summer progress as children. The apartments in the Citadel are grand, but being in the center of the city, surrounded by all those streets—somehow, it makes the heat even worse." She laughed, light and airy. "Where did you spend the summers?"

"The streets," Lore answered.

Silence at the table. Well, silence other than Bastian's single snort of laughter.

Not entirely true. There was always a bunk in the warehouse for her if she wasn't on a job. But Lore couldn't pass up that kind of opening.

"Admiral Legrande," Bastian said, changing the subject and turning to a portly man seated on his left. "The last report I received said a new ship should be ready by the end of the month. How goes the progress?"

Despite the fact that Legrande had been loudly complaining of the increased tax on his acres of farmland to all with ears to hear, he seemed pleased to talk about a new ship. "It's coming along quite nicely. Once she's out on the waters near the Isles, the Kirytheans will think twice about cruising so close."

"Is that so?"

"Certainly. The cannons on her could knock out a vessel from a mile away." The admiral hitched up his belt. "We'll have nothing to fear from the filthy imperials come fall."

"That's certainly the hope," Bastian replied.

The rest of the dinner proceeded in stilted conversation, and it was all Lore could do not to heave a sigh of relief when the same bell that had gathered them all to dinner chimed again, this time to dismiss them into the ballroom. Bastian lingered by her chair until the other courtiers had gone, and only once they'd left did her spine lose its rigidity.

"Gods dead and dying," she muttered.

"Quite." Bastian held out his arm. "Not done yet, dearest."

The song playing when they reentered the ballroom was a waltz, Lore thought, though everything sounded like a waltz to her, since it was the only dance she reliably knew the name of. The other courtiers swept immediately into the dance, swirls of glitter and lace skirts like night-opening blooms.

It reminded her of her first night in the Citadel, Gabe by her side, dressed as a foxglove. Next to her, Bastian had a similar preoccupied look on his face, and she wondered if he was thinking of him, too.

In the center of the room was a dais with two thrones, slightly elevated so whoever sat on them could easily observe the ball. Both chairs were silver, and both were tangled with what looked like dead vines.

"The florist must be upset that we haven't engaged their services for Horse yet," Lore said.

"That's on purpose." Bastian's voice was steely.

She frowned. "Explain."

Bastian gestured for her to step up first; hand on her waist, he followed behind, then gave her a wide-but-weary grin. "Demonstration number two."

Oh.

Lore gnawed on the inside of her cheek as she examined the dead vines. Roses, what else? The thorns were sharp, woven into the silver lattice of the chair backs, woody and dry and dead as dead could be. At least it wasn't hemlock, to really drive the point home.

She shook out her fingers, already feeling the curl of Mortem in the dead matter, sensing the gleam of Spiritum far beneath. "Are you going to tell them all to look? Play ringmaster?"

“Not necessary.” Bastian turned and situated himself behind her, his hips rustling the fabric of her skirt as he pressed close. “They never stop looking.”

There was no need to talk through the plan. Every time they did this, it felt more natural, more instinctual. Bastian held out his hands on either side of Lore, the same stance he’d taken at the farmlands. She placed her hands in his, knuckles-to-palm.

The world around them dimmed, faded into black and gray and gold.

It was so easy. Lore threading out the death, Bastian feeding the life, the strands of both powers cycling through them like tributaries on the way to the ocean. When the roses opened, the pall of channeling-space lifted, color bleeding in again.

“Perfect,” Bastian whispered. It didn’t sound like his voice, not right then. Too resonant, too low. But when Lore looked back at him, Bastian seemed fine. More than fine; he seemed ecstatic.

The roses were blood-colored, full as powder puffs. There was silence for just a moment, but then someone started polite applause.

Bastian took her hand, turning her around on the dais. He held out his arms like a showman, laughing. Lore tried to do anything but grimace.

Across the room, in the corner, Caius stood. He raised his wineglass, eyes glittering, though he didn’t join in the applause.

Chapter Nine

Never let those you love be parted from you, as I never allowed them to be parted from Me.

—The Book of Holy Law, Tract 1347

In a move that both surprised her and made her give thanks to all gods dead and dying, Bastian didn't make her dance. When Lore asked about it, he gave her one raised brow. "We *are* trying to look intimidating."

She swatted his leg.

So instead of dancing, they spent the ball seated on their rose-festooned dais, sipping wine and people-watching. Bastian was very good at catching every minor embarrassment of his court, lightly tapping Lore's thigh and jerking his chin to tell her where to look. She saw at least three hissed arguments, four stomped toes, and one attempt at a grope in the corner by two very drunk noblemen who stumbled out of the room before things got too debauched.

Lore also saw Alie talking to Caius.

Her hand on Bastian's leg wasn't playful, this time. She gripped his thigh, cold fear pouring down her nerve endings. "We have to go over there."

Bastian followed her eyeline and frowned, but didn't spin into Lore's panic. "There's no need. Alie has things well in hand."

And it appeared she did. She even laughed at something Caius said, her pretty face arranged into a gentle smile. She looked at Lore once, something unreadable flashing across her eyes, before turning back to the Kirythean.

"I don't like it," Lore murmured, her grip on the King reluctantly softening.

"Try not to worry." He placed his hand over top of hers. "Alie is much better at secrecy than you ever were. And if you watch, you'll see she's not talking much. She's letting him steer the conversation. It will be interesting to hear how he introduced himself."

True, but watching still made Lore nervous. She twisted the gauzy fabric of her skirt between her fingers.

A nobleman stopped in front of the dais. She recognized him, vaguely. Lord Demonde, one of the few courtiers of the older generation who didn't openly oppose Bastian's new rulings. That didn't commend him much, however. Alie had told her that Demonde was a slippery sort of man, his convictions malleable. And he wasn't one of the wealthier nobles, so the new taxes hadn't hit him quite as hard.

He also had the distraction of a recent marriage. The new Lady Demonde clutched his arm lightly, her eyes cast away. A pretty woman, not much older than Lore. Demonde himself had to be over sixty. And not a well-aged sixty, at that—the man's cheeks were clearly rouged, the whites of his eyes jaundiced. The padding in his coat couldn't quite hide the skeletal thinness beneath. He'd certainly been dosing poison.

Bastian looked at Demonde as though he was already bored of whatever the other man was going to say. He adjusted his circlet, the movement designed to be casual, though Lore knew it was anything but.

"It is wonderful to see you, Majesty," Demonde finally said

through a simpering smile when it became clear he'd have to speak first. "We missed you at our wedding, but understand how busy you've been."

"Yes," Bastian said. He didn't offer anything else.

Lady Demonde raised her eyes to Lore, just a split second, then cast them down again. They were a pretty cornflower-blue, set nicely against the gold of her hair. Her features looked vaguely familiar, though Lore was sure they hadn't met before.

Which was strange, because that split-second look was filled with venom.

"May I present my wife," Lord Demonde said, undeterred by Bastian's coldness. "Amelia Demonde, née Devereaux."

Amelia Devereaux. *Oh.* Danielle's older sister, Danielle who'd conspired with Bellegarde and Anton, whose story about the docks had been one more step on the path toward the catacombs and raising an undead army.

"Amelia," Bastian said, his voice veering from disinterested to somewhat frosty. "How fortunate, that you found yourself someone who could save you from the rest of your family's fate."

Amelia dropped her eyes and moved into a curtsy, but not before Lore saw the flare of rage in her pretty eyes again. "I am fortunate indeed," she said softly to the floor.

Demonde nodded with a manufactured serious expression, all the subtext of the conversation flying over his head. "The Devereauxs and I were in talks before all that messy business happened," he said. "When you handed down your sentence—a very merciful one, I must say—my lawyers said I would be well within my rights to dissolve the betrothal." He raised Amelia's hand to his lips and gave it a kiss. "But I was far too in love, by then."

Amelia gave her husband a sunny smile, one that highlighted just how beautiful she was. Lore recalled what Danielle had said at Alie's tea, that Amelia was furious with her parents for marrying her to Demonde when she'd had her sights set on Bastian.

She'd played it smart, though. Pretending to return Demonde's infatuation had saved her from the Burnt Isles.

Lore would've preferred the Isles.

"I only hope that you're able to find such happiness one day," Demonde continued, staring adoringly at his bride.

"Thank you," Bastian said simply.

"And when you do," Demonde said, winking at Lore, "Amelia can help the lucky lady plan. She'd like that, wouldn't you, my love? Put together a positively beautiful ceremony for us, and on such short notice."

Amelia's lips blanched, pressed hard against her teeth. But her voice was entirely even when she spoke. "I would be happy to. Just let me know when, my lady, and we can discuss."

"I'm sure that won't be necessary." But she meant it as a reassurance, to let this woman who obviously despised her know she wouldn't have to help her plan a nonexistent wedding. It was already out of her mouth when she realized it was probably an insult. Lore stumbled over her words, trying to find better ones. "I mean, I don't think there will be any need to—"

"Noted, Amelia." Bastian squeezed her hand, and Lore fell silent. "Thank you."

Amelia's lips pinched into an approximation of a smile. "Being an Arceneaux Queen is no small matter," she said. "It takes great preparation. Of course I would be honored to help where I can."

Demonde and Amelia took their leave with a bow and a curtsy, fading into the throng. Amelia didn't look back at them, but it was with the kind of determination that said she wanted to, badly.

Lore blew out a relieved breath, making one of the carefully cultivated curls on her forehead toss sideways. "That... well." She turned to Bastian. "Does *everyone* think we're getting married?"

He let go of her hand and leaned away on his opposite elbow with a shrug. "It seems so."

Normally, he would make a joke here. Say something pithy

about how no one in the court thought for themselves. But he didn't.

Her dress was itchy. Lore shifted in her chair. "That was kind of you," she said finally, changing the subject. "Letting Amelia stay in the Citadel."

"Not exactly kind, when staying meant she had to marry that oaf." He adjusted his circlet again, pushing it back like he couldn't find a comfortable angle to wear it. "Amelia's father swore she had nothing to do with the rest of the family's plans. She was pious, ridiculously so, but she was willing to make an oath promising that she'd never plotted against me specifically, and never would." He paused. "She cried so much, at the trial. Call me soft, but I couldn't send her to the Burnt Isles after that."

"Seems that tears sway you easily," Lore murmured.

"Don't be jealous." But his smile was wan and tired. "I just… knew she was innocent, I suppose." He shook his head. "No, that's not quite right. It was intuition. A feeling like keeping her here was right, like it would set the correct tone for my reign. Something to do with Spiritum, maybe." He frowned slightly. "It seems as though I should pay attention to such things."

Lore lumped up the chiffon of her skirt again, dug into it with her thumbnail until a thread in the delicate fabric broke. "Maybe."

"You seem less than convinced."

"You were less than convincing. *Intuition*, Bastian? That's what you're ruling with?"

He gave her a sardonic look. "Remember when you raised the body in the vaults? When it said some claptrap about awakening, about finding the others, and you just knew what it meant?"

She bristled. "That's different."

"Is it, though?" He leaned her way again, looking almost eager. Bastian had never been one for theological debate, not like Gabe, but the man did love to argue. "Both of our powers are misunderstood. Both of us can use them in ways never seen before. Is it really so unbelievable that it might push us in the right direction from time to time? Give us a dream, a vision, something?"

Lore's frown deepened. But before she could ask him to elaborate, the doors at the front of the room opened.

On the other side, Gabe.

The daggers on his chest harness gleamed, the pendant of the Bleeding God's Heart hanging on a shorter chain than Anton had worn. Right over his own heart, glinting back refracted chandelier glow. The candles tattooed on his palms showed in fragments as he walked, snatches of black ink.

It made Lore think of the deep dark before dawn, of those hands on her skin and the cold of a window at her back. She swallowed.

There was a pause in the party, this time. Dancers stopped their swirling, one of the violinists missed a note. Lore didn't blame them; Gabe looked like an oncoming storm. It didn't seem that his mood had improved since the coronation.

From the corner of the dance floor where she'd been standing with Lore's mothers after leaving Caius, Alie started forward. Mari's hand on her arm stopped her. Brigitte, Alie's friend who'd also been at that ill-fated tea party, had joined their group moments before, and now seemed equally apprehensive of the looming Priest Exalted, taking a step back toward the corner.

Gabe didn't look at any of them. He strode right up to the throne dais, glaring, and crossed his arms. The stance emphasized the Heart pendant against his chest. "You called?"

His voice was even and steady, but in the momentary quiet, it rang clear as Church bells. Especially the stretch of silence where he didn't add *Your Majesty*.

The pause didn't last long—the courtiers of the Citadel knew how to mask their interest, knew how to act as though nothing was amiss while keeping a shrewd eye on proceedings. The string quartet began again, the dancers swung back into measured steps, wineglasses were once again lifted to already-stained mouths.

"I did," Bastian said quietly. All the quick energy he and Lore's brief debate had brought him was gone now; Bastian seemed nothing but determined.

Gabe's eye flickered her way, so quickly Lore could've imagined it.

Slowly, Bastian placed his empty goblet on the floor, then stood, turning her direction. He looked almost apologetic. "This sort of thing has to be officially Church-witnessed."

Then he went down on one knee.

Every system in Lore's body froze, from muscle to marrow. Alternative explanations flickered past, were discarded—surely this meant something else, surely it wasn't what it looked like—

If the room had paused before, now it stood arrested, every subtly watching eye casting out its secrecy in favor of open staring. The quartet didn't just miss a note; it stuttered, a discordant jangle of strings, then went silent.

Alie had a hand over her mouth. Beside her, Brigitte's dark brows were in the vicinity of her hairline, her wineglass half raised like she'd been arrested mid-sip.

In the corner, where he'd been speaking with Demonde and Amelia, Maxon went silent, turning to the dais with narrowed, curious eyes.

All of this entered Lore's mind and was briskly, emotionlessly cataloged, distractions against the fact that Bastian Arceneaux was currently kneeling in front of her. Lore gazed out at the crowd until they blurred, then her eyes sought Gabe.

He looked as shocked as she felt. And he was looking *at* her, finally, as if that shock had broken through every other barrier they'd built between them. Bastian was aware of Gabe, too; she could see it in the way he was turned just slightly, so he could keep the other man in his sights. That triangle, again, three points that left them all bleeding.

"Lore."

Bastian's voice, different than she'd ever heard it. No, that wasn't quite right—it had the same unreal, earnest quality it'd had that night in the atrium three weeks ago, when they were headed down into the catacombs. When he said that his father being a bad man meant his hatred must make Bastian good.

And that resonance she heard when they were channeling, sometimes. He seemed both more and less himself, here on the floor in front of her.

Slowly, with effort, Lore lowered her eyes to the Sainted King's.

He took a deep breath. "I don't think this should really be a surprise," he murmured, meant for only her to hear. "And not just because of what the court thinks. This is meant to happen. Us. You feel that, too, don't you?"

And here was another echo from their recent past, that plaintive note, almost begging. *Tell me I'm not alone in this.*

She'd had an answer, then. Now she couldn't find one.

But the sight of him like this, laid bare and earnest, felt like something beautiful and awful, something no mortal eye was meant to look on and no mortal heart could hold. This was one more step in a dance, as inevitable as everything that came before it. There'd been something about him from the beginning that called to her and made her *want*. Something about both of them, him and Gabe. And maybe this wasn't exactly where the wanting pointed, but gods, it was as close as she could hope to get.

She looked into Bastian's eyes, glinting dark. She nodded.

Behind him, Gabe stiffened.

Bastian reached into his doublet, pulled out a ring. The band was braided gold and silver, much like his throne. The diamond had a nearly golden cast to it, shimmering like a piece of captured sun.

"Before my gathered subjects." His voice was still quiet, but the room had grown grave-silent, and his words carried to every corner as he spoke rote phrases, decided centuries before. "I ask that you, Lore, take my hand in marriage and become the Queen of Auverraine."

It sounded strange, for there to be no surname in the pronouncement, a gaping hole that everyone had to notice.

If they were just Lore, just Bastian, it wouldn't even be a factor—they'd be together already in every way that mattered. She knew that. But they were a King and a deathwitch, two channelers of leftover god-power. And though the titles shouldn't matter, though something like this should be just about *people*, it couldn't be. Not now, not when the titles were so damn heavy.

But still, she wanted.

"Yes." She barely felt her mouth move, but she heard herself answer. "Yes."

And the ring slid over her finger.

And he kissed her. And Lore kissed him back.

While his lips were still on hers, while the crowd whipped itself from shock to cheering, her eyes opened and looked at Gabe again. His lips were parted, his cheeks flushed. One hand raised, fingers twitching toward her and Bastian.

Then he turned and left the room.

Chapter Ten

There is always something different to want.
–Fragment from Marya Addou, Malfouran poet

Her hands were on the tree again.

It didn't take her long to recognize it was another dream. As soon as her eyes registered sensory input, she knew.

Lore expected fear, along with that knowledge, expected panic to drip icy down her spine and make her limbs clumsy. Having the dreams meant that her forest wasn't working, that the influence of a dead goddess might be seeping into her mind, no matter that Bastian didn't believe it. But no fear came.

Maybe there's nothing to be afraid of, she thought, but it was a faded thing, fleeting as smoke. In this dream-world with her dream-mind, the words hardly made sense together, something the person she was here had no context for.

Her hands—palm unscarred, paler—caressed the bark in front of them like it was a long-gone lover, a thing she'd never expected to touch again. Her mind felt split down the middle, dream-her and real-her, each with a different set of thoughts and memories and beliefs. Dream-her was louder. Dream-her thought if she could concentrate hard enough on this tree, narrow all the noise in her mind to only the feel beneath her fingers, maybe she could forget.

Forget what? real-Lore asked, another bare impression of thought that barely made an impact. There was no answer.

"It was kind of him."

A voice she both recognized and didn't. She glanced over her shoulder.

Her eyes wouldn't quite focus on the figure behind her, glancing off at all the salient points. Tall. Broad-shouldered. His hands were freckled, but his face was a wash of light and color, like water thrown across a canvas that hadn't dried.

Dream-her scoffed lightly, turning back to the tree. "I don't think he knows how to be kind anymore," she murmured. "Kindness is a human thing."

The figure shifted on his feet. "Did you give him an answer?"

She sighed, leaned forward so her forehead pressed against the tree as surely as her palm. "I need time."

"That does seem to be the one thing we have plenty of, now," the other voice said ruefully. A pause. "And what answer will you give, after all that time?"

The dream-mind fluttered over answers, unsure which was right. Did she love him? Of course she did, she wouldn't have come here if she didn't. Wouldn't have done as he asked, over and over again, even when she wasn't sure he was making the right decisions. But did that mean she wanted to marry him?

"I don't know," she murmured, an answer for the question in her mind and the person at her back.

The atmosphere shifted. She knew he'd raised his hand, could feel the way his fingers flexed as surely as if they were already on her skin. Her breath caught, waiting. Wanting, though she tried to bury that.

"Don't," the other voice said, so softly it was barely sound.

Lore didn't wake up gasping. Her eyes opened calmly, staring up into her canopy, the fabric waving like a ghost in the breeze through the cracked-open window.

Instinctively, she knew that this dream had harmed no one. It wasn't her own mind turned against her like Anton had done; it was her own.

Though that phrasing didn't fit quite right. There was *something* about these dreams, something more than just tired firings of an overworked brain. They felt too real.

Whatever the dreams were, they were clearly being triggered by channeling. And even if these particular dreams weren't harming anyone, they still made her uneasy.

Something tugged at her hand when she stood, kept it flush to the bed. Frowning, Lore looked down.

Her ring.

A thread from her bedsheet had gotten caught in one of the silver prongs holding the diamond. Lore had nearly forgotten she was wearing it—ludicrous, the thing was huge—but it sat comfortably on her finger, a weight that seemed like it'd always been there.

She stared at it a moment, lips pressed together. Then she gently untangled it from the loose thread.

There hadn't really been a discussion of sleeping arrangements when she and Bastian returned to his apartments. He'd gone to his room and hadn't asked her to accompany him. She'd gone to her own. None of it felt real, like it was a play they were putting on for the benefit of everyone else, for all that she wanted him and he wanted her.

Lore didn't think he would have stopped her, if she'd followed him. Maybe she should have. Made this something familiar.

Sleep wouldn't come again, not tonight. She knew that like she knew the shape of her scar. So Lore defaulted to what she'd done before, when her mind refused to settle.

She walked.

No candle this time. She didn't need it. When she left her room, closing the door softly behind her, the moon illuminated the solar, casting dark shadows of palm fronds on the tiles.

Illuminated Bastian, standing at one of the tall, arched windows, his face tipped toward the sky.

Lore stared at him a moment, idly twisting her ring around her finger. The time after Bastian's proposal was a blur in her mind—the roar and applause, the congratulations. Her memory was narrowed only on two things: Bastian's eyes, brown-gold and glimmering as he still knelt in front of her, like he thought something might break if he moved.

And Gabe's face behind him, his expression carefully blank. Gabe, whirling to leave, just like he had before. He was always leaving.

She didn't realize she was walking toward Bastian until her feet were already moving. Same as it ever was, him holding her tether, pulling her along.

Bastian glanced at her as she approached, no surprise to be found on his face, then turned back to the window. He didn't touch her as she came to his side. Strange, for two people who would presumably be married. Maybe he would have stopped her if she'd tried to follow him to his room after all. Maybe they needed time for this to settle before they could treat it like something normal.

As much as anything ever was between them.

Lore scrutinized the window, trying to see what he was looking at so intently. All she could see was a wide swath of sky, a scrim of summer storm clouds over stars.

"They won't stand for it," Lore murmured. She twisted her ring around her finger, the tic as ingrained as if she'd been doing it for years. "You know that, right? The nobles won't allow you to..."

To marry me. The words stuck in her throat. Here was the part that had to settle: Lore believing it could ever actually happen. That her life could change that much.

A scoff. "They don't have a say. This is between you and me."

She sat on the wide sill. "Why?"

The question that had presented itself moments after this ring was on her finger. The question that had chased her into sleep. It couldn't just be a question of *want*, not for the two of them. Not under circumstances like this.

He was quiet for a long moment, ticks of her heartbeat that landed like punches. Lore dared a glance sideways. Bastian's head hung low, his overlong dark hair hiding his face.

She'd been right, so many weeks ago, when she'd thought about how Bastian's too-long hair would probably be the next fashion. Most of the younger nobles were growing their own out now.

Gabe still kept his brutally short.

"I want to keep you safe," Bastian said finally, his face still hidden. "This is about as close as two people can be, isn't it?"

Her face heated.

"And it legitimizes you in the eyes of the Kirytheans," he continued. "Shows them you aren't going anywhere. That your power is Auverraine's."

She twisted the ring faster. "Does that mean it's just for show?"

"No." He finally looked up at her. The two of them were arranged in opposition, him facing the window and her the room. Him in light and her in shadow.

"No," Bastian repeated softly. "I have every intention of marrying you."

Her heart knotted in on itself. "I'll be a terrible Queen, Bastian. You can't have thought this through."

"I don't need to. It was always going to be you, Lore. Our magic reflects each other. We *know* each other in a way no one else can."

He paused. "And you're one of the only people who makes me feel like I'm not alone."

One of the only people. She knew the other, one blue eye and inked palms.

"Fine," Lore murmured to the floor. "You know what you need. What about what I do?"

"You need me," Bastian answered, low and easy. "Just like I need you. It's why you're still here." He gave a slight shake of his head. "If we were different people, Lore, you would've been long gone by now."

He was right. She was only good at running. But she was trapped here in his gravity, a star in his orbit, and leaving hadn't even crossed her mind.

A dark garden, a plea by an open well. *Run.*

No.

"So I'm what you need." She made herself lift her eyes, made them meet his. "But what about what you *want*?"

It was the first time she'd seen Bastian Arceneaux at a loss for words.

But maybe that wasn't exactly right. He didn't look so much like he couldn't find the words—more like they were dammed up somewhere within him, and blocked from getting out. A war playing across his face, fought in the increments of a tightening jaw and a carving line between his brows.

"Lore," he said quietly, like it was the beginning of a confession. But the rest of the confession never made it out of his mouth. Nothing but her name.

Her eyes went to his mouth, slightly open. He'd kissed her, when she said yes, and it was real and warm and it felt like sunlight after winter. The memory of it kept creeping at the edges of her every thought, and the memory made her think of how he'd kiss her if they weren't in the middle of a ballroom, if every eye in the Citadel weren't watching.

One eye, in particular.

"Why did you make him come see it?" She hadn't meant to ask. But this was an answer she truly wanted. Yes, royal betrothals had to be officially witnessed, but that just meant they had to be recorded, and couldn't Malcolm have served as the Church's emissary? "That was cruel, Bastian. For all of us."

"Because I wanted you to make the decision where you could see us both," Bastian said. "I don't deny it was cruel. But I wanted to know that I was the one you chose."

The stone on her ring had turned in toward her palm. It felt like ice against the raised lines of her scar. "You shouldn't have done that."

"Add it to the list." He sighed, running a weary hand over his face. "But you . . . you did choose, right?"

Uncertainty sounded strange from Bastian. It bolstered her own certainty, the Law of Opposites at play again. "I did," she said.

But Bastian's deep breath didn't sound like relief. Like he didn't really want her to make a choice at all.

Bastian turned from the window, his hand rising to her arm. His skin was a pleasant heat, like water that had soaked up the sun. His hand on her arm went to her cheek, pressing gently so she turned in his direction, a flower to light.

"Tell me what you're thinking," he murmured.

Lore sighed, closed her eyes. "I'm thinking that I wish we weren't who we are. I'm thinking that if I'd met you on the street, and you weren't the Sun Prince, we would already own a row house together." Her nose wrinkled. "We'd rent one, at least." Maybe Gabe would be there, too.

He laughed quietly. "We'd be poor, and we'd have no magic, and you think that sounds better than this?"

"It does to me."

His breath was so warm, so close. It wouldn't take much to kiss him. And if she did, they wouldn't stop there, they'd be inside each other on the floor in the moonlight, searching for something simple when everything around it was so complicated. They'd circled that kind of togetherness for so long, but never let themselves get that close.

Lore tipped back her head, his lips a mere hairbreadth from hers. She moved to close the gap.

And Bastian leaned away.

It didn't hurt her, not really. Things were raw, things were fragile.

Bastian's breath was shaky. "I'm sorry," he said. "Any other time…I don't know, I just feel like I shouldn't…"

She didn't understand that. But she didn't have to. Lore just nodded, and stepped out of his arms.

He didn't stop her.

She considered going back to the garden, but she didn't. She went to the atrium instead. There was no reason to assume Gabe would be in the garden again, but she didn't want to chance seeing him, not with Bastian's ring on her finger.

Maybe Gabe had fully let her go. Maybe she was looking for something that wasn't there. An indication that she was still important to him, somehow, that she was more than the thing that had trapped him here beneath the thumb of a King he hated. Or at least wanted to believe he hated.

It was selfish of her to *want* to be something different. But Lore's selfishness was nothing new. The pull she felt to both of them hadn't changed, no matter who she was engaged to.

"That's horrible," she muttered to herself, but was it, really?

The moon through the windows was bright enough to light her way down the stairs of the turret, through the winding halls that led to the glass-domed room full of poison plants. Lore encountered no one, but a few of the rooms she passed bled the sounds of laughter and music into the silence. The ball had been eventful; such parties didn't end quickly. She wondered how many times her name had been uttered behind those closed doors. She wondered what rumors were brewing. Cold comfort, that none of them could be as strange as the truth.

The atrium opened around her, a cloud of warm, somnolent scent from the night-blooming flowers—evening primrose, climbing datura. Lore knew Gabe wouldn't be here, either, but she looked for him anyway, searching for a shadow that might hold a monk.

No monk. But someone was here.

The figure was slender, taller than Lore, standing by one of the windows. A pale, thin hand caressed one of the blooms next to the glass. Hellebore, its bloody color leached pale by the moon. A fall of golden hair covered the figure's face, but Lore recognized her almost instantly.

Amelia Devereaux. Demonde, now. Dani's sister, the only member of her family who'd escaped the Burnt Isles, whose tears had moved Bastian to mercy. In the dim light, she almost could be Dani, the way Lore remembered her—laughing with Alie and Brigitte in Bastian's solar, eating macarons, feeding her the tiny bread crumbs of information that would lead to Anton's trap.

Lore made no sound, but the other woman knew she was there anyway. She lifted her hand away from the hellebore as she glanced over her shoulder.

Distantly, Lore wondered if she should try to run, to hide. The look on Amelia's face was all malice.

"You don't deserve it," the other woman murmured. "You stole the greatest blessing the Bleeding God could grant, power beyond imagining, and you don't even care. Stupid girl."

Any other time, Lore would have some sort of arch rejoinder that would make someone think twice about talking to her like this. But she was so tired, and Amelia had a right to be angry, really. She was here while her family was gone, trapped in marriage to an old man. She just rubbed a hand over her face. "You aren't the first to think that."

"Just remember that it's your fault," Amelia continued as if Lore hadn't spoken. Slowly, she walked toward Lore, meeting her in the center of the atrium, the moon overhead a spotlight on them both. "If you had done as you were bidden, the rest of this wouldn't have to happen."

"The rest of what?" Lore asked, her brow furrowed. "Don't do anything stupid, Amelia. Demonde will probably die soon, and then you can have your pick of eligible bachelors. I mean, other than Bastian."

The other woman's face twisted. "This isn't just about Bastian." She nearly snarled his name. "This is about a new world. *His* world. This is bigger than any of us, deathwitch, and you've made it so much more complicated than it had to be. You just couldn't go down alone; you had to take everyone else with you. Selfish."

It sounded like her mother, and it made Lore recoil.

Amelia's hand rose, her cold fingers brushing across Lore's cheek before dipping to her hand. She picked it up, held it before her, turned it this way and that to inspect her ring.

"Hemlock Queen," Amelia scoffed. "Such a fierce name for someone ruled by fear. Who damned the world because she was afraid."

Then she was gone, drifting out of the atrium and into the darkness of the nighttime Citadel.

Lore sighed. Then she made her slow way back to Bastian's apartments, too tired to sort through what Amelia meant.

Something is happening.

The thought felt alien, as if someone was whispering inside her skull.

Then, a word.

Catacombs.

Not her inner voice, not the mundane monologue of her own thoughts. This came from somewhere else, just like it'd seemed to the first time she heard it, the night she went to the stone garden and saw her mother, saw Gabe.

But it was stronger, now, and finally she could place where she'd heard it, this voice lurking in the back of her mind, both like her own thoughts and not.

The same voice she'd heard at the Mortem leak, a lifetime ago.

Lore closed her eyes tight. "Go away," she muttered through her teeth. She looked like a madwoman; felt like one, too. "Go the fuck away."

Her head was quiet, but the pull she felt in her bones remained. Lore ignored it, stalking purposefully toward her bedroom, hurrying past the Citadel door as if afraid some monstrous hand would reach through and pull her into the night.

Chapter Eleven

I would deem it unwise to make a move on Auverraine just yet, despite their current upheaval with the new King. We should see if the rumors are true.

–Kirythean correspondence, intercepted at the Ourish Pass by Caldienan border guards

Bastian did not often attend First Day prayers. Lore didn't blame him—Anton and August's designs on his life centered on religion, so it made sense that he might want to avoid it. Lore didn't often attend, either.

But damn her if she was going to miss this one.

Lore had woken with the dawn and immediately gone to her closet. She dressed, and considered calling for Juliette to do something about her sheet-creased face and her tangled hair. Instead, Lore took care of them herself, braiding her hair, rubbing something lotion-like from a pot on her vanity into her face to smooth the creases. The end result was less polished than she was used to now, with a phalanx of maids at her disposal. She looked more like the person she had been, rather than the one she'd become.

The night before picked at her mind as she tucked down tufts of hair. Amelia in the atrium, apparently wandering at night to escape her elderly husband. Part of her wondered if Gabe could shed some light on what Amelia meant, when she said something about Lore taking Apollius's greatest blessing. Surely, she wouldn't refer to *Bastian* like that? But no, she'd said this wasn't all about Bastian, that it was bigger. If there was more religious dissent brewing at court, Gabe needed to know. Maybe she could catch him before prayers began.

That was the reason she was up so early, getting ready on her own. To see Gabe, by himself. To make sure he was all right.

Maybe, perhaps, to mention the voice she heard in her head, and seek reassurance that she wasn't going mad. That Anton hadn't been right.

"Dressed already?"

Lore whirled around.

Bastian stood in her doorway, leaning against the jamb with a cup of coffee and one dark brow arched. He'd dressed, too, and more nicely than usual—golden threads shimmered through the billowing sleeves of his white shirt, constrained by an embroidered linen vest. He'd even buttoned it, this time, not left it open like an afterthought.

"Couldn't sleep," Lore said. "Since when are you awake this early?"

"Turning over a new leaf." He came into the room, growing larger in the mirror. His hand twitched like it'd land on her shoulders, then fell to his side instead. "It seems we suffered the same affliction. I couldn't sleep, either."

He said it like he expected it to be new information, as if she hadn't seen him last night. As if he didn't remember their conversation at all.

Bastian's hands rested on the back of her chair instead of her shoulders, concern drawing his brows low. "Are you well, Lore?"

She forced a smile. "Fine."

Bastian set his cup down on the vanity, gestured that she was welcome to it. "Today seems like a good day to be punctual."

Lore shrugged.

A tremor went through Bastian behind her, a disturbance in the air. When she turned back to look at him, his eyes were closed, his jaw a tight line, like he was trying to fight off a sudden headache.

"I hope he doesn't hate me," he murmured, so quietly. Like a secret he wanted to keep, even from himself. "Stupid thing to hope. But still."

Lore stood, her fingers closing around his tightly fisted hand. "He couldn't hate you."

"I guess we'll test the limits of that theory." Bastian lifted her hand, stared down at the ring on her finger. It'd twisted around, the stone slipping sideways. "Little big for you. We'll have to get it resized, before..."

Before she became his Queen.

When Bastian looked up at her, his momentary vulnerability was gone. "Sorry," he said. "Headache." He lifted her hand to his mouth, idly kissed her fingers. Then he tucked her hand into his elbow. "This will be our first outing as an official betrothed couple, won't it? Auspicious, that it should be a prayer meeting."

Lore didn't respond as she let him lead her from the room, sunlight flooding around them like parted golden curtains.

The North Sanctuary was nearly full when Lore and Bastian arrived. Curious eyes crawled over her, lighting on her ring, her face, the black dress she'd hurriedly pulled from the closet, spinning whispers from it all. The floor was an easier thing to look at than the gathered nobles, still bleary from the ball and the parties that came after, hoarse from a night full of gossip that bore her name.

Bastian let go of her arm when they sat in their places at the front of the Sanctuary, allowing a bit of distance. Gone was the tradition of the Arceneaux King and heir kneeling at the altar to begin First Day prayers—Bastian hadn't attended since the eclipse, and there was no heir to accompany him.

The thought of an heir made heat rise to her face. Lore supposed it would be on her to provide one, as Bastian's wife. She couldn't picture them as parents.

The Sanctuary gradually grew silent, a sea of quiet nobles in stained-glass-colored light. Lore felt when Gabe entered the room—the collective intake of breath, the way Bastian stiffened beside her.

She looked up.

He was staring at her. Gabe stood in the center of the dais, the Bleeding God's Heart on its shorter chain gleaming against his broad chest. The leather of his eye patch stood stark, like a badge proclaiming he didn't belong in this role.

Bastian coming with her meant she hadn't had the chance to speak with Gabe, to tell him about the voice in her head. Maybe she could bring it up to Bastian instead, but something warned her against that. He'd either panic or think it was nothing, and neither extreme was helpful.

She didn't realize she was imagining her forest until a heartbeat later. Lore closed her eyes, and it swept around her mind, green leaves and brown bark and the open sky. A barrier, yes, walls to keep her safe.

A cage.

But maybe that was what she needed, if she was hearing voices in the dark.

A moment of silence, then Gabe started speaking, his voice a low rumble. The same prayer from every First Day service. It felt unnatural, to hear Gabe saying things she'd heard Anton say first.

Lore and Bastian rose and knelt with the rest of the congregants, an ingrained performance none of them had to think about. The stained glass making up the Bleeding God's Heart in the window shone bloody, the brazier smoke making her eyes water.

"We ask that You make a vessel for Your light," Gabe murmured, nearing the end of the prayer. The words were jumbled, like he couldn't wait to get them out of his mouth, to leave this Sanctuary and everyone staring at him.

"We ask that You return and make us holy—" the gathered nobles murmured back, Lore's voice lost among them. But then, that collective voice broke off, dissolved into gasps.

Lore's eyes went to Gabe again. He was staring, but not at her this time, his eye wide and fixed on Bastian.

Dread chewing at her heart, Lore followed his gaze.

Bastian glowed. Not just from the light through the window, though that certainly heightened the effect—there was a golden luminescence wafting around him, the antithesis of a shadow. His eyes were closed, his face tipped up to the window, as if completely unaware of the pause in the prayer.

But then his eyes opened, and Lore knew he wasn't unaware, not at all. He glanced at her, smiled, reached out and took her hand.

His touch was light and warmth and summer, a rush of blood, a rush of air. For a moment, Lore's vision flickered, and the man holding her hand didn't look like Bastian at all. As if some other form was superimposed over his own, like two sheets of vellum laid one atop the other.

"Beloved," he murmured, and then she blinked, and the not-quite-doubling effect was gone.

As soon as it had come, the golden phosphorescence surrounding Bastian fizzled out, the shimmer dimming slowly and dying away. All the nobles were staring, all with similar awed expressions. Some had the telltale gleam of tears in their eyes.

Lore's middle twisted along with her ring, nerves driving them both.

Straightening her ring, Bastian lifted her hand to his mouth, kissed the backs of her knuckles. He winked at her while his lips were still on her skin.

"Seemed like a good time to show off," he whispered.

She glanced toward the back of the room, knowing what he meant. Caius and Maxon stood there, still dressed as if they were being passed off as country cousins, just like she had been. But Lore didn't think she'd ever had such a strange expression as the two of them did, a blend of awe and rage.

Now halo-less and acting completely unaware of what had just interrupted prayers, Bastian turned to Gabe. "Your Holiness, should we continue? There are things to be taken care of once prayers are concluded, you'll remember."

Gabe eyed him warily, something almost hurt flickering across his face before he schooled it into indifference. He finished prayers quickly, half the courtiers forgetting their part of the call and response, too busy staring at their King.

Then Gabe stepped back from the front of the dais, his movement quick enough to make the incense smoke dip and whirl. He looked at Lore again, blue eye blazing.

And he left.

That wasn't supposed to happen, and the momentary stutter in Bastian's steps said as much. But a look of relief spasmed across his face right before he took to the dais. He shook his head slightly, a wince like the headache he'd complained of this morning hadn't completely gone, but his face was calm as he stood before his court.

Bastian raised his hands, and a hush fell over the congregants. "I have people to introduce you to." Straight to the point, forgoing any additional theatrics. His expression went from serene to wry, his grin crooked and disarming. "Last time this happened, you were introduced to my future wife, so I'd suggest you pay attention."

Some of the answering smiles in the crowd thinned.

"This introduction promises to be just as important." Bastian's arms fell, wafting incense smoke. He gestured at the back of the sanctuary.

Lore turned. So did everyone else. Maxon quickly arranged his face in a tight smile and followed the Sainted King's direction, walking gracefully up the center aisle. Probably much more gracefully than Lore had, when she was introduced to the court. Caius trailed behind him, eyes shifting from one side to the other, as if cataloging every face he passed.

Manicured brows lowered over reddened eyes as the two men stepped up on the dais next to Bastian, hands that had never known calluses twitching nervously.

"It is my pleasure," Bastian said when the Kirytheans had reached the dais, "to introduce you to Maxon Agripolus and Caius Sentia."

The Kirythean names made a ripple of unease wind visibly through the crowd.

Bastian saw it. He grinned, wolfish. "Delegates sent from Emperor Jax himself."

He paused, then, like a priest waiting for an objection in the middle of wedding vows.

Silence in the sanctuary, but not the calm kind. The Court of the Citadel was too well bred to voice their displeasure in public, but it simmered beneath the air like a pot near boiling over.

"This is a historic time," Bastian continued. He didn't pitch his voice like someone making pronouncements; he spoke to his nobles as if they were gathered around a casual dinner table, as if they were at one of the parties he'd thrown as the Sun Prince. "The rules are changing. Threats of the past have no place in the future; instead, we must find ways to work together. Ways to coexist as we usher in a new era."

Quiet but for the rustle of small, nervous movements, the

near-silent sound of hundreds of breaths in and out of anxiety-tightened lungs. Lore dared a glance around—she couldn't see Alie, but Malcolm stood near the back of the sanctuary, his scarred arms crossed tight over his chest, his face all hard lines. He caught her eye, then looked quickly away.

Up on the dais, Bastian clapped Maxon on the shoulder. The other man stood stiffly, refusing to be moved.

"I expect you to make them welcome as we work toward preserving the peace we have so long trusted," Bastian said. He lifted his hand from Maxon, like a release, and cast a pointed look over his shoulder, highlighting the absence of clergy. He turned back to the crowd with a wry smile. "I suppose it falls to me to dismiss you, then. Go on."

He came back down the stairs with a spring in his step, as if relishing the confusion he'd just wrought, and took Lore's arm. "That went well."

"Other than Gabe leaving."

Bastian's self-satisfied grin faltered, just a little. "Perhaps that's for the best." He winced, his hand rising to his temple, then falling. "Come on. That damn headache is coming back."

Chapter Twelve

I am never far from my faithful.
–The Book of Prayer, Tract 56

Lore waited until the door to their chambers closed behind them before asking the question that was no doubt ringing through the entire Citadel. "How did you do that?"

"Do what?" Bastian seemed completely nonplussed by what had taken place at First Day services. His step was jaunty, his manner relaxed, someone watching a plan fall neatly into place. It was so different from how he'd been last night at the moonlit window, seeming just as lost as she was.

"That trick at the end of prayers," Lore said, not trying to keep the irritation from her voice. Surely he knew what she was talking about. "The *glowing*."

"Oh, that." He shot her a wicked grin. "Just channeled a little Spiritum on a whim, strengthened my own aura a bit. Wasn't sure it'd be strong enough for any non-channeler to see, but apparently it was. Left an impression, don't you think?"

"Seems like a rather frivolous use of magic."

"Beloved, for us, there's no such thing."

The alcove in the corner—the same one where Alie had hosted her tea party—was now set with a sumptuous breakfast, piles of fruit and pastries that two people could never hope to eat. Bastian made a quick line for the table, as if his impromptu magic trick had left him hungry.

He poured a cup of coffee, dosed it with cream, and held it out to her. "Maybe next time you could do something similar. Make yourself look like a walking corpse."

A joke, but not one she liked. Lore's lips tightened as she took the proffered cup and went to add sugar before taking a sip. Usually, Bastian knew just how she wanted her coffee, with enough sugar to scrim her teeth, but this morning he'd apparently forgotten. Maybe it was a side effect of all that Spiritum, making him not think before he spoke and forget coffee preferences.

"Come now," he said, fixing his own cup and flopping into one of the chairs. "I was kidding."

"So you just wanted to make an impression?" Lore asked, ignoring the halfhearted apology.

"That, and to see if I could do it." Bastian took a bowl of fruit, sorted out the strawberries from the blueberries, and pushed the latter to her side while keeping the former. At least he remembered which berries she liked. "Anything that shows our friend Jax the extent of our power is a good idea, I think."

Her appetite was gone, but Lore made herself eat, knowing she'd be starving later if she didn't. "You should be careful, Bastian. We still don't know what the consequences of channeling could be."

Consequences like a voice in her head. Maybe it was just anxiety, a manifestation of all that trauma she buried as deep as the fucking goddess. But it could be more. She'd heard that same voice at the Mortem leak, and it could be more.

He chewed deliberately, swallowed his strawberry. "So we're on this again." With a sigh, Bastian sat back in the chair, looked out the window. The view showed the back grounds of the Citadel, the green space between the main structure and the North Sanctuary. If you craned your head to the side, you could just see the glass dome of the vaults, the roses planted on the tops of the crypts reaching for the sun.

Bastian stared at that as his mouth worked, like he was looking for words in the glint of the glass. There was something pained in the way he moved, though every motion was minute—the muscles around his eyes as they closed, the way he reached up and rubbed at his mouth with his fingers, flashing a glimpse of the eclipse carved into his palm.

"I understand your concerns," he said finally, so quiet it was almost like he was afraid of being overheard, though they were the only people in the whole palatial apartment. "But you don't have to worry about me, Lore. I know what I'm doing."

She dropped an uneaten blueberry back into the bowl. "Do you?"

"I know that Anton made it seem like we should be wary of our power," he said. "But clearly, he was wrong. And we can't *learn* about it without *using* it."

Her lips twisted to the side. "Maybe we should ask him about it."

Silence. Bastian's fingers tapped against the side of his china cup.

Lore nervously ate another blueberry. "He might be one of the only people who can tell us how this is supposed to work."

"You aren't wrong." He leaned forward, braced his elbows on his knees. "But I highly doubt Anton is still alive. Even if he is, I don't know where the Mort keep him."

"I could ask Gabe," she said, feeling slightly ashamed for bringing up the Priest Exalted when they'd both been dancing around him so carefully. Maybe she'd feel like that every time she mentioned Gabe in Bastian's presence from now on, fingers digging into a shared bruise. "He'd know where Anton was kept."

"If that would make you feel better," he said with a dismissive wave.

Her hand stretched over the table, rested lightly on his. He didn't look at her again, but his eyes closed.

"I think," she said quietly, "that maybe we should give channeling a rest for a few days. For both our sakes. You look exhausted."

The thought of not channeling was both a relief and a disappointment. She wasn't sure what answer she hoped for.

"That has less to do with channeling and more to do with the general fuckery of being the Sainted King," Bastian said. With another spasm of his jaw, his eyes opened, and something in them was subtly changed. A new resolve. Bastian extracted his hand from under hers, not unkindly, but with unmistakable finality. "I'm afraid it's not an option, beloved. Not now."

They fell into silence. Bastian put the strawberry back on his plate, uneaten. Lore chased blueberries around her bowl but didn't pick up another.

Bastian left soon after, when the silence became so heavy Lore felt like she was suffocating under it. He kissed her on the forehead as he got up from the table. "Nothing exciting," he reassured, though Lore hadn't asked where he was going. "It's time to bother the treasurers again."

"More payments?" Despite herself, there was a bright note to her voice. The direct payments to Auverrani citizens were still something she could feel good about.

He smiled at her, though it never climbed all the way into his eyes. He didn't answer. "And how will you be filling your hours?"

"Probably seeing the Priest Exalted." His title felt safer than his name. "Some extra lessons might be a good idea, if channeling isn't something we're going to get away from."

And she was going to ask about Anton. The need had ballooned in her chest over the rest of breakfast until it pressed against her sternum, set to burst. She needed answers wherever she could get them, if only to lay her own anxieties to rest.

The curve of Bastian's smile went sharper. "I think that sounds like a splendid idea. Tell Remaut hello from me."

Her brows knit. "I doubt that will go over well."

But Bastian was already out the door.

Lore let her head drop against the back of her chair. Bastian wanting to taunt Gabe was nothing new, really. Though she thought things had changed in that regard. That Bastian didn't want to hurt him, either.

Maybe that was just her own wants talking. Her own desire for the three of them to find some sort of resolution.

She forced herself up, prepared to go spill her guts to one of the men who made her life immeasurably harder.

A bloodcoat guard stood next to one of the potted palms outside the door. Lore reeled back when she saw him—after ten years as a poison runner, the sight of guards still made her uneasy, perhaps even more than the Presque Mort did. Her time in the Citadel hadn't done much to raise them in her estimation.

The bloodcoat said nothing. Lore cleared her throat. "Why are you here?"

The guard's eyes cut her direction, nonplussed by her rudeness. "King's orders," was the clipped answer. "I'm to accompany you around the Citadel when he can't."

Her lips pressed together, anger building quick. "I've been moving through the Citadel just fine."

The bloodcoat didn't respond, but his eyes dipped down to Lore's ring, then back up to her face.

Ah.

"That won't be necessary." She drew herself up to her full height, tried to put the weight of future queenliness into her voice. "I'll inform the King that I relieved you of your post."

The bloodcoat shifted on his feet but didn't leave. "I'm afraid you can't do that, my lady."

Her smile was frosty. "I assure you, I can."

"I can only be dismissed by the one who gave the order." Dammit all, this bloodcoat had more spine than Lore had prepared for. She was used to scaring them, and the one time she wanted to use that, it wouldn't work. The guard continued, "If you want me to call His Majesty back—"

"No." She snapped it, turning on her heel. "No need."

Because she wouldn't win that argument, and she didn't want to see the satisfaction on this man's face when she lost.

Lore swept down the hallway toward the stairs without another word. The guard, whose name she didn't ask for, fell in behind. She entertained fantasies of him tripping on the stairs and falling ass over feet all the way to the ground floor.

So focused was she on this particular daydream that she didn't see Alie until she nearly ran her over.

"Hello to you, too," Alie said, slapping her hands to Lore's shoulders to keep her steady. There was a laugh in the words, but her eyes were jade-like, glittering and stony.

"Sorry." Lore righted herself, cast a glance over her shoulder. The bloodcoat had stopped a few feet away, standing with his back to the wall, his hands at his sides and his eyes straight ahead. A casual enough posture, one that wouldn't make it immediately obvious he was following Lore.

That was probably the idea.

Alie's gaze followed Lore's, the wariness in her face honing to a harder, flintier edge.

"Of course," Lore said, loudly enough so that the bloodcoat could hear. "I'd be happy to accompany you to your apartment, I know how that time of the month can be such a bother."

Confusion barely flickered over Alie's face; she gave Lore a subtle nod, responding, "Oh, thank you, the cramps are so terrible. A cup of Brigitte's tea would be just the thing, if you happen to have some with you."

"Always." Lore felt like a particularly untalented mummer putting on a morality play at a market festival, but another quick glance over her shoulder said the inelegant ploy had done its job. A look of faint distaste bent the bloodcoat's mouth, and when she and Alie moved back to the stairs, he didn't follow quite as close behind.

"Gods," Alie said under her breath. "Anyone who doesn't bleed acts like it's catching." She gave Lore an unreadable look. "Bastian's orders?"

"Minutes ago, apparently."

"Hmm." If Alie had any insight, she didn't offer it.

The bloodcoat followed them back up the first flight of stairs, down the hallway to Alie's door—rather than potted ferns, like Bastian's, Alie's door was instead bordered with a climbing pothos vine, growing riotously in the light through the window across the hall.

"Won't be a moment." Lore followed Alie inside and shut the door behind her. They both paused, staring at the handle to see if it would turn. It didn't; apparently, the bloodcoat was content to wait outside while they discussed the matter of monthly bleeding.

Alie's apartments were much smaller than Bastian's, on par with the rooms Lore and Gabe had stayed in while she pretended to be Eldelore Remaut, though much more finely decorated and maintained. The door opened on a small sitting room with a white marble fireplace and a whole wall of windows looking out on the northern Citadel green. A propped-open door at the back of the room showed a sliver of plush, unmade bed, and an open archway led to a small study, housing a velvet-upholstered chair and a desk scattered with books and letters.

But Lore didn't have much chance to study the apartment. Alie whirled to her. "What," she said, clipped and hard, "in all the *myriad hells* are you doing, Lore?"

Lore's mouth opened, closed again. She hadn't been prepared to be interrogated. But Alie was looking at her almost like an enemy, her copper-brown cheeks flushed and her eyes sparking, her arms crossed tightly over her chest.

One near-white brow rose over Alie's eye, her gaze going pointedly to the ring on Lore's finger.

Ah, Lore thought again. So Bastian *had* done this without speaking to anyone first. One more important decision he'd undertaken completely on his own.

She let out a shaky breath and twisted the diamond into her palm, like she could hide it. "That's the thing," she said. "I don't really know."

Alie sighed, her shoulders slumping, arms loosening. "Well, that makes two of us." She crossed to her couch; Lore followed, the both of them sitting down in a *whump* of chiffon and silk. "Did he ask *you* about it? Before he did it, I mean?"

"No." Lore barked a weak laugh. "I had no idea. We've never talked about anything like that before."

But was that true, really? Bastian had said over and over how he would keep her safe. Keep her close. In his mind, maybe this had been a natural progression.

Alie was looking at her like she had three heads. "And you just went along with it? Even though you'd never discussed marriage to an Arceneaux King? That's not something to take lightly."

"What exactly was I supposed to do, Alie? Just say *thanks but no thanks* in the middle of a royal ball, with the fucking Kirytheans watching? They're reporting everything back to Jax—that's the entire reason Bastian invited them. Word of the Sainted King's deathwitch turning down his marriage proposal isn't going to make us seem like paragons of stability."

Another deep sigh from Alie. "You're right." She rubbed at her forehead. "Malcolm and I were completely blindsided, but we assumed he'd at least spoken to you. Did he tell you why?"

They all knew this wasn't just because he cared for her. It stung, a little. Lore shrugged. "To keep me safe, he said. To show the Kirytheans that I'm a permanent fixture, that I'm not going anywhere."

To see who I chose. But she kept that part to herself.

"Seems more like he put a target on your back," Alie muttered.

"Thus the guard, I think."

"Still. I don't understand..." Alie trailed off before finishing, but it wasn't a statement that needed an end. Neither of them really understood. It was becoming the common thread when it came to Bastian's actions. And what could they do about it? He was the King.

"Something is wrong," Lore said finally, quietly. She didn't realize she was gripping her hands to fists until she felt the ring digging into the meat of her palm; she rotated it back around, slow and deliberate, and stared at it as she spoke. "Inviting the Kirytheans, proposing to me, channeling so much magic. He's being irrational."

Alie's lips pressed flat. "Probably just the stress of becoming King, though *Bastian* and *rationality* have never shared close quarters, especially when it comes to things he wants."

"I don't think that's—"

"How well do you know him, Lore?" Alie turned to face her, chin lifted and expression stoic. "I know you have this...this magic connection, but the fact is that you've only known Bastian for a few months. You aren't exactly the best person to be making judgments on what's normal for him or not. This isn't outside the realm of what we expected, when Bastian became King. He's always put more stock in his own opinion than anyone else's."

Lore stared at her, wanting to defend Bastian but unable to completely disregard the sentiment. If she was selfish, so was Bastian. Both of them had rejected what Anton and August wanted that night. Both of them had told the greater good to go hang. "Then what are we supposed to do about it?"

Alie stood, crossed to the teapot on her marble hearth. She stuck a poker with a gilded handle in the fire, stirred up the embers, hung the teapot over the first flickers of the fire. It was too hot for such a thing; she fanned herself with her hand, billowing the white curls of her hair. "You," she said finally, "don't need to do anything."

A subtle emphasis on that *you*. Unease pricked along the back of her neck. "Are you planning something, Alie?"

The teapot began to steam; Alie pulled it off the hanger and poured hot water into a mug, not bothering with tea leaves, for bleeding cramps or otherwise. "He has a council," she said quietly. "Even if he seems to forget. Trust that we will be weighing all our options."

"What *options*?"

"There are always options." Alie's eyes flickered her way, peering at her through the steam of her teacup. "Just because you can't see them doesn't mean they aren't there." She paused, her next words quieter. "Have you talked to Gabe?"

The question caught Lore off guard. "That's where I was headed when I saw you."

Alie nodded, watching the water as it cooled. "So you haven't really chosen between them yet."

Talking about Gabe with Alie—talking about him in this context—made discomfort coil in Lore's stomach, a serpent waiting to strike. She knew Alie still cared for him, but wasn't sure exactly what it looked like. Whether it was the way Lore cared, or something softer, a leftover love that hadn't died but wouldn't grow again.

"I don't want to," Lore whispered.

Alie chewed on the corner of her lip. After a moment, she nodded.

The air sat strange. Lore shifted on the couch again. "Alie, I..." But she didn't know how to follow that, changed direction. "You and Gabe..."

"Don't worry about me and Gabe." Alie watched steam rise from the lip of the teacup. "I'll always care about him. He'll always care about me, presumptuous though that may be to say." Her lip quirked. "But it was never going to be him and me, Lore. Things were never going to be that simple. Not for any of us."

She picked up the steaming cup of tea and went to open the door.

The bloodcoat stood across the hall at military attention. Alie inclined her head his direction, then turned to Lore, taking her hand and steering her over the threshold. "Thank you so much for the tea, I'm sure I'll feel better in no t—"

But it wasn't just Lore's new guard at the door.

Caius stood with his hands clasped behind his back, almost the same stance the bloodcoat took. The light in the window behind him flushed his edges and made him hard to look at directly, but when he stepped forward, his expression was easy to see.

Eager.

"Alienor," he said, ignoring Lore entirely.

Confusion creased Alie's brow, but only for a moment. She slipped into her diplomat self as easily as a well-worn cloak. "Caius. How lovely to see you again, especially now that the court knows who you are."

She said it playfully, but there was a splinter she couldn't quite sand away. A place where that well-worn cloak had gone threadbare.

Caius grinned. It was not the kind that would set a person at ease. "You would never have been so fooled. You seem like someone who knows when trickery is afoot."

Lore didn't think she had ever heard someone use the word *afoot* unironically. She also couldn't believe how easily this was going—was the whole court accepting the presence of the Kirytheans as if it were nothing? Even her guard seemed nonplussed.

Yes, she thought, answering her own question. Yes, she supposed they were. Auverraine was desperate to avoid a war and all the costs associated; this gesture of peace, strange as it seemed, would hold up the illusion that everything would be fine. And the illusion was all they needed.

Alie smiled back, but her eyes stayed shrewd. "I do admit that I didn't quite buy your story about being a distant nephew of an ill viscount, but I can't say I expected the truth. I suppose I should have; it's not the first time a new acquaintance has come to me through such means."

She threaded her arm chummily through Lore's. There was a slight tremble in it.

"Seems more like a friend than an acquaintance," Caius said, with another one of those sharp half smiles. "I hope it can be the same for us, in time. Bastian speaks so highly of you."

Lore patted Alie's arm. "Go rest, Alie," she said, trying to sound light and breezy. "I know your time pains you."

"Don't let me interrupt your plans." He was an operative for an enemy government, but at least Caius was polite. "I came to see if you would take a turn with me through the gardens, but if you're not feeling well..."

"She isn't." Lore gave him a tight smile and nudged Alie back over the threshold of her apartments. "But it is so nice to see you, Caius." Then, because she couldn't leave well enough alone, "Bastian and I hope you've enjoyed what you've seen of Auverraine so far."

"It's certainly been impressive." With one more glance at Alie, he turned the full weight of that predator smile on Lore. "And a late congratulations to you, my lady. We are all anxious to see the kind of Queen you will become."

He inclined his head, not as deeply as one should to a lady and the future Queen, and disappeared down the stairs.

Lore let out a shaky breath and whirled to Alie. "Are you—"

"Fine," she said faintly. "Go see Gabe."

Then she shut the door.

Chapter Thirteen

There is no path thornier than that between two people who once grew love.

—Emilie Beligne, Auverrani poet

The sun beat down with heated fists on Lore's hair as she crossed the Citadel green, entered the heavy doors of the Church. She kept a brisk pace and didn't look to see if her guard was following as she stalked down the corridor of stained-glass windows.

It shouldn't be a surprise that Bastian wanted Caius to spend time with Alie. She was their best diplomat, able to pull information out of anyone before they realized they'd let it go. Still, this was one more thing he hadn't discussed with her, and it made irritation flare, made her teeth clench.

But she wasn't *surprised*. No, Bastian doing what Bastian thought best was nothing new. It felt like an ingrained truth, now, something that hadn't shocked her before and shouldn't shock her again.

Alie was right. How well did she know him, really?

Lore twisted her ring around and around her finger, rubbing the skin raw.

She approached the doors to the unused confessional room, and her guard found his place against the wall a polite distance away. "The Sainted King ordered it," he said in response to her skeptical brow. "You're to have privacy when you meet with the Priest Exalted."

Lore didn't press that bit of luck. With a nod, she slipped into the confessional room, closed the door behind her. A moment, then she turned the lock, just to be sure.

She didn't want any part of this conversation to be overheard.

Hurrying down the aisle, flicking aside the curtain, letting it fall behind her. But Lore didn't sit on the bench, instead striding right up to where the lattice kept them apart, pressing as close to it as she could without touching. "I need to talk to you."

The shadows moved over the floor as Gabe sat down on the other side of the lattice, bisected by delicately twisted metal and the wavering light of the single sconce. "Excellent news," he rumbled, exhaustion and irritation mingling in his tone. "You're doing that right now."

"Don't be an asshole, Gabe." Lore reached up and hooked her fingers in the curving metal, as if making him see her skin could somehow imbue her voice with urgency. His shadow stiffened; it worked. "I mean about..."

She didn't finish, but her fingers tightened in the lattice, curled like she could tear the metal out herself, make him *look* at her.

A sigh from the other side. "Fine," Gabe said wearily, his head lolling back against the wall. "Talk."

And when she did, it wasn't to ask about Anton. Not yet. "I'm still dreaming."

"We've discussed that. As long as your defenses—"

"No," she cut in. "They still don't feel like the dreams I had with Anton, they feel...solid. They feel almost like memories. But not mine."

Silence from the other side, though she saw him shift. Lore

had never asked him what he still believed about Apollius, Nyxara, about her power being the harbinger of the world's end. Bastian had taken the lack of apocalypse as a sign that Anton was wrong, but he'd never really believed to begin with. Gabe had. Gabe had believed so *much*.

And Lore still didn't know where she fell. A fulcrum, the tipping point between Gabe's piety and Bastian's indifference.

"I guess it's possible they mean nothing," Lore said, when it became clear Gabe planned to hold his quiet. "But since the whole point of us meeting here is so my magic doesn't somehow bring back the Buried Goddess, I think they're worth discussing." Her voice snapped, there at the end. "Now is the part where you say something, Remaut."

His surname made him stiffen. Slowly, Gabe sat up straight. A shadowy blur as he ran his hand over his face, his hair, adjusted his eye patch. "What do you want me to say, Your Majesty?"

"I want to know whether you think they're important." She let go of the lattice and clasped her hands in front of her, because this next part felt like a confession. "I do."

A pause, heavy.

"Tell me about the dreams." His tone was even, but the shadows moved as Gabe stood, paced back and forth. "As much detail as you can."

Lore sank onto the bench. "I'm in a forest," she said quietly. "Or kind of a forest, at least. It feels like the one on the green—something planned, not natural. It looks a lot like the one I imagine as my barrier."

"That could be why you dream of it," Gabe murmured. "You've built it up often enough that it stays in your mind without you trying."

But Lore was already shaking her head before he finished. "It's not like that. It's more like... like I *remembered* this forest, and that's why I chose it as my barrier." She waved a hand. "Anyway, I guess that part isn't important. I'm in the forest, and my hands are on a tree, except they don't look like mine. They aren't scarred."

A brief pause in his pacing, the memory of how she'd gotten that scar arresting his movement. But then the pacing started back up again.

"And I'm talking to people, sometimes," Lore continued. "Having these full conversations that don't seem odd at all, inside the dream, but make no sense outside of it. I can't remember the specifics when I wake up, but it's something about a decision being made..."

The more she talked, the more foolish she felt. Maybe she was ascribing meaning to something meaningless, just like trying to find a sign in Gabe that he cared about her when all he'd done was show he didn't. When it was cruel of her to still want him to.

A long sigh, her head dropping into her hands. "Forget it. I'm being stupid, this doesn't mean—"

"You aren't being stupid." He was standing directly on the other side, as close as she had been before. A moment, then his fingers hooked through the metal, blunt and callused.

"Have you told Bastian?" he asked quietly.

She tried to parse out the nuances in his tone, separate the hurt from the longing and the anger. But they were braided together and wouldn't come undone.

"I told him that I dreamed," Lore answered, "but not what was in them." She laughed, quick and breathless and a little bit desperate. "They scare me, Gabe. And I just want to know if I should be scared."

His fingers twitched, like he didn't like that answer. But the fragmented light from the sconce flickered over the golden-red of his hair as he nodded. They stood in silence, a fragile moment that could shatter if either of them moved in the wrong direction.

Finally, Gabe sighed. "You know I want to trust you, Lore."

And her heart shouldn't leap up at that, not with Bastian's ring on her finger.

"So I'm going to," he said, almost a challenge. "A little bit, at least."

He was not a man accustomed to giving in to what he wanted. Gods knew Lore hadn't given him a good reason to trust her, but he was going to do it, simply because he wanted to.

She wanted to touch him. Wanted to feel the move of his skin under hers, the tender thrum of his heart. She still remembered every beat of that kiss in the southeast turret so many weeks ago, like a dance her muscles hadn't yet forgotten.

Gabe's other hand went to a notch in the wall, twisted something. With a long-rusted squeal, a piece in the middle of the metal lattice popped open.

A door. It seemed logical now that there would be a door, a way between the different sides of the confessional, but Lore hadn't considered it until she saw it open, hadn't even seen hinges anywhere in all that twisting iron, it must've been a delicately wrought thing, very subtle—

All of those details were just distractions her mind provided her, trying to take away the impact of Gabriel Remaut standing in the now-open door, looking at her, close enough to touch.

There were dark bruises beneath his visible eye, and his face was wan beneath his faint scattering of freckles. There was a red mark on his temple, like the strap of his eye patch had rubbed him raw, like he'd been wearing it too long without giving himself a break.

"Follow me." A turn on his heel, as if it didn't even occur to Gabe that she wouldn't.

"There's a bloodcoat outside of the confessional room," she said as she stood. "Bastian told him to stay with me."

Gabe tossed a dark look toward the front of the room, as if the bloodcoat could feel it through the velvet curtain and oak door. "I'm surprised you were able to come in here without him, then."

"That, apparently, was also part of Bastian's orders. I'm to have privacy when I'm with you."

Surprise made Gabe freeze, made him look over his shoulder at her with his forehead so furrowed it nearly nudged his eye patch out of place. “Well,” he said, and didn’t finish.

“Well,” Lore agreed.

A moment, then Gabe turned back around, continuing his stride through the priest’s half of the confessional, to a small stone door beyond. “Thankfully,” he said, “we can get to where we’re going without leaving this room, so Bastian’s guard won’t see you leave.”

“And where is it we’re going?”

He tipped his head back, loosing a sigh at the ceiling. “The stone garden,” he said, resigned. “I’m going to show you why I was there that night.”

Chapter Fourteen

> Upon My return, the earth will be united, one Holy Kingdom that spans all land and all sea.
>
> –The Book of Holy Law, Tract 173

Labyrinthine stone passageways twisted through the bowels of the Church, all of them appearing clean and well maintained. Apparently, the Presque Mort and other clergy often needed to move through the Church without entering the Citadel grounds. Lore supposed it made sense, the Church's construction being what it was—a huge stone circle around the Citadel and surrounding area, as much a wall as a structure in and of itself. The North and South Sanctuaries were like beads on the granite necklace, places where the building expanded, while the eastern and western sides were thinner, housing storage and cloisters.

Despite the fact that these passageways clearly weren't secret, Gabe moved swiftly, like he didn't want to be seen. Not that the chances of encountering anyone were high. Since half the Presque Mort and all the clergymen who'd conspired with Anton were in the Burnt Isles, the number of people traversing Church corridors was significantly reduced.

They approached a door that looked like any number of others they'd passed. Gabe produced a key from his pocket, slotted it into the lock. It opened into an arch of harsh summer sunlight, heat so thick it was nearly visible. Gabe slipped out the door, and Lore followed like a shadow.

The garden looked smaller in the daytime, without the seethe of mist to obscure its corners. The light made the changes easier to see, too. The banks of geraniums were thicker than she remembered, eating up the humidity and light. The living roses bloomed so densely that they nearly covered the stone ones, hiding the gray among green stems and brown thorns.

There was less Mortem to channel out of the catacombs, now. There'd been one minor lunar eclipse since the ritual—on a night that Lore spent huddled in her room around a bottle of wine—but apparently, it hadn't yielded much magic.

She wished she could be comforted by that.

Gabe led her through the winding pathways, a different route than they'd taken the first time he'd brought her here. Up ahead, the well loomed out of the banks of flowers. The statue of Apollius sat small in the shade, hands outstretched. It seemed to Lore like He beckoned her forward. Taunting.

But Gabe didn't linger at the well; he took a sharp right turn, moving back into the roses, toward the wall of the garden and the small greenhouse settled into the corner. With one last look at Apollius—and a lifting of both middle fingers—Lore followed.

Gabe paused outside the greenhouse. His one eye closed, opened again. "It's not pretty," he warned.

She'd forgotten to ask about Anton, in the rush of emotions left over from talking to Alie, confronting Gabe with the dreams. And yet here he was. Of course this was what Gabe had been doing that night.

"I'm not afraid," she lied.

He nodded, squared his shoulders, and pushed open the door.

The greenhouse was divided into two rooms, one at the front with shelves along the glass walls, and then one at the back, covered by a half-open door, nothing but darkness visible beyond. The shelves were cluttered with broken pots and half-dead plants, clearly neglected and stuck here because there was nowhere else to put them. Gabe strode toward the back of the greenhouse and slipped through the open maw of the door.

With a gulp against preemptive nausea, Lore followed.

The back room was dark, the walls and ceiling nearly covered by climbing roses and ivy. Despite that, they thrived, blooming lush and thick. The air smelled heady, like petals and loam. It was almost beautiful.

Until you saw what the plants were drawing from, richer than any soil.

Anton was barely visible beneath the flowers. His back was flush to the wall, as near as Lore could tell, his head tipped up as if he were a bloom himself, seeking the sun through crowded leaves. Ivy covered his torso, growing onto the wall behind him like living shackles, keeping his arms spread to his sides. The posture evoked Apollius, and Lore had to swallow hard again to keep bile in her stomach where it belonged.

The roses were worse than the ivy. They wove in and out of Anton's skin, breaching it as easily as dirt, the thorns tearing through the delicate membrane to unfurl gory petals. The one that had grown through his eye stretched up past his head, one red bloom opening wide while new buds studded its length, pushing against his eyebrow, his forehead. The socket was a hole of viscera, complemented by the deep-purple scarring all down the side of his face; a souvenir from his vision, the one that had shown him Gabe and Bastian and Lore and the destruction they would allegedly bring. Viscous fluid ran down his cheek—the remains of his eye.

But the very worst part was how he was still breathing, his chest rising and falling easily, like he was asleep.

Lore found herself angling her head so she didn't have to face the former Priest Exalted directly, but Gabe stared right at him, not allowing himself to look away. "I couldn't let him die," he murmured. "Bastian promised me that much, at least, the night of the ritual. He let Anton keep his life; I couldn't let it pass."

The leaves rattled as Anton pulled in a breath. He was listening, Lore knew, conscious in all that thorn and blood. "Why keep him secret?"

"Because it's undignified to leave him like this out in the open." The Presque Mort who'd been part of the coup had all been sent away; Gabe would be the only person in the Church who knew this had happened to Anton, who knew the former Priest Exalted wasn't dead.

"He refuses water sometimes," Gabe continued. "It'd been a hot day, that time you saw me here, and I was making sure he drank something."

The image of Gabe watering his mentor like a plant in a pot made her shudder.

"He begged for Apollius, at first." Gabe's voice was almost trance-like, reciting this litany of horrors now that he finally had a listening ear. "To save him. He never did. I moved him in here from the garden—it was hard, I had to uproot the roses one by one, and if I so much as ripped a leaf, he screamed." A frown. "Well, not screamed, really. He couldn't get that loud. I tried trimming back the blooms for a while, but that seemed to hurt him, so eventually I stopped."

"Gabe." Lore pressed a hand to his arm; his muscles were stone-tense. "If he's in that much pain—"

But he shook his head, knowing what she was going to say and already negating it. "I can't," he said hoarsely. "I tried. I can't."

She lifted her hand away.

All thoughts of the questions she would ask Anton if given a chance, the reassurance she would seek about her magic, fled her mind at the actual horror of him. He'd been a terrible, murderous man, but the punishment Bastian had wrought was almost worse.

"You."

It was barely sound, a breath from a dry throat full of leaves and thorns.

But it made Lore's voice dam in her own throat, made her vision involuntarily focus again, see the man in the mess of bloody flowers.

Anton's one eye rolled down from the sky, slowly, obscenely. It fixed on her, sharp as the day he'd had her trussed up and drugged in the bowels of the Church. "The deathwitch," he rasped. "Still alive when you shouldn't be."

Lore's hands balled to fists by her sides, though they shook, and her voice did, too. "You're one to talk."

A terrible huffing sound; a laugh, she guessed. "Point taken," Anton said, rustling the ivy leaves on the vine snaking out of his mouth. "Though this fate is not as awful as you would think. It gives me so much time to commune with the one true god. So much time to speak to Apollius, and know He is listening." Anton made that rustling laugh sound again, vocal cords rubbing against flower petals. "His plans have changed, deathwitch. He is mutable. Adaptable. All gods are."

The shivery feeling in her stomach slipped down her spine.

The one whole eye that had rolled down from the sky to regard her had rolled back up again, staring into the punishing summer light. "He grew her a forest," Anton said, low and hoarse, stirring another rustling of ivy leaves. "He asked all of Them to stay, to help Him hold the power He'd found. But She was the one on whom the isolation grated most, and She was the only one He gave something back to. He asked for Her vow, and She gave Him Her fist."

A forest. Like the one in her dreams. Lore's eyes narrowed. She looked to Gabe, searching for explanation. But he shook his head, held a finger briefly to his lips. Quiet.

"He gave Them all the gift of divinity, but that was not enough." Anton spoke as if entranced, his face tilted toward the sun. But the fingers splayed out on the wall twitched, like he would've made fists of them if he could. "And that is why They are not fit to be remembered as gods. Because They threw it all away, They left Him alone. What else could He do?" A tear slipped down his craggy cheek. "He has only ever done the best He can with what He has been given. Changed as He had to."

Anton fell silent. Lore realized she'd leaned away from the man, her arms clasped tightly over her chest like she could make herself smaller. She slid a look to Gabe.

"The wording changes," he said quietly, divining her unspoken question. "But the gist is the same. The story about the forest, the betrayal."

"And you." Anton's eye slashed down from the sky again, latched onto Lore. The movement of the muscles tripped something in his ruined face, pumped more viscous fluid from the rose-choked socket of his other eye. "You lived when you should not. You bring about destruction, make more work for Him, and yet still He calls you favored. Because you won't stop, will you? You will channel and channel, sink yourself into death and darkness, and nothing anyone says will stop you. He wants that, now. A second chance."

"Where is he *getting* all that?" Surreptitiously, Lore glanced up, squinting through the vines at the midday light like she might see someone up in the clouds, whispering to the mad holy man.

"The story he's telling maps loosely onto some of the legends about the gods on the Golden Mount," Gabe said quietly. "Before the Compendium was written."

"Back when you were allowed to tell stories about Them," Lore muttered. In antiquity, when the gods were still alive, there'd been just as many stories about Them as there were Tracts now. Their worship was informal, and They were regarded more like fairy-tale characters than all-powerful deities, remembered both as the people They had been and the gods They'd become. Religion ossified as it aged, allowed less room for interpretation. Most of the stories about the gods that hadn't made it into the Compendium weren't written down anywhere, instead told through word of mouth down through generations. Eventually, even those oral traditions died out. The telling of stories about the gods—especially ones that painted Apollius in a less-than-flattering light—wasn't necessarily outlawed, but it was frowned upon.

An arch look from Gabe, but he nodded, allowing her the point. "I've looked through the library, just to confirm. Malcolm helped me locate some old manuscripts—"

"Wait." It shouldn't be a surprise, she supposed, but it still hit her like one. "Malcolm knows about Anton? About what he's been saying?"

Gabe's lips pulled flat. He nodded. "There was no other way to get ahold of those manuscripts."

"Have you told Bastian?" The same question he'd asked her earlier, an echo of distrust.

His lips pulled, if possible, even flatter.

Alie, Malcolm, Gabe. All of them subtly positioning themselves in opposition to Bastian—or if not in complete opposition, at least at odds. Distrust grew unless you pulled it out at the root, and Bastian seemed in no hurry to allow himself to be checked.

No Arceneaux rule had ever been challenged, not until August. Maybe they should've expected a domino effect after that, one coup leading to another, an endless line of falling Kings.

Gabe read the quicksilver thoughts on her face, the spark of betrayal and understanding that flared and burned out. He sighed, rubbed at the red marks on his temple left by the strap of his eye patch. "Bastian is volatile," he said quietly. "You've known that from the beginning, Lore. He took over violently, and while some of the changes he's made have been good, you can't deny that he's angling down a dangerous path. And he's taking you with him." He didn't look at her ring, but it seemed to sit heavier on her finger, like his invisible regard imbued it with terrible weight. "If he thought Anton was spouting off about Apollius and Nyxara, about channeling bringing about an end that the gods wanted, what do you think he'd do?"

He'd finish what he started. He'd kill his uncle. And though Lore knew that was a mercy, she also knew Gabe would never allow it.

The idea of one more wedge driven between the two of them made her chest hurt.

"The stress of everything is getting to him, and he's using whatever he can to firm his hold. I understand it." Gabe said that part begrudgingly. "But he can't continue ruling as if he has absolute power."

The part he left unsaid hung around them, thick as cigar smoke in a windowless room. Bastian *did* have absolute power, but they were all trusting him not to use it. To trust a council, to take other opinions into account.

"I agree," Lore said slowly. "But what alternative does he have, Gabe? The fields had to be healed if we wanted a harvest. And showing the Kirytheans that we have power they don't will keep them from invading." She said these things like she believed them, and she did. Part of her did, at least.

"Then you know very little about power, Lore."

"And you do?"

"More than you." With the sun lighting the glass ceiling behind him, his hair looked more red than gold. "Showing the Kirytheans your power won't cow them. It will just make them think of ways to take it for themselves."

"Good thing they can't, then." She had to squint to glare at him, but she did it anyway. "Only Bastian and I can channel Spiritum. And Bastian would never give up to the Empire."

Another rustling laugh behind them. Anton hung in his bloody bower of roses and ivy, his head tilted up. The leaves by his mouth feathered, the rose growing through his scarred and empty eye socket bobbed back and forth.

"You are so eager to think less of what you are," the former Priest Exalted murmured, when his painful mirth subsided. "This plan may not have been His first, but I see now how He moves the pieces." He shook his head, as much as he was able. A thorn dragged across his cheek, pulled it open into gaping red meat. "You will bend to Him, daughter of the dark. You always do."

Lore swallowed. "Does he say things like that often, too?"

"No." Gabe took her elbow and steered her away from the thorn-riddled priest, back out into the greenhouse. "That's new."

Gabe led her back into the Church, back through the serpentine corridors and into the small door that led to the confessional. They'd only been gone a few minutes, but Lore still poked her head through the heavy velvet curtain warily, making sure the bloodcoat hadn't gotten curious.

The confessional room was empty, as always, refracted light from the rose window illuminating the dust motes floating over unoccupied pews. No bloodcoat. She breathed another prayer of thanks for whatever strange notion had made Bastian ask for Lore's privacy.

Lore turned back to Gabe, let the curtain fall behind her. He stood closer than she thought, and she took an unconscious step backward, her heel catching on the curtain's hem.

She tripped; he caught her elbow. He'd touched her there before, steering her out of the garden, but it seemed weightier, now. More tactile, like being in this room, away from any threat of prying eyes, somehow roughened his calluses and amped his heat.

"I want to help," Lore said, because the moment begged for something to break it, and words were the safest option. "We can make Bastian see reason. This doesn't have to be a war."

"He made it part of a war when he brought in Kirythea," Gabe said darkly. But he still didn't let go of her elbow. "Quite literally."

Lore shook her head. "We can't think like that. We can't *afford* to, Gabe. There's too much at stake."

"*You* are at stake." His grip tightened on her arm, pulling her subtly closer. "You came here because those dreams are scaring you. Dreams you have after channeling. And you know he won't let you stop."

She'd wondered before what Gabe still believed about her power, what it would turn her into. She supposed this was a kind of answer. "I can take care of myself."

"You have demonstrated over and over again that you absolutely cannot." Gabe tugged her forward again, just a bit, and it felt like something inevitable, inching closer, gaining unstoppable momentum. "When it comes to him, you fold every time. You want to talk about things we can't afford? We can't afford a weakness, and he's yours. Always has been."

He was too close, his eyes trained on her mouth. They hovered on the precipice of something, here, just waiting to see who would step over the edge first.

"You think he's my only one?" Lore murmured.

He stared, a muscle twitching in his jaw, the tendons in his neck tight enough to snap. She wanted him to touch her, wanted to close the tiny distance between them. Wanted to run the finger wearing Bastian's ring along his collarbone.

But she didn't. He didn't, either.

"So who else knows about this?" she asked, crossing her arms. "That you think Bastian is getting out of control?" Her thoughts grasped at that moment a few nights ago, when she'd found Amelia Demonde in the atrium, talking about Bastian and Apollius.

"And is there any chance Amelia Demonde has been talking to Anton?"

"What?" Shock made the word slice through the humid room. "No one knows where Anton is but you and me, Lore. Even Malcolm doesn't know his location, just that he's alive."

Yet another secret to hold between them.

Gabe shook his head. "Where in all the myriad hells did you get *Amelia Demonde* from?"

"I saw her in the atrium the other night. Talking some religious nonsense. Sounded a lot like the kind of thing Anton is fond of throwing out."

"Amelia used to come to Anton for counseling. She was very... devout." But the way he said it made it sound distasteful. "She wanted to draw as close to Apollius as possible. Anton instructed her in the Tracts." He ran a weary hand down his face. "But she thinks he's dead, just like everyone else does. Her family was part of Anton's sect, but she's harmless. The only person we have to worry about right now is Bastian."

"Something is affecting him," she said quietly. "He's not acting like himself."

Gabe gave her an incredulous look. "He seems perfectly like himself to me. Selfish and careless. Except now it's a problem for the whole damn country, not just us."

Lore sighed. "I'm serious. He seems... distracted, lately." She thought of the night before, when she'd moved to kiss him and he'd moved away. "Maybe channeling is affecting him, too. Maybe he's also having weird dreams and just won't tell me about them. I know we have to focus on ruling, on war, but I want to make sure he's fine before—"

"Before you marry him?" There was another question behind that one. *Are you really going to marry him?*

Lore chewed her lip. Nodded.

He stared at her, a slight slump to his shoulders. Then, with a curt nod of his own, he pushed aside the curtain, strode to the front of the room. "I'll see you at the King's dinner this evening. I assume we'll all be discussing your betrothal."

Her eyes narrowed at his back. "Shouldn't we make plans to study this more? I can meet you in the library—"

"No." He stopped in front of the door, turned to face her. Any trace of softness in his face was gone, any hint of what had almost happened behind that curtain completely wiped away.

That was for the best, probably.

"Then what's *your* plan?" she asked.

"I told you I would give you some trust," Gabe said wearily, headed for the priest's side of the confessional. "Not all of it."

She supposed the fact that she couldn't sleep shouldn't be a great surprise.

After the fifth time she'd changed positions, flopping over in bed and throwing her pillows down to the floor, Lore admitted defeat and got up. Part of her was relieved that sleep was so elusive. The last thing she needed was another strange memory-dream.

Go find him.

The voice was faint, a slither through her head that could easily have been imagined.

She knew it wasn't. She'd heard it too many times, now.

The deep of night made everything feel unreal, not quite as tethered to reality. Once, that line of thinking had led to her kissing Gabriel Remaut. It would've led to more if he hadn't suddenly recovered his monkish sensibilities when she was reaching for his belt. Now, she was sure, it would lead to something equally reckless.

What are you?

The question was fired off into the darkness of her mind before she could overthink it. Before she could decide if it was an answer she actually wanted, much less needed.

But not before she knew it was necessary. There was something else in the dark of her head with her. She'd tried to ignore it, hadn't mentioned it when she was telling Gabe about the dreams. But there was a voice in Lore's head, and it was stupid of her to pretend like she didn't know what it was.

When the answer came, it sounded almost bemused. *Do you really need Me to tell you that?*

Lore slammed her mind closed as if it were a trapdoor, hunkering down like a burrowing animal. She'd wanted this, wanted an answer, but now that she had it, she wanted to hide. Before, when the voice just whispered *catacombs* in her head as she wandered at night, it'd been easier to ignore. Full sentences were a different matter.

Something like a sigh echoed through her, gossamer-thin, then gone. Lore tried to grow her grove, tried to make dense trees and blue sky. But that just reminded her of the dreams, and the barrier never solidified.

Lore took a moment, breathing in deep. She opened the teeth of her mind, just a bit. *So now You're telling me to go find Bastian, instead of telling me to go to the catacombs?*

I'm adaptable.

She closed off her mind again, as well as she could when her tree-barrier seemed out of reach. Slowly, Lore sat up, painstakingly extricating herself from the tangle of her sheets. A glass of water sat on her bedside table, and she gulped it, rivulets running down the corners of her mouth to wet her nightgown.

Upstairs, a crash, like something heavy falling to the ground.

Myriad *hells*.

Lore pushed up, stalked across the room, into the hallway. She wasn't sure of the time, but it was full night, the windows black velvet cut by white moonlight.

Her stride became a stomp as she reached the spiral staircase leading to Bastian's rooms, an anger she didn't really understand seeping through her nervous system, making her palm tingle where the eclipse scar interrupted her life and heart lines. It felt like an echo, an emotion reverberating back from some past moment when it'd been suppressed, only fully realized now in the dark.

When she reached the top of the stairs, her eyes were filmed with tears that felt like they didn't belong to her.

Bastian was awake, though the sheets of the bed were knotted and pillows tossed to the floor, as if he'd fought his mattress before rising. Bare-chested, wearing only a pair of trousers in the same white gauze as Lore's nightgown, he stood at the window, his scarred hand flexing open and closed. His dark hair was tousled, his cheeks flushed, like he'd woken from either a nightmare or a particularly good sex dream.

Maybe both.

Next to the window, a small table had toppled to the floor, a vase of roses lying on its side in an expanding pool of murky water. That explained the crash.

He knew she was there. She could tell by the way his muscles tensed, lines limned in moonlight, a map she could follow to his center. Lore hadn't seen him at all before she went to bed. Dinner had been brought to her room on a tray, and when she'd inquired about the King's whereabouts, the servant who brought it just said that His Majesty was indisposed. Lore was too overwhelmed by her meeting with Anton and almost-kiss with Gabe to try seeking him out. If he didn't want to see her, that was fine.

Now she wished she'd come to find him. Wished she'd made Gabe come with her.

Bastian braced his hands on either side of the windowsill, head bowed. A low, huffing sound—a laugh, or an attempt at one. "Which one are you?"

Her brows drew together. "What the fuck are you talking about?"

His head hung further forward. "I guess that's a stupid question."

Lore's jaw firmed, her hands in fists as she strode across the room. The first touch of her palm to his shoulder shivered through her like something alive, a blush in her cheeks and a gasp of fresh air in her lungs. She pushed until he faced her, all glare and loom, though he didn't do it quite so well as Gabe. Bastian's face wasn't built for glaring; he was the honey to Gabe's vinegar.

She met his eyes just for a moment, then pointedly looked away from him, to the upended table. "They told me you were indisposed, but I didn't think you'd take it out on the décor."

"Whatever works." He wasn't rising to her bait. There was something almost awed in Bastian's eyes, something wondering, softening his glare until it was gone completely. His hand rose, cupped the side of her face. She didn't pull away, though neither did she lean into his touch. Balance, always, poised on a tightrope over a yawning chasm.

Bastian searched her face, looking for something she didn't know how to give him. The wonder in his eyes took a turn, almost jealous. "How do you do it?" he murmured. "How do you hold so much, and still keep yourself? I'm slipping, more and more every day, but you're still *you*."

"So are you." She covered his hand with her own, not quite sure what to make of this.

Yes, you do, whispered the voice in her head.

"I wish I was," Bastian murmured. His thumb brushed across her cheekbone. "I want so much, Lore, but I can't have it."

"You can." She swayed toward him, wanting to close that distance. Nighttime, making her reckless.

For a moment, he let her be.

His lips were warm, and they were hungry, pressing hers open at the same time that he surged forward and trapped her between him and the wall. Lore's foot slipped in the spilled rose water, and he used the off-balance moment to nudge his knee between her thighs. She gasped, and his tongue slipped into her mouth.

They both moved so quickly, like they were trying to outrun something.

He won't like this, said the voice.

And almost like he could hear it, Bastian pulled away, his hands falling from her hair as he stepped back. He reached up and tenderly touched his lip, just once.

"Even now…" But he didn't finish, giving her a quick, furtive look that said he was afraid to.

And she wanted to soothe that fear, wanted to have this honesty between them, here in the deep of night where the sun was as far away as it was ever going to be. She wanted to tell him about the dreams, so she and him and Gabe were all together in something. "Bastian, I have to tell you—"

But he shook his head, a quick, sharp negation. "Don't."

Don't, echoed the voice.

She'd learned to trust intuition. To trust deep feelings, especially when it came to this man.

So she kept her mouth shut.

Bastian sighed, hands hanging on his hips again. "Why did you come up here?"

"Heard the crash."

He nodded, and they stood there like that a moment, neither sure what to do next. When Bastian broke the silence, it was so quiet.

"Stay," he said. "Please."

Lore nodded, and the acquiescence felt echoed, mirrored, everything within her agreeing to stay here with him for the night.

Even the parts that didn't feel wholly like her.

There were no overtures of sex, despite the kiss. Bastian slid into bed, and she got in the other side; they chose their sides like they'd been doing it for years, natural as breathing. She smoothed the sheets as best she could. They smelled like him, red wine and cologne, the musk of sweat.

Bastian rolled over to face her back, throwing an arm across her middle, pulling her to press against his chest. His breath stirred her hair, slowing, evening.

Lore stared into the dark. Eventually, the dark became the back of her eyelids, oblivion creeping up on her.

A ghost of words in her mind, just before she tipped over into sleep. Almost a confession.

I missed this.

Chapter Fifteen

Some bonds don't break. They only bend.
–Caldienan proverb

She woke facing him, having somehow twisted in her sleep, her head cradled beneath his chin, his arms wrapped around her back. Lore stiffened when her eyes first opened, her mind taking a moment to catch up with last night, with why she was here.

She stiffened further as she waited for the voice, sure it would have something to say. But her head was silent, empty of all thoughts but her own.

It wasn't quite dawn—outside the window, the sun was slowly rising, painting the indigo of the sky in violet swaths, inching into pink and orange. The light reflected in the pool of water on the floor, the vase of roses neither of them had bothered to clean up.

Lore craned her neck to look into Bastian's face. He was awake, looking down at her with an expression of…of loss, almost. It made her brow furrow, made questions she didn't have words for swirl in her head, looking for an outlet to her mouth.

He put a finger to her lips. "I don't know how safe it is," he murmured. "How much of what I know stays my own. Better to not talk."

Her brow furrowed further, an awful understanding blooming. "Bastian, we have to—"

He shook his head. Gently, he kissed her forehead, as the sun rose fully into the sky.

When he pulled back, something was different. It was subtle—a coldness around his eyes, the angles of his face somehow more austere. Subtle, but there, and Lore had to fight not to jerk away from him.

If he noticed, he didn't comment. Bastian rolled out of bed and stretched, making the muscles on his chest stand out in sharp relief. Last night, he'd been just as near-naked as he was now, but there hadn't been anything overtly sexual in it—at least, not any more than there always was with Bastian, who was too handsome for it to be ignored. But now, he watched her watching him, a self-satisfied curl to his mouth.

Lore got up quickly, crossing to a table holding a crystal pitcher of water with lemon and two glasses. Her cheeks heated. The lemons were fresh; a maid had undoubtedly brought this in while they were asleep. There was no reason to be embarrassed at being caught in her betrothed's bed, but she felt the same needle of shame she'd felt that time Mari walked in on her with some girl she'd met the night before, whose name she'd never asked. Unearned intimacy, baring parts of yourself to someone you didn't know.

Because the man she fell asleep with seemed completely different from the man watching her now.

"What's on your agenda for today?" she asked as she poured, mostly to dispel the aura of expectant silence. She gulped down one glass, poured another.

"Our agenda, more like." She heard Bastian stand up, heard his closet doors open. "You'll be accompanying me."

That was enough to make her turn away from her careful examination of the blank wall. "Accompanying you where?"

Bastian grinned at her over his shoulder as he pulled a white shirt—his staple—out of the closet. "To the harbor," he said, as if it was the most natural answer in the world. "With our good friends Maxon and Caius and most of the court. We have to christen the new ship, remember."

She did, vaguely. The new naval ship he'd been discussing with the admiral the night of his coronation, an answer to the increased oceanic presence of Kirythean war vessels near the Burnt Isles—one of the only projects of August's that Bastian hadn't halted. The party on the docks had been part of her social calendar for weeks, but the days all seemed to blur together lately.

"Who knows, maybe we'll get a chance to show off our magic some more." His eyes flashed, the brown of them flecked in gold. "Two birds, one stone, and all that."

"I won't."

"Why not?"

"I don't think it's a good idea, not today. The consequences—"

"I thought we'd all agreed that the consequences were a silly thing Anton made up to scare you."

Lore gritted her teeth. "That seems to be yet another decision on which you consulted no one else."

Across the carriage, Malcolm watched them argue like someone might watch a boxing match. He was their official Church escort today, but he'd stayed near-silent on the short ride to the docks. Lore had invited him to ride in the carriage instead of beside it in a rush, not wanting to be alone with Bastian.

Bastian, who was different now that the sun ruled the sky.

As much as she tried to ignore it, tried to leave the realization at the back of her mind, the conclusion was obvious. Anton had warned them of the consequences if she continued to channel—that she would become more like Nyxara. So far, all she'd gotten was the voice in her head.

There'd been no such warning for Bastian, but what if that was because Anton *wanted* him taken over? The Church desired Apollius's return. It'd always been depicted as a bodily return, a triumphant emergence from wherever the god had been hiding for five hundred years, but what if it was this instead? A captured body, a shackled mind?

She wanted to tell Gabe. But what if he thought it was a good thing, too? Even if he didn't, he and Malcolm and Alie already thought Bastian was acting erratically. If she told them that was because Bastian wasn't Bastian anymore, not all the time, what would that do?

Nothing good.

Malcolm apparently took Lore's lost stare as a prompt to speak. He sat up, making a slightly irritated face at her before smoothing out his expression. "I agree with Lore. The Kirytheans have seen what you can do. There's no need for another display today. Besides, there's nothing Spiritum or Mortem can do with water—you'd need Caeliar's power for that."

Bastian glanced at him from a narrowed eye, like he might argue, but then settled into his seat. "We'll see," he said simply.

His arm was slung across the back of the carriage seat, his fingers dangling close to Lore's loose hair. No time for Juliette this morning; he'd dressed quickly and bid her do the same. When he came to her bedroom door, she'd greeted him with the pronouncement that she would not be channeling today. His response had been to smile and shepherd her down to the carriage.

"As I've said before," Bastian said, twitching his fingers to gently tug a lock of her hair, "not using your abilities is bowing to Anton's fearmongering. You have nothing to fear from magic, Lore."

He said it like a joke, but a shadow flickered across his eyes.

"Caution isn't fear," Malcolm said. "Caution is good."

Bastian said nothing, but gave him a withering look.

Absently, Lore twisted her engagement ring around her finger.

Bastian picked up her hand, glancing down at the ring he'd put there. A subtle change in his face again; he looked at her like he couldn't quite believe she'd let him do this. There was a momentary softness in his eyes that seemed out of place as he lightly touched her cheek.

Then that change again, swift as sun slicing through cloud cover. The touch on her cheek became less wondering, more like ownership.

Lore leaned back, just enough to make his hand fall from her face.

Bastian leaned back, too, settling into the corner of the seat, and turned his eyes to the covered window, ignoring her and Malcolm both.

A flicker in her mind, like the brush of captured moth wings against a palm.

Part of Lore wanted to scream, to shout at Malcolm for not noticing that something was desperately wrong here. To push this awful knowledge onto someone else and make them deal with it instead. She glanced at him, a flash of panic spasming across her face.

Malcolm's brow furrowed.

The carriage came to an abrupt stop. Gull caws echoed in open air, and the light through the gauzy curtains seemed brighter, reflecting off the sea.

"I still won't do it," Lore said quietly. "I mean it, Bastian."

He said nothing.

The door opened. Bastian climbed out, giving a theatrical stretch, smiling to the gathered audience she could hear milling beyond the curtain.

The bloodcoat came around, opened her own door. With a weary sigh, Lore let him help her out.

Malcolm followed, the irritated look he'd given her before melting into concern. "Lore, is everything all right? Did something happen?"

But she didn't answer him. Didn't know how to, not in a way that wouldn't make Bastian either more of a villain or an acceptable sacrifice on the altar of the greater good.

Lore couldn't live with either.

"I mentioned it to Gabe," Malcolm continued, watching Bastian as he started working the crowd. His dark eyes narrowed, his jaw a firm line. "That Bastian seems . . . off. He knows it. Gabe doesn't miss much when it comes to Bastian. But he didn't want to talk about it."

"He's fine," Lore said faintly, hoping that Malcolm and Alie hadn't had a chance to talk since yesterday. That between Malcolm noticing Bastian's change and her telling Alie that she thought something was wrong, they weren't able to come to the same terrible conclusion knocking at the back of Lore's skull. "Just tired, I'm sure."

Malcolm made a skeptical noise.

Leaving the conversation where it was, Lore drifted toward the crowd.

The docks didn't look anything like she remembered. The weathered wood had been cleared of barnacles and gull shit, the salt-lashed planks scrubbed until they didn't gleam, exactly, but looked much cleaner than they'd been since they were nailed in place. Velvet ropes lined the edges, keeping the gathered courtiers from accidentally tripping into the sea.

Gods, it looked like the entire Citadel was here. At least four docks had been cleared, a perimeter established by bloodcoats and a few dark-clothed Presque Mort at the ends of the road that wound around the harbor. Keeping the rabble out, creating a sanitized space for the nobles to feel like they were experiencing the city.

"I thought it was a good idea to get the court out of…well, out of the court." Bastian had apparently greeted everyone at the fringes of the crowd, and now came to Lore's side, taking her arm. "It's high time we actually interacted with Dellaire, don't you think? Most of the nobility won't set foot outside the Citadel Wall while they're here in the summer, and gods forbid they make a stop on their way back to their winter holdings."

"Looks like there's still a wall." Lore jerked her chin toward the bloodcoats and Mort clustered on the dock roads, blocking them. "Just a lower one."

Bastian shrugged. "Slow progress is still progress."

If Lore craned her neck, she could see people gathered on the other side of the bloodcoats, giving them a wide berth while still peering in on the courtiers. Were there people she knew in that crowd, people she'd drunk with or run poisons for? Her stomach gave an uncomfortable lurch at the thought, wondering what they thought when they saw her now.

She'd attempted to keep all the pieces of her life separate—catacombs, poison running, Citadel, three distinct phases, three distinct Lores. But they bled into one another more and more every day, those three pieces inevitably making a whole.

She thought of her and Bastian and Gabe.

Bastian tucked her hand into his elbow. "And we're off."

The first few rounds of courtiers Lore managed to mostly ignore, a flurry of pastel-colored summer clothes and refined accents that blurred into an indistinct wash. She smiled and made her clumsy curtsies, mostly kept up with banal small talk. Bastian was a good enough conversationalist that she didn't have to engage much, riding the wave of his charisma.

The crowd parted briefly, giving her a glimpse of white, curling hair.

"I see Alie." Lore disentangled herself from Bastian's arm, not caring that she'd just interrupted Lady Whatsherface's treatise on how to effectively grow flowers on the cold Caldien border. "I'll be right back."

Bastian let her go without a fuss, placating Lady Whatsherface with a charming smile as Lore wove through the teeming courtiers. Alie stood near the velvet ropes blocking the edge of the dock, talking to Brigitte with her head bowed low. The other woman's saffron-yellow dress made her dark-brown skin glow; matching threads had been woven into the ends of her long locs. Alie wore blush-pink today, a short-sleeved gown that left her freckled shoulders bare, and her cloud of white curls was gathered into a bun on top of her head. She managed to make the hairstyle look effortless. When Lore attempted similar things with her own hair, she looked like she'd been in a terrible accident with an oil drum.

Brigitte saw her coming before Alie did. "Lore! It seems congratulations are in order."

"I suppose they are." Lore wasn't sure how to navigate this part, whether she was supposed to act thrilled or serene. She would excel at neither, since her true feelings were a churn of anxiety and desire that mostly made her feel like screaming.

Next to Brigitte, Alie turned, subtly signaling a passing servant to take her empty wineglass. Her eyes snagged on Lore's ring, and she smiled and gestured to Bri, though her eyes kept tracking nervously over the crowd. Probably looking for Caius. "Here it is, Bri. Take a gander."

"*Finally.*" Bri held her own wine near her chest and leaned in close to Lore's outstretched hand. "I've wanted to get a look at it for ages."

"Look to your heart's content," Lore said, wiggling her finger. This was nice, acting like she was just a normal woman being normally excited about her normal engagement.

"Gods dead and dying," Bri murmured, angling Lore's hand back and forth to make the golden-hued stone catch the light. She eyed it as a scientist with a particularly rare specimen might, like she wished for a magnifying glass. "That diamond is, quite literally, priceless."

"Aren't most Arceneaux jewels?" Alie asked with an arch look.

"Well, yes, but that jewel in particular is special." Bri smiled like someone finally being given an opportunity to expound on a beloved subject. "Ask me why, please. I get so few opportunities."

A smile tugged at Alie's lips. "Brigitte is an amateur jeweler herself," she explained for Lore's benefit. "And as such, she knows far too much about gemstones."

"I made this." Brigitte ruefully dropped Lore's hand and held out her own, as if she were the newly engaged one. "Go on, ogle."

The ring was gorgeous, a silver sunburst cradling a deep-blue sapphire. The band was carved to look like wind gusts, curling over Brigitte's finger.

"It's beautiful," Lore said. "An earned ogle, certainly."

"Thank you." Bri dropped her hand and gave a little curtsy, then looked to Alie. "Now Alie has to ask me about your ring."

Alie rolled her eyes with a smile. "Fine. Tell us."

"That diamond," Bri said, launching directly into her answer, "was mined from the Golden Mount."

Lore's brow furrowed. "Wait. That can't be true, can it?"

"It can." Bri beamed, thrilled to have a reason to explain. "It's been tested by the best jewelers in the world, and its structural makeup is different from every other diamond mined anywhere else—it's most like the others from the Burnt Isles, but even those aren't a perfect match. Apparently it shares some other component, another type of stone rare enough that no two jewelers agree on what it is. Between that and its yellow coloring, the only explanation is the Golden Mount."

"Or an extremely creative salesman," Alie said.

Bri shrugged. "The Arceneaux family has believed that it's from the Golden Mount for generations. Not that any of them got a great look at it—after the stone was tested, Gerard Arceneaux had it hidden within the Church somewhere. Most people thought it was a myth, especially since Gerard said it had been given to him by Apollius." She grinned. "The fact that Bastian knew where it was, and gave it to you as an engagement ring, is quite the scandal. I find it terribly romantic, personally."

Lore tried to smile, but the muscles in her cheeks would only twitch.

"Bastian." Alie said his name like a warning; Lore turned to see her fiancé striding toward them, wearing a wolfish smile and a glint in his eye. Bri and Alie gave quick curtsies; Lore wasn't sure if she should follow suit, or if such things weren't required of her.

The King answered the question by taking her arm and planting it once again in the crook of his elbow. "Ladies."

"Majesty," Bri murmured, dipping her head. Alie said nothing, her lips pressed tightly closed.

Something in Bastian's stance withered a bit at her silence, but it didn't make his smile falter. "I have to steal my Queen away from you for just a moment."

"Of course." Bri took Alie's arm. "We were just going to tour the new ship."

"If you have any ideas for a title, let me know," Bastian said. "I have to name the thing in half an hour, and I have nothing."

Lore let him lead her gently away, her ring-heavy hand pressed against his arm. She'd known the ring was valuable—it was an Arceneaux heirloom; it'd be astronomically expensive from that alone—but mined from the Golden Mount? That pushed it from valuable into mythic, regardless of the story's veracity.

The Golden Mount existed—pre-Godsfall maps confirmed it—but no one knew where it actually *was*, other than somewhere in the miasma of fog and ash surrounding the Burnt Isles, just off the coast. There wasn't a consensus on if the Mount even still existed after Apollius had thrown Nyxara into the Isles during Their final confrontation, before directing His early followers to take Her body and inter it in Dellaire. If the diamond in Lore's ring really was from the Golden Mount, it would've had to be mined before the Godsfall happened. Which made sense within the context of Bri's story, Lore supposed. If one believed that Apollius Himself had dictated the Tracts to Gerard Arceneaux, it wasn't much of a leap to think He'd given him a ring, too.

Though she hadn't the foggiest idea why. Or why such a thing would've been kept in Church storage, rather than displayed as another sign of the Bleeding God's favor. Myriad hells, if the story was true, August would've had the thing permanently attached to his face, if Anton didn't beat him to it.

As for how Bastian knew where it was…she thought she understood that part.

"You're thinking hard about something," Bastian murmured, leaning close so his lips brushed her ear. "Care to let me in on it?"

"It's nothing." Lore followed his lead, leaning into his shoulder to soften the impact of her refusal.

A few more empty greetings and equally mindless conversations later, Bastian turned the two of them with purpose toward the yet-to-be-named ship. It was open for tours like the others on the docks, the gangplank guarded by two Presque Mort, the daggers in their harnesses glinting afternoon light. They had to be sweating buckets. The sun was high, and the midsummer heat was making itself known. More than one carefully created hairstyle was frizzing in the humidity.

"Once we go up there to name the ship," Bastian murmured, "we'll channel together, like before. It'd be nice if we could do something useful, but like Malcolm said, that's currently out of our scope, so maybe just something like that day at prayers—"

"I told you I won't, Bastian." Lore's voice was small but not timid.

He didn't look at her, eyes fixed on the ship and the horizon beyond. But a tremor went through the muscles her hand was trapped between, still tucked into his arm.

"I want to honor that," he said, a tremor in his voice to match the one in his arm. A *but* lingered at the end of the sentence, one he didn't say.

He turned away from the new ship, meandered around the velvet ropes to the other dock, going back to working the crowd.

The King's demeanor changed as they stepped onto the dock nearest the barricade of bloodcoats and Presque Mort. He straightened further, squared his shoulders, as if shoring himself up for battle. "We should go see our honored guests."

No question who he meant. The Kirythean diplomats stood near the velvet ropes lining the dock's edge, sipping wine and chatting with two other courtiers. The lady of the pair laughed, throwing back her head. Amelia Demonde, gorgeous as ever, with a pleasant expression on her face that didn't recall midnight meetings and hissed religious pronouncements.

Maxon inclined his head as Bastian and Lore approached, a slight smile on his face. He dressed in Kirythean fashion, now—more austere than what most Auverrani favored, a flowing dark shirt with no vest tucked into simple trousers and shorter boots than Lore was used to seeing. A golden laurel wreath was embroidered around the shirt's collar, open nearly to the middle of Maxon's chest, just like the tunics they wore over their armor. The man was almost as ridiculously handsome as Bastian. "Quite the party you've thrown. I've seen less lively gatherings for Consecrations than you're having for a new ship."

"Oh, I don't know," Amelia purred, sipping her wine, her eyes flicking to Lore. "The last few Consecrations I've been to have been quite diverting."

Lore was honestly impressed that the woman managed to turn the whole bloody mess of the eclipse ritual into a delicate court barb, as common an accessory as a ribbon in your hair. She probably *would* have been a better Queen.

"It's not saying much, from Maxon," Caius said. "Consecrations in Kirythea are somber affairs. The honor is for the Bleeding God, not the one reaching the age of ascension." He lifted his cup in salute to Bastian. "For an Arceneaux, though, I'm sure Lord Apollius appreciates a bit more revelry."

Sidestepping the subject of Lore's disastrous Consecration entirely, though surely he knew the story. Amelia looked put out.

"We do love any excuse for a party," Bastian replied. "I hope the two of you have been made welcome by the court. I like to think they've kept an open mind."

"We've been received cordially enough," Maxon answered. "Though *welcomed* might be pushing it."

"They'll come 'round," Lord Demonde assured him, clapping the other man on the back. He'd clearly been indulging in the offered wine; his cheeks were flushed, his eyes glassy. "Better to make new friends than keep old enemies, I always say."

"Indeed." Bastian's eyes were flinty, though the smile beneath them stayed warm. From her place by her husband, Amelia watched him avid as a bird on a worm. Her golden hair was piled atop her head and held in place with what looked like hundreds of tiny glittering pins, and even with the humidity, she managed to look dewy rather than sweaty.

Despite herself, Lore felt a tug of possessiveness run through her. No, *possessive* wasn't quite right—*protective*, then, like Bastian needed a shield.

Foolish of her. No amount of shielding would protect a rabbit that insisted on wandering into the wolf's den.

"We've had a splendid time, actually," Amelia said with a smile. "It's been illuminating to discuss our cultures, especially since August forbade talk of the Empire for so long. For instance, did you know that in Kirythea, Lereal's power could be used up until nearly two hundred years after the Godsfall? Some researchers believe there are still traces of air magic left near Laerdas, since that's where Their body was found." She laughed, high and musical. "I daresay Kirythea got the better deal, in that regard."

"I'd certainly rather have a surplus of air magic than Mortem," Demonde agreed. "Far more useful."

"Perhaps," Bastian replied. A passing servant came by, carrying a tray of small pastries iced in the same purple as the flag of Auverraine; he snagged one off the plate. "From a certain point of view."

Maxon said nothing, only quirked an eyebrow.

"Amelia and Hugh have been most enlightening about how Mortem issues have affected Dellaire, and Auverraine as a whole." Caius cocked his head, the queue of his golden hair falling over one shoulder. "It seems there was a fairly large leak a few weeks ago, after many years without?"

Can't run from what you are, daughter of the dark.

"There was, yes." Bastian tightened his hold on Lore's arm. "Thankfully, my fiancée was there to help channel it all before it could cause any harm."

"I wouldn't say *that*." Amelia kept her voice light, but there was venom beneath. "She channeled it all into the farmlands."

"Fortunately," Lore said, matching the other woman's tone, "I also healed them just last week. Or did you not hear about that part?"

"Oh, no, I did." Amelia sipped her wine. "I only hope it wasn't too late to impact the harvest."

"It wasn't." Bastian's tone was icy, and for once, his face reflected it, dropping the mask of charming civility. "Lore did admirably. Both in her initial management of the leak and in the cleanup afterward. It was one of the things that convinced me she would make a good Queen, in actuality instead of just court nickname."

That, finally, made Amelia be quiet. She almost seemed to

shrink into herself, like the statement had been pointed beyond just a rebuttal. Lore's heart softened toward her, slightly. Amelia had been dealt a rough hand, and Lore knew that had she been given the same, she probably wouldn't be pleasant company, either.

Apparently, Hugh Demonde didn't notice his wife's shrinking. He smiled, wine-widened, and clapped Bastian on the shoulder in a show of familiarity he probably would have reconsidered if sober. Shoulder-clapping seemed to be the man's go-to gesture. "Delightful to see you in love, Your Majesty. Just delightful. It's been a while since the King and Queen of Auverraine actually liked each other."

The mention of his parents, however oblique, made Bastian stiffen. But it was momentary, small enough to miss if you blinked, and he nodded at Demonde's words as if he weren't the child of just such a union. "Hopefully it bodes well for the country as a whole."

"I'm sure it does," Caius said, with another smile delivered over another sip of wine.

Bastian swept his hand toward the end of the dock, as if to change the subject. "Have you all availed yourself of the décor? It's very impressive, if I do say so myself."

Lore didn't know much about boats beyond that they floated, despite living in close proximity to the harbor for a majority of her life, but the ship bobbing in the tide at the end of the dock looked impressive indeed. Heavy cannons bristled from the port and starboard sides like ribs from a spine. Another cannon was secured to the prow, its open mouth poised right above the figurehead. Caeliar of the sea, Her hair flying behind Her to caress the ship's sides, Her arms outflung to embrace the coming tide. Her eyes were narrowed, Her mouth open in a battle cry. Caeliar was always depicted as the most warlike of the original pantheon. Images of the elemental gods were technically outlawed but for special circumstances—the windows in the Church, and figureheads. She looked fierce in them all.

"Extremely so," Maxon conceded, turning bright-green eyes from Bastian to the ship. His gaze lingered on the depiction of Caeliar, a small, smug smile hanging on the corner of his mouth. "I haven't had a chance yet to go inside, but I'm anxious to see what it's like. Kirythea is known for its battleships."

"Yes, Malfour is renowned for their shipbuilding." Bastian gave Maxon a sly smile. All of the Empire's ships were constructed in conquered Malfour, a smaller coastal country known for sea voyages before the Empire took over. "Allow me to be your tour guide."

"We've already been," Demonde said, taking Amelia's arm. He jostled her; only by a graceful sway of the hip did Amelia manage to keep from spilling wine down her pale gown. "And we should make our rounds before the naming. Come, dear, I saw Lord Gauthien and his new wife, we should invite them to our fete next week—"

Amelia seemed less than pleased to be prized away from Bastian and the Kirytheans, but she dutifully followed her husband. As they moved away, she shot a sharp glance at Lore over her shoulder. The venom had drained out of it. Instead, the other woman looked almost hurt.

The Sainted King towed Lore toward the warship, and she lost Amelia in the crowd. Maxon and Caius fell in behind them, but far enough away not to overhear if she whispered.

When she leaned into Bastian's shoulder, however, it came out more hiss than whisper. "Do you really think showing the enemy the interior of our best ships is a good strategy?"

"It is if these aren't our best ships," Bastian murmured back with significantly less hiss. "Or even naval ships, technically. These are borrowed from August's personal fleet. The cannons are just decoration. The new ship is still docked up the harbor, fully guarded. When we name this one, it will be named by proxy."

Her death grip on his arm slackened, but Lore still frowned up at him. "That's... clever."

"Don't sound so surprised." He tapped a finger on the end of her nose. "It's good to keep some secrets, even from potential allies."

Lore wrinkled her nose and ducked away. "Calling the Kirythean Empire a *potential ally* seems overly optimistic."

"I am a very optimistic man."

Two Presque Mort guarded the gangplank, but clearly only in name, granting entry to anyone who approached with nothing but a cursory nod. When they saw Bastian, they stepped all the way aside, letting him and Lore and the Kirytheans pass wordlessly.

The ship was nearly as fine as the Citadel, which Lore guessed made sense if it was really from August's personal fleet. She only had a moment to marvel at the gleaming boards of the deck, the gold worked into the railings, before Bastian led her to a small spiral staircase cut into the floor, leading down into the bowels of the vessel. "The best way to experience it is bottom-to-top," he called back to the following diplomats. "Trust me."

"Is that bullshit?" Lore murmured to his back as she followed him into the dark. "It sounds like bullshit."

"Only partially." He hopped off the bottom step, reached up for her hand to help her down. "I have plans for us once we reach topside, and I'd like for our guests to be among the audience rather than sharing the stage."

Plans like channeling. Lore frowned, but in the sudden dark after the brightness of outside, she didn't think Bastian saw it. "I told you I won't."

"Lore, please." And he sounded so much like he had last night—so wounded, vulnerable, all the soft parts of him bared—that she didn't say anything more.

She expected relief from the heat beneath the deck, but the enclosed space just made the humidity oven in on itself. Her hair stuck to the nape of her neck, heavy and uncomfortable.

It didn't occur to Lore until they were in the depths of the ship that there were no bloodcoats down here, no Presque Mort. If either of the Kirytheans decided to try to take them out, there would be no one to stop the attack but themselves.

When she looked at Bastian, there was a near-feral gleam in the smile he gave her. Almost like he'd relish the opportunity.

Wooden steps creaked as Maxon and Caius made their way down the spiral stairs. Bastian turned away from her, gesturing to the open expanse of the hold, about half as large as the throne room in the Citadel and just as finely outfitted. "Gentlemen, welcome aboard."

The tour was a bit of a blur. Lore had become inured to the finery of the Citadel; at this point, her eyes slid past jewels and gilding without much thought. There was a bit much down here for it to be a convincing warship, between the ballroom with statues of scantily clad mermaids and the giant canopied beds in what was supposed to be barracks. But maybe the Kirytheans would just think that Auverraine was swimming in money, that even their engines of war were luxurious.

The fact that August's terrible taste could bring down the ruse would be funny if it weren't a legitimate concern.

But the Kirytheans didn't seem to see through the deception. Maxon nodded and made the appropriate awed noises when cued. Caius kept his silence, giving no indication to what he thought.

Tour concluded, Bastian led them all back up the spiral stairs and into the unforgiving sunlight. Two Presque Mort waited at the top of the stairs; he waved a hand with some meaningless words of parting—*enjoy the wine, we'll rejoin the party momentarily*—then took Lore's arm and started strolling toward the prow, gait unhurried but purposeful.

The front of the ship was hung with colorful banners, deep-purple pennants whipping in the salty breeze. Rosebushes had been brought down from the Citadel in huge copper pots, flanking the prow. It made the space look almost like a stage.

Lore halted, planted her feet. She didn't say anything; she'd said it all before, and had nothing to add to her refusal. She wasn't channeling.

"Lore." Bastian stopped, came in front of her. Picked up her hand. "You have no reason to be afraid. You've channeled with me before, and I know Malcolm's talk of consequences wasn't anything new. What's changed, really?"

A shrewd spark in his eye, even as his voice stayed soft. His eyes searched hers, as if looking for something lurking behind them.

And Lore knew, then, that she wasn't really talking to Bastian. Knew that he flickered in and out like a candle in high winds.

Dread wrapped its fist around her spine.

He stepped a bit closer, tipped up her chin. The sun blazed behind him, haloed his dark hair almost auburn. "Do you trust me?"

No. "It's not about that."

An infinitesimal flinch backward, like he'd seen the true answer in her face. His expression changed, softened, the austere lines of it becoming something more familiar. "Lore."

Just her name. He sounded different. More himself.

Still.

Lore shook her head. "I can't."

He stared at her a moment, something almost like fury lurking behind his eyes, trying to surge forward. "Listen to me—"

The rest of his words were swallowed in the explosion.

Chapter Sixteen

Time is something we created to make sense of the world. It is a river to step into and out of, a way of thinking that gives us structure. It rules all, and does not exist.

–Norun Loe, Ratharcan philosopher

Lore was used to death. It had dogged her steps since she was a child, a tangible thing she could wrap around her fingers, braid into ropes of her will. That day at the Mortem leak had been the most she'd ever felt before, a river of it flowing from Nyxara's body deep beneath the city. Even that she'd managed to control, run it through her system and into stone. It'd knocked her out for a week, sure, but she'd done it.

This was so much worse.

Now death surrounded her like a cloud. None of the Mortem was hers—how in all the myriad hells was none of it hers?—but that didn't make it hurt any less, didn't mitigate its horror. She couldn't see anything but a deep well of darkness, prisming, diamonds of entropy and unraveling. Her orientation was a mystery, upside down or backward or inside out. Lore could only be sure of the reality of her body because she could feel her fingers, stretching toward all this dark and feeling it stretch back to her in turn, ready to be woven.

A light in front of her. Bastian. Spiritum blazed from him like a miniature sun, rays of light cutting through the black. It reached for her, too, ready to be channeled, directed, made into what she wanted.

Lore turned—she thought she turned—looking through the cloud of death.

Spiritum, everywhere, hundreds of dying stars. Tendrils of it grew slowly, so slowly, expanding outward from the people who'd held it, leaking away from bodies that were dying, turning into Mortem.

Something next to her. A gap, a hole, a mouth of eternity. She stood in death's antechamber, where the threads of life were picked apart. Time was a river and she stood on the shore, watching the work of seconds stretch into impossible proportions, a massacre in arrested motion.

A massacre she could stop. Lore was something different, something that could hold life and death in her hands. And she was going to have to use them both.

Spiritum first. Lore reached out—assumed she reached out—and grasped the threads of Spiritum racing into the air, the ribbons of life escaping their vessels. She ran them through her veins as quick as water to the sea to imbue them with her will, then pushed them out to the people they belonged to.

It all went back, as easily as a knife into softened butter. Life spooled into the places where it had been, weaving into auras, stopping its slow drain. The dormant Mortem that had been rushing up to take its place was shoved away, forced into stasis again to wait for a different death.

Most of it, anyway.

Some of the Mortem was too far gone, overtaking Spiritum,

the change already begun as one power alchemized into another. The bodies nearest the obliterated ship, other than her and Bastian. The bodies in pieces, limbs flung to far corners. If Lore had been fully aware of her physical form, she would've gagged.

Good thing she could channel them both. Good thing she could put them back together, here in this space between seconds, where souls lingered on the threshold of life and death and neither had fully taken over.

Mortem came to her like a childhood pet, twisting around her fingers, breaching her arbitrary barriers. When she ran it through herself, this time, she changed it. She wasn't sure how, didn't know the mechanics, but the Mortem she took in came back out as Spiritum, and she put it back where it was supposed to go, arresting death in its tracks, giving it back as the life it had been.

There was a moment when she was afraid of the consequences—afraid that she was somehow making these people living corpses, like the bodies in the catacombs—but as soon as the thought came, it was gone. This was different. This wasn't giving an unearned life, this was returning a life stolen, snatching it out of the second where it could become death.

Something lurched beneath the city.

Slow at first, then it came in a rush.

Death crawled out from beneath Dellaire, a huge wave of it knocking her backward, like a flood surging for a crack in the levee. It rushed through rock, through wood, through dead matter, making a path to Lore that was paved in nothingness. It wasn't like a leak, a mindless surge eating away everything in its path. This was calculated, an assault.

A homecoming.

She should stop. But Lore was nothing but a conduit, now, pulling up Mortem and channeling it inward. It gathered in her hollow places, and she'd almost accepted it, the inevitable end. No mere mortal could survive.

But you're no mere mortal, Lore. Haven't been, ever.

The Mortem kept coming, but Lore felt none of what she assumed would be the signs of dying—seizing breath, slowing heart. Whatever had changed within her, whatever she had become, it made her something that could withstand this.

Lore was the depository. Lore was the holding cell. Mortem crashed into her, endless waves, a pulsing torrent of black thread. And it coiled into her, and it stayed.

And she stayed alive.

Rushing, rushing, and she didn't mark the point when the world started to come back into focus, when color began to leach into her vision, when her ears ceased to be filled with soft white noise and instead heard screams, cries, raised voices.

Scared, and hurt, but alive. All of them alive.

Because she'd kept them that way. Stepped out of time and stopped death, held life where it was supposed to be like a hand on a spurting artery.

The cool lap of water, welcome in the heat. A tangle of voices, some familiar. One in particular.

"You," Bastian murmured in Lore's ear, "are a *wonder*."

It was a nice thing to hear, right before she lost consciousness.

There was no death toll. That was the most important and most unbelievable part. All three of the ships at the ends of the docks had exploded, and there was no death toll. No one on the ships or the docks had died, neither had the commoners gathered beyond the barrier. Many had wounds they *should've* died from, awful scars and blood loss, but everyone was alive.

The second most important and most unbelievable part was how the explosion had happened in the first place.

"It had to be someone in attendance." Malcolm had a finger hooked thoughtfully over his lips, sitting forward in his chair, one leg jittering up and down in an anxious dance that hadn't let up once in the half hour they'd all been in Lore's room. "A courtier, a guard, someone. Those ships were checked and rechecked over and over."

"Unless someone planted the bomb during the checks," Gabe rumbled. He stood by the door, his arms crossed, his one eye pointed anywhere but at Lore on the bed. He'd looked at her when he carried her here, drinking in the sight like he wanted to catalog every wound and was almost bereft that there were none to count, nothing to use as a barometer against his worry. But after putting her down, he'd looked away, and hadn't once looked back.

"No." Malcolm shook his head. "It can't be one of ours. Everyone in our ranks or the bloodcoats' who wanted to get rid of Bastian is in the Burnt Isles."

"Which is why the Kirytheans are the most obvious culprits," Alie said. Again. She sat closest to Lore, right next to her pillow, a bandage on her wrist and another at her temple. She'd been at the very end of the dock road when the explosion happened, and her wounds were minor, mostly cuts from flying wood splinters. Still, her hands trembled in her lap.

"Surely they wouldn't be that stupid," Malcolm muttered, running a hand down his face. He'd been out of the blast radius and sustained no injuries, but his shirt was dark with someone else's blood. "There are a million easier ways to assassinate you. At least, one would have assumed there were, before this."

Before Lore had demonstrated a power over death beyond what anyone could have imagined.

No one had a response to that, least of all Lore. Five pairs of eyes went surreptitiously to her hands, lying flat on the bedding.

She wanted to press them into her sheets, wanted to try to hide what lay on the other side. But Lore turned her hands over, almost unconsciously.

From the center of her palm, a charcoal-gray star spread

outward, darkness tracking from the middle and out to her fingers, as if that part of her hand were long dead. It dyed her eclipse scar in mottled colors, almost like a bruise, and it wouldn't wash off, no matter how she'd scrubbed when she was first brought up here, carried in Gabe's arms like a dying bride.

Even in that state, her consciousness slipping in and out, she was surprised Bastian allowed such a thing. But she recalled him walking next to them, his shoulder nearly touching Gabe's, his fingers threaded through hers. The three of them entangled.

Bastian had kept his silence ever since they arrived at the apartments, and he still kept it now. He stood by the window, almost preternaturally still, sunlight seeping through the thin curtain to outline him in gold.

"There's that old saying about the simplest answer often being the correct one," Alie said drily. "And the impact of such an attack might outweigh the relative intelligence. They know we're vulnerable, for all Lore and Bastian's magic."

The mention of magic made Gabe's eye go flinty, his arms tighten across his chest. "Well," he said. "There's an option to consider, isn't there?"

The ships themselves were too obliterated for there to be any quick evidence of what the bombs had been made of, but a handful of debris was on its way to the university up in Farramark, the capital of Caldien, to be tested for gunpowder or other clues. Even now, mere hours after the attack, rumors flew about what could've caused it. A Mortem leak (proving that the common citizen had no idea how Mortem actually worked), an act of Apollius (which made Lore feel an unpleasant twist in her gut), a cannon malfunction. Surprisingly few courtiers seemed eager to point the finger at Kirythea. The shadow of war was cold, and they did whatever they could to scramble out from under it.

Besides, the why and how of the attack were much less interesting than the aftermath. Or lack of it, rather.

The consensus of the court, at least for the moment, was that the lack of death was a mark of the Bleeding God's favor. How that squared with those who thought the attack itself was an act of Apollius, Lore wasn't sure, but religion always found loopholes. She assumed that the North Sanctuary would be very full come First Day, that a new sense of religious fervor would run through the Citadel like a virus.

A mark of favor. A show of power.

Just like Bastian wanted.

None of them said anything, Gabe's implication settling slow.

Bastian lifted his eyes from the floor.

Gabe didn't move, the Heart pendant on his chest gleaming in the light from the candles. "Tell me you didn't do this." Gabe's voice was low and dangerous, a hiss like a sputtering flame. "By all the *gods*, Bastian, tell me you didn't do this as some sort of power play."

The Sainted King was across the room in two steps, his face inches from Gabe's, crowding the Priest Exalted back into the wall. His teeth were bared, his eyes blazing. "No," he spat. "Of course it wasn't me, and the fact you'd ever fucking *think* that..." The rage in him alchemized, an infinitesimal change, and his wordless snarl became a sneering grin. "If I was going to blow up a ship, Remaut, don't you think I'd wait until you were on it?"

"*Bastian*," Lore said, her voice hoarse from exhaustion and disuse. But even as she said it, she knew he wouldn't hear, lost somewhere in his mind, another consciousness taking over.

Disbelief flickered across Gabe's face, chased by a deep hurt. He banished it quickly. Two inches, and he straightened to use it all, looming over the King as much as he could manage. "That's unsurprising. At this point, I think you'd sacrifice any one of us—"

Bastian's fist, too quick for Lore to shout. It met Gabe's nose with a crunching sound, and the Priest Exalted's head turned to the side, a spurt of blood spattering across the pale wallpaper.

Alie cried out; Malcolm pressed back against the wall, out of the line of fire.

"Bastian!" Lore called again, stronger now but too late, because Gabe was rearing back his own fist, it was cracking against Bastian's jaw, and Bastian was turning with a laugh and a feral smile full of bloody teeth, and this all felt like a memory, like something that had happened before, a snake eating its own tail again and again—

"*Stop it.*" Lore didn't realize she'd stood until she felt her knees wobbling; the force of her voice was undercut by the way she collapsed to sit on the bed again. "This is the last fucking thing we need."

Her words broke some spell; the two of them backed off each other, but not before Bastian reached up and grabbed Gabe's chin. He jerked the other man close enough to kiss, their bloody mouths mere inches from each other, both breathing hard. The moment vibrated, caught at the moment of possibility.

Then Bastian smashed his palm over Gabe's nose. When his hand came away, Gabe's nose was straight and unbroken again. Spiritum at work.

Slowly, the already-blossoming bruise on Bastian's jaw faded, smoothed away. The only sign of their brawl was the blood on the wallpaper.

Lore collapsed back into bed. Alie's hand reached out, as if she'd help, but Lore shook her head. Both of them should be resting; neither of them should be trying to referee a brawl between the Sainted King and his Priest Exalted.

"Are you done?" Malcolm asked warily.

Neither Gabe nor Bastian answered, still staring at each other with a heat in their eyes that could mean anything.

Malcolm threw up his hands and went to the door. "There's supposed to be a minor lunar eclipse in half an hour. I have to go help the others prepare the well for the extra Mortem. Try not to kill each other while I'm gone." He slammed the door behind him.

Bastian straightened as Malcolm left, wiping his hands off on his shirt, leaving a smear of Gabe's blood. He seemed completely unruffled, now, like the brief fight with Gabe had happened to someone else entirely. "We will get to the bottom of this. I've already had the Kirythean delegates arrested; questioning will begin tomorrow."

Stunned quiet.

Then a frustrated noise from Alie. "So you just arrested a foreign delegation with no due process? Without consulting anyone?" Her bandaged hands fluttered in the air, like she could grab the moment this decision had been made and crush it. "That's not how diplomacy works, Bastian! Are you *trying* to start a war?"

"It won't come to that." He shrugged. "If the Kirytheans are innocent, it will be found out quickly, especially once we get the report from Caldien about the debris. Until then, all Emperor Jax will have are rumors of an attack, and how Lore prevented any casualties."

"If you don't think those rumors will also include how his diplomats were arrested and held without trial, you're an idiot," Alie seethed.

Bastian gave her a placid smile. "I don't doubt they will. But I also don't think that will be a problem."

She pressed her lips tight and closed her eyes, as if it took all her willpower to keep from calling him every foul name she could come up with. "I'll need to speak with them," Alie said finally, deceptively even. "To try and smooth over this fucking mess you've made."

"Feel free," Bastian replied. "You can today, even. They're in the holding cells beneath the northwest turret; those were in the best shape." A sharp smile. "I am nothing if not hospitable."

Alie said nothing, but her eyes were poison.

The door banged open. On the other side, a Presque Mort Lore didn't know, sides heaving and eyes wide. Lore's mind flashed back to that day in the throne room, when Malcolm had run in to tell them about the Mortem leak. Memories, snakes eating tails, time moving in endless gyres.

"We opened the well in the garden," she said as she caught her breath. "There's nothing."

Gabe stiffened, his teeth still bloody though his nose was healed. "What do you mean, Marie?"

"I mean there's nothing." Marie flung her hand back. Lore noticed, distantly, that she was missing three fingers and most of her palm. "There's always at least a little Mortem, tiny bits of it to channel out. But it's gone." Her eyes tracked to Lore on the bed, her marked hands, scarred with an eclipse and marked with darkness. "All the Mortem is gone."

Chapter Seventeen

> And on His* return, He will have a new body—one unmarked by the violence of the wayward goddess, one perfectly suited to His purpose.
>
> —The Book of Holy Law, Tract 893

Lore expected some resistance to the idea of her coming with them to see the well for themselves, but everyone was too shocked to give much protest when she levered herself out of bed and threw a thin robe over her thinner chemise, rushing to follow Marie back out into the open hall. Gabe shot her a slantwise look, his eye tracking from the top of her head to her hastily slippered feet, snagging on the slight tremble in her hands. But he said nothing.

As they approached the stairs that led down into the solar, Bastian reached back and took her scarred hand. Squeezed it. She couldn't see his face, but somehow, she knew he was grinning.

She should be, too. This was a good thing, all the Mortem gone, none of it left to possibly surge. Wasn't it?

---

*In some early translations, the pronouns *He* and *His* are instead *They* and *Their*, understood to be meant in the plural rather than the singular.

Still, her stomach churned.

There was no breath for conversation as the four of them rushed through Bastian's apartments, down the stairs of the northeast turret, into the southern expanse of the Citadel green.

Marie led them through the iron gate into the maze-like warren of the Presque Mort's stone garden. Lore's heart kicked up to her throat for just a moment when she thought the other woman might veer away from the well, head toward Anton's greenhouse. But Marie kept to the path.

The well was open, the cover canted off the far side, the small statue of Apollius that held it in place pushed to its notch in the stone. One of the Mort she vaguely recognized—Alexis—leaned over the lip of the well, looking down into the shadowed depths as if they thought the Mortem was hiding. Next to them, Malcolm stood with his hands on his hips, his expression stricken.

"What happened?" Bastian had wiped the grin from his face; he was all business now, his voice stern. "Details, please."

Alexis stepped back, waving their hand at the well. "Nothing happened, that's the problem." They pushed sweaty blond hair back from their forehead. "There's always *something* when you open the well."

"Especially on a lunar eclipse." Another Mort, one whose name Lore didn't know. He was nearly as tall as Bastian, his arms crossed over a barrel chest. A scar cut from his forehead down to the corner of his lip, narrowly missing the flinty eye he had trained on Lore. "And especially lately."

Well, no one could ever accuse a Presque Mort of subtlety. Lore stared right back at the Mort, refusing to be the first to look away. Eventually, he caved, swinging his gaze back to the open well.

"I'd hardly call a lack of Mortem a *problem*." Bastian walked to the lip of the well and mirrored Alexis's stance, hands braced on the side, his head eclipsed in shadow from the roof. "In fact," he said, the stone echoing his voice down into the dark, "it seems more like a solution." He straightened, turned to Lore, beaming. "You did it."

She took a step back on instinct, putting space between her and the well. When she blinked, she saw this place in darkness, the flames of dry flowers licking up into a sky where the moon had overtaken the sun. Her hands clenched closed, hiding her palms. "I did what?"

"This!" Bastian swept his arms wide, encompassing the well, the stone garden, the blank-faced Presque Mort with nothing to channel. "Somehow, when you saved everyone at the docks, you must have channeled all the Mortem left." He came to her, hands on her shoulders, his forehead tipped against hers. His touch felt foreign, a golden glitter in his dark eyes. "You are a *wonder*."

The same thing he'd told her after it happened, when they both realized they were still alive. The same pleased note in his voice, things going according to a plan no one else knew.

"I didn't," she said, because she didn't know what else to say, and even though it wasn't true it's what came easiest to her tongue. "At least, if I did, I didn't do it on purpose. It should be impossible for one person—"

"Impossible for everyone but you." He was close enough that he barely had to give the words sound; they floated in the space between them like ghosts. "You were special before, but now you're irreplaceable." His gold-flecked eyes closed as if he were overcome. When in all the myriad hells had Bastian Arceneaux *ever* been overcome? "I knew I was making the right decision."

He was talking about proposing, right? She wasn't sure. It sounded like something that could apply to more than one instance, a chain of decisions that led them here.

"Wait." Alexis stepped forward, their eyes wide. "You mean… if it's *all* gone…"

"It is." Bastian turned to the gathered Mort, away from Lore, but kept cradling her hands. She closed her fists tighter. "We've been liberated by our future Queen." He shot Lore a dazzling smile over his shoulder. "If she didn't hate socializing with the courtiers so much, I'd throw her a party."

Malcolm had been silent since they reached the well. He stood with his arms crossed, staring at its open maw, expression blank. "I can't feel anything," he murmured, almost to himself. "Before, I could always feel at least a little, if I tried, but now..."

Lore pressed her mouth flat, directed her gaze to the cobblestones. This should be a good thing, but Malcolm looked almost pained.

Behind them, Gabe stared at the well with a similar lost expression, his one eye wide. He shook off whatever emotion had him pinned, glared at Bastian. "There's no way to be certain unless we send someone down there."

Bastian raised a brow. "I don't think that's necessary, but if you do, I won't stop you."

Surprise made Lore raise her head from her contemplation of the ground, her eyes meeting Gabe's for a shared beat of shock. That was the easiest she'd ever heard Bastian concede to the other man.

The King noticed their quick glance, and his mouth lifted in the tight smile of someone who'd gotten what he wanted but wasn't yet sure of the cost. There was something nearly pained in the line of his jaw, like he was fighting off one of those headaches again. His eyes slid upward, to a sky slowly sinking toward twilight. The attack had been this morning; Lore had only lost a few hours to recovery.

An improvement on a week. Especially since she'd channeled so much more Mortem this time around.

All of it, even.

"This should free up some of your time," Bastian said. "Now that you won't have to go to the Priest Exalted for help with your forest."

Lore's brows knit. "I beg to differ."

The pleased look on Bastian's face faltered, a shadow passing over it. "Do you."

Not a question. He said it flat.

"If it's all... escaped," she said, her voice skipping over saying exactly what had happened, "I'll need my barrier more than ever."

Her forest, he'd said. Had she ever told him it looked like that?

"It would be a waste of time." Bastian's voice brooked no argument. "You and Remaut both have better things to do than hide away in a dusty confessional booth."

"I highly disagree."

"As do I," Gabe said quietly.

Bastian's eyes swung between the two of them, more gold than brown. "I see."

"Bastian," Lore said, starting toward him, passing close by a bank of stone roses. "We should keep things as they are until—"

Her arm brushed a stone stem, and it gave, as if the rock had suddenly become ice and melted at her heat. Lore lifted it quickly, backing away from the flower bed.

The rose only cracked, at first. Then it shattered. All of them did, down the line, the rock becoming so brittle it flaked like ash before nearly disintegrating, a cloud of gray grit in the humid air.

She'd seen rock do this before, but only when huge amounts of Mortem were channeled into it.

That's when she noticed her hand. The gray star on her palm had extended outward, nearly covering her fingers, every vein etched in ink. The cold set in slow, the pins and needles as her blood went sluggish.

Mortem. She'd channeled Mortem into the roses, with barely a touch. But that was impossible, if it was gone—

Not gone.

The voice was faint, like a whisper through a door that was only cracked.

Just in you now.

"Fuck," Lore whispered, staring at her hand, staring at where the stone roses had been. Staring at Bastian, who looked at her with something both thrilled and almost worried in his eyes.

"I'm going to keep working with Gabe." Lore didn't know how to hold her hands, afraid that she might channel death into anything she touched. "In fact, I think we should go practice right now."

Bastian didn't say anything, even as Gabe nodded and turned to walk back into the Church, even as Lore followed him. He just watched them go.

"I don't understand."

She'd said some version of those three words at least five times in the few minutes she'd been following Gabe through the labyrinthine back hallways of the Church, taking the long way like they had the day they went to see Anton. Gabe didn't try to hide, this time, apparently unafraid of being followed.

Lore kept her arms crossed tight, her stained hands hidden. "I didn't even feel it, Gabe. There was no warning. It just *happened*."

"We'll have to guard your mind more," Gabe said, stating the obvious. He walked with no thought for her shorter stride; Lore scrambled to keep up. "Stronger barriers. If all the Mortem is in you now—"

"Wait." She stopped in the middle of the stone hallway. "How do you know that for sure?" The voice had told her, quiet in her head. Did he have a voice, too? Something whispering to him when the sky grew dark?

He turned, confusion written across his features. "I don't know," he said finally. "But am I wrong?"

Lore shook her head.

He nodded once, decisively, then started down the hall again. Knowing things they shouldn't about each other wasn't a shock at this point.

What is happening *to us?* Lore could feel it approaching, like the charge in the air before a storm, a dread and anticipation she couldn't put words to.

They reached the confessional room, but Gabe didn't stop, leading her through the lattice and then the velvet curtain, down the deserted aisles to the door. He opened it, waved her through, turned right, and went down the hall. She recognized the path, after weeks of taking it daily a little over a month ago. He was going to the library.

"Think on your barrier," he said as he walked, a lesson given on the move. "You know how to do it by now. Think on it hard, Lore, guard your mind like your life depends on it."

It had this whole time, but never had she felt it quite so acutely.

She could imagine her forest without closing her eyes now. It sprang up around her thoughts, thick and green, a mirror image of the forest she saw in her dreams. Lore could nearly smell it—the thick sap, the sharp bite of greenery, salt on the breeze—

When Gabe reached the library door, she was calmer, the panic in her stomach soothed enough to pull in full breaths. Experimentally, she reached out, touched the stone wall. No melting, no sudden brittleness.

It's more settled, the voice in her head said. Stronger now, as the sky outside dimmed to dusk. *You can contain it.*

Lore lifted her hand away.

When Gabe threw open the door, Malcolm was waiting, already gloved, shoving books beneath the glass dome running down the center of the reading tables. His mouth was a thin line, his eyes determined, but there was a barely-there shake in his hands. "I've pulled everything that mentions channeling mechanics," he said, not looking up from his work. "Between the three of us, we should be able to check all of these in an hour or so, just keep it quick, and I can send to Farramark and maybe even Kettleburgh for more—"

"I don't think we need all that, Malcolm." Gabe's voice was gentle.

Still, Malcolm scowled, his gloved hands sliding the last book under glass. He moved toward the shelf for more—the pothos vine growing along it twitched at his approach. "Then what *do* you think we need, Your Holiness? Because the Mortem is gone, and while that seems great in theory, in practice I am *extremely troubled*."

"What we need," Gabe said, "are the myths."

"Why?" Lore asked, even as Malcolm, with a shrewd look at Gabe, diverted his course from the shelf. He went toward the small alcove in the corner, the one where he'd once told her the prophecies and other things deemed too important for common eyes were kept. "What could you possibly think the damn myths are going to tell us? It seems like Malcolm has the right idea about how to figure out what happened to the Mortem, how to reverse it."

"Reverse it?" Gabe arched a reddish brow.

Lore hadn't known that's what she was hoping for until the words were already out of her mouth.

Too late for that, the voice said.

Shut up. Gods, there was a very real possibility she was completely mad now, no slow descent for her. She was talking to the fucking voice in her head like it was an irritating sibling.

Not quite, the voice rejoined. *This would be much easier if you stopped pretending you don't know who I am.*

Lore concentrated on her forest very, very hard. "I don't want this," she murmured. "Gabe, there's no way anyone could want this."

Someone could. Lore wasn't sure whether the thought came from the voice or from her.

He sighed. His hand twitched up, tentative, before he smoothed back her hair, tucked it behind her ear. It'd been at least a day since it was brushed, a frizzed and tangled halo around her head—Juliette would have heart palpitations if she knew Lore was traipsing around the Church in such a state, and in a nightgown, too.

But he didn't turn to stone. That was something. The cold fear that had trapped her eased, somewhat.

"This doesn't feel like something that can be reversed," he said quietly.

The fear came back, albeit in a different shape.

"Here." Malcolm came out from the small alcove room with only one book in his gloved hands. He slid it beneath the glass, then pulled two other pairs of gloves from his pocket, tossed them at Lore and Gabe. "This is the only one I could find." He barked a rueful laugh. "There's apparently volumes of technically non-canonical stories in Laerdas, if we wanted to ask our Kirythean friends in the gods-damned holding cells. Maybe Alie can bring it up."

"Hopefully not," Gabe rumbled. Alie hadn't accompanied them to the well, instead going to her own apartments, ostensibly to prepare for the sudden diplomatic crisis. "I think we should keep this as quiet as possible."

"You might need to adjust your expectations of *possible*." Lore slid onto the bench in front of the book as she pulled on her gloves, now confident that she could touch things without sending death into them immediately. "I don't think me saving everyone from an explosion will be news that goes away quickly."

"Probably not." Malcolm reached through the door to turn the book's delicate pages. "But the part about you somehow absorbing all the excess Mortem leaking from Nyxara—and keeping it—can hopefully be left out."

That could be true. The average courtier didn't keep up with the eclipse cycles; there'd be no reason for them to know that Lore had taken in all the Mortem left in Nyxara's dead body.

"There's just too much we don't *know*," Malcolm said, still leafing through the book. "Can we still channel the Mortem in dead matter, when there's no extra coming from the Buried Goddess? What about people who dose poison? Will it even do anything anymore? Will you still get the high, will it still make you live longer—"

"It should." Finally, something Lore had concrete answers for. "Most poisons have mild mind-altering effects when taken correctly, even outside of Dellaire—that's why poison runners are able to do business elsewhere, shipping out poisons grown here, since they're more potent." Or they had been. Maybe she'd ruined Val and Mari's business, too. Lore was breaking records for ruining things lately. "The life-lengthening effect utilized the Mortem within a person more than the Mortem leaking from the Buried Goddess. Anyone who bought some years should still have them."

"Wonderful," Malcolm said, sarcasm thick in his voice. "At least our criminal enterprises won't be harmed." He scrutinized the page beneath the glass, straightened the book, then stepped back. "Here's a myth for you. *The Fount of the Golden Mount.*"

"Who named it that?" Gabe scrunched his nose in distaste. "The rhyming is unnecessary."

"Clearly, they didn't let that person name anything else," Lore said. "The Sapphire Sea would be 'the sea you want to flee.' The Ourish Pass would be 'the pass that's a pain in my ass.'"

"If you aren't going to be helpful, don't talk." Gabe sat down across from Lore, peering through the glass to read. "Lo, I tell of the Fount of Power, the source of all magic—"

"The *lo* is also unnecessary."

"Attempting to hide your fear through humor is never effective. Also, that wasn't funny."

Lore shut up.

Malcolm gave her a sympathetic glance from the other side of the table. "The bit about the Ourish Pass was funny, though."

"Got one," Lore muttered.

Gabe ignored them. "The Fount of Power, the source of all magic, was found on the Golden Mount by He who would become Apollius. And feeling the weight of all power, He invited those He loved most to the Mount, to partake of the Fount and receive power in turn."

"The weight of all power..." Lore repeated slowly. "Does that mean what it sounds like it means?"

"Yes." Gabe sat back, a thoughtful look on his face, though there was no hint of surprise. "In the beginning, Apollius was the god of everything. Just like He is now."

No, said the voice in the back of her head. *That's just what He wanted them to think.*

"That doesn't tell us anything about what happened with Lore and the Mortem." Malcolm stepped forward, flipped through the book again, looking for another myth. "Here. This one is about the Dissolution."

The capitalization was clear in his tone. "What's that?"

"When the gods first left the Mount, before the Godsfall," Gabe answered. "All of Them but Nyxara and Apollius, anyway. He couldn't leave. Had too much power to be far from the Fount."

Not true, again, the voice said. *Not like that, anyway.*

Malcolm read aloud, this time. "When eons of time had passed upon the Golden Mount, with the power of the Fount shared among the pantheon, the gods grew restless and wanted to leave Their paradise. Even Nyxara, who had wed Apollius, desired to leave with Hestraon and the others. Apollius, stricken with woe, begged Them to stay. Nyxara did, but the rest departed and left Him alone. This was when Nyxara began to plot Her husband's demise, and when Apollius began to realize He was better as the only god."

She expected another negation from the voice, but it remained silent. Lore twisted her fingers in her gloves. "Rather harsh."

"That's gods for you." Malcolm was already turning pages again, his agitation clear. "And that's why I can never understand why we're supposed to try to be like Them. It's not like They were paragons of morality." He gave another one of those rueful snorts of laughter. "I guess August took that in the opposite direction, didn't he? Apollius's flaw was that He was *too* loyal to His wife, and no one could accuse August of that."

A muscle in Gabe's jaw twitched at the word *flaw*, clear discomfort with the idea of a god having such a thing. But he just sighed and rubbed at his eye patch. "No, they certainly couldn't." He shook his head. "I heard more than one tale about August ordering people to his bed. Nobles' wives, servants, whoever caught his eye."

"You don't have to use force to be a rapist," Malcolm said, still flipping pages. "I hope his hell is particularly gruesome."

Lore thought of the brief stories she'd heard of Gabe's boyhood, of his mother and Bastian's mother, Ivanna, their friendship. Ivanna was an unhappy woman in an unkind marriage. Extremely unkind, apparently. August was even more repugnant than Lore had known.

Malcolm reached the back of the book, flipped it to the front again, his ire rising. "The only other myth in here is about the sacred grove on the Mount burning the night the elemental gods left." Mindless of its age, he slammed the book shut. It made Lore start, made her lean back from the table. Malcolm must be beyond furious, to manhandle a book like that.

With rough movements, Malcolm took the book from beneath the glass. "This is useless. The most religiously significant events to happen since the Godsfall are happening right under our noses, *to us*, and we have no reference points because—"

His voice died in his throat as he spun on his heel to take the book back to the alcove.

When Lore looked at the bookshelf behind him, she saw why.

The pothos vine had grown. *Grown* was too tame a term, really—it'd rioted, spreading more leaves, more green tendrils, climbing up the shelf and down to the floor. It'd happened soundlessly, and so quickly none of them had noticed it until now.

A moment's shocked silence. Then Malcolm whirled, his dark eyes wide and fixed on Lore. "Did you do that?"

"No!" She clenched her hands tight, as if stray magic might leak from them. Maybe it would. "I didn't feel anything."

"Like you didn't feel the Mortem at the well?" But Malcolm sounded distracted, not accusatory. He opened his own hands, staring into his palms, an inverse reflection of Lore's stance. Dark eyes went from his hands to the vine, tracking along its length.

"I can't channel Mortem anymore," he murmured, almost to himself. "There's none to pull out of the catacombs, and I can't even feel it in dead matter. But I feel..." He closed his hand and didn't continue.

A weight on Lore's shoulder. Gabe's hand. He gently nudged her up from the table. "We should go, Lore."

She stood on shaky legs. Briefly, she considered reminding Gabe that they hadn't actually worked on her barrier yet, but her forest grew riotous in her mind, thick and green.

It'll hold, the voice reassured her.

Lore grimaced. *Aren't You what I'm supposed to be keeping out?*

No reply.

Gabe looked to Malcolm, still standing by the bookshelf, still studying his hands. "I'll be back after I return Lore to her rooms." Bastian's rooms, but none of them voiced the correction. "We can look through more books."

"Not unless I write to Farramark," Malcolm said distractedly. "I've looked at our other books, they don't have anything useful."

"Seems like allowing one god to tell all the stories before disappearing wasn't the best plan." A yawn punctuated the end of the sentence. Lore wasn't sure how late it was, now, but her body seemed to think it was the middle of the night.

Malcolm just grunted.

Right before she stepped through the arched doorway, Lore looked back. Malcolm still stood by the bookshelf, though his attention had gone from his hands to the vine stretching across the books. Tentatively, he raised his finger, touched one of the leaves.

Lore turned and followed Gabe into the hall.

When they were a few steps away from the library, Gabe turned, face thunderous, and backed her into the wall.

Lore wasn't sure what to do, caught between his body and the stone behind her. Warmth emanated from him, as if he housed some internal fire, and the light from the sconces flickered in his one eye.

"Tell me the truth." The warmth she felt was nowhere to be found in his voice. It was all hard edges with no blunting. "Did you make the vine grow?"

"No." It came out hoarse and small; Lore swallowed and tried again. "There's something else happening here. Something bigger than Mortem or Spiritum."

"Bigger than you and Bastian," Gabe growled. "Imagine that."

He was very close. Her chemise and robe were very thin.

"Most things are." She matched his tone, a lacing of anger around something far more volatile. "If you'd get your head out of your ass long enough to realize it. I thought we'd finally left all this shit with me and you and Bastian behind, but you keep trying to narrow everything down to just this."

They'd never left it behind, could never leave it behind. It would haunt them through this life and any other.

"*This*," he repeated. The hand fisted on the wall came close to her face instead, his thumb skating over her cheek. "And what is this, Lore? You've never said." His rough fingers feathered over hers. "You're wearing his ring, but you're here with me, and you aren't going anywhere. How does that figure into *just this*?"

She didn't have an answer for him. Barely had one for herself. The voice in the back of her head was silent.

"You made a choice," she murmured. "That night in my room. You left me, and then you betrayed me. Whatever could've been between us, you stomped it out. If you regret that, you have no one but yourself to blame."

"And I do." His mouth was so close to hers, now, so close she felt his breath across her lips, took it in as he gasped it out. "Every fucking night, I do."

His hand dropped down the wall, slowly, like he was waiting for her to run away. She should. She didn't.

Gabe's hand landed light on her shoulder. A gentle friction, raised ridges from the tattoo on his palm, where it hadn't healed quite right. His thumb traced her collarbone.

"Tell me to stop," he breathed. "Tell me to stop, tell me you want him instead."

His voice hitched on *him*, a longing he couldn't hide, not this close together.

"I can't," she murmured. "And neither can you."

The hand on her shoulder gently wrapped her neck, not enough to hurt, just enough to make her heart speed.

The sconce on the wall flared.

A rush of heat, a flash of light. The flame burst upward, like someone had thrown gas on it, nearly singing the ceiling. Then, as soon as it had grown, it shrank again, once more just a flickering flame rather than an inferno.

Gabe pulled away from her, breathing hard.

"What was that?" Lore's voice came ragged. She should pull away from him, but the wall was at her back and there was nowhere to go.

His eye closed. Opened again. Slowly, deliberately, he stepped away.

"A sign, probably," he said. He didn't look at her. But he did look at the sconce, his face drawn in an expression she couldn't read.

Something like fear.

The atmosphere rushed back in, their pocket of unreality punctured and leaking. Lore's face flushed; she pulled her robe tighter around herself.

The Priest Exalted straightened his shirt. He turned and started back down the hall, toward the door that led into the Citadel green, toward the apartments Lore shared with Bastian.

Lore followed.

Chapter Eighteen

Hell is a life with no constants.

–Seen carved on a vault in Kadmar

Gabe didn't go with her into the Citadel. He held the door open when they reached the entrance of the Church, staring straight ahead, bowing his body just slightly away as she passed him, as if he couldn't bear to get too close.

Lore stepped out into the humid green. The door closed softly behind her.

With a sigh, she tipped her head upward.

Night fell like layers of veils, each darkening the sky further. Lavender became indigo became midnight-blue, pricked through with stars. The crescent sliver of the moon shone on the curve of the horizon, a crescent slice into some light-filled reality beyond what she could see.

"Go back," she muttered, on the off chance Apollius could hear. "Go back to Your Shining Realm and leave us alone."

He can't.

Her inner voice, the one that came from elsewhere. The one she still refused to name.

We're all awakening, slowly, the voice continued. *What's begun cannot be stopped.*

She refused to cry. Crying did not come naturally to Lore; anger presented itself much more easily as a response to emotional overwhelm. Even now, it wasn't simple sadness that made tears threaten. It was frustration, it was crushing hopelessness.

Lore gulped in a deep breath of summer-thick air and stalked into the Citadel.

It was early for courtiers to be out—most revels started when the night was deeper, they'd be dressing and preparing right now—so Alie walking purposefully across the foyer was a startling sight.

"Alie?" Lore had banished tears on her stomping walk across the green; her expression now was just confused. "Where are you headed?"

The other woman stopped, her slippers soundless on the tile floor, and sighed. She'd changed into a filmy cream-colored dress that left her shoulders bare and shimmered when she moved, tendrils of white-blond curls falling artfully from her piled hair to brush her neck. If Lore didn't know better, she'd think Alie was meeting a lover.

Maybe she didn't know better. She and Alie had drifted; and really, had there been much to drift from in the first place? Lore had few friends and held the ones she did tightly, but Alie had so many. Losing Lore from their number would be no great blow.

When Alie looked over her shoulder, there was no flush of anticipation on her face. Just resignation and a spark of wariness. "To see the Kirytheans," she said quietly. "To see just how big of a mess Bastian has made."

Oh.

She looked so fragile, standing there all alone. There was a tiredness in Alie's eyes that Lore hadn't noticed before. It reminded her of Bastian, a little. When had they all become so exhausted?

She strode up, took Alie's arm. "I'll come with you."

"Lore, you don't have to—"

"I won't mess anything up, I promise." Now that the idea had come, it wouldn't easily leave, and Lore realized that she deeply didn't want to go to Bastian's apartments just yet. She needed a moment, first. And she didn't want Alie to do this alone. "They don't even have to see me. I'll stay back, won't make a sound."

She wanted to object, Lore could see it in her face. But Alie didn't want to be alone any more than Lore did.

Alie nodded.

Lore had never been to the holding cells. Now, walking down the stone stairs that led to them, she realized how ironic that was. Anton had threatened her with them when she first came to the Citadel, but with hindsight, she thought the threat was probably empty. He needed her close to Bastian so their opposite powers could coax each other out. The damn Law of Opposites.

For what was ostensibly a dungeon, the corridor to the cells was well-kept. There was no dampness to the stone, and though it was cold down here, it was a welcome respite from the heat outside.

One bloodcoat stood guard at the end of the empty corridor, in front of a heavy wooden door reinforced with iron bars. He'd been told to expect visitors, apparently, but when he saw that one of those visitors was Lore, his eyes widened.

"The King asked that Her Majesty accompany me," Alie said smoothly, already slipping into her diplomat self. "To observe."

Somehow, she managed to imbue those last two words with an air of mystery, implying that Lore was here for magic reasons. Overkill, maybe, especially when coupled with the *Her Majesty*, but the guard nodded and opened the door in a hurry. Lore tried to hold her head high and make her steps even and gliding. The stance did not suit her.

The room beyond the door was dark, lit only by one sconce, flame flickering low. With a squeeze of Alie's hand, Lore settled her back against the wall in the corner, staying out of the ring of weak light. The barred doors to three cells lined the room, and it took Lore's eyes a moment to adjust enough to see which were occupied.

The utter stillness of the inhabitants didn't help.

In the center cell, Maxon sat on a bare cot, his legs crossed, his hands placed atop his knees. Lore couldn't pick out his expression in the gloom, but what she could see looked serene. Her mouth pulled down, an involuntary lurch of disgust; something about that stance in this room, in these circumstances, felt extremely wrong.

Part of her expected the voice in her head to offer commentary. But It was quiet, though she could feel that alien consciousness listening. As if It was as baffled as Lore was.

It. She. Eventually, Lore would have to admit to herself what was living in her head, but now was decidedly not the time.

In the cell to the left, Caius stood, his hands clasped behind his back, his chin tilted up in a contemplative posture. When Alie closed the door—louder than she needed to—he was the only one that moved, looking at her over his shoulder. Maxon stayed where he was.

"Alienor." Caius sounded as if he were greeting a guest to his home, not seeing an enemy diplomat in a glorified prison. "How kind of you to come see me. But alone? Surely Bastian would want you to have an escort."

Lore shrank back against the wall.

"Bastian doesn't know." Alie's voice was soft and breathy, on the brink of some overcoming emotion. If life had dealt her a different hand, she could have made an excellent actress. "I just wanted to make sure you were being treated well. It's dreadful, the way he tossed you in here with no recourse, with no real proof. Even if the others think it's necessary, I can't abide it."

A clever bit of work, there. Establishing that most of the court agreed with Bastian, that he was a ruler unquestioned, except by Alie. Making herself a safe place for honesty.

"I've heard stories of how interrogations sometimes go down here." Alie let a tiny shiver work through her slender shoulders, took half a step closer to the bars. "Has it been awful?"

"Hardly," Caius said, soft and warm, taking on the role of reassurance. "You're the first person we've seen, in fact. It's given us ample time for meditation and prayer."

Alie was the first person they'd seen? Lore's brow furrowed. She supposed it wasn't that unusual for Bastian to wait a few days before sending an interrogator, but he'd seemed so convinced the Kirytheans were to blame for the explosion, she'd assumed he would want answers as quickly as possible.

Another small step closer to the cell. Alie's back was to Lore, but she could hear the small smile in her friend's voice. "Meditation and prayer? I didn't realize how pious you were, my lord."

"Auverraine is not the only country Apollius favors." For the first time, there was a bite of venom to his words, a fierceness to his smile. "The whole world is His kingdom."

"Of course." It almost pained Lore to see Alie act like this, even though she knew it was all for show. Meek and obliging, her innate kindness become something to be trampled on. "It must be hard to keep faith, when you're treated so unfairly."

"We submit to Apollius's will, whatever it may be." Caius stood very close to the bars, now, close enough that he could reach out and touch Alie with no problem. His hands stayed respectfully at his sides. "There is freedom in it. You'd find great comfort in bending to His will, Alienor."

"I do my best, my lord."

"I'm sure you do." Caius gestured to the cell. "Don't worry overmuch about us. Imprisonment here is no great hardship. I'm sure that means your father is doing just fine, since he is only confined to his home, and not a cell."

Alie stiffened, her façade cracking for the first time since they'd come down here. "What do you know about my father?"

"Oh, we all know of Severin Bellegarde," Caius said. "He and Anton Arceneaux make quite the cautionary tale about thinking Apollius's will is set in stone, don't they? To be truly faithful, one must be adaptable."

A slight twitch in Alie's fingers as she recovered, slipped into her false persona again. "Indeed," she murmured. Then, she made a show of glancing backward, starting, as if she were a fairy-tale princess looking at a nonexistent clock. "Oh, it is getting late, and I have somewhere to be. I'll be back if I can, but I do hope Bastian continues to be kind, even though some encourage him not to be."

"I'm not worried." Caius smiled at her. There was a genuine warmth to it, though the dim lighting made it devilish. "Though a visit from you will always be welcome."

She curtsied, a slight bob of her head and flutter of shimmering skirts. Her smile fell away as soon as she turned from Caius, her expression drawn and thoughtful.

"The guard told me that he would only let me in if I brought out the sconce," she said, taking it gingerly from the wall. A cut of her eyes to Lore; she was trying to hide her presence. "I'm terribly sorry to leave you in the dark."

"Think nothing of it," Caius said. "Apollius will be lord of all, even the deepest night."

Alie held the sconce to the side, away from Lore, and slipped through the door.

Lore followed after, a wraith in almost total darkness. But she felt Caius's eyes on the back of her neck.

Neither of them spoke until they reached the main floor of the Citadel again. The sounds of courtiers rousing for late-night parties echoed ghostly in the halls, but for now, Alie and Lore were still alone.

"Well," Alie said finally, "it sounds like they aren't angry. That's something."

"Why hasn't Bastian had them questioned?" Though the meeting with the Kirytheans had gone about as well as could be expected, Lore was still unsettled. Their placidity at their capture felt unnatural—surely, even the best damn diplomats the world over would be perturbed at such an imprisonment, guilty or not? Though she supposed she wasn't the best judge of such things.

Alie shrugged. "He could be trying to wear them out mentally. Leave them alone in the dark, see if it makes them more willing to talk."

"Except they don't seem to mind being alone in the dark."

"True." Alie sighed, shook her head. "Either way, it seems Bastian hasn't fucked this up quite as much as we'd thought. I'll take that as a win. And now I am going to bed."

They walked together up the northeast turret. Alie gave a half-hearted wave when they reached her wing, eyes still thoughtful as she disappeared beneath the pothos vine.

When Lore reached Bastian's apartments, she closed the door and rested her back against it, chin tilted up, eyes closed. She was exhausted, all the sudden, as tired as Bastian looked, as Alie seemed down there in the holding cells. Twenty-four, and she felt centuries old, too many years packed into her frame.

After three weeks spent in a blur after the eclipse ritual, scrambling to keep up with how quickly and irrevocably her life had changed, Lore had looked forward to some sort of calm. An eye in the storm. She'd gotten it, somewhat, though it was only through sheer force of will. Ignoring how Bastian changed, trying to smooth it over, make it something normal.

It wasn't an option, not anymore. She had to find out how to fix him. How to banish whatever changes had been set into motion by the eclipse, if such a thing could even be done.

Don't think like that, she admonished herself.

Then there was the question of the Kirytheans, the Empire breathing down their necks, the apparent assassination attempt that had left her with all the Mortem in Dellaire trapped inside her body.

"So stop a war," Lore muttered to herself, "and stop a god. Sure. Fine. Certainly two things I can do."

Lore pushed off the door, trudged up the stairs to her room. No light but the moon, lending just enough glow to help her navigate without tripping. Lore flopped into bed, staring up at the billowing canopy. Her hand snaked under her pillow to support her neck; something crinkled against her fingers.

Paper. Frowning, Lore pulled it out, squinted to read what was written on it in the gloom.

I'm sorry. In an elegant hand she'd seen before, though the ink was smudged, like it'd been written in a hurry. *Try to talk to Gabe, he'll help you.*

A note from Bastian. One that made hardly any sense. She couldn't keep up with his changing tides, especially where Gabe was involved—one moment, he seemed to begrudge the air the Priest Exalted breathed, and the next, he seemed to long for him just like she did. Some of that she could attribute to the affliction that she suspected was a mirror to her own, but not all of it.

"What is your angle, Bastian?" she murmured into the moon-glow dark of her bedroom.

To try and keep you safer than he's been able to keep himself, answered the voice in her head. *I'm not offended.*

Lore closed her eyes, teeth bared. "Are You ever going to give me real, full answers? What's the point of having a voice in my head if You don't tell me anything useful?"

I can only tell you so much, like this. Tried to get you to the catacombs, where we can… communicate… more effectively, but that never worked.

"And it won't," Lore said quietly. Even the thought of going down there made her skin feel like it was going to crawl off her bones.

I gathered. The voice sounded almost as tired as Lore felt. *I'm bound to Him, as you'll remember, if you've let yourself get that far. Let yourself think that hard.*

Lore squeezed her eyes shut. Yeah, she'd let herself think that hard.

Can't speak ill of Him directly, the voice continued. *Not this way.* A pause, the next words wry. *But I think I answered enough of your question, didn't I?*

"Fuck." Lore sat down on her bed, hard. "*Fuck.*"

Precisely, Nyxara agreed.

Chapter Ninteen

Existence is a loop. Everything comes back around again.

–Armand Jeroux, Auverrani philosopher

Dreaming again.

Lore was mostly shocked that she'd managed to fall asleep, after her extended conversation with the apparently-not-completely-dead goddess in her head. But needs must, and her body was exhausted, and so here she was, in this forest that seemed all too familiar, in this dream that seemed more like a memory.

Her mind was already retreating, going backward to make way for the other dream-self—*come on, Lore, you know who it is*—to come to the forefront. The goddess had said She could only share so much through their intra-brain conversations; Lore supposed this was one more way to pass information.

Hands, pale and unscarred. Trees, green and lush. Blue sky behind, the smell of salt on the air.

Where *was* this?

"You'll have to give him your answer soon."

This was a voice she hadn't heard here before, one that thankfully didn't have that edge of recognition. Feminine and haughty, more than a little irritated.

Lore turned. The figure's face was obscured, like everyone's was in these dreams, a swirl of color that never quite resolved into actual features. Long dark hair, though, and arms crossed over a willowy body, an impression of beauty even without concrete evidence.

"If you won't marry him," the figure said, with a toss of that long hair, "one of us will. *I'd* be happy to. It should be an honor, not some terrible fate."

The pale hand that both was and wasn't Lore's reached out for the tree next to her, the bark a grounding grit against her palm. "Whoever marries him is stuck here," she said softly. "Just like he is."

"Aren't we anyway? He said if we decided to stay, it was forever." The other figure cocked her head to the side, gesturing at the world around them. "But he's powerful. If he chose one of us, loved one of us more, maybe he could break the ties of the island." She paused. "He told me that he can change things, sometimes. Because he's the most powerful of us. He said if we did as he asked, he would try."

"He lies." Dream-Lore's hand tensed on the tree bark. "He lies."

"Rise and shine, beloved."

A not-dream voice, a real-life voice, and one that made Lore's spine tense even as she slept.

Her eyes opened, breaking apart the too-real dream in a flood of bright sunlight.

Bastian stood at the window, pulling aside the curtains to bask in the warmth of midmorning. The light burnished his hair, gleamed across his skin, made him even more heart-wrenchingly beautiful than he already was. And true to form, Lore's heart *did* wrench. Both for his beauty, and for fear. For how much she cared for him, even now.

Lore groaned and flopped over, burying her head in the pillow.

He crossed to the bed, pulled the pillow out from under her, bopped her with it lightly. "I let you sleep far too long. Come on, up, we have places to—"

Cut off, like his voice had died in his throat. Frowning, Lore sat up, following his arrested gaze.

The table. The note.

The light behind Bastian obscured his expression as he reached down and picked up the paper. "Curious," he said softly. "I don't remember this."

Frozen, she watched him like a mouse before a hawk. Fear flooded her system, rooting her in place.

His head turned, the angle of it making his face visible beyond the glare. Her same Bastian, too handsome by half, his dark eyes searching. "When did you get this?"

Lie, lie, lie, the thought coming quick and so loud she thought maybe the goddess in her head was joining the chorus. But Nyxara was quiet, now, as if She could only speak with the night. "Found it in a book," Lore said, cobbling something together. "I think it was from earlier in summer."

His gold-sheened eyes narrowed. Bastian looked at the note again, then tucked it into his pocket. "Interesting."

Lie, distraction; Lore took his hand and tugged it so he sat on the bed. She sat up, kissed his cheek, and wished it was just for changing the subject, or just because she wanted to, and not for a messy tangle of both reasons.

Bastian smiled, the warm and unguarded one she remembered from before he became King, the one she'd seen so rarely and treasured every time she did. "Good morning to you, too," he murmured, his hand cupping her cheek.

His skin was warm against her own, calluses gentle on the curve of her cheek. He'd gotten them boxing; she wondered suddenly if he missed that, sneaking down to the docks to get the shit beaten out of him. His small chosen penance for the privilege of being born royal, born with the knowledge you'd never have to worry about being warm in the winter or fed when you were starving.

She knew what he was going to do, recognized the warmth in his eyes, for the moment still familiar. Their kisses had been few and far between, and she couldn't keep herself from comparing his to Gabe's. Gabe kissed hungry. Bastian's were gentler, not tentative, but not forceful, either. If kissing Gabe let her desire lead, kissing Bastian let her curiosity. One she wanted to consume, the other she wanted to explore.

Bastian leaned forward, so subtly she couldn't see it, could only tell by the way his breath felt stronger against her mouth.

But he didn't kiss her. They stayed there a moment, so close that one wrong move would send them crashing into each other, but he didn't kiss her.

She thought of the night of their engagement. When she tried to kiss him, and he pulled away. Of the night he let her, and it stopped almost as quickly as it started.

And she thought of the voice in her head, how she was certain now that Bastian had one, too. What was it—*He*, she knew who it was as much as she knew the identity of her own mental passenger—telling Bastian?

She waited for Nyxara to say something. Offer some sort of advice. But there was nothing, as if the sun in the window washed Her out.

Bastian straightened. His eyes narrowed, slightly, flicking across her face as if she were a book to be read. His mouth opened; he took a breath.

The door opened. A servant whose name Lore didn't know, a

pretty girl with big blue eyes and dark hair, carrying a tray with a smell that made Lore's stomach growl. She placed it on the table by the door, curtsied with her eyes sliding curiously between the King and his betrothed, and left.

"Eat quickly," Bastian said, following Lore to the tray to pour himself a cup of coffee after she'd made her own. "We need to leave within the hour."

"Where are we going?" she asked around a mouthful of cherry tart.

"Summer progress starts today, beloved. You desperately need to keep better track of your social calendar."

"Maybe I should stay here." She needed to be researching, needed to be finding answers, not gallivanting around Auverraine with a bunch of nobles who didn't even like her. "I'm sure none of your chosen courtiers really want me coming along, anyway."

Weak.

"No, Lore, you're coming." His voice was playful, like they were just bantering for the sake of it, but his eyes were cool. "Anyone who makes you feel unwelcome can come speak to me about it."

She chewed the corner of her lip.

Bastian smiled. "The garden could always use more statues."

All her dresses were already packed, a bit of industriousness from Juliette that Lore should really have expected at this point. They were riding out at noon, accompanied by a handful of Presque Mort and a few courtiers handpicked by Bastian.

Bastian left as the maids descended with the instruction to meet him down in the foyer in no less than two hours. It seemed like plenty of time, but Juliette's pinched expression as she surveyed her hair said that the other woman doubted her ability to make Lore presentable within such constraints.

Lore's hair was partially braided into some intricate knot before she finished half a cup of coffee and found her voice. "So where exactly does one go on summer progress?"

"Through the estates that have volunteered to be part of the journey," Juliette said, frowning at a particularly recalcitrant strand. "If I remember—the Demondes, the Viscount Allairs, and Lord and Lady Leclaire."

Juliette rattled off the names easily, for all her show of having to recall them.

"The journey will be shorter this year, with only three nobles selected to host," she continued. "None of them left the Citadel to get ready, instead leaving all the preparation to their summer staff. It's a bit of a scandal."

How easy Lore's life would be, if all scandals in the Citadel were so banal.

Recalcitrant strand vanquished, Juliette took a jeweled pin from the vanity and slipped it into place. "The King was quite choosy with who he invited to accompany him this year, as well. All the hosts will be traveling with the progress, and only two other families were invited besides." She shook her head. "The size of the court is certainly smaller these days."

"With good reason," Lore said.

"Well, yes, of course." Juliette tugged on her hair again, then twisted her head back and forth in the mirror, admiring her handiwork. "Otherwise I wouldn't have nearly enough time to make you look queenly every day."

Lore choked on a laugh. The other woman smiled, fleetingly.

Footmen carried her trunks—yes, plural, there were three of them, which after nearly twenty-four years of owning perhaps five outfits in total seemed astronomical—painstakingly down the northeast turret stairs. Lore, Juliette, and three other maids whose names Lore hadn't been told followed behind. Apparently, in addition to three whole trunks, Lore was also traveling with a retinue.

This should be expected, with future Queens. It still made her feel completely out of place, like she was the rock caught in the bottom of a particularly fine slipper, ruining what was otherwise a perfect picture.

In the foyer, Bastian and the others who'd been selected for summer progress milled about in bright colors. Tinkling laughter that somehow managed to be both polite and an obvious ploy for attention echoed down the halls, in the clear hope that some less fortunate courtier might pass by and see the chosen few. Lore recognized them all from various court functions, curtsies and bows and introductions.

Amelia and Hugh Demonde stood near Bastian, closest to the door. Bastian was saying something, his head bent low as if he didn't want to be overheard. It looked like he was telling a joke; Hugh grinned, and Amelia's eyes sparkled, the blue of them made even lovelier by the sky color of her traveling gown. Jealousy made Lore want to scowl, but she knew that was ridiculous, so she schooled her face into placidity. Tried to, anyway. She found herself thankful for her lack of a mirror, so she couldn't examine the resulting expression and compare it with Amelia's.

Across the room, Gabe stood at attention, his arms clasped behind his back, his Bleeding God's Heart shining on his chest. He watched Amelia, too, Lore noticed. She wondered if he was also having to smooth jealousy from his expression at the way she blatantly flirted with Bastian.

Gabe's eyes met hers. They stared at each other a moment, and her cheeks flushed, remembering the hallway. Remembering what he said, when she told him he had only himself to blame for the way things were between them.

Every fucking night, I do.

A breakfast service had been laid out on a long table, reminiscent of the way lunches were made available during summer days in the Citadel. She'd eaten the tart Bastian brought her this morning like a ravenous thing, but Lore's stomach still growled.

Alie stood by the table; Lore went straight to her, grabbing a handful of blueberries. "I truly cannot tell you how thankful I am that you're coming."

"Couldn't miss it," Alie replied, in a voice that said she deeply wished she could miss it. She sighed around her cup of tea. "It makes sense for me to stay here. Talk to Caius and Maxon some more. But Bastian was very insistent that I accompany you." She pulled a face. "It was strange. I asked him yesterday about skipping progress this year, and he all but ordered to me to attend. Then last night, right before you and I went to the holding cells, he showed up at my door. Said he was sorry, that he didn't want to force me to go, but he wanted to make sure someone was around that could keep an eye on you." One pale brow arched. "I told him in no uncertain terms that I was not going to be your nursemaid, and that you didn't need one."

"Staunchly agree, on both accounts," Lore murmured. "So you should stay."

"No." Alie shook her head and chewed the corner of her lip. "No, I do feel like I should go." She snorted. "Intuition, I guess. That's what Bastian is calling all his whims now, right?"

Lore said nothing and nervously ate another blueberry.

A warm hand on her shoulder. Bastian leaned over her, his chest pressed against her back, and plucked up a piece of cantaloupe. "Ready?" He smiled as he popped it in his mouth. "Time to go, beloved."

Lore tried to smile as the party moved toward the doors in floating swaths of silk and chiffon, as parasols were opened against the blazing heat, as horses pawed at the ground before well-appointed carriages.

Bastian hated cantaloupe.

Chapter Twenty

Empathy does not require friendship.

–Fabien Allier, Eroccan monk

Summer progress, it turned out, was virtually indistinguishable from business as usual at the Citadel. The only difference Lore could surmise was that now all the parties took place in different locations, and the travel between them was much more irritating.

Also irritating was the fact that being stuck in this hellish cycle of traveling and parties meant she had no time or resources to look for a solution to her and Bastian's god problem. She hoped Gabe and Malcolm were still hitting the books back in the Citadel. Maybe she'd return to the issue solved. Shit, maybe they'd receive the debris tests back from Farramark, too, and have an answer for what had happened on the ship, a concrete reason either for imprisoning the Kirytheans or for letting them free.

One could dream.

The first progress stop was at the palatial estate of the Lord and Lady Leclaire, Maison de Lune. Lore was informed of the name by the intricate wrought-iron archway over the entry drive. The sharp-edged letters were woven through with woody vines dripping pale datura flowers.

"Seems overt," Lore murmured as the carriage passed beneath the arch.

Next to her, Bastian grinned. "Lord Leclaire's great-grandfather named the place after a particularly nasty tussle with the first Priest Exalted—something about an agreement to name one of the new monasteries after him. The Leclaires leaned into it."

As the house came into view, the windows of the top floor glinted down at them in the late-afternoon light. Eight windows for eight phases, the moon waxing to fullness and waning down to a sliver in sharp-cut glass.

Lore gnawed on her lip. The sun was still high in the sky, the dark passenger in her head silent. "They certainly did."

She expected Bastian—or, more accurately, the god she knew was in Bastian's head somewhere—to be upset by the choice of décor. But he grinned widely as the carriage pulled to a stop beside the silver-tooled doors, and clapped a nervous-looking Lord Leclaire on the back as a liveried footman opened up the Maison.

Lady Leclaire stood at the door, welcoming the guests. Despite the heat, the woman wore long opera gloves, covering her from fingertips to above the elbows. Lady Leclaire saw Lore looking as she approached, and after glancing around to make sure no one else was paying attention, gently rolled down the top of one.

Livid scars marked her arms, freshly healed. "From the explosion," she said, a soft whisper as she quickly pulled the glove back into place. "We were afraid I would be...afflicted...with channeling, afterward. But I wasn't." Her eyes shone. "You saved me, Your Majesty, and I will always remember that. No matter what they call you."

Lore gave her a tight-lipped smile and slipped into the house.

It was beautiful, of course, with the moon motif continuing in carvings down the grand staircase and more datura flowers trained to grow over the doorways. But Lore paid more attention to Bastian than to the manor.

His gaze ate up the interior, his grin almost triumphant as he trailed his hand along the moon phase carvings. "Do you know who exactly did the banisters, Vincent? I might have them come make a few adjustments to the Citadel."

Vincent—Lord Leclaire, apparently—stammered out an answer, color high in his cheeks and his smile near to splitting them. Bastian looked at Lore, that triumphant grin pulling up his mouth, his eyes sparkling almost gold.

She found herself returning the smile, found relief weakening her knees. Maybe Bastian had his own mental passenger well in hand. Maybe she was worrying over nothing, and she could speak to him about what to do, now that he'd figured out how to live with it. That night after Gabe had taken her to Anton for the first time, Bastian had stopped her when she tried to speak to him about the voice in her head. But he was the only other person on earth who could understand, and Lore felt like she might rip apart if she couldn't talk to someone soon.

"My lady?" Lady Leclaire's voice was timid, still. "I'll show you to your rooms, if you'd come along. They adjoin His Majesty's."

Good. Maybe they could talk things through. "Thank you." Lore followed Lady Leclaire up the stairs. At the top, she glanced back down at the foyer.

Bastian stared up at her. The triumphant grin was gone. Now he just looked lost.

Lore didn't mean to take a nap, but when she saw the gigantic canopied bed in the room the Leclaires had prepared for her, she couldn't help but flop onto it. And the stress of traveling, and sleepless nights, and being the future Queen of a country on the edge of war sent her quickly into blessedly dreamless sleep.

When she woke, her traveling gown tangled around her legs and her hair in knots, the window was dark.

With a curse, Lore sat up, scrambling off the bed. She didn't know what kind of party the Leclaires had planned, but surely she'd missed it—

"Calm down, my lady, you'll turn yourself into even more of a mess, and I already don't have enough time to set you to rights."

Juliette, seeming completely unperturbed at Lore's unexpected nap. She was perturbed at something, though; she arranged her implements of beautification on the table like someone else might lay out torture tools. "When the evening plans changed, I decided it was best to let you sleep. I didn't bring enough powder to completely hide the bags under your eyes."

"The plans changed?" Lore's mouth felt like she'd gargled half the Sapphire Sea; she grabbed the glass of water waiting on the bedside table and took a long drink.

"It was supposed to be a costume ball," Juliette said, waving her over to the vanity, "but the Leclaires decided that it would be an astronomy party instead. At midnight." She shook her head. "As if every handmaid in the Maison hasn't been putting together costumes for the last week..."

I don't like that.

The voice in her head, returning with the night.

Seems like You of all people should like that, Lore fired back as she sat down before the mirror. Behind her, two other maids laid out a long white gown, threaded with silver.

Not a person, technically, the voice rejoined. *And who do you think told them to change the party theme?*

Bastian, of course.

"Thankfully, they decided to tell us the change of plans right after we arrived." Juliette pulled a brush through Lore's tangles, gentler than usual. Having a verbal outlet for vitriol made her not take it out on Lore's hair. "If they'd waited until nightfall, it'd be a disaster. Even still, I decided you'd wear the same dress that we packed for the costume party, we'll just accessorize differently."

A small case by the vanity held everything Juliette used to make her presentable. Small moon-shaped pins gleamed from the depths, pearls and diamonds fashioned into crescents. Lore's mouth felt dry again. "Who picked my costume?"

"The King, of course."

I don't like that, Nyxara repeated.

She didn't, either.

An hour later, when Lore was dressed and coiffed, a knock came on the door. Alie stood on the other side, in a sky-blue dress with cap sleeves made of cerulean feathers. "I thought you might want company on the walk to the observation tower."

Lore did. With a final approving look from Juliette, she hooked her arm through Alie's and let the other woman lead her down the hall. Bastian was nowhere to be seen; Lore assumed he was at the party already. Maybe she could talk to him there.

Careful, the voice in her head warned.

"Any idea why the sudden change in party plans?" Lore said as she and Alie crossed the hall, mounted a set of stairs at the end.

"I was going to ask you the same thing. Leclaire announced that the theme was changing soon after everyone was shown to their rooms. Said it was by special request." She grimaced, scratching at her feathery sleeve. "I suppose I should be grateful. My costume was a bluebird, and the headpiece itched like every hell."

Lore thought of that lost look Bastian had given her as she left the foyer. He'd orchestrated this, she was certain. She only heard Nyxara at night; maybe he only heard Apollius during the day. Maybe he was trying to give them an opportunity to speak without the god listening. Trying to seize the chance to act as King while he was the only one in his mind.

"I have no idea why he'd change the theme," Lore said, the lie coming easy. "I can't say I'm upset, though. I'm over masquerades."

Alie huffed an agreement.

When they reached the observation tower, Alie drifted away, going to greet Lady Leclaire and the other ladies traveling with them. Everyone wore a gown that was clearly supposed to be part of a costume, subtly altered. Alie motioned Lore over, but Lore waved her off, looking for Bastian.

There he was, by the long table holding flutes of champagne, talking to Leclaire. He looked different—tired, again, his face wan, despite the smile he gave his nobles. One of his hands was bound in bandages.

Lore rushed over. "Bastian? What happened to your hand?"

She expected him to be eager, to pull away immediately. He'd planned this, surely, trying to give them time. But instead Bastian looked at her and held up a finger. Telling her to wait.

And she did, too taken aback to react any other way.

The nobles finished their conversation—something inane, mentions of weather and gardening, Lore wasn't listening over the nervous roar in her ears—and then left, heading to the telescopes arranged around the room's floor-to-ceiling windows, pointed at the sky. Half-moon tonight.

"And again, Your Majesty," Leclaire said, nervously turning his glass in his hand. "Please don't worry about the window. We can have it fixed in no time." He chuckled. "Truth be told, I've wanted to put my own fist through the glass more than once. I hope whatever angered you so has been resolved, and if there's anything I can do..."

"No need, Vincent." Bastian drained his flute as he pulled his bandaged hand closer to his chest. "The matter is closed."

Vincent nodded gratefully and walked away.

Finally, Bastian faced her. He put down his empty champagne flute, picked up another. There was a slight tremble in his fingers.

Some of her anger seeped away. "What happened?"

"Nothing." His hand twitched, as if he might hide it behind his back like a caught child. "Like I said, it's taken care of."

"So you're coping with your anger by punching windows now? Mature of you." But even as her voice came cutting, worry tightened its hold. "It's past midnight; we don't have much time. We need to talk about—"

"Lore." His voice was pained. "We can't."

Her mouth hung open, the rest of her sentence poised on her tongue, words tangling with the conversation's new direction. "What do you—Bastian, I know you changed this on purpose—"

He stepped close, like he might kiss her, their bodies pressing together and turning so her back touched the chill glass of the window. To anyone looking, it would be the start of an embrace, expected between the King and his betrothed. But there was no lust in his expression, only longing as his bandaged fingers touched her lips, bidding them closed. "I tried," he said quietly. "I tried, and He punished me. He hears everything, even when I'm the one in control." His eyes, so deep a brown now they were nearly black, looked pleadingly down at her. "I'll keep trying, but you have to give me time."

Then he left, weaving through the party, leaving Lore standing by the cold window with the moon hanging over her head.

I guess You were right, she thought at Nyxara.

The goddess was silent.

Lore didn't try to ask Bastian about the voices again. Not when they left the Maison de Lune the next morning, everyone exhausted and hungover from the night before. Not when they reached the home of the Viscount Allairs, without a fanciful name over the door, and not when they had to endure the costume ball they'd previously avoided at the Leclaires'. This time, Lore was dressed as a night sky, in a midnight-colored gown dotted with stars. Bastian was dressed as the day, his doublet a soft blue with golden thread.

"You look lovely," he said, slightly strained, as they walked into the ballroom arm in arm.

"Did you pick it out?" Lore asked.

He swallowed. "No."

Her throat went rough.

They spoke often enough. In front of people, at least, playing their parts of King and deathwitch, now betrothed. Lore held his hand and laughed at his jokes, feeling completely outside herself. She tried not to look too closely at him when the sun was high.

And at night, she would beg the goddess in her head for a solution, hoping maybe She could give her what the books of myths hadn't. *Tell me how to free him.*

There isn't a way to free him, Nyxara said. How did a disembodied voice manage to sound so weary? *Not now.*

"You're lying." Lore sneered it at her canopy, though her voice wasn't necessary to speak to the Buried Goddess.

Nyxara stayed silent.

Alie tried to speak with her, sometimes. Asked what was wrong. But Lore didn't know what to tell her, so she just said she was overwhelmed, and it wasn't a lie. Alie tried to help, told Lore she could talk to her about anything. Lore nodded and kept her own counsel.

Occasionally, someone would ask about the Kirytheans, what Bastian planned to do with them. He would wave the questions artfully away, reassuring the asker that everything was taken care of, that there was no need to worry, that peace would hold stronger than it had before.

Then it was time to leave the Allairs estate and head to the home of Hugh and Amelia Demonde.

Lore barely paid attention when they arrived, though in a distant way, she recognized that this estate was the finest they'd visited so far. Amelia greeted them at the huge doors, a rose wreath in her hair to match the pots that grew riotous on the deep porch.

"Your Majesties, it is truly a thrill to host you." A curtsy, her golden hair falling to hide her face.

It was certainly a change in attitude from the last time Lore had seen her. There was something she recognized in Amelia's stance, something she'd felt often in her first month at the Citadel. A wariness. An impending defeat.

Bastian seemed to recognize it, too. His face, usually stern and austere during daylight hours, seemed to soften as he looked at Amelia. "Lady Demonde."

She looked up, almost hopeful.

But the shutters fell over Bastian's face again; the softness grew edges. "How brave of you, to host a summer progress." He left the bizarre statement for a moment, dangling, severed. "When you are so new to this estate. Of course, such a lady as yourself would find no hardship in managing a great house. This is what you were raised for."

Amelia pressed her lips tightly together, then nodded. "Of course, Your Majesty. Do come in. We've planned a garden party for all our guests, but you have plenty of time to freshen up first." Her eyes flickered to Lore. "We have prepared separate rooms, but if you wish—"

"No," Bastian said. He sounded ragged; when Lore looked at him, that softness was back in his expression, a flash of regret, almost pained. "Separate is fine."

After being shown to her separate room, Lore was outfitted in a new dress, though she'd only worn the other for the hour-long carriage ride between the Allairs estate and the Demonde mansion. Juliette brushed out her hair and arranged it with a wreath of white roses, which Lore assumed after seeing Amelia's was the custom for garden parties.

Bastian waited outside her room. He smiled when she emerged, a cold glitter in his eye. "Roses have always suited you."

Lore didn't say anything. She threaded her arm through his

and let him lead her down the stairs, out into the sprawling garden.

She tried to pull away when they reached the green, but Bastian held her arm tight. His eyes were closed, a line between his brows. "I'm trying," he murmured. "Just give me a little more time, and I promise we'll talk about this."

"How much time?" She was going to burst. She was going to go stark raving mad if she was unable to tell anyone about the goddess in her head soon. Lore had held the truth of her Mortem channeling close for eleven years; she'd used up all her secrecy. "We need to come up with a solution, as soon as we can. Before it gets worse."

He huffed a laugh, pressed the heel of his palm against his forehead. "I never took you for an optimist."

An echo of what Nyxara told her, deep in the night when the moon was high and Lore couldn't sleep. There was no way to fix this.

"Go." Bastian released her arm. "He's coming back."

"But I—"

"*Go*, Lore." He all but pushed her away as his head bent, his eyes closing again. From afar, it would appear to an onlooker like he was fighting off a particularly bad headache. But up close, Lore could see the veins throbbing in his temples, the sheen of golden magic gathering around his clenched fists.

Lore turned on her heel, walking into the green as fast as she could without running, not paying attention to where she was going. The Demonde garden was divided into two separate parts—the first, near the manor, was filled with the typical beds and trellises. The second was a hedge maze.

She blundered into it, the points of the leaves scratching her skin, catching on the billows of her skirt. The hedge was as tall as two of her, cool and dark against the summer heat, and the sounds of other courtiers echoed ghostly through the greenery, laughing and calling to one another, sighs of lovers who'd found privacy.

Lore only allowed herself one moment of pressing into the green to close her eyes and clench her teeth and try very, very hard not to sob.

So when she heard the sob, soft and muffled, at first she thought it was her own escaping.

She held her breath. The sob came again.

Slashes of pink and red crisscrossed Lore's arms from the leaves of the hedge maze, stinging as she extracted herself. She'd barely noticed before, too focused on fleeing from Bastian, on getting somewhere private where she could fight back an imminent breakdown. Now a curse hissed through her teeth as she turned around in the middle of the maze, trying to pinpoint where that crying was coming from.

Laughter. A sigh. A flicker of pink tulle as someone ran around the corner. Then a hiccuping breath, on the other side of the hedge.

Lore started forward.

A few twists of the maze brought her to another corner like the one she'd taken refuge in, though this one had a bench settled into the three walls of close greenery. Someone sat on it, their back to Lore. Someone with long golden hair and a circlet of roses.

Amelia.

She should leave. Lore was certain she was the last person a crying Amelia wanted to see. But before she could melt back into the maze, the other woman turned around, her face as red as her roses.

"You." But it didn't sound vicious. It sounded weary.

For a moment, Lore just stood there, caught in Amelia's blue gaze, shifting back and forth in her muddy slippers. "Are you..."

"No." Amelia snorted, a surprisingly un-lady-like sound from such a poised woman. "No, I'm not."

A moment's decision, and Lore walked over to the bench, sitting gingerly beside her. "Me, either."

Silence, but a disconcertingly comforting kind. This wasn't like that night Lore had seen her in the atrium, when Amelia had been full of righteous anger. That had bled out, somewhere along the way. Now they were just two people who barely knew each other. Sitting together was, in a way, like being alone.

"I suppose you're pleased with yourself," Amelia said finally.

"Not particularly," Lore answered. She risked a glance at the other woman. "What's gone wrong? Was the punch not mixed properly? The foxgloves didn't bloom to their full potential?"

"Gods, you'll be an awful Arceneaux Queen." Amelia ran her wrist beneath her nose, another un-lady-like gesture that Lore was sure she'd never make in the company of another. And it felt like that when she spoke again, too, like Lore was something inanimate, beneath her notice. A substitute for talking to herself. "It's all fucked, now."

Lore traced the scratches from the hedge on her hands, so like the scars Lady Leclaire hid beneath her gloves. "I know the feeling."

They sat in silence, neither requiring explanation from the other. Lore assumed something had gone wrong with the party, or Amelia had fought with Hugh, or she was still upset that Lore had usurped a place meant for someone of her social stratum. But misery loved company, and sitting here with someone who was miserable over mundane, understandable things made her feel marginally less lonely.

After a while, when Lore started to worry that she might be missed, she stood up. Her legs were stiff from sitting on the hard stone. She didn't say goodbye to Amelia as she left, picking her way back through the maze.

Amelia stayed where she was, staring into the greenery, her rose crown askew on her head.

Chapter Twenty-One

Trust that your god knows all.
–The Book of Holy Law, Tract 457

Lore wanted to sleep late the next morning—Nyxara had been uncharacteristically quiet, and she hadn't been plagued with dreams the entire summer progress, she wanted to enjoy it—but Juliette flung open the curtains barely past dawn.

"Up," she commanded, passing Lore a cup of bitter coffee, no sugar to be seen. "The King wishes to be on the road in an hour."

Finally, it was over, and they could go back to the Citadel. Back to the library, and hopefully to answers. Lore sipped the coffee, pulled a face, placed it on the table never to be touched again. "He's in a rush to get home."

"Not home." Juliette seemed troubled as she bustled over to Lore's trunk. "At least, not for you two. You're going to Courdigne."

Another impromptu stop. Fantastic. "What's in Courdigne?"

Juliette looked back at her, her arms full of a gauzy blue traveling dress. "Courdigne is the estate where Severin Bellegarde is serving his house arrest."

The bottom fell out of Lore's empty stomach. She hadn't

thought of Bellegarde in weeks, confined out of sight and out of mind, a problem to be dealt with some other time. "Why in all the hells are we going to see Bellegarde? And just Bastian and me?"

With an imperious wave, Juliette motioned her over to the vanity. Lore went. "His Majesty says he believes Bellegarde might have some insight into the attacks by the Kirythean spies," she said as she pulled a brush through Lore's hair. "It is . . . unusual . . . for such matters of state to be taken care of during progress, but since we are close to Courdigne, the King thought it expedient."

Lore wondered which person in Bastian's head had made that particular decision. Thus far, Apollius had seemed uninterested in the Kirytheans—that was the only explanation she could come up with for why Bastian seemed content to let them rot in the holding cells. But if it was Apollius making that call, maybe this was a good sign. Maybe Bastian was wresting back control. Then he could force Apollius into a relationship like the one Lore and Nyxara had. Distant, only speaking occasionally, with Lore in full authority.

They could live with that, couldn't they? If there was no other way forward?

"Where is the King this morning?" Lore asked.

"Already downstairs and ready to go. You're late."

Figures.

Lore riffled through her mental catalog of what she knew about Bellegarde as Juliette continued to draw and quarter her scalp into an acceptable coiffure. Alienor's father, though they had an estranged relationship, even before he'd been confined to his estate for treason. He disliked the Church, but not because he didn't like religion—it was because he liked religion too much, thought that the Church should be the governing body of Auverraine rather than the Sainted King. He'd allied with Anton, who thought the same thing, and as the leader of the Church in Auverraine was in the unique position to do something about it.

That *something* being killing August so that Bastian could take the crown.

Juliette tugged at the loose hair she'd left down Lore's back, threading pearls through the strands with the deftness of a spider spinning a web.

"Is there a reason I need to look nice?" Lore asked, tilting her head obediently when Juliette gave her hair another tug. "If we're just traveling to see a prisoner?"

"You're the future Queen." Juliette tilted her head up again, then turned it left and right as if Lore were a doll. "You must look the part, regardless of where you're going."

Despite Juliette saying he was downstairs, Bastian was waiting in the hallway when Lore finally emerged, her hair suitably ornate, her gown a flowy, floor-brushing number in summery green, with large sleeves that gathered at the wrist and a golden belt around her waist. He smiled as she approached, holding out his hand. "That's a lovely color on you."

He looked like himself, this morning, his hair slightly mussed, his eyes dark. There was a tiny tremble in his hand. That was a tell, she was learning. A sign that he was holding on to himself as tightly as he could.

She took his hand. "Should hide grass stains better than some of my gowns have in the past."

"That day in the forest," he said quickly, as if he wanted her to know he remembered. "When you first arrived."

Everything had been complicated then—things between them always had been—but in comparison with now, that time seemed almost idyllic.

He raised her hand to his lips, tapping the diamond in her ring with his thumbnail. A servant in the hallway opened the curtains, and the sunlight through the window sliced across Bastian's face. A barely perceptible shudder ran through him, and when he looked up from her ring, his eyes glinted golden.

"We've come a long way since then," he murmured.

They proceeded down the hall, down the stairs. It was early, and most of the courtiers were asleep. So seeing Alie in the foyer was a surprise.

Seeing the packed traveling trunk next to her was another.

"Alie?" Lore passed Bastian, who'd stopped in the center of the floor with a bemused expression, going to her friend's side. They hadn't seen much of each other during the progress, both preoccupied with other things. Lore with her betrothed's apparent possession, Alie with diplomacy and catching up with friends. "What's going on? Are you all right?"

"I'm fine." Alie's face was drawn into resolute lines, her delicate chin tilted up. She didn't look at Lore, though she briefly reached out and squeezed her arm. All her attention was fixed on Bastian. "I heard where you're going. I'm coming with you."

The Sainted King arched a brow. "Why would you want to do that, Alie?" A flinty tone to his voice, almost suspicious. The sun climbed in the windows, bright and unencumbered by clouds. "I didn't think there was much love lost between you and Severin."

"There isn't, but he's my *father*," she replied. There was no real emotion in the emphasis; it was there for its own sake, underpinning her argument.

Bastian's brow rose farther, picking up on the lack of warmth in her tone. "A fact that has not engendered in you any deep emotion before." He placed his own meticulous emphasis there. *Fact* came out like it should be part of a question.

"And it doesn't now." Alie crossed her arms, sighed. "But the man is useless with the actual running of an estate. I don't have high hopes that the paperwork at Courdigne has been kept in order as it should be, and since it will someday be *my* estate, I have an interest in making sure such things are seen to."

"You know I'd take care of that."

"Yes, but I'd really like to see it done myself." Alie straightened her shoulders, prepared for war. "I was planning to visit soon anyway; I simply thought traveling together would be more efficient."

Bastian's lip quirked; then his eyes closed, as if stricken with a sudden pain. When they opened, they were softer.

Softer, and maybe a little bit afraid.

The moment passed; he waved his hand. "Come along, then. You can travel with Lore in the carriage, I think I'd like to ride." He moved toward the doors.

This was a change to the traveling arrangements, apparently—one of the footmen rushed toward the doors that led out to the stables. At the same time, Hugh Demonde came down the stairs, fully dressed but obviously still half-asleep. He clapped Bastian on the back, the two men speaking in low tones.

Alie let out a breath, deflating a bit as Bastian turned away from them. "That was easier than I thought it'd be," she murmured. She smiled at Lore, tiredly. "I apologize in advance if I fall asleep on you in the carriage."

"I'll probably join you." But Lore's words were faint; she was watching the King.

Bastian finished his conversation with Demonde, then turned to push the doors open, sunlight streaming in to burnish his hair. He paused there, his hands on either door, his head hung low. Like he'd run out of energy to do anything else.

As if he felt her looking, Bastian glanced back over his shoulder. Gods, she'd never seen someone look so anguished.

Then the expression was gone, so quick it might never have been there at all. Bastian stalked into the sunlight, spine straight, gait unhurried, a King in every aspect.

Lore had no idea how long it was supposed to take to get to Courdigne, but the relatively small size of their traveling party—five bloodcoats, three footmen, plus her and Bastian and Alie—made her think they'd get there quickly. Juliette and Alie's personal maids had been sent back to the Citadel. Apparently, there was no great need to be regal when visiting a criminal, for all Juliette had said about looking the part of a future Queen.

"We'll be there by nightfall," Alie said through a yawn when Lore asked about timing. "After dinner, but before midnight. I think, anyway. It's been ages since I've been."

Her tone leaned introspective, almost sad, like the place didn't hold pleasant memories. "Courdigne was the smallest of the Bellegarde estates," she said after a moment, quietly. "It's where my mother lived, after my father turned her out."

"Gods." Lore didn't know much about the Bellegardes other than that Alie's mother was dead, and she and Severin never seemed to like each other much. Severin turning out her mother would surely be a reason for their estrangement.

Alie gave a delicate snort, leaning bonelessly back into the upholstery. "She had an affair. Right after I was born, or maybe even before. I never remember them living together. They kept separate apartments when we were all in the Citadel." Her dark-green eyes went stormy. "Affairs aren't uncommon within the court, but my father acted like she was a leper. Didn't treat me much better."

Lore thought of the few times she'd seen Alie interact with Severin—they'd entered First Day prayers together but mostly seemed to ignore each other. The only other time was at the ritual, when Alie had tried to come stand with her and Gabe and Bastian. When Bellegarde had wrenched her arm so hard she'd cried out.

Severin Bellegarde hadn't treated anyone in his family kindly.

"I could only visit her once in a while," Alie continued quietly. "Other than summers in court. I think I was ten the last time I actually visited her at Courdigne."

The same age Gabe had gone home to Balgia after a fight with Bastian. When Jax had torn out his eye.

"She seemed like she was doing well, though," Alie said.

"Better than she did living with Severin. She had a lover—at least I think so; she seemed very close to Blaire for her to be just a 'lady's companion.'" She smiled. "She died when I was thirteen, and Severin acted like she hadn't existed at all. At my Consecration earlier this spring, he didn't even have her name listed as a parent." Her hands balled to fists on her lap. "It'd be just like him to let Courdigne fall into ruin because it was once her home. That's the kind of petty, small man he is."

Silence fell, and with it, Lore's thoughts turned to her own childhood. She was thirteen when her mother told her to run from the Watch; Alie was thirteen when her mother died. Strange, how all their tragedies seemed to orbit one another, this small, dysfunctional family she'd found in the Citadel.

"You know what happened with my mother," Lore said quietly. "Gabe told you."

Alie nodded, solemnly. "He told me and Malcolm, yes."

The intricacies of her identity—that she was the Night Priestess's daughter—had been kept from the general population, just like the fact that the Buried Watch still existed. Lore couldn't see it being made common knowledge anytime soon, if ever. One massive paradigm shift at a time.

"Well," Alie said, amending, "Gabe told us that you were born in the catacombs. To one of the members of the Watch." Her eyes flickered to Lore, curious and a little sad.

"She wasn't just a member of the Watch. At least, not anymore." Lore huffed a laugh. "She's the damn Night Priestess."

Alie's eyes widened, briefly.

Here came the biggest part. Lore could only stand to have so many secrets. "And I was able to channel Mortem from birth."

Silence in the carriage, but for the rumble of the wheels over the cobblestones.

"Well." Alie's mouth had dropped open to match her widened eyes; now she closed it with a click of her teeth. "That's..."

unique? Isn't it? I thought most people had to nearly die in order to channel."

"Not just most. Everyone." Lore shrugged, flattened her mouth into a parody of a smile. "Everyone but me."

Everyone but her, and she was starting to realize what that meant.

Alie's teeth dug into her bottom lip. "Is that why . . . I mean . . ." She sighed, blinked, tried again, and then the words came in a rush. "Is that why Bastian wants to marry you? Why you want to marry him?"

She said it almost apologetically, as if she was sorry to bring it up but needed to know.

"That's part of it," Lore said slowly, trying to straighten the knot of her thoughts into lines language could follow. "Our magic is . . . compatible."

"So he's using you." Alie said it flat, anger in undercurrent.

"No." Lore shook her head, stopped, winced. "I mean, yes, kind of, but not . . . not like that. He cares for me. It's complicated."

Alie looked to the ring Lore still twisted around her finger. "And how about you?"

Did she think she'd already come to the hard part? This was harder. Her past was a wound that hadn't healed, but it was at least scabbed a little. This was fresh, a new realization, a still-stinging aftermath. "I care for him. I do. But . . ."

It wasn't like she could tell the truth, not about Bastian, not about her. It wasn't like she could tell Alie that they had gods living in their heads and there might not be a way to fix it. That all this distance from Bastian, seeing him fight against Apollius's influence, made her care for him more.

But it made her long for someone else to care for him. The job was too big for one person. She'd pushed Gabe to the back of her mind so often these last few days.

"But you care for Gabe, too," Alie said softly.

For a fleeting moment, Lore wondered if she'd voiced her thought aloud. But no, Alie was just like that, perceptive enough to pick out what someone else was feeling by the expression on their face.

"I do." What was the point in denying it?

They rode in silence. Then Alie, quietly: "Maybe you can love them both. Maybe everything doesn't have to be some impossible choice."

Lore didn't know what to say to that.

Alie turned to the covered window, watching the blurred outlines of trees go by. She closed her eyes again, and her breath slowly evened, sinking her back into sleep.

Lore stayed wide awake.

Courdigne might have been the smallest of the Bellegarde holdings, but to Lore, it looked like a behemoth, just as large as any of the manors they'd visited on summer progress. She wasn't as awed as she might've been two months ago—living in the constant opulence of the Citadel had numbed her senses—but when the footman called that they were approaching and she pushed aside the gauzy window coverings, her eyes still widened.

If the Citadel gleamed, Courdigne ate the light. The massive gate they headed toward was black wrought iron, capped with steel. The manor beyond was dark stone, looming against the darkening sky like a gargoyle.

"Home sweet home," Alie said wryly, leaning over to open her own window. "Mother tried to brighten it up, when she lived here. I remember roses by the door."

There was no sign of roses now. Bellegarde must've let them die.

Maybe that was uncharitable. It'd rained a bare handful of times in the past few months, and never in a helpful way—the spring had brought pounding rainstorms that drowned crops, and the summer had been all but bone-dry. No plant life in Auverraine was looking its best.

Nowhere on the entire Enean continent was having normal weather. The summer burned too hot; natural disasters were on the rise. One more crisis in a long line of them, getting steadily worse.

There was a pause at the gates before they opened. When Lore craned her head to look, she saw the footman from their carriage and a few of the accompanying Presque Mort dismount and speak to someone on the other side. Apparently, Bellegarde's gatekeeper had been let go.

A sleek black charger stood a few yards away from the carriage, its rider still mounted. Bastian. He stared at the manor with a sharp jaw and narrowed eyes, the horse beneath him sidling back and forth, as if sensing his tension.

Bastian turned their direction. His eyes met Lore's, brown flashing gold. He gave her a wolfish smile.

Lore let the curtain fall.

Alie was awake, now, covering her yawn. She idly picked up Lore's left hand, inspecting her ring. "Was Bri right? Is it really Mount-mined?"

"Not sure," Lore said. "Honestly, I haven't had time to look into it."

"Understandable." The ring glimmered on Lore's hand as Alie tilted it back and forth, making it catch the falling light. "Bri will be disappointed to not have confirmation. Though she'll probably still believe it's from the Golden Mount."

"It'd be nice to have faith in something so easily."

"Wouldn't it, though," Alie murmured.

The gate was unlocked, then pushed open by the footman and the Presque Mort. As they went back to their mounts, out of breath, Bastian rode through into Courdigne, not waiting on the rest of the party.

Alie frowned through the window after him. "Seems Bastian is in a hurry."

Lore didn't say anything, keeping her eyes on the sky as it

faded from blue to lavender, twilight chasing the sun's downward arc. Her shoulders tensed as the dark fell, expecting another missive from the goddess that had taken up residence in her mind, but She was silent.

A *hup* from the footman, now reinstalled at the reins, and the carriage rolled forward through the gate and into Courdigne.

Alie pulled the curtain back over her window, staring straight ahead. Her dark-green eyes were wide, her breath coming in deliberate pulls in through her nose, out through her mouth.

Lore stretched out her hand, settled it over her friend's. "It will be fine."

The other woman's eyes fluttered closed, a rueful snort taking the place of all those careful breaths. "Seeing him is never fine," she said quietly. "But it has to be done."

She opened the carriage door and stepped out into the encroaching twilight.

Unease spiraled in Lore's middle, laddering up her ribs. She leaned her head back against the velvet seat and took her own deep breath, then opened the door.

The footman waited beyond it, one hand outstretched, his eyes looking anywhere but at her. It almost made her laugh. Deathwitch *and* future Queen. She must be terrifying.

"How was the trip?"

Bastian, appearing at her side. She expected a limp from being sat in the saddle so long, but he stood tall despite the bags under his dark eyes. His hand rested briefly on her shoulder, then fell.

"Fine," she answered. But he was staring off into the hazy horizon instead of looking at her, watching the night close in, and she knew he'd only asked to be polite.

The distance between them shrank and expanded like a tide.

"Good." He turned his eyes from the darkening sky back to her. "I wanted to give you and Alie time to talk. I know things have been..." He trailed off, his mouth cramping to the side, as if someone had twisted his throat to change the words waiting in it. "Difficult," he settled on quietly.

"It was nice," Lore responded when it became clear Bastian was done speaking. "Nice for us to... to talk."

He nodded, something unreadable flashing across his face before he turned toward the manor, offered out his arm. "Good."

Lore took it and let him lead her silently to the door of Courdigne.

The manor couldn't be called beautiful. *Imposing* was a better descriptor. Black spires pointed accusingly upward from the four corners, an imitation of the Citadel's construction. The arched windows were few and far between, indicating that the inside of the manor house would be just as dark as the outside. The door was arched, too, and crowned with bronze fashioned into a spiking pattern that crawled over nearly the entire front of the house.

It took Lore a moment to recognize that it was supposed to be sun rays. They looked sickly, twisted. A hobbled sun, crushed into a shape that was technically correct but seemed somehow wrong.

Alie waited by the door already, her packed trunk by her feet, her arms crossed and her fingers tapping a nervous tattoo on her travel-wrinkled sleeve. Lore didn't know if the bell had already been rung, or the door knocked, or whatever it was you were supposed to do to signal that a royal traveling party had arrived. She shifted from foot to foot, watching shadows grow longer over the ground.

Next to her, Bastian stood tall, with the kind of stiffness that spoke of supreme effort. As if he'd topple over with the slightest gust of wind.

The door opened, finally, with a creak as if the hinges were decades from their last oiling. Lore expected a butler or another footman, but Bellegarde himself stood on the opposite side of the door, ghostly in the dim light.

"Well," he said after a moment, in his haughty voice. "I would say this is unexpected, but I suppose it shouldn't be."

Chapter Twenty-Two

There are two stages to truth. When you first know it, and when you finally speak it aloud to another.

–Alia Meroux, Auverrani poet

That was all the greeting they got. Bellegarde stood aside, nearly hiding himself behind the door. Bastian and Lore entered first, wordless. Bellegarde barely acknowledged Lore but gave Bastian a deep bow.

"Stop," Bastian said, his voice hoarse.

Bellegarde did, his back at an angle. He didn't raise his head, but he did lift his eyes, narrowed in the gloom as he watched his King. They darted from side to side, searching Bastian's face, and came away disappointed.

"As my King commands," he said, and landed hard on *King*, as if something else should be there along with it and he was upset it stood alone.

What the fuck is his problem? The thought was idle, one that slid through Lore's head many times on any given day.

The Kingling isn't playing along, came Nyxara's voice in answer. *He made us get here late, when the sun is gone, when Apollius's hold isn't as strong.*

Lore's eyes widened, a look of quick confusion that she turned her head to hide. *That was rhetorical*, she said to the goddess in her head. *But thank you.*

Something like a laugh feathered through the back of her mind.

Alie walked over the threshold, a footman carrying her trunk behind her, and sighed as she gave the foyer a once-over. "Are times so hard you can't spare a lamp, Bellegarde? It's darker than the bottom of a wine barrel in here."

If his daughter calling him by his surname rather than Father bothered the lord, he didn't show it. He didn't even look at her as he pivoted on his heel, striding to one side of the massive staircase curving like a horseshoe over the back of the room, leading to the second floor. "There's plenty of light where I spend my time," he answered, though he managed to make it seem like he was simply thinking aloud rather than addressing Alie. "Seeing as I am the only one living in Courdigne at the moment, more light seems a waste."

So when Bellegarde was confined to his estate, he'd lost all his servants, too. Lore was surprised the man hadn't starved to death. He didn't strike her as self-sufficient.

The news didn't seem to surprise Alie. Her lips twisted to the side, almost pleased.

Bastian said nothing, turning to follow Bellegarde to the stairs. He dropped Lore's arm, but it was just so he could grab her hand instead. His palm was clammy.

Bellegarde glanced over his shoulder, his eyes flicking down to their clasped hands, then back up to Bastian. The dim light hid most of his expression, but the corner of his sneer was unmistakable.

"Congratulations," he said, sounding anything but congratulatory. "News of your betrothal has reached even the ears of the exiles."

"Good," Bastian said.

Shadows slid over the lord's face as he looked to Lore. If he'd had his way, she would be long gone.

Lore twitched her finger, making the golden gem on her ring catch the light. Bellegarde frowned at it; she gave him a beatific smile.

The circumstances of her betrothal might be fucked through all seven days, and she might be at a loss for how to save one of the men she cared about from a god in his head, but annoying Bellegarde would always bring a bit of comfort.

The old man held a torch, and he lit a few sconces on the wall as they passed. Gas lamps were set into the wall, too, but Bellegarde passed them by. Lore wondered if he'd used up all the fuel. Such things weren't cheap.

The additional light helped her see the inside of the manor better, even if it only deepened the shadows. The huge, curved staircase made up most of the foyer, its dark wood railing intricately carved into jagged swirls that reminded her of the sun over the door. Small statues of Apollius stood at either end of the staircase, the white marble made ghostly in flame-light.

One Apollius was carved in an attitude Lore had grown familiar with—His hands held open at His sides, studded with garnet blood, face tilted to gaze peacefully at the heavens, a shallow basin where His heart should be.

But the other Apollius had been fashioned in a way she hadn't seen before. His chest was open, and not in the manner of the wounded Apolliuses she'd seen scattered in the more morbid corners of the Church. Those empty-chested gods still had *something* there, the sculptor opting simply to scoop out material from the middle of the statue, a symbolic removal that didn't really mar the body's basic structure.

This Apollius's chest was gone. A perfectly circular hole was cut where it should be. And instead of the prayerful peace that

His face usually displayed, this Apollius howled, mouth wrenched wide, hands clenched in fists over the hole of His center.

He looked furious. Furious, and in so much pain.

The second-floor hallway was lined with dour portraits, most of them depicting people with the same milky-pale skin as Bellegarde, the same severe faces. Alie's mother may have lived here, after Bellegarde set her aside, but it looked like only his family had pride of place on the walls.

"My rooms," Bellegarde said, sweeping his hand toward the largest door at the end of the hall. "I cede them to you, Majesty, as is only proper."

"I don't want your rooms, Bellegarde." Bastian's voice was honed to sharp points, for all that he still sounded exhausted. "The last thing I want to do is spend my nights where you've spent yours."

The man's lips pressed to a tight line, but the sound he made was closer to a laugh than anything else. "I suppose you wouldn't," he said, turning to make his way up another grand staircase at the end of the hall. A turret like Lore had seen from the outside, an obvious nod to the Citadel. "There are other rooms you can take," Bellegarde said as he climbed the stairs. "Plenty for you, and Alienor, and your betrothed—"

"Lore is staying with me," Bastian said, still in that same sharpened tone.

Her hand jerked a little in his, but she didn't let her surprise show. Not in front of Bellegarde.

The older man made that same almost-laugh again, echoing and eerie in the staircase. "I suppose I should've anticipated that, too."

At all their other stops, Bastian had wanted separate rooms. Something had changed.

It remained to be seen whether that was a good thing.

The staircase seemed to wind up for at least three more floors, but Bellegarde stopped before it did. He led them into another dark hallway, the only light coming through a small window in the middle of its length, moon-silver and weak. Most of that light was blocked by the Apollius icon in said window, anyway. Lore didn't want to look at it too closely, afraid it might be another one with a hollow chest and a howling mouth.

Bellegarde lit one lone sconce on the wall, next to the stairway door, and gestured to the right. "Largest room," he said, clipped and cool. He waved the same hand down the hall. "Alienor, you know where the guest rooms are. Take your pick." The flames made caverns and mountains of Bellegarde's thin face as he turned to Bastian, like an apparition in the gloom. "We will speak in the morning. When the sun is high."

When Apollius's hold was strongest. He knew. Of course he knew.

A month ago, Lore would expect Bastian to have some cutting remark for the old lord for daring to give him an order, and if he was in a really bad mood, possibly a ticket to the Burnt Isles. But the Sainted King, the highest authority in Auverraine and one of the most powerful men on the continent, simply closed his eyes.

"We will speak when I deign to speak with you, Severin," he said, eyes still closed. When they opened, they were clear and steady and only brown. "Whether under the sun or moon is up to my discretion. Don't forget that I am your King."

The lack of light made it near impossible to tell if Bellegarde was cowed, but the man was at least quiet. He ducked his head—not a bow like he'd been about to give downstairs, but a deference that would suffice—and went back down the hall, taking the torch with him.

Lore, Bastian, and Alie stood in the dark. Alie looked to Lore, her face settled in determined lines. "I'll have the footman bring my things to the room at the end of the hall," she said. "There's plenty of space there if it's needed." She walked off, apparently knowing these corridors well enough to navigate them without light.

When she was gone, swallowed up by the dim, Bastian leaned back against the wall, head tipped up, eyes closed.

"Are you all right?" Lore kept her voice quiet. It seemed Alie, Lord Bellegarde, and the footmen who'd come with them were the only other people in Courdigne, but secrecy was ingrained in her now, for all she hated it.

Bastian huffed a laugh, rueful and pained. "No, Lore," he murmured. "I'm not."

He turned, opened the door Bellegarde had indicated for them. Lore followed, worrying the inside of her cheek with her teeth.

When the door closed, she didn't bother being quiet anymore. "Tell me." She took a step, advancing on his tired form. "We can't keep tiptoeing around this, Bastian."

He'd been bent over a small table against the wall beyond the door, his hands braced among vases of flowers long dead, but at her words, he stiffened.

Lore swallowed. Then, hating herself a little for it, "We're on the same side, aren't we?"

He stiffened even further at that, the muscles of his back bunching visibly against the thin weave of his shirt. "Always," he murmured.

Don't tell Him I'm here. Nyxara's voice, urgent. *He suspects, but don't let Him know.*

Why? If it was possible to snarl through a thought, she was doing it.

He wants Me to do to you what He's doing to the King, Nyxara said. *Don't tell Him I'm here.*

Telling Bastian isn't telling Apollius.

A moth-wing flutter of frustration in the back of her mind. *I wouldn't be so sure.*

It made her want to sob, the idea that she had to keep this quiet still, but Lore pressed her mouth closed. She remembered Bastian saying something similar when she tried to talk to him at the astronomy party, telling her not to say anything.

But even if she couldn't tell the whole truth, she couldn't leave it like this. Completely unspoken, and Bastian alone.

"It started when we began channeling together," she said carefully, not saying what *it* was, trusting he would follow. "Didn't it?"

Bastian didn't turn around. His fingers twitched on the dusty table. She couldn't see his face, but the movement of his shoulders betrayed some struggle. "Not quite," he said quietly. "Before, for me. I started…it started right after the ritual."

The spark in his eye, that night. The imperious way he'd tilted up his chin as he put the crown on his head, bisecting the bloody line through his brow. Long live the Sainted King.

Lore drifted into the main part of the room as he spoke. Not an apartment, like the chambers in the Citadel. Simply a bedroom, with a small sitting area at one end and a large canopied bed at the other. She looked at that bed, then jerked her eyes away. "Mine is worse at night," she said.

Too close. Nyxara sounded more afraid than angry. *Have a care, girl. Do you not think He is still more powerful than I am? He designed godhood to suit Him.*

Lore swallowed.

Silence, for a moment. Then Bastian straightened, running a hand over his face. "*Fuck*, Lore."

She sat on the edge of one of the chairs, body held tense. It took her a moment to realize she was poised to run.

Bastian stared into the desiccated remains of a bouquet in one of the vases. She could almost see the resolve travel through him, just like Spiritum or Mortem might. All the secrecy he'd held, the distance, channeled out of him as he decided to finally tell her. "At night, I'm free. Mostly." He spoke quickly, the words jumbling over themselves in his haste, like he only had so much time. "He's quiet, then. But He's still there, waiting in the back of my damn brain. He can't…can't hear me, not if I try to keep

Him out, but when the sun rises, I feel Him looking, getting an idea of what happened the night before."

Nyxara's caution wasn't completely unfounded, then. Lore waited to feel some kind of satisfaction from the goddess in her head, but She didn't seem vindicated. Just worried.

"That's why I haven't wanted to speak to you about it." Bastian ran his hand over his face. "I don't know what He'll do, when He knows *you* know."

Cold slithered from the top of Lore's head all the way down her spine. "Don't worry about me. You can tell me anything."

Even if she couldn't return the favor.

"I can't, but I'm going to." He made a broken sound, hanging his head low. "Because I can't be alone with it anymore. Lore, I feel like I'm going to *explode*."

She wanted to go to him. But if she did, she would tell him about Nyxara. So she knotted her fingers tightly in her lap and stayed still.

"I don't know how much I can do," Bastian continued, still staring at the dried-out stems of what used to be foxglove, gathered in the dusty vase. "How much I can say. Because during the day, He takes over. Not always, but more and more. He..." Bastian trailed off. His head turned to the side, hiding his face from her, so all she could see was the night-spill of his overlong hair. "I shouldn't have done this," he said, so quietly Lore wasn't sure if she was meant to hear. "I thought I was helping. I thought I would be better than *him*."

No capitalization there, just vehement hate. Lore swallowed. "You mean... do you think your father heard Apollius, too?"

Another burst of that awful not-laugh sound. "It'd be easier if he had, don't you think? Something outside of him to blame. I wonder if he'd have been in the same hurry to kill us and gain our power if he knew it came with a god holding your reins."

Lore didn't think that would've deterred August much.

Bastian paused a moment, still facing away from her. "It's getting worse," he murmured, as if he could be quiet enough to keep Apollius from overhearing. "Every day, when the sun comes up, it feels like I have to fight a little harder to have any sort of control. Like He's getting stronger while I get weaker." A pause. "And the worst part is, I don't really know why I'm trying to hold on. Surely, Apollius would be a better Sainted King than I am."

"Don't say that." It came from Lore's mouth, but it was echoed by the voice of Nyxara in her mind, the two of them spitting the words at the same time. "You're a good King, Bastian."

"I've never been *good*." Dry, like it was a joke. Bastian finally let go of the table, his hands leaving prints in the dust, and came into the room proper. No sconces had been lit, but the window by the bed was open, and the full moon shone more than enough silvery light to see by, even if it kept everything shadowed.

"Then that makes two of us." Lore reached out and caught his hand, the scarred one. She fit her palm to his, laced their fingers. "Be morally ambivalent with me, then. Stay. Don't..."

Don't give up. Don't fade away. Don't let the god of everything have you, too.

The shadows hid his eyes, but his head arced toward their clasped hands. "I'll do my best," he said finally.

The door opened. One of the footmen slipped in two trunks, one for each of them, then bowed and left as quickly as he'd come. They probably made a very dramatic picture, the King and his betrothed, clearly in the throes of some important discussion.

When the goddess's voice feathered through Lore's head, it was subdued. She'd been listening, too. *He is working harder to keep Him at bay than I anticipated.*

I told you he would. Lore shot it at the back of her mind like an arrow.

It is no small feat, Nyxara murmured. *It is not a battle he can fight forever.*

There had to be an end to it. An answer in the books; maybe an answer from Anton, if she could go interrogate the mad old priest again when they returned to the Citadel. There had to be *something*.

Bastian still stood in front of her, his head hung low, the dark waves of his hair obscuring his face. He didn't move, but his hand in hers was heavy, weighed down.

"Hold on," Lore murmured, clasping his hand tighter, their scars marrying into the image of a melded sun and moon. "Bastian, just hold on for me, and we will figure something out."

His other hand came to rub at his eyes, a weary sigh lowering his shoulders. "For you," he said finally. Then, "Come to bed, Lore."

She rose, went to open her trunk. Pulled out a chemise, shucked out of her gown with no thought for modesty, left it in a heap on the floor. By the time she turned around, Bastian was already in the wide bed, his shirt gone, the moon tracing pale lines across his bare skin. Faint scars there, sleek muscle. He'd always looked rougher than a prince was supposed to.

Lore wasn't sure what to expect. Wasn't sure what she wanted. She slipped quietly into bed, into his arms.

Their faces were close, his breath humid against her cheek, feather-light.

Lore melted against his hardness, scarred muscle and angular bone. He stirred against her thigh, but his hands didn't roam anywhere that the heat in her wanted them to, one cupped at the nape of her neck, the other on the dip of her waist, the softness of her stomach.

"I want you," he murmured against her mouth, "but I think… we shouldn't…"

And she understood. With a nod, she turned over, settling her back against his chest.

"It feels like a waste to sleep," he murmured against her hair, his fingertips lightly tracing down the curve of her arm. "Night is the only time I'm alone in my head, but I'm so fucking tired."

"You're with me," she said, running her hand along his arm. She kissed his dry knuckles. "You're yourself. Sleep, Bastian."

He shifted behind her, his breath fluttering her hair. "The worst part is that there are parts of us that are the same," he said, with the slow, viscous quality of words formed half in sleep. "We both want this." His arm tightened slightly around her. "We both love you."

A wet sting pricked at the corners of her eyes. "Sleep, Bastian," Lore repeated.

He did, slowly, his breath evening, the weight of his arm across her middle growing heavier. But Lore stared into the shadows of an unfamiliar room, her mind quiet of both her own thoughts and a dead goddess, and sleep didn't come easy.

Chapter Twenty-Three

The best attack isn't necessarily unexpected. It's one that your target refuses to expect.

–General Omari Ventus, First Kirythean Naval Division

Lore wasn't sure what to expect in the morning, but by the time she peeled her eyes open, Bastian was gone. The fact filled her with something very akin to panic.

The sun blazed bright, which meant his head was full of Apollius. Apollius, who might have heard all of their conversation the night before, dormant as He was in the back of Bastian's mind. What would He make of it, if He had? What would He do?

She dressed as quickly as she could, barely marking the gown she pulled out of the trunk—long-sleeved and shimmering golden, far too fine for a day-dress—and ran her fingers through her hair as she opened the door, rushed down the stairs Bellegarde had led them up the night before. He hadn't shown them the breakfast room, but surely it was on the first floor somewhere. Next staircase, the horseshoe one; she all but slid down the banister in her haste, keeping her eyes resolutely forward as she passed the statues of Apollius with the holes in Their chests.

Some innate knowledge of how houses should be constructed led her down a small corridor behind the stairs, then she caught the scent of coffee. Lore followed it to a door leaking light from its edges and the soft sounds of stilted conversation. She pushed it open without pausing to catch her breath.

A small room, somehow still dreary despite the large windows. A table at their apex, with four chairs that looked like they'd been brought in from other parts of the manor. Bellegarde sat in one, an odd look on his face, like he wasn't sure what to make of his circumstances. In another, Bastian. Alie was nowhere to be seen.

Bastian gave her a wide, sunny smile, like he'd soaked up all the light that should be coming through the windows. "You're up early, beloved."

Lore plastered on a false smile and sat in one of the mismatched chairs. There was a small plate of stale pastries in the table's center; she helped herself to one.

"Apologies," Bellegarde said, turning to speak to Lore though his eyes remained on Bastian. "Our stores are low."

Lore shrugged. It tasted fine to her. And Bellegarde clearly didn't care—he studied his King like a code he was close to cracking, the curiosity and puzzlement on his face slowly breaking into awe.

Shit.

"Your Majesty," Bellegarde said, sounding much more obsequious than he had the night before, "as you know, there are things we should discuss, and I think today is a fine time—"

"I want a tour," Lore interrupted.

Bellegarde looked like he would happily strangle her, but Bastian slowly lowered his coffee mug, a small smile playing at the corner of his mouth. "I didn't expect you to be so eager to see Courdigne."

She shrugged. "Seeing fine houses is still a novelty to me."

Across the table, Bellegarde sneered.

Last night, Bastian had said that Apollius picked through his memories as the sun rose, getting an idea of what happened the night before. And he'd said they both loved Lore—a fact she wanted to savor, having finally heard it from Bastian's mouth. But pragmatism had to win out at the moment, and she had to think of that confession as something she could use.

Maybe Apollius had been distracted by Lore in Bastian's bed. Distracted enough not to look too closely at the other memories, the shapes of conversation kept intentionally vague.

Still, she expected Him to see through this as an obvious ploy, clearly a ruse to keep Him from speaking to Bellegarde during sunlight hours. Especially with that look in Bastian's eyes, studying her in a decidedly un-Bastian-like fashion.

It wasn't love she saw in that look. It was ownership.

Her plan was hasty and unrealistic, but it was all she had. Hopefully, Lore could make herself annoying enough that Bastian and Bellegarde wouldn't get a chance to talk. At least not about anything that mattered.

"I think that's a splendid idea." Bastian set down his coffee, stood from the table. "A tour through the grounds. Bellegarde, you'll show us?"

Quiet panic bloomed in Bellegarde's eyes, but he stood, too. "I can, certainly," he stammered, "but, Majesty, we should really speak on other matters, both regarding Kirythea and your future rule—"

"Your future Queen desires a tour, and a tour she will get." Bastian's eyes were still on her, molten. He smiled, and she tried to smile back.

Bellegarde's mouth thinned. "As you wish. We can begin with the gardens." A quick flick of disapproving eyes in her direction. "There are a variety of poison plants that I'm sure will be of interest to your betrothed."

"She has a name," Bastian said idly.

"Of interest to Lore." The way Bellegarde said it was strange. A pause, then landing hard on its one syllable.

"Better." Bastian held out an arm for Lore, smiling. "Lead the way."

Lore wasn't sure what time it was, but as Bellegarde led them out of the gloomy manor and into the stone-walled gardens beyond, the light had the brassy shine of midmorning. She was half afraid that the reason Bastian—not really Bastian right now, her brain reminded her—had conceded to a tour so easily was because he'd already spoken with Bellegarde, started making plans for Auverraine as Apollius. Bellegarde's attitude made that seem unlikely, but she was leery of putting too much trust in that alone. The man would be unpleasant if Apollius Himself came down and made him a birthday cake.

All she had to do was keep them occupied until night fell and Apollius went dormant in Bastian's brain. As dormant as He ever went, anyway. Then Bastian could speak to the old lord about whatever he wanted, but as himself.

And then she'd have to find something else to keep him distracted tomorrow.

Gods dead and dying, how long could she keep *that* up?

No time to worry over it now. Lore lifted her hand, squinted against the sunlight. It hurt her eyes.

"Too bright for you?" Bastian pitched his voice low, tugging her a bit closer to his side. All her muscles tensed. "It always was."

She wasn't sure how to respond to that. The words were meant for someone else.

He looked in her eyes, his own turned golden by daylight. The alien consciousness behind them was obvious, not quite drowning out the man she knew, but coming too damn close.

Whatever he found in her face made him grin. He didn't speak but tucked her arm into the crook of his again and ambled on after Bellegarde.

"Foxglove." Bellegarde was not a very involved tour guide. He simply threw his hand out at the banks of flowers and announced their names. "Hellebore."

"It's strange that the hellebore is still blooming." Lore peered at the dark-red blooms. "They're usually in season around early spring."

"Courdigne is north of Dellaire." Bellegarde sounded rather disgusted that he had to point this out to her, Lore's ignorance of geography just one more way she didn't measure up. "It doesn't get quite so hot so quickly. Spring flowers stay longer."

Well, there was one item of conversation to stall him with, and it'd used up barely a minute. Lore cast her eyes around, searching for something else to comment inanely on, but Bastian interrupted her just as her mouth opened to ask what different colors of foxgloves bloomed every year.

"As much as I love a horticultural exposition," he said, "I find I'd prefer a stroll with less botany." He started down the dirt path, the heels of his boots kicking up dust clouds. Her hand slid out of the bend in his elbow, but he caught her fingers instead. "Come with me, Lore. You can tell me about the flowers if you really want to."

She glanced over her shoulder. Bellegarde's expression was a mask of gentility, but fury lived in the slash of his mouth. He knew exactly what she was doing.

So why not drop the charade? Tell Apollius that Lore was clearly stalling, trying to run them out of time? The only answer she could come up with was that Bellegarde didn't think her plan would work. That, for whatever reason, Apollius was purposefully allowing her silly indulgences, her vain attempts at fixing this.

That terrified her.

The gardens really were lovely, despite the spots of browning leaves that pointed to the lack of rain plaguing the whole continent this summer. A stone wall hemmed the grounds, containing a disorganized chaos of greenery. It had been cared for once, she thought, and meticulously so. But at some point, the garden had been left and gone to seed, only to spring up again in a wild, tangled profusion of flowers, both poison and not. It must've belonged to Lise, Alie's mother, left to ruin when she died just like the rest of the estate.

Bellegarde had left his mark here, though. Those unsettling statues of Apollius lurked in corners and at the sides of benches overgrown in creeper vines. In one of them, next to the stone wall, a creamy datura bloom opened directly in the center of His chest, poison where His heart should be.

Fitting.

"Is he following us?"

Bastian's voice ripped her from her consideration of creepy religious icons. It was *his*, unadulterated, tinged with fear. Her Bastian, Apollius momentarily contained.

Lore turned, sweeping her eyes over the path. "Doesn't look like it."

"Thank fuck." He pulled her aside, underneath an arbor grown thick with weeds, hiding them from the rest of the garden. His whole face had changed in an instant—instead of haughty lines, there were dark circles, strain in his eyes. He'd fought past the god to the surface, but Lore didn't think it would last long.

"Worse today," he said in explanation. "That was quick thinking, to want a tour."

"Quick, yes, but not especially good. A tour won't eat up an entire day."

"It will eat up enough." A spasm of pain across his face; Bastian closed his eyes tight, but when he opened them, they were still his. "They want to talk about Kirythea. Some plan moving forward. I don't know all the specifics; I can't rifle through His mind like He can mine."

"War," Lore said numbly.

"We can assume." Bastian shuddered slightly, like a branch in a windstorm. "He isn't displeased by this development, though. He likes spending time with you."

Lore tried not to recoil back from that.

He winced. "But He's... not here right now," Bastian said. "Or, He is, He always is, but I'm..."

"You're you," she murmured, echoing what she'd told him last night. Her hands raised nearly of their own accord, settling on his arms, pressing at the muscle there.

A pained nod. A rueful sound. "Mostly." Slowly, his hand came up, settled on her cheek. Slipped down, her chin cradled in the crook of his finger, his thumb. "This is me."

He paused. Those words were a question. Every time, with him, it was always a question, making absolutely sure this was what she wanted.

And she did. Gods help her, she did.

Lore closed the difference between their mouths, and Bastian sighed into hers like it was rest.

Kissing Bastian and kissing Gabe were such different things. Every time with Gabe was an accident, a slow explosion, the tension coiling and bursting out in whatever release it could find. Want took them in its grip and didn't let go until Gabe regained his sense of who he was, the things he'd promised. Lore thought, distantly and ruefully, about how it was never her that had to regain that sense. The want, the recklessness—all of that was congruent with who she was. Not Gabe, though. All he had was the fire.

But Bastian... kissing Bastian was a dance, careful, every step plotted and reined. Not because there was any falsity in it, though. The opposite. She was almost certain that when he kissed other people, it was different. But with her, he kept it soft, like he was afraid to press too close, afraid he might let something out of himself.

She could never decide which she preferred. Didn't think she had a preference, really. Both felt vital.

"It's always been me," Bastian murmured against her lips. "I want you to know that. Every time I've kissed you, it's been me."

Lore ran her hands into his dark hair, anchored him close. Her back was pressed against the overgrown arbor, tiny thorns and itching leaves scoring her skin through the thin fabric of her dress, but she didn't care.

He gasped into her mouth, his hands framing her waist, one rising to tug down the neckline of her gown. He thumbed at the raised peak of her breast, his calluses a heated friction that made all her insides melt. She bit off a moan, pushing herself into his hands, wanting this to be some kind of anchor. A way to keep him here, a way to give him back to himself.

Bastian's hand trailed down her thigh to her knee, hooking it in his hand, pulling it up around his waist. He broke from her lips, lowered his head instead to her breast, his breath warmer than the summer air. The tip of his tongue circled her, lightly. "*Gods*, you taste good." Then he drew her deep into his mouth.

Lore's turn to gasp, heat spilling through her middle as she let him jerk her forward, one hand braced on the arbor behind her head. It gave a warning creak, but neither of them paid attention to it.

He let her breast go, his mouth rising to hers again, his fingers taking up the work his tongue had begun. His kiss became hungrier, less careful, more claiming. Bastian ground against her, a low growl in his throat, hard against her thigh as the heated core of her pressed into the jut of his hip. "Tell me what you want," he murmured breathlessly in her ear. "I want you to make me do exactly what you want."

Her hand covered his on her breast, his lightly circling fingers. "Harder."

He obeyed. He *pinched*.

A sharp, helpless sound burst from Lore's throat; the hand that wasn't wreaking merciless havoc on her breast came up to press against her mouth, keep her from making too much noise.

Stars blinked in the corners of her vision, a breaking coming on fast, coiling in her middle as she bucked against his hip. Lore's mouth opened to gasp, and his tongue was in the space she made, slipping along her own, a skill clearly honed. Her heart was beating too fast, her lungs felt too full of air, making her light-headed—

Bastian wrenched away from her.

Lore's eyes opened, dazed, but the heat-filled fog around her thoughts dissipated the moment she saw his eyes. Golden, golden through and through, with a smile on his face that could only be called cruel.

"Are you in there, wife?" Even his voice sounded different. Warmer, but not in a kind way. She thought of those roses ripping through Anton, something with all the pieces of beauty turned awful instead. His voice was like that. "She kisses like you did. Eager."

She tried to jerk away, but they were tangled up too closely; she was trapped between him—*Him*, Apollius, staring at her out of Bastian's face—and the arbor. But the arbor was dry-rotted, decrepit, she could probably knock it down if she had to, every thought in her head centered on *gone, away, get away*...

He saw it in her face and laughed, low and rumbling and thrumming at her center, still wet and heated from kissing him, still pressed against his hip.

"I'm not Her." Even now, she kept her voice low, not wanting Bellegarde to find them. She righted the bodice of her gown with a jerk, the thwarted heat in her middle turning to dread. "And You aren't him. He isn't Yours."

He laughed again, His hand fisting in her hair, bringing her mouth close. "He has *been* Mine, daughter of the dark," He whispered, His lips brushing Lore's, His voice a sneer. "He was made for Me. Do you really think you can change that?"

His thumb went to her bottom lip, pulled it down; she tried to tug out of His grip, but His other hand left her knee and came to the back of her head, holding her fast.

Tears leaked from the corners of Lore's eyes, hot and stinging. "Get out of him," she snarled. "Go back to Your Shining Realm or wherever the fuck You were, this world isn't for You anymore."

"It has always been for Me." His breath scraped harsh against her face, fury lashed down. "All of it, every piece. I will go nowhere, because all of this is *Mine*."

Lore clenched her teeth, tried to turn her head away, but he held her fast, insisting on the posture of lust when it'd curdled into something far more dangerous.

"This has been in motion for eons," Apollius said, His lips still brushing her own, a parody of the embrace she'd shared with Bastian. "And you aren't doing much better, Lore. I know who's in your head. I know Her *intimately*." He said Lore's name like a joke and punctuated the last word with a drag of His mouth up her neck. "Eventually, you'll be just like Her. She'll take you over. She'll be upset with Me at first, maybe, but I could always convince Her to forgive Me. And then We'll have such fun—"

The god in Bastian's body broke off with a strangled sound. His head tipped backward, the shape of his Adam's apple stark and straining against white flesh. A choking sound, like he was trying to swallow back something far too large, a convulsion of his hands in her hair that brought more painful tears to her eyes.

But she didn't try to run, though she could break from his grip now. "Bastian." Her hands, lacerated from scrabbling against the arbor, came to his shoulders, trying to pull him up from the dangerous way he bent backward. "Bastian, hey! Wake up!"

There was a moment when he went limp in her hands. A horrible moment that only lasted for a heartbeat, maybe two, but seemed to stretch into its own little eternity, where the deadweight of him pulled her down and fear blunted the edges of her every thought.

I do love him, she thought to herself, a simple statement of fact she hadn't let herself fully articulate until now.

It happens, came the ghost of a voice in the back of her head, barely strong enough to really be words at all.

The awful, endless moment ended, and Bastian straightened painfully. Slow at first, then jerking from her grip, his eyes wild. His hands came toward her, like he wanted to check for damages, but then he wrenched them away, nearly hiding them behind his back like a child. "Did He hurt you?"

"No." She reached out and caught his arm, tugged until he yielded and let her hold his hand, their scars lining up. "No, I'm fine, are *you*? What happened?"

"He's getting stronger." Bastian only let her hold his hand for a second; gently, he disentangled their fingers, rubbed his hand over his face. Exhaustion was carved into his shape; he looked like someone taking ill before her eyes, his shoulders bowed forward, his skin dull. "He's been more than just a voice for a while, now, but He wasn't... wasn't..."

"Possessing you completely."

"Right." He shook his head. "It's taking more effort to keep Him from pushing me all the way out." His lips quirked, then fell, like he didn't have the energy. "And you know how I hate effort."

Lore took his arm. She pushed his hair behind his ear. Bastian closed his eyes, and she let her touch linger.

"There has to be a solution," she murmured.

"We'll see," Bastian whispered. He leaned into her hand, turned his head to kiss her scarred palm. Then he stepped from the arbor, straightening his shoulders, holding out his elbow. "Come on. We have hours of daylight to kill."

"Will He let you?"

"He wants to spend time with you." Bastian didn't look at her as he said it, but his arm went tense.

She'll take you over, He'd said. Lore's fingers dug into Bastian's arm, like he could anchor her. "I don't think I'm who He wants to spend time with."

Slowly, they made their way through the browning garden, the sun beating down overhead. The lack of rain seemed to crisp the air, make it brittle.

They'd only gone a few steps when Bastian stiffened under her arm. Lore stopped, sliding her eyes his direction. Ready to run, if she needed to.

But Bastian—not Bastian, not wholly, not now and maybe not ever again—only looked at her, his eyes tinged gold. The ghost of that cruel smile touched the corner of his mouth.

"Come, Lore," he murmured. "Let's continue our tour."

Chapter Twenty-Four

Knives are just as sharp in the day as in the dark.
—Caldienan proverb

The tour took most of the day, because Lore was very, very good at being annoying. After the gardens it was the mews, not empty like Lore had anticipated, but full of livestock that, apparently, Severin Bellegarde was taking care of on his own. She felt a surge of begrudging respect, but it was snuffed out when he kicked aside a goat who'd come to investigate the newcomers. The goat didn't seem fazed, but Lore made a show of petting it anyway, even though the poor thing smelled awful. She made Bellegarde tell her the name of every single goat, and tell her which ones had sired them, tracing out little goat family trees until the man's face was nearly purple with rage. Through it all, Apollius lounged in Bastian's body, a small, knowing smile playing around his mouth.

After the mews, the stables, where Bellegarde seemed less resentful of his new animal husbandry duties. Only three horses remained there, though there was room for four times that many. Bastian petted one of them gently, and it made Lore think of Horse, of Bastian's strange tenderness for the not-dead beast.

Apollius wouldn't give a shit about an undead horse.

When the shadows grew long—when some of the tension in Bastian's shoulders eased—Lore finally excused herself from the tour, claiming tiredness and wanting to clean up before dinner. Bellegarde grumbled that dinner would be no fine affair, but she gave him some inane response about tradition anyway, and pulled at Bastian's arm as she moved toward the manor house. He followed easily behind.

When they were inside and safely in their rooms, she turned to him with her hands on her hips. "Bed. Sleep."

"Can't." But he sat on the end of the bed anyway, sinking into its softness. "Gotta talk to Bellegarde tonight."

"You have all night for that—you're his King, you can summon him whenever." She pointed imperiously to a pillow. "Take some time to rest first, Bastian."

He looked at the bed. He looked at her. "Are you coming?"

And she was tempted, thinking of the garden, the arbor, what came before Apollius did. But she shook her head. "I should go find Alie. Make sure she's doing as well as she can."

"Where's she been all day?" Despite his protestations that he shouldn't waste this time when his mind was mostly his own, Bastian eased back onto the bed, his eyes fluttering closed and then open again, as if he had to fight against the pull of sleep. "Haven't seen her."

Even when the tour had diverted from the grounds and into the manor, the last hour before the sun began to blessedly set, they hadn't run into Alie. Lore wasn't sure if that was by the other woman's design, or if maybe Bellegarde had purposefully bypassed the places he thought she might be. Father and daughter had barely spoken to each other since they arrived.

"The reason she came was to put the estate's matters in order,"

Lore said, "so I assume she's found a study somewhere. It seems Bellegarde has been content to let this place rot."

"All that business with Lise." Bastian nodded sleepily, fighting back a yawn. "Gods, my father was a prick."

Lore wasn't sure how that thought followed, but it certainly wasn't a false one.

This time, when Bastian's eyes flickered closed, they stayed that way. It didn't take long for his breathing to even. Fighting against the god in your head was tiring work.

For him, at least.

It's because He and I want different things.

Nyxara, Her voice still faint as the last dregs of sunlight faded from the sky.

Our methods are the same, She continued. *But Our goals are not.*

And I don't suppose You're allowed to come right out and tell me what those goals are? Lore asked, making her interior voice as irritable as possible.

Unfortunately not.

Lore rolled her eyes.

With a sigh, she started toward the door, resigned to opening every gloomy room in the damn house in order to find Alie. She had maybe an hour before dinner, and she supposed she could wait to see if Alie showed up then, but she wouldn't bet on it. Far more likely for her friend to go to the kitchens for a plate of leftovers late in the night, when her mind swam up from whatever work she'd found long enough to realize she was hungry.

Her hand landed on the door handle, cold against her scarred palm. But then Lore turned, walked back to the bed and the sleeping King sprawled across it. She bent, kissed his forehead.

"For what it's worth," she whispered, as though he'd just said the words moments ago instead of last night, "I love you, too."

Part of her wondered if he could hear, deep in his dreaming, if he'd give her the corner of a smile that let her know her voice had landed home. But when Bastian's mouth moved, it was in a snore, and he turned away from her to burrow into a pillow.

Lore rolled her eyes again and went to find Alie.

She assumed the rooms on their floor were all bedrooms, so Lore grabbed a candelabra from its place on the wall—shaped like the Bleeding God's Heart, of course—and started up the side staircase. Night had fallen with unseasonable haste, coating the sparse windows in darkness, and Lore moved slowly so that the candles wouldn't burn out. Hot wax dropped onto the back of her hand; she cursed and wiped it on her skirt.

"Would it kill the man to light some of these damn lamps?" she muttered to herself, knowing even as she did that Bellegarde probably couldn't afford the fuel. She couldn't bring herself to feel sorry for him. That's what happened when you were a seditious theocrat.

A seditious theocrat who seemed to have gotten exactly what he wanted, all things considered. Bastian on the throne, every day further reduced to a mouthpiece for Apollius.

Lore picked up her pace.

The top floor of Courdigne was no better lit than any of the others, but there was a large window set into the middle of the hall. It faced the back gardens and was nearly as large as one of the walls in the room where she and Bastian stayed, though something blocked a bit of the light, something she couldn't make out in the shadows.

Placing the candelabra carefully on the ground, Lore crept closer, suddenly nervous, as if this wasn't a place she was supposed to be.

Another statue of Apollius, the one with the empty chest. Wait, no, not empty—an eclipse had been carved into the circular space, the rays of the sun reaching out to the edges of the cavity, the crescent moon hanging in space below it. The same symbol carved into her palm, Bastian's palm.

The marble eclipse wasn't the only difference. Instead of howling in pain, Apollius's face was a rictus of terrible triumph, His mouth stretched in a cruel grin that looked disturbingly like the one Bastian wore sometimes. One hand reached to the side, holding what looked to be a chunk of rock carved with a sun. The other stretched over His head, holding another rock, this one marked with a moon.

And on His head, the sun-rayed crown of Auverraine.

I told you, Nyxara murmured in the back of her mind. *Our goals are different. His is to regain what He lost, and more.*

And Yours?

A pause. *To find a way for the world to live with what We've done.*

Lore stared at the statue for a moment, her hands opening and closing on her skirt. Then she thrust her middle finger at it and went to pick up her candelabra, searching for a door to open.

The first she tried led only to darkness, and the statue had spooked her enough that she didn't relish exploring the shadows. Three more doors were the same, one cut with enough moonlight to show that it was a shabby and understocked library, but the fifth one she tried opened on soft light.

A study, and Alie in it, sitting at a large oaken desk, surrounded by a storm of open books and files. Her head was in her hands, her pale curls flattened with dust and the day's work. A portrait leaned against the far wall, next to a wrinkled canvas covering.

The woman in the frame had pale, coiling hair, her skin a shade or two darker than Alie's coppery brown, a smile lurking around full lips and putting a shine in her dark eyes. Lise, it had to be, her portrait hidden away up here. Freckles scattered across her small nose in the same pattern as her daughter's.

Lore stepped inside, closed the door, raised a brow. "Was the room like this when you found it, or did I miss a very localized hurricane?"

"Neither." Alie didn't look up, as if she'd been expecting Lore to show at some point. "This mess is mine."

Lore put down her candelabra, blowing out the candles since this room was a tinderbox. She picked up one of the folios scattered across the floor.

At the desk, Alie finally raised her eyes, as if she might ask Lore not to look. But she just sighed again and waved her hand, an invitation.

The leather binding creaked when Lore opened the folio. She expected a ledger, and it was, kind of. But instead of tracking things like grain costs, food expenses, and livestock numbers, it was a list of payments. The same amount every time, a mind-boggling sum, and careful dates of when they'd been received.

Her eyes narrowed in the dim light, peering at the spidery lettering of the first date. "Is this your birthday?" She knew it'd been just after Gabe's; there was a list of nobles' Consecrations etched into one of the stones of the South Sanctuary, and she remembered seeing Alie's there, the score-marks still fresh.

"Sure is," Alie said quietly.

Lore frowned at the dates and payments for a moment, then picked up another folio. This one held what looked like separation papers, a simple contract drawn up to set parameters when a noble couple decided to live apart. The contract, surprisingly, seemed to heavily favor Lise Bellegarde over Severin.

"For as huge an asshole as your father is," Lore said, "he was much kinder in these negotiations than I anticipated."

"Helps when you're being prodded along by the King," Alie said, poison simmering in her tone.

Lore's fingers curled over the folio, an awful realization twisting in at her gut. She looked up at Alie, mouth agape.

"Did you put it together?" Alie stared straight ahead, her eyes glazed with hurt and fury and sorrow all at once. "August is my father."

Everything slotted into place with perfect clarity. What Malcolm said about August never being faithful, Alie's parents' separation, the payments—August coerced Lise into his bed, and when a child came of it, he paid Severin to keep her true parentage quiet and raise Alie as his own. Lore wondered how many other illegitimate children August had in the Citadel, if all of them had been somehow paid off. If they knew, or if it was kept secret.

"Notice," Alie said coldly, "that those payments weren't to Courdigne. They went to Theris, where Severin lives most of the time. Not a coin of it went to my mother." She glared at the ledger. "He must've moved the records here when Bastian put him under house arrest."

Another quick look at the folio proved it true, *Theris* penciled in that same spidery handwriting next to the payment dates.

"Alie..." Lore didn't know what to say. What could you say, to this? "Gods, Alie, I'm so sorry."

"Not as sorry as he's going to be." Alie pushed up from the desk as if she carried pounds of stones on her back. "My mother gave in to August because she had no choice—no one he set his sights on did. When I was born, Severin got paid for my *upkeep*, to pretend that I was his, and he still treated my mother like... like..." She turned away, the gas lamp catching the shine in her eyes. "I will ruin him," she murmured, almost to herself. "I will make sure everything is taken from him, and I will see him in the fucking Burnt Isles. Bastian will do it in a heartbeat."

And he would, Lore thought. If Apollius would let him.

She went to her friend tentatively, not sure if Alie wanted physical comfort. But when she got close, the other woman threw her arms around her and buried her head in Lore's shoulder. She didn't sob, but her breath hitched, and warmth soaked into Lore's sleeve.

"Whatever you want," Lore said into her cloud of white hair. "Whatever you want done to him, I'll make sure it happens."

Alie nodded, trying to regulate her breathing, make it even. When her head lifted, her eyes were still wet, but her mouth was a snarl. "If August was still alive, I'd kill him. Maybe you could raise him for me, just so I have the pleasure of killing him again."

Lore thought of the former King's body, ensconced in a vault on the highest level in the center of the Citadel, the back of his head stomped in. "I'm glad he died dirty," she said. "And I'm glad it hurt."

"It wasn't enough." Alie dashed her wrist against her eyes. "It should've hurt more."

Her anger was still there, but it burned itself out and became a sorrowful exhaustion almost instantly. Alie sagged, and Lore helped her stack up the mess of folders and folios into some semblance of order, murmuring soft reassurance. Then she helped her friend down the stairs, to her bedroom. "Do you want me to bring you something to eat?"

"Not hungry," Alie said, rubbing at her eyes. "I'm just...I'm just going to sleep, I think."

"Let me know if you need anything."

Alie nodded again, softly closing the door.

In the dark, Lore closed her eyes. Her breath rattled in through her nose, out through her mouth.

Logistics. Pragmatism. It seemed August was invested in keeping his by-blows secret, from them and from the court—that was good. The last thing they needed was someone challenging Bastian for the throne. One less thing to worry about. She could weather this. It was cataclysmic for Alie, but just one more straw to add to Lore's growing pile, and she could hold it up because she had no choice.

Lore made it halfway down the hall before she broke down.

It came in waves. She'd shoved this off for so long, this *rending*, that it couldn't come on her all at once. First, a sob, clawing its way out of her throat like a live thing caged, and the force of it made one knee buckle, then the other. One hand went out to steady her on the wall while the other clapped over her mouth, like she could gag it back down.

But it'd started, now, and it wasn't going to stop. Stinging tears flooded her eyes as Lore collapsed against the wall and curled up as small as she could and wept and wept and wept.

It was for Alie, at least it started that way. Lore had always had an easier time crying for others than for herself. But it quickly coalesced into everything—the inherent corruption that allowed what had happened to Lise, the way the powerful got to do whatever they wanted while everyone else bowed under the weight of divine expectation, the girl she'd been in the catacombs and the way her mother must've loved her, once. Her life with Mari and Val and how she could never get it back. Gabe, the way she kept hurting him and he kept hurting her. Bastian, oh gods, Bastian, shackled to the god who'd orchestrated it all, drowning in his own head.

Lore didn't know how long she cried. Until she wrung herself out, at least, all that emotion finally given a valve.

When it was over, she still huddled by the wall. Her muscles ached as she stretched out her legs, let her arms flop to her sides, boneless. Her head tipped back, salt on her tongue when she licked her tear-sticky lips.

I don't suppose, she said to the back of her mind, *that You could check into August's hell and make sure it's sufficiently hellish?*

No reply from the goddess. "I'll take that as a no," she muttered, and pushed herself up.

Her stomach growled. Surely, it was dinnertime, despite the way the sky outside the windows seemed closer to midnight.

I don't suppose, she said again, in the same tone, *that You have anything to do with the weirdly early moonrise?*

The eclipse ritual brought Us into the world again, at least after a fashion, Nyxara said. *The world responds.*

That was a shitty answer, but probably the one Lore should've expected. She shrugged off a shiver and started down the shadowy hall, regretting leaving the candelabra back in Alie's study, but unwilling to go retrieve it.

She really didn't want to walk past that statue of Apollius again.

Instead, Lore made her way to the bedroom she was sharing with Bastian. She opened the door gently, trying not to make noise. Gods knew he needed his rest.

The idiom was fleeting and ingrained, but Lore's lips still twisted. Gods knew, indeed.

He was asleep, curled up on his side, shoulders rising and falling with gentle breath. At some point, he'd roused enough to pull off his shirt, and it lay in a heap next to the bed.

Lore cocked her head and let herself stare at him for a moment, her hunger forgotten. For a man whose presence loomed so large, who was known to throw his legs as wide as possible on the throne and take up all available space, Bastian made himself as small as he could when sleeping. He lay on his side, knees pulled in, head craned toward them. Fetal, almost, reverting to the boy he'd been beneath the weight of a sickly mother, a cruel father, and the threat of a crown.

Moonlight shifted around her as Lore made her way across the room, sat on the bed. She pushed his hair aside, pouring through her fingers like dark water. With a sigh, Lore lay down beside him, her chest to his back, an inversion of how they'd slept before. She hooked her arm over Bastian's middle, rested her cheek on the broad expanse of warm skin between his shoulder blades.

His breathing never quickened, still the slow slide of sleep. But his hand came and rested over hers, their fingers tangling.

When Lore woke, he was gone.

The pillow was cold next to her—he'd been up for a while,

then. A tray of bread and hard cheese sat on the table beside the bed, a consolation prize for the dinner they'd undoubtedly missed, assuming Bellegarde had managed to cobble one together. She choked something down without really tasting it, mostly to stop the complaints of her stomach, and got up in a hurry. The sky was dark, but that didn't tell her much. She went out into the hallway without bothering to find a candle.

The side staircase was marginally better lit than the hallways, and once Lore got there, it was an easy trek to the first floor, to where she remembered that breakfast nook being. Soft voices sifted through the crack in the door, Bastian's recognizable baritone, Bellegarde's reedier replies.

Some habits were hard to break. Lore stopped outside of the room, her back pressed against the wall, and leaned forward to hear better.

"This will never work, Severin." Bastian sounded like himself, wholly, not the strange amalgam of King and god that he was in the daylight hours. It made her chest ache. "I don't know what you and Anton expected, but this is untenable. I can't rule a country and try to hold on to a god in my head. You have to tell me how to revert this... this..."

He didn't know how to finish, apparently, and his voice trailed into silence. Silence that Bellegarde didn't seem inclined to fill. The other man stayed quiet, the only sounds the creaks of an old house settling.

A window was cut into the wall at the end of the hallway. The darkness outside was starting to fade, slowly lightening with the creep of dawn.

A loud crash, porcelain thrown against a wall. "Fucking *answer me*, old man," Bastian seethed. "You lost. You're here, locked away, and Anton is living in pain while a whole damn rose garden grows through his spine, do you really want the same?"

"We did not lose." Bellegarde didn't sound perturbed by

Bastian's show of violence. "We got what we wanted, Your Majesty. Only one thing went wrong with the ritual, and it seems that one thing is affecting you far worse than us."

One thing. Lore, still alive. She huddled into herself outside the door, trying to slip farther into the shadows.

Quiet from Bastian, though she could hear the heave of his angry breath. "Tell me," he said, emphasizing every syllable, "how to revert it."

"It cannot be *reverted*." Bellegarde's tone was pointed and cold. "You are fulfilling your purpose. The divine office you were created for. It is not a journey that allows for backward steps."

She could nearly *feel* the curl of Bastian's fists, that look he got on his face when receiving news he didn't like. A distance in his eyes, a bladed grin.

"The girl is a liability," Bellegarde said, softer this time. "We have known it since the beginning. She served her purpose by strengthening your power, but her continued presence here—on this plane of existence—is making things harder for you." A pause. "It will make it harder for everyone, in time. Apollius knows this. He dictated the Tracts to Gerard Arceneaux specifically to prevent other gods from rising, so He would be the only one to return. You let Nyxara live—"

"Lore." Bastian said her name like a prayer. "She isn't Nyxara. She's Lore."

"Whatever you want to call her," Bellegarde said flippantly. "She is a weakness. She is the one flaw in the execution of this plan, a plan that was centuries in the making. Allowing her to live allows Them all to rise."

In the frame of the window, fingers of lavender dawn inched into the sky, grabbing at the veil of night and ripping it slowly.

"I need her," Bastian said. "We need her power."

A scoff. "That isn't true, and you know it. You are more than capable of channeling all the Spiritum and Mortem you need."

There was a plaintive note in Bastian's voice. It was ill fitting. He wasn't someone used to asking for things, and even now, he didn't phrase his words like they were asking for Lore's life. He just laid out reasons why she should live. "She saved everyone, that day on the docks."

"You could have."

"Was that you?" Barely leashed fury. "Did you set the bombs on the ships, instead of the Kirytheans? Trying to get me to use more power, get Apollius more firmly lodged in my brain?"

"Of course not." And though Lore didn't make a habit of trusting Severin Bellegarde, the horror in his voice rang true. "I have no idea who did, but I assure you, it was no one working with us."

He didn't heap more blame on the Kirytheans, though he had to know about Maxon and Caius's presence in the Citadel. A fact to file away, though Lore didn't know what to do with it yet.

"You want me gone." Strain in Bastian's voice, now. Scrabbling fingernails, fraying rope. "You want me gone and Him in my place. Fully."

"Eventually." Bellegarde didn't try to talk around it, at least. "But I will admit it is happening far faster than we planned. Rather... abrupt, and disrupting, to be completely honest. This, too, you can lay at the feet of your poison runner." The sneer was obvious in his tone. "Nyxara draws out Apollius. Corrupts Him. If you'd let us send her with the Night Sisters, let them force her into the tomb and to her death, things would be going much easier for you. You signed the warrant on all this yourself when you insisted on sparing her life."

"Did I?" So little of Bastian left in his voice. Instead, something dark and light at once, the sun in its awful burning, painful life where it should not be.

The sky was turning rose-colored.

Bellegarde didn't seem bothered by the subtle change. A creak, as if he leaned closer across the table. "It can be corrected," he said. "Kill the girl in the tomb, allow her power to be absorbed into Nyxara's prison, and His divine light will seep into you bit by bit. It will inhabit you comfortably, gradually, without her corruption to make it a flood. He will become you, you become Him. A holy thing. Paradise."

Lore's hands clenched to useless fists, thinking of Bastian subsumed into Apollius, Bastian lost.

Fervor rose in Bellegarde's voice. "This is what He wanted—a vessel, but also a partner. An Arceneaux, chosen from the beginning, made in His perfect image. Kill the girl, and the world is saved. The rains will return, the seasons shake back into their proper patterns, this subtle warping fixed before it can become too noticeable. The earth creaks under the weight of too many gods; it will tear asunder if the full pantheon is allowed to rise, to stand against You again. You said so Yourself."

He'd transitioned seamlessly from addressing Bastian to addressing Apollius as the sun rose higher in the sky. The silence after his words faded had a brooding quality as the man across the table—man, god, something between—thought them through.

"Perhaps," Apollius said through Bastian's mouth, "this world deserves whatever happens to it. Perhaps *you* do, if you think I cannot handle the rising of a few paltry gods. If you think I cannot change My mind."

A nervous pause. "You are our god," Bellegarde said quietly. "Your word is law, Your every thought full of goodness. As You direct us, we will go."

"Good to know." The screech of a chair pushed across the floor as someone stood. "In that vein: Tell me again, Bellegarde, what you think I should do about My wife."

Spluttering. At first, Lore thought it was due to Bellegarde not knowing how to answer. It took a moment for her to realize it was due to a hand wrapped around his throat.

"Whatever You want." His voice came thin, ragged. "Whatever You want, Your Majesty, Holy One—"

"Easy to say when you feel death crawling nearer," Apollius murmured. "But not true. You wanted Her dead. You still do." His tongue clicked in his mouth, the sound one would make to chastise a wayward child. "None of you ever understood, not even the ones who saw Us together on the Mount. I never wanted revenge on Nyxara. I never wanted Her gone. I just didn't want Her to be a god anymore, and neither did She. With Us here, in new bodies, She won't be a goddess. She will simply be My Queen, to use Her power at My command. Mine, in every way."

Lore pressed her knuckles against her teeth, hoping neither of them could hear her quickened breathing.

"That's the difference between you and the other faithful still in the Citadel." His voice was smooth and quiet, a lover's whisper. "They trust Me, instead of just pretending to. They don't try to direct My decisions like a horse at the rein." A harsh wheeze was Bellegarde's only answer.

"I love My wife," Apollius said simply. "I plan to keep Her, this time."

And then there was a *crack*, and the sound of something heavy hitting tile.

She swallowed her surprised scream, forcing it to be nothing but a painful catch in her throat.

On the other side of the door, there was a scuff of boots across the tile, a slide of fabric as something was lifted, a meaty thud as it dropped.

Then a low chuckle.

The door opened before Lore could run. She whirled away from it, barely avoiding being hit. She still covered her mouth, like she could keep from being seen as long as she didn't make any noise, a child's safety measure.

Bastian didn't seem surprised to see her there. *Apollius* didn't seem surprised. He stared out from Bastian's face as the sun rose higher in the sky, a blaze of gold in His should-be-dark eyes.

"Good, you're here." His hand latched onto Lore's arm, sending a bloom of warmth and life that made her head light, made the gem on her engagement ring flare like a sun shard. Too much blood in her veins, too much air in her lungs. "We're leaving. Now."

CHAPTER TWENTY-FIVE

Our love is one that will never be destroyed. It will echo through ages.

–The Book of Holy Law,
Tract 789 (Apollius's marriage
vows to Nyxara)*

The muscles of Bastian's chest pressed against her back as they rode, felt through the thin fabric of her gown as if she wore nothing at all. He hadn't spoken to her since they set out, hadn't said a word other than to order her to ride with him instead of in the carriage with Alie. Lore complied. She knew better than to fight with a god.

Because that's what He was, now. Fully. She looked at His face, and nothing of Bastian looked out. Something had changed, there in the darkness of Courdigne when He killed Bellegarde, and whatever bits of himself Bastian had managed to hold on to in daylight hours were gone. He was all Apollius, now.

*Stricken from the Compendium in 1 AGF, by order of Apollius to Gerard Arceneaux.

It made her want to cry. She didn't. She'd had her one breakdown; there was no time for another.

Alie, for her part, hadn't seemed fazed by their abrupt departure. Still reeling from having her true parentage confirmed, she'd roused easily when Bastian—Apollius—politely knocked on her bedroom door, Lore's hand held in a vise-grip, and told her they were leaving. Alie had just nodded, her eyes dim, and packed up the few belongings she'd brought with her. Lore saw her slip a folio into her trunk. Presumably the one with documentation that proved she was August's daughter.

She wondered what the other woman planned to do with that information.

Luggage had been gathered, footmen rallied. Lore followed behind Bastian docilely as this all happened, spinning her ring around her finger and trying to work through what to do next. If there was anything she *could* do next.

Bellegarde's body had remained in the breakfast room. Even though she'd never seen it, Lore knew what a breaking neck sounded like, knew the timbre of a corpse hitting the floor. Severin Bellegarde was dead and apparently would be left to rot in the house he'd surrendered to the same fate.

A fitting end, really.

Now they rode toward Dellaire, clattering down the road at a punishing pace that had to be rattling Alie in her carriage like a coin in a beggar's cup. The sun was fully risen, though Lore's internal clock said it shouldn't be, not yet.

The world responds, she thought dully.

The morning light illuminated the passing fields, and Lore found herself paying more attention to them than she had before. The crops were dry and listless, drooping in the humidity. The road was near-silent other than hooves and carriage wheels, no birdsong or insectile hum. The world, rotting, shifted off its axis.

Guilt clawed long-nailed fingers into her gut. *Kill the girl*,

Bellegarde said. *Kill the girl and slow the changes.* He'd meant the changes in Bastian, the way that Apollius had taken him over so swiftly, but what if it could slow the changes in the world itself?

The fields transitioned from wheat to corn. A bulbous, swollen stalk bent, broke as they rode past. Lore craned her neck to watch it slowly split, brown fluid leaking from the wound.

"Don't worry," Apollius murmured into her hair, slowing the charger to a trot and then an easy walk. She expected another statement to follow it, an addendum with *why* she shouldn't worry. None came, as if the blight on the world was simply beneath them, something too small to be concerned with.

Lore turned back around, her jaw set tight, her back stiff against the give of His chest. "Is he in there?"

She felt more than heard the rumble of Apollius's chuckle, the same one He'd loosed when inspecting Bellegarde's body. "Oh, he's in here. Still screaming to get out. This whole trip to Courdigne was an attempt to get *Me* out, him thinking he was so clever to go speak to Bellegarde, but it seems to have backfired quite spectacularly. He should have known I wouldn't allow him to go if there was a chance he could succeed, but it seemed cruel not to let him try." He held the reins in one hand, and the other snaked around her waist, palm laid against her stomach. "He doesn't like it when I'm the one close to you. Silly, honestly. I have far more right to you than he does."

"Neither of you has a right to anything." The quarters were far too close for her to cringe away, and Lore wasn't keen on falling off a damn horse, so she pinched the back of His hand, hard.

Apollius raised Bastian's brow, a lascivious smile curving His mouth. "You like that, I recall. Pinching."

She pulled her hands away from His, letting them hover awkwardly in the air. That was better than touching Him any more than she had to.

He laughed fully this time, letting His hand fall away, putting it on His own thigh with exaggerated slowness. "We have no right to you, maybe," He said. "But I absolutely have a right to *Her*."

The goddess in Lore's head was quiet, as She always was when the sun shone. But Lore still felt Her awareness in the back of her mind, knew She was listening. "Not Her, either," she said quietly. "And I won't become Her. She won't do that to me, not like You're doing to Bastian."

She wished she sounded surer of that.

Apollius laughed again, full-throated, making the footmen riding behind them toss curious looks their way. "She won't have a choice, *dearest*. We are what We are, and so are you."

Him calling her *dearest*, like Bastian did, made Lore's stomach knot up. "Bastian will be back," she said, mostly because she had a sinking feeling that maybe, eventually, he *wouldn't*. "He's fought You off so far, and You can't have him when the sun goes down, anyway."

The god at her back was quiet for a moment, contemplative. "He has been...combative, true. But every day, that resolve weakens."

He didn't wrap an arm around her waist again, but He shifted on the saddle so they were closer. Her teeth ground audibly. Apollius knew she was afraid, and He liked it.

"Part of him wants it," Apollius whispered into her hair, like He could read her mind. "Wants the release, the rest, of letting Me take over. He said it himself: He's not a good King, especially while he's so distracted. He knows I would be better. The only thing holding him back, really, is you. He thinks he loves you, and maybe he does, in his inadequate, human way. But you are destined to be Nyxara, and Nyxara is *Mine*." His lips brushed her ear. "Silly of him, to let love for you keep him holding on. On his own, he is only an angry man with the misfortune to be born royal, small and petty and mean. And how could you want that? Want *him*, stripped of everything but himself? The only way he'll get to keep you is by becoming Me. He'll figure that out."

"That's not true." She couldn't lean any farther forward without the pommel cutting into her stomach, but Lore tried, a vain attempt to put space between them.

"Isn't it?" Apollius asked. "Before the ritual, you were caught up with the monk. You think Bastian didn't notice? That he doesn't long for you both, so full of wanting he can't see anything else? Just like you. Inadequate human feelings that do nothing but destroy." The scrape of another laugh, but this one had no humor in it. "How much of what you feel for either of them is actually yours, Lore?"

"All of it," she snarled, but doubt crept into the corners. "And leave Gabe out of this."

"Gabriel Remaut," Apollius spit, and despite everything, it struck Lore as a little unfair, that the god Gabe had sacrificed so much for spoke his name with loathing, "has nearly as much to do with this as you do. What's happening to him and the others is your fault, too. Your stubborn insistence on living. I'm obviously not upset that things didn't go according to the old man's plans, but that side effect is unfortunate."

The old man had to be Anton. "What do you mean? What's happening to them?"

But she had a horrible feeling that she already knew.

No answer. The god was apparently done giving her useful information. He fell silent, but his hand twitched by his side, then went to her knee, grasping as if her body were a lifeline. "Lore."

Bastian.

She straightened on the saddle, turned her head as much as she could. Bastian stared at her with all the concentration of someone lining up a gunshot, his jaw tense, his eyes whiskey-brown and bruise-stained.

"I don't know how long," he said, every word strained. "I'm sorry if He did anything—it was different, this time, I couldn't see, couldn't hear..."

The confession sent fear skittering through every nerve ending, but Lore tried not to let it show on her face. "I'm fine," she said, taking Bastian's hand and putting it on her waist. "I'm fine."

"When we get back, you have to tell them." His voice was strained, his fingers twitching against her abdomen. "Gabe and Alie and Malcolm. You have to tell them what's happening to me. I'll go up to our rooms, say I'm not to be disturbed. I'll try to… try to stay myself for as long as I can, wait it out until nightfall." His hand tightened, pulling her in close. "You have to be careful of me, Lore. Can't trust me."

How surreal, to hear the things Gabe had said about him coming from Bastian's own mouth.

She felt Bastian's head turn, taking in the road. "I don't remember…why did we leave Courdigne? The last thing I recall is sitting down with Bellegarde."

Tears, again, threatening at her eyes. Gods dead and dying, cry one time, and then it's a hair-trigger. "Don't worry about it," she said, fighting her voice to evenness, so it wouldn't sound as ragged as she felt. "I'll tell them. You just concentrate on…on staying you, for as long as you can."

And he did, kicking the horse back into a run, the footmen and carriage following suit. Lore didn't have to look at Bastian to know he stayed himself as they ate the miles between Courdigne and the Citadel, as she felt the jolt of crossing into Dellaire. The way he balled her skirt in his hands said enough, the way he'd occasionally bend his head to the curve of her shoulder, the way that she felt the warmth of tears when he did.

They clattered through the Citadel gates and dismounted. Bastian, still stiff, eyes still dark, just nodded to Lore and kissed her hand before marching through the gold-and-oak double doors. Lore watched him go, swallowed a couple times to level the thorns in her throat, then whirled to the carriage, where Alie was climbing out and attempting to stretch at the same time.

"Apollius's wounds," she cursed as Lore approached. "That went much faster than it should've. Why was Bastian in such a hurry? That carriage is not meant to travel at a canter."

"Try actually riding the horse." Now that she had a shred of attention to show it, Lore's body felt like one large bruise. She ignored the pain, taking Alie's hand and turning her down the path through the gardens that led to the South Sanctuary. "Come on, you and I need to find Gabe and Malcolm."

The other woman's pale brows drew together, but she didn't argue. She opened the trunk the footman had just set at her feet, pulled the folio from the top, and clutched it to her chest. "I won't waste time asking you why, since I assume you'll only want to say it all once."

She was almost too good a diplomat. "Precisely," Lore said.

Alie waved a weary hand. "Then lead on."

Lore only led until they actually entered the Church, the cool shade of the stone building a balm on her sun-reddened skin. Then Alie took point, walking confidently through the warren of hallways and naves and stained-glass-lit corridors. "Gabe is usually in his study at this time of day," she said over her shoulder. "When he isn't meeting with you, anyway."

The fact that Gabe had a study was news to Lore, though she supposed it made sense. The title of Priest Exalted seemed one that would come with a study.

It was hard of her to think of him that way, still. As the highest religious authority in the land—the highest authority, period, other than Bastian. She recalled the disgust with which Apollius had spit his name from Bastian's lips.

The aforementioned study was in a part of the Church that Lore hadn't been to before, up a few flights of wooden stairs that creaked ominously beneath their weight, every landing laden with a statue of Apollius. Most of them looked normal enough, but the one on the last landing, right before the small, arched wooden door that led out of the staircase, was the mirror image of the one she'd seen in Courdigne. Apollius with an empty chest, a moonstone in one hand and a sun-stone in the other.

"What do you call that?" she asked Alie as they paused on the landing. "The only other statue like that I've seen was in Courdigne."

"They're rare, and old as dirt," Alie answered, digging in the small reticule hanging from a ribbon around her waist. The digging produced a key; she slipped it into the lock. It sent a pang through Lore's chest: concrete proof that the others had been meeting without her and Bastian, not trusting them. Though it wasn't like she could blame them, now.

"They were carved right after the Godsfall," Alie continued as she opened the now-unlocked door. "As far as I know, there are only a few in existence—one here, the one in Courdigne, and one in Laerdas, the Kirythean capital. Maybe a couple others." She gave the statue a withering glance over her shoulder as she passed into the shadows of the hall beyond the door. "It's called Apollius Avenging, I think."

Lore frowned at the statue, giving it as wide a berth as she could as she followed Alie through the door.

The corridor beyond was smaller and shabbier than the rest of the Church. The dark wood didn't do much to amplify the light from the small windows at the end of the hall, and though there were gas lamps on the walls, they weren't lit. The carpeting below Lore's feet was short and nubby, a stark contrast with the plush luxury inside the Citadel and the austere hardwood in more traveled areas of the Church.

"Anton didn't use this study much," Alie said, almost by way of explanation. "There are other, grander offices down on the first floor, where he could be seen and admired for his holiness more easily. That was always more important to him than actual study."

"Not there at the end," Lore said quietly, following the other woman to an arched door that matched the one at the staircase. "He studied quite a lot, before the ritual."

"I suppose he did." Alie knocked, four sharp raps, a pause before the fifth. It reminded Lore of the specific knock Val and Mari's crew used at the warehouse, and for a second it nearly pulled her heart in half, these incongruous similarities between her two lives.

Alie turned to her when her knuckles fell away from the wood. "This is where we've been meeting," she said, with an undercurrent of apology. Meeting without Lore. "To discuss what to do about Bastian."

"And what to do about me?" Too threadbare to be a joke.

Alie didn't reply.

The door opened, Malcolm on the other side. He didn't look surprised to see Alie, but his eyes widened when he saw Lore. "Um, hello, what are you—"

"It's fine." Alie pushed past him, all business now, into the study beyond. Gas lamps lit the small space in yellow, illuminating a messy desk and an overstuffed bookshelf sporting a fine layer of dust. Gabe sat behind said messy desk, his reddish-gold head bent over an open book. "Lore knows something is wrong."

At that, Gabe's head shot up, his one eye fixing on Lore in a stare that went from surprised to scrutinizing in an instant. She didn't let herself drop it.

Malcolm didn't look wholly convinced. He perched on the edge of Gabe's desk, crossed his arms. "What changed, then?" He spoke to Alie as if Lore weren't there, and that hurt, a little. She'd counted the Presque Mort as her friend, still did. But this had superseded friendships. "You said you didn't trust her."

That stung, however justified.

"Well, now I do." Alie took a seat in a velvet-upholstered chair near the room's one window, leaned her head on her fist with a weary expression, and waved her other hand at Lore. "She has something to tell us, it's about Bastian, and I assume that in five minutes or so, we're going to know if we're right or not."

Through all this, Gabe didn't speak. He stared at her, expressionless, his only tell of tension the way his fingers had gone white-knuckled on the cover of the book he'd been reading.

Well. There was no easy way to say your friend and fiancé was sometimes possessed by a vanished god. "Apollius is inhabiting Bastian," Lore said. "And it's getting worse." Then, after a deep breath, smashing the words together as if they could outrun the alien presence waiting for nightfall in the back of her mind: "Nyxara is in my head, too."

Silence. The brittle, harsh kind that came because no one wanted to step from one moment into all the moments that would have to come after.

"Damn," Malcolm said. "We were right."

Chapter Twenty-Six

Make those of us who are worthy in Your image. Mold us into what You need.

–The Book of Prayer, Tract 590

Lore's mouth worked for a minute before she managed to wring words out of it. "Pardon me, but what the *fuck* do you mean you were right?"

Gabe opened the book in his tense hands. Wordless, he flipped to the page he'd been reading, held it out to Lore. "Those mythology records from Farramark came in. This morning, actually."

"We'd had suspicions before then," Malcolm said. "But this confirmed everything."

From her perch by the window, Alie leaned her head back against the sun-warmed glass, closing her eyes. "I've never been so upset at being right."

Snatching the book from Gabe's hand, Lore scanned the page, almost too jumpy for her eyes to organize the letters into words. *The Opening of the Fount*, the story was called, and she skimmed the paragraphs afterward, the first letter of each beautifully illuminated—a thick-trunked oak, a wave rising over a shore, a pale woman with an upturned crescent moon in her long black hair.

On the Golden Mount, the Fount of All Things stood, holding within It power like lightning caught in a bottle. And when Apollius, then mortal, found the Fount, He knew It was a place of great power, and desiring to know It fully, He opened the Fount with a mighty heave, breaking It into four pieces.

The Fount opened to His strength, and He asked of It the question that had long pulled at His heart. The Fount made no answer.

But Apollius was not content with this. He brought His friends, those with whom He shared His heart, including Nyxara, whom He loved above all others. And He told Them, Drink from the Fount with Me, that We may know all things, and hold all powers.

But the Fount did not give up Its powers easily, and when It did, it was with a caveat: that all the powers that made the world must be held equally, or the world would fall to ruin and rot. For those who hold the soul of the world shape it in Their image, and mortality cannot be completely conquered.

And so They took of Its power, and Apollius and Nyxara did drink first, and at the same time, from each other's hands. They took the larger share, two sips to Their fellows' one. And the Fount railed against this, but could not stop it, for all godhood passes thus: in selfishness and desperation, in a wish for more than can be.

At the end of the story was another illustration, this one of a fountain. A crack ran down the fountain's side, and the lip of it was jagged, three places where rock had obviously been broken off. Words were carved into the fountain's edge, in a font so tiny and layered upon itself that Lore had to squint to read it. *What was contained must always be contained. Divinity is never destroyed, only echoed.*

Lore hadn't realized she was reading aloud until she stopped, the soft cadence of her voice fading into the dust and books and gas lamp glow, her finger tracing the etching on the illustrated fountain. The silence lay like a spell.

She snapped the book closed and brandished it in the air with one hand. "Anyone care to explain that to me in plain Auverrani? I thought the mythologies were supposed to be entertaining instead of dry as toast, isn't that the whole reason they're all but banned?"

Malcolm hurriedly roused himself from the corner of the desk to take the volume from Lore, looking at her as if she were handling a newborn baby instead of a book. "Vessels," he said simply, dusting off the cover. He wore his gloves from the library, she noticed. "The Fount was one, and the gods took from It. They became the vessels, and when They were gone, new vessels had to be found. Like... like when you break a cup. The water has to go somewhere. And if that cup breaks, you find another, and so on."

The wheels in her head were turning, laying out an awful truth. "And you think Bastian and I are becoming cups."

"Not becoming." Gabe's voice was low and graveled, like he hadn't slept in days. "*Are.* You are the vessels of Apollius and Nyxara. Just like Anton said you'd be."

He sounded so defeated already. So... accepting.

Well, fuck that. Lore crossed her arms. "So we find a way to fix it. Find another cup, or... or put the power back where it was before." She glanced at Malcolm. "It *was* somewhere before, right?"

"Theoretically," Malcolm replied. "Nyxara's power was here—obviously—but Apollius's wasn't. It didn't manifest until the eclipse ritual, when it showed up in Bastian."

"But it had to be held somewhere. The Shining Realm, maybe,

or wherever it was Apollius was biding His time before He jumped into Bastian's head." Her arms went up, down, a futile gesture that meant everything and nothing. "So we...we find a way to send it back."

Alie gave a delicate snort, eyes still closed. "Just like that, huh?"

"You found something in these incredibly lackluster mythology books to confirm your theory," Lore said. "So we keep looking through them until we find out how to reverse it."

"And what happens then, Lore?" Gabe's elbows were propped on the desk, his fingers steepled in front of his mouth. "You read the story. You've seen what's happening. The power has to have a vessel."

No rain, broken seasons, blights on crops. The world, rotting.

When Lore spoke, her voice wavered. "So you're just going to let Him have Bastian?"

Gabe's eye closed.

"You can't do that." Her throat felt clotted. "Gabe, we can't just give him up."

He didn't respond, but a tremor went through his clasped hands.

"We aren't giving up." Malcolm frowned down at the book in his hands as if it might help him find the words. "There might be a different solution. I still think we should look at the prophecy."

His eyes darted toward Gabe, gauging his reaction.

Alie leaned forward in her seat, her eyes intent on the Priest Exalted as if this was a continuation of a larger argument, one she'd been waiting to start again. "Yes. We should."

"That document is sealed," Gabe said to the desk. "*Ritualistically* sealed. The only prophecies with that level of security are ones that could have dire consequences if read by anyone other than the prophet."

"That has happened exactly once," Malcolm rebutted.

"And that *once* got us the Night Witch," Gabe replied.

"I thought it was a Tract that made her go mad," Lore said quietly. "She misinterpreted a Tract, isn't that what you told me?"

Gabe shifted uncomfortably in his seat, the first sign of real emotion he'd shown. "That's what happened, in the simplest terms. She read a prophecy, that prophecy referenced a Tract."

It shouldn't surprise her by now, but the way the Church twisted itself into knots of apologetics was enough to do her head in.

"I mean," Lore said, huffing out something that was decidedly not a laugh, "it sounds like maybe she wasn't that far off, if you think *I'm* supposed to be Nyxara's vessel now. Was she just the first one Nyxara tried?"

It was daylight, so the goddess in Lore's head couldn't make a real reply. But there was a dark flutter at the back of her mind, like the ghost of a nod. Nyxara hadn't wanted her to tell anyone that She'd taken up residence in Lore's mind, but it seemed She was resigned to it now.

"We were only taught to prepare for Apollius's return," Malcolm said. "Not *all* of them."

And that dragged in a realization that should've been obvious, one that made Lore's stomach pit. "This is what you wanted," she murmured, speaking to all of them but looking at Gabe. "Isn't it the whole point? Paving the way for His return?" Lore put out a hand on the desk to keep herself steady. It made her fingers come very close to Gabe's arm, and she saw him flinch. "This is what every Priest Exalted has been waiting for since the fucking Godsfall. All of you must be thrilled."

"No." It came harsh, punctuated by Gabe's hands slamming against the desk, making her jump back. "No, we are *not*, Lore."

She shook her head, another one of those mad not-laughs clawing out of her. "You've been devoted to Apollius since you were a kid, Gabe, forgive me if I don't believe that you aren't jumping for joy at the confirmation that you were right—"

"We weren't." He'd schooled his voice even again, but he rose from behind the desk like something avenging, looming over her with lightning crackling in his one blue eye. "We weren't *right*. Apollius was supposed to return from the Shining Realm and bring paradise to the earth, restore it to a place of peace for His faithful. Not...not live in the head of an Arceneaux asshole and play power games!"

The hard-won evenness eroded as he spoke, and by the end, he was nearly shouting.

A moment, then Gabe drew in a ragged breath, ran a shaky hand over his disheveled hair. It'd grown out more than he usually let it. "This isn't how it's supposed to be," he said finally, and he sounded so...so wounded, like this was a personal failing, a personal slight.

"If you haven't noticed," Alie said drily, "none of us exactly believe the Church's teachings as written anymore. At least, not the way they're presented in the modern Compendium."

Gabe frowned.

"Some of us have taken it harder than others," Alie murmured.

Lore's anger alchemized to something harder to name, guilt and shame and something almost, maybe, hopeful.

"So what do we do?" Lore asked quietly.

"The gods were all human once." Malcolm put the book back down on the desk, satisfied that Lore hadn't hurt it. He took off his gloves with small, meticulous movements, making a show of not looking at Gabe. "There has to be a way to...not stop Them completely, maybe, but put Them off somehow."

"And the way is probably in that prophecy," Alie finished. Where Malcolm refused to look at Gabe, that was all she did, her dark-green eyes fixed on the slumped, dejected figure of the Priest Exalted like she could haul him up through will alone.

"The story of the Fount said there have to be vessels for Its power." Malcolm's voice put capitalization on the pronoun, just like the book had. "I don't think we can change that. But we can delay it, maybe, lure Apollius and Nyxara back into dormancy until more . . . appropriate vessels can be found. Now is not the best time for physical manifestations of the gods to suddenly reappear. And They clearly aren't at Their best if They're choosing you lot."

Gabe knuckled at his exposed eye. "Will that exacerbate the issues with the crops? The weather?"

"Maybe the opposite, actually," Malcolm said. "If you look back at the records, none of those things started until Bastian was born."

That put a funny hitch in Lore's middle. Bastian was older than her, though only by a month or so. She'd never lived in a world he hadn't touched. All of them were of an age, here in this room, and the changes in climate and landscape had always been a volatile thing, starting subtly, getting worse in such small increments that she hadn't known to be wary of it until she was told.

And there was what Apollius had said as they rode back from Courdigne. About Gabe being just as much a part of this as she was. About the others.

There were four more gods other than Apollius and Nyxara. Four more gods, and three more people in this room.

But surely, if things had gotten that far—if her friends had gods in their heads, too—they would have said something? Maybe they could stop this before it got to that point.

With a sigh, Gabe leaned back in his chair. When he spoke, it was quiet. "Fine. We can look."

Neither Alie nor Malcolm seemed to know what to make of his sudden capitulation, after what Lore suspected was weeks on weeks of resistance. For a moment, they were still, then Malcolm all but jumped toward the door. Gabe followed reluctantly. Lore fell in next to Alie, bringing up the back of their small crowd.

She still had something to tell her. Something she probably should've said before they entered Gabe's study, but she'd been distracted.

Gabe and Malcolm gained a longer lead as they made their way to the staircase again, to that unsettling statue of Apollius. Lore hung back on purpose, and Alie followed suit.

Much like telling them she had a goddess in her head, she didn't know how to finesse the news that Bastian had killed Alie's father. Well, not-father. And not-Bastian. So she just said it.

"Alie," Lore said quietly. "There's one more thing."

The other woman arched a brow.

"Before we left, Bastian—Apollius, really, He'd fully taken over—He killed Bellegarde."

Silence. The only sign Alie had heard her at all was the widening of her eyes, gone glassy in the afternoon light.

"Is he still there?" Alie asked, her voice barely sound. "In Courdigne?"

Lore nodded.

"Good," Alie snarled. "Let him rot."

Chapter Twenty-Seven

When does religion cross from faith into governance? Where is the line between what a god says, and what a priest claims They say?

–From the writings of Moira Killory, Caldienan scholar. Fled to Ratharc when orders for her arrest came from the Auverrani Priest Exalted, 150 AGF.

The ritualistically sealed prophecies were kept in secure rooms below the Church. That sounded a little too close to the catacombs for comfort, but Lore had a dearth of choices at this point, and none of those she did have were pleasant.

It was a long walk, winding through wooden corridors and more now-defunct confessional rooms, a small hallway lined in extra Apollius icons whose marble had gone dingy. Then the halls narrowed, their path taking them from the wider expanse of the Church that housed the South Sanctuary into the thinner part of the building that held storage and cloisters. Every few feet, they passed an empty room with nothing but a bed made up in white linens.

They spooked her a little, these empty cloisters. But the walk gave her time to think. A small detail from the mythology text stuck in her mind, and after turning it over in her own thoughts as much as she could, Lore picked up her pace to come level with Malcolm.

"In the book," Lore started, "the pronoun for the Fount was capitalized. And It spoke. Neither of those things are typical for normal fountains, in my experience."

Malcolm shot her a smile, the one that said she'd tripped upon some obscure theology question he was simply thrilled to explain. "It isn't typical, no. There's not much documentation about the state of religion before the rise of the pantheon, just a few murals painted in Myrosh and some extremely old texts kept in the archival libraries in Caldien, but the leading theory is that the Fount was actually considered a god Itself."

Lore could barely conceive of a time before the pantheon. Everything she'd ever known centered on Apollius and Nyxara and the elemental gods. "You mean they worshipped a fountain on an island? *Everyone* did?"

"Not worshipped, per se." Malcolm waved his hand in the air, as if balancing an invisible scale. "*Revered* may be the better verb. The Fount wasn't a person, not at any time, and It wasn't anthropomorphized. As best scholars can tell, the Fount was considered the source of the earth."

Her brow furrowed. "The source of *what* of the earth?"

"Of the *earth*." He grinned. "All the powers that made up the entire world, the...the world's soul, I guess would be the easiest way to put it. The Fount was the soul of everything. It didn't require worship or tending or prayer. It just existed."

"Until Apollius found It."

"Until Apollius found It, and opened It, and spoke to It." Malcolm shrugged. "And wrecked It, apparently."

All godhood passes in selfishness and desperation. It didn't paint a rosy picture of divinity.

"But was He looking for it? Did He just wash up on the shore of the Golden Mount and stumble upon the world's soul?" Lore barked a laugh that had nothing to do with humor. "That seems far too convenient to be a coincidence."

"Who knows? Maybe He was looking for It. Maybe He just got lucky."

Lore fell silent, but the open questions didn't sit right with her. She couldn't believe that Apollius—human Apollius, who surely wasn't that different in personality from the god He became—had simply happened upon something as ancient and powerful as the Fount.

The myth said He'd asked It the question that had long pulled at His heart. And seemingly hadn't liked the answer. Surely, He'd been seeking the Fount, thinking It could tell Him something.

Lore shook her head. "If the Fount held the world's soul—for lack of a better term—and Apollius and the others took Its power, then does that mean They're the soul of the earth, now?" She didn't like that prospect, though the world hadn't necessarily made a good case for itself as being something with an immaculate soul.

Malcolm shrugged again. "I don't think that's the kind of question one can answer easily. Like I said, the Fount isn't the earth's literal soul—as much as such a thing can be called literal—It's just the concentrated essence, a place of great power." A scoff. "You know, assuming It actually exists at all. But as for the question of the world's soul..." He trailed off, frowned. "I feel like that can't be determined by one person. Or even a group of people, even powerful ones. The world belongs to more than the powerful. Its soul has to be something we all have a say in, right?"

Lore didn't have an answer.

She and Malcolm had kept their voices pitched low, not because they didn't want to be overheard, but just because the atmosphere of these deep places in the Church seemed to call for quiet. Alie kept a few feet behind them, listening but not feeling the need to add to the conversation. Gabe was yards ahead, his back straight, his arms swinging by his sides, like someone marching into a battle instead of a storage room.

Her teeth worried at the inside of her cheek as she watched him. Gabe, who just wanted to be right. Gabe, who just wanted to be good.

How did a man like that cope when both of those things became too complicated to grasp, too ephemeral to hold on to? When the paradigm shifted so far it was nearly unrecognizable, the god you served becoming the evil you guarded against?

She loved him, too. Like with Bastian, it was an obvious thing to admit, once she let herself. The love here was more complicated, tangled up in knots from his betrayal the night of the ritual. But Lore was starting to wonder if she was even capable of feeling love simply. Who she was—what she was becoming—didn't leave much room for simple.

And should she tell him? That was another thing. She was engaged to Bastian, and even if she couldn't necessarily see a wedding going forward while they were dealing with all this god mess, surely it wasn't fair to either of them for her to admit that she loved them both. That she could never make a choice that excluded one or the other.

Eventually, the cloister hallway ended at a small door, another staircase behind it. This one was stone, and already underground. The cold was enough to raise goose bumps on Lore's arms despite the heat outside. Eventually, the sconces on the walls went dark, and Gabe had to stop and cobble together a torch from some supplies lying by the wall. It lit with barely a touch to the flame.

The supplies pile itself looked old when Lore passed it, the cloths mildewed enough that she was surprised they'd caught at all. Clearly, it'd been a while since anyone came down here.

Right as her thighs were beginning to severely protest the seemingly endless stairs—not the best idea right after the long ride from Courdigne to Dellaire—the corridor leveled, stairs becoming a long, cold hallway, lined in small doors. The walls were damp, and though the flame of Gabe's torch was steady, its light didn't do much to illuminate the shadows. Instinctually, they all crept closer to one another, huddling around the yellow glow like children afraid of the dark.

"Well," Malcolm said, looking to Gabe, "you're the Priest Exalted, surely you know where the prophecies are kept."

"I have a vague idea," Gabe grumbled, his one eye scanning the hall as he moved slowly forward. Malcolm, Alie, and Lore clustered around him; Gabe gave them all a withering look, but didn't comment, his attention focused elsewhere.

There were no doors in the stone walls. Instead, numbers, but not set out in order, just a senseless chaos. Gabe glanced at Lore over his shoulder, face stern. "When we find the right room, you'll have to open it. Some of these locks can be opened just by using the Mortem in the stone, but some need more, and I assume Anton's prophecy will have more security than the rest."

Right. Because Lore had all the Mortem that once leaked from the catacombs.

"*That's* taken some getting used to," Malcolm said, in a falsely bright tone that hid what he actually thought about it. "I barely know what to do with all my newfound free time."

"Apparently, you've been reading obscure theology," Gabe grumbled.

"To be fair, I was doing that before. There was supposed to be a minor lunar eclipse tonight, actually. Just think, if Lore hadn't gone wild that day on the docks, I'd be preparing instead of trekking down into the bowels of the Church with you three."

Gabe grumbled.

Bringing up the rear of the party, Alie was still quiet, her delicate features composed in an unreadable mask. Lore kept shooting her covert glances, in case the righteous anger she'd displayed when Lore told her about Bellegarde had somehow collapsed into grief, but the other woman's face gave no clue to what was going on in her head.

Alie was Bastian's half sister. Lore didn't plan to tell anyone—it wasn't hers to tell—but dread chewed up her middle when she thought about what that kind of information might do. What it might mean.

Alie was an Arceneaux heir, another one of Apollius's chosen line. Did He know? What would He do about it?

What would Kirythea do, if they found out?

Finally, Gabe stopped his seemingly endless trek down the dark, damp hallway, the light of the torch wavering over the number-marked blocks of stone. Lore squinted to see the number they'd arrived at: 918.

The number didn't have any special significance to her, but when she looked at Malcolm, his eyes were wide. "Tract Nine Hundred Eighteen," he murmured. "*Only the Fount is eternal.*"

Lore frowned. "I've never heard that one."

"You wouldn't have." Gabe didn't take his attention from the stone, as if his eye were a hammer that could break the stone room open. "It was never officially in the Compendium. One of the first priests brought a letter from Apollius back from the Mount with that line in it. The letters were included in the first few drafts of the Compendium, but they were taken out later."

"Looks like I'm not the only one reading obscure theology," Malcolm muttered.

"So the prophecies down here are organized by…what? The Tract most relevant to the content?" Lore took a small step closer to the wall. Mortem was thick in the air around them, all but humming through the stone, making her palms itch and her heartbeat slow.

"Not exactly." Gabe sighed. "They're organized by the Tract that the prophet was meditating on when they had the vision."

"Of course Anton was meditating on stricken Tracts that

no one can access but Church officials," Lore grumbled. "Why wouldn't he be?"

Malcolm gestured to Lore, then to the door. "Neither Gabe nor I can sense enough Mortem to undo the lock. All you, Sainted Queen."

"I will give you whatever jewel strikes your fancy from the treasury if you promise never to call me that again." Lore said it like a joke, but they all knew it wasn't.

"You'd better get used to it," Gabe said darkly, with no trace of a joke at all.

Shaking out her hands, Lore moved forward again, the Mortem awareness growing until she could nearly hear it, a soft not-sound like the hush of the tide against the shore. Lore wasn't sure how much of it was the magic in the stone and how much of it was the magic within her.

When she touched the wall, the force of it nearly threw her head back, a curl of cold seeping through her hands and down through her core. Her breath hissed between her teeth, and vaguely, she was aware of Gabe, moving forward as if he could help her. But he left her alone. There was nothing he could do.

The lock on the secret room was basically the same as the lock in the catacombs where the bodies from the villages had been hidden. A knot with a trip mechanism, a puzzle box that would straighten when solved and outline the door. This one used quite a bit more Mortem than the one in the catacombs. The prophecy must really pack a punch if it was more closely guarded than an army of the undead.

A few moments more and Lore untangled the puzzle, the Mortem within her pushing out through her hands to turn over the knot within the wall. The rock around it was brittle, but not terribly so. She found herself very thankful for that, when she thought of the miles of dirt and Church above their heads.

Lore dropped her hands as the lock unraveled, turned up her palms to inspect the gray stars there. Strands of Mortem still clung to her, like they had in the catacombs. For a moment, that set panic into her middle, but then Lore took a breath, centered herself. Pulled a little bit at that shining length of gold that lay alongside her darkness, the sun to its moon.

Spiritum shone around her fingers, a pale-gold glitter that lasted only a heartbeat and then was gone, leaving only the gray starbursts. They looked slightly larger than before, climbing nearly to her first knuckle.

She turned, jerked a thumb at the door, now clearly outlined. "All done."

Malcolm and Alie moved forward eagerly, pushing open the door with the groan of unused hinges and rubbing stone. Gabe entered more warily, torch still burning in his hand.

With another steeling breath, Lore followed.

For a ritualistically sealed room holding a very volatile prophecy, it wasn't much to look at. Stone walls, stone floors, though not damp like the corridor outside. Lore supposed rats and other vermin weren't an issue, what with the Mortem-locked door. One sconce on the wall, illuminated by Gabe's torch; he touched the flame to its wick and it went up immediately, a tall spike of fire.

The weirdly steady light from the sconce cleared shadows from the corners of the small room, finally lighting up the prophecy itself. A stone lectern stood in the center of the room, holding a single scroll beneath a glass dome. The dome was similar to the ones lining the tables in the library, but without a door in the top—the glass was a tomb, and the paper within was never meant to leave it again. A reliquary, holy and untouchable.

Malcolm was already standing over the glass, nearly vibrating with anticipation, ready to read as soon as he had enough light. Alie stood a bit behind him, not hovering like he did but still close enough to see, worrying at her bottom lip.

Lore didn't approach the glass-protected prophecy at all. She'd look at it, eventually, but the prospect of it sent dread swirling through her, a cold storm of it rising through her chest and making her throat feel too narrow.

Gabe set his torch into an iron ring on the wall, crossed his arms. "Well?"

"It's long." Malcolm frowned. "And there's something at the bottom I can't read, that doesn't look like written language at all. Just swirls and lines."

Silence. They all waited.

Malcolm cleared his throat, then read aloud in a clear, unwavering voice. "Two things must occur for Apollius to return within His chosen vessel, and two things must be prevented. The things that must occur: The unfaithful King must be dethroned, and the daughter of the dark must be brought to the chosen, just before his ascension."

Things that had already happened. Apollius was here.

"The things that must be prevented," Malcolm continued. "The dark's daughter must not linger past fulfilling her purpose. And the..." He trailed off, brow furrowed, leaning in closer as if to make sure he was reading it right. "The war must not be allowed, for no one faithful to Him is an enemy, and our task is to make a Holy Kingdom that spans the earth."

"Sounds like an Empire to me," Alie muttered darkly.

"Also sounds like we've fucked up most of this prophecy already," Lore added.

Waving a hand at both of them for quiet, Malcolm kept reading. "If these requirements are not met in full, the power of the Fount will find new vessels. One for each It lost—for Nyxara, for Apollius, for Caeliar and Braxtos and Lereal and Hestraon. The cycle will continue anew, and it will spell woe for the world."

Six gods. Four people in this room. Bastian, waiting in the Citadel, trying to hold on to himself.

Malcolm leaned back, frowning, then looked silently to Gabe.

"So we aren't just dealing with two gods," Gabe said. "We're dealing with Them all."

Chapter Twenty-Eight

The world is not eternal.

–Carved on a seawall in Myrosh

It was wildly inappropriate, but the first thing Lore felt was relief, her suspicions proven correct. She and Bastian weren't alone.

The next thing she felt, far more appropriately, was terror.

She looked at Gabe again, trying to gauge his reaction. But Gabe wasn't looking at the floor with that furrow across his forehead that said he was deep in thought. Instead he was looking at the sconce on the wall, with its steady, nearly flickerless flame.

"So what do we do with that?" Alie, as usual, taking the information in stride and moving forward. "As Lore noted, most of these parameters have been fucked up already, but that didn't stop Apollius from possessing His vessel."

"But neither did all the predictions come true," Malcolm said. "No one has prevented a war. In fact, I'd say one is far closer than it was before, after that explosion."

Alie's brows drew together, her expression going distant. Lore wondered if she'd been back to speak to Caius, to see if she could get unequivocal proof that Kirythea was behind the attack that day. If she had, she hadn't shared it with Lore.

"And if the other gods taking vessels manifests the same way Nyxara and Apollius have for Lore and Bastian, I'd think it'd be obvious," Malcolm continued. "They'd be exhibiting elemental powers by now…"

He stopped, silence like a stopper in his throat. His eyes went to his hands, then to Gabe. "The plants," he murmured. "In the library."

Slowly, his eyes still on the flame, Gabe nodded.

"Shit." Malcolm stared at his hands a moment more, then rubbed one over his shorn head. "Shit on the Citadel Wall."

Still standing by the prophecy, Alie's green eyes were so wide that the whites showed all around her irises. None of them had to spell out what Malcolm had just realized, the truth running through them clear and sharp as a bayonet end.

"Can you hear Him?" Alie breathed. "Braxtos?"

Malcolm shook his head, his candle-inked palm pressed to his temple, like he was listening very closely to the space between his ears. "Haven't heard anything, nothing like a voice." His eyes swung to Lore. "When did it start, for you?"

"I've heard Her a couple times in the last year," she said, "but I didn't know what it was—who it was—until She told me."

Was that true, though? Had she not known? Who else could it be, speaking in her head, calling to her from the death she could braid and shape and bend? Lore was practiced at avoiding things she'd rather not think about, and she'd employed those skills to their fullest.

"It's gotten worse since Bastian and I started channeling together," she continued, quieter. "After we set the bodies to rest in the catacombs. After we healed the fields."

Malcolm nodded slowly, something like hope seeping over his features. "So I just don't use it. Whatever I did with the plants—"

"Earth magic," Gabe murmured, apparently not wanting anything to be kept vague.

Another nod from Malcolm, this one stilted. "I just won't do it again," he said, weakly triumphant. "I'll just…just keep an eye on it, make sure it doesn't happen, and then He can't get into my head."

The pronoun staggered out of him, like he didn't want to say it. Didn't want to acknowledge who exactly he was talking about.

"I don't think it's that simple," Gabe said. His eye was still watching that flame, a sinuous tongue of light dancing against the backdrop of the stone wall. "It can't be. If a god wants you, They'll have you."

"I don't fucking accept that!"

In all the time she'd known Malcolm, Lore had never heard him shout. He wasn't a quiet man, but he was a measured one, able to keep his moods pleasant and even regardless of the circumstances.

This circumstance, apparently, was the one to break him. Malcolm's eyes were bright with furious tears, his hands clenched to fists by his sides, as if he could keep any magic from leaving them by keeping them closed. He advanced on Gabe as he spoke, the Priest Exalted having become the receptacle of his anger since the actual culprit wasn't there to receive it. Since the actual culprit was a god, and the Fount that gave Him power.

"It makes no scientific or spiritual sense," Malcolm continued, all but spitting the words. "There is no magic left in the world. Lore took all the Mortem; Spiritum isn't available to anyone who isn't Bastian. If the gods are returning now, it's in the wrong way, and we have to fix it!"

"We're still going to try," Alie murmured. She looked at her hands, long, delicate fingers splayed wide. With a deep, hitching breath, she twitched one of them.

A gust of a breeze filtered through the dark room, feathering Lore's hair. Of course. Of course.

"We're still going to try," Alie repeated, closing her hands. "If you haven't heard Braxtos, Malcolm, and I haven't heard Lereal, that means there's still time."

Alie hadn't mentioned anything about feeling magic, but she'd kept herself apart for almost the whole of summer progress. Maybe this was why.

Two elemental gods down. Two to go.

Malcolm's eyes were glassy, swinging from Alie back to Gabe. "I don't want a god in my head."

Gabe finally turned away from the flame on the wall. It leapt upward, as if protesting, painting lurid light across the stone. "I don't, either," he said, so quiet it was nearly a whisper. "But trying not to use the power doesn't seem to have slowed Him down at all."

Three out of four.

Lore swallowed down the dry, thorny lump rising in her throat, scouring, bitter guilt. Of course the leftover gods would take over her friends, people close to her, just like the elemental gods had been close to Nyxara. Another sacrifice she'd unwittingly made.

"How long?" she asked Gabe.

He sighed, his muscled shoulders slumping. "Couple weeks. Since we started working on your mental barrier, after you told me about the dreams." A hoarse bark of not-laughter. "Fat lot of help *that* did."

The thorny thing in her throat got larger. Every breath was a saw, the pressure of not crying pushing at the back of her eyes as if it'd shove them right out of their sockets. She'd gone soft. The dam on her tears had been torn down.

"It isn't like you, though," Gabe continued. He refused to look at the sconce again, but apparently didn't want to look at any of them, either, fixing his gaze instead on the floor. "Where you hear a solid voice, have... *conversations*." He said the word like it repulsed him. "The elemental gods were never as powerful as Apollius and Nyxara. It's more like having ideas that aren't my own. Impulses."

His eye flashed to Lore, then. One burning look.

"Hestraon was the most powerful elemental god, though." Gabe spoke clipped and sure, as if reciting academic facts with no attachment to him. "If Alie and Malcolm aren't feeling those... those impulses yet, maybe they won't at all. Maybe the other gods are too weak."

"That's Braxtos and Hestraon and Lereal, then." Alie sounded the surest of them all, no trace of a waver in her voice, though the hand she'd used to manipulate the air still trembled a bit. "That leaves Caeliar." She trilled a high, half-mad laugh. "Anyone see someone floating by the harbor recently?"

"We can't just leave this." Lore crossed her arms tight over her chest. "We can't just sit by and let it happen."

Everything was already broken because she was still alive. Still here, a wrench in the prophecy, allowing the ascension of Them all rather than the ascension of one.

Guilt knocked on her ribs like doors, slipping in and making a permanent home.

Gabe seemed to have the same thought she did. His mouth firmed to a hard line. "We don't know who will get Caeliar's power."

"So far we've been lucky, relatively," Malcolm said. "We're all on the same side. Who knows if that pattern will hold?"

It made her think of moon shadows and Bastian's tense shoulders, when they'd first arrived in Courdigne and she made him admit what was happening. *We're on the same side, aren't we?*

They were. But that side wasn't winning.

"It has to be someone in the Citadel," she said. "Every other god has been someone close to me. People who have relationships to me like Nyxara had with the other gods." Lore laughed, hoarse and thin. "At least, I assume so, since there are barely any fucking myths still around for us to read."

Gabe nodded. "So we keep an eye on the other courtiers. Anyone you've spent time with."

"And then what?"

He had no answer. None of them did.

Alie's fingers tapped a nervous rhythm on her forearm as she stared at the prophecy, like she could make the words change shape and become answers instead. "We should talk to Anton."

Two pairs and one lone eye swinging to her, all wide.

She shrugged. "He's the one who heard this prophecy, right?" Her hand cut to the glass like it held a spider instead of paper. "Maybe he remembers more than he wrote down."

"I agree. We need all the answers we can get." Even if they made no difference. Lore tried not to think of that. All the answers in the world meant nothing if there was no loophole to get them out of this.

"He's mad," Malcolm said. "*Extremely* mad, madder than when he was the Priest Exalted."

"Having a rosebush grown through you will do that," Gabe growled.

"And has he said anything lucid since, Your Holiness?" Venom in Malcolm's tone. "I know you've been speaking to him regularly. What wisdom has he imparted? Or has he just raved?"

Gabe didn't respond, but the flame behind him climbed higher.

"I don't see what other choice we have," Alie said, frosty. The room seemed to go colder, like winter wind pushed at its edges, but maybe that was Lore's imagination. "Who else are we supposed to ask?"

Malcolm threw up his hands. "The man doesn't have enough mind left to tell us anything useful, and even if he did, how would we know he isn't lying?"

"We wouldn't." Lore tapped her temple with a rueful half smile. "But the goddess in my head probably would."

"And you're willing to trust Her?" Gabe's voice was a low rumble.

"I don't have much choice, do I?" Lore replied.

"A theme appears," Malcolm muttered darkly. "Fine. We'll talk to the mad priest."

The plan was made as they walked back through the damp stone hallways beneath the Church, as they made their way back up the narrow, rarely used stairs with Gabe's un-guttering torch lighting their way.

At midnight, when the sun was gone and Nyxara was loudest in Lore's head, she and Gabe would sneak out to the Presque Mort's garden, to the greenhouse where Anton's ravaged body was rooted. They'd hear what the priest had to say, measure it against Nyxara, and tomorrow morning, the four of them would meet in the confessional room to extract what sense from it they could.

"What about Bastian?" Even as she asked, Lore knew what the answer would be. What it'd have to be. "Shouldn't he be involved? Apollius is weak at night, he could come with us and get some answers."

She brought up the rear of their procession, and thus saw the other three exchange furtive looks. They weren't even trying to be subtle. "That isn't a good idea," said Malcolm, the unofficial spokesman. "Not if he's as far gone as you say."

All of them had a god's influence, now, and Lore wanted to call them hypocrites. But Malcolm was right. Bastian was the furthest gone. Still. "It's different at night—"

"No." Gabe's answer was a cudgel, beating out any further questioning. Even as he said it, though, he wilted.

The thought of Bastian shackled to Apollius seemed to weigh on him as heavily as it did on her.

He looked at Lore, worry in his eye. "Is he…I mean, how bad…"

She wanted to reassure him. Didn't want to infect him with

the same endless dread she felt every time she thought of Apollius forcing Bastian out of his own body. But ignorance wouldn't help anything.

"Bad," she murmured.

Gabe pulled in a shaky breath.

A few strides ahead, Alie's lips pressed together, her eyes finding the floor before flickering up again. Lore wondered if she was thinking of her father, of what Apollius had done in Bastian's body.

Maybe she wasn't quite as cold to Severin's fate as she wanted to appear. Even though he wasn't her father, even though he'd been cruel, he'd still been part of her life for twenty-four years. Those knots were hard to untangle.

Gods, Lore's birth mother had only been in her life for thirteen years, none of them pleasant, and she still didn't know how to navigate *that* maze. Her mind kept dredging up images of the Night Priestess—Lilia, her name was Lilia—in the stone garden under the moon, begging her to run. Telling her that she could throw a rose into the well to signal for help. Was she waiting down there? Checking the packed dirt floor every day, waiting for a crumpled bloom?

It didn't matter. Lore didn't want her help. Lilia wouldn't know any more than Anton would, and Lore would rather deal with Anton. She'd rather do just about anything than ever have to deal with the catacombs and who lived in them ever again.

Even if Nyxara wanted her to go there. *Especially* if Nyxara wanted her to go there. Lore had to keep reminding herself that she couldn't fully trust the Buried Goddess, for all that they seemed to have largely the same goal.

And maybe that felt a little bit like an excuse. But it was an excuse she would cling to.

In her head, something like a sigh.

The thin cloister hallways opened back up into the soaring

ceilings and stained-glass alcoves of the Church proper. Gabe looked at Lore. "Tonight."

"Do you want to come see him?" she asked.

Malcolm and Alie looked away, pretending not to hear.

Gabe wavered. His eye fixed to the wall, like he didn't want to look at her; his tattooed hands twitched. "No," he said finally. "I can't . . . no."

And she couldn't make him.

With a final glance, Gabe turned away. He'd gotten rid of his torch when they reached the top of the stairs, but the sunset light in the windows still outlined him in flame colors, lit his hair like a wick.

Malcolm gave her and Alie a nod and headed in what she assumed was the direction of the library. Lore sighed when he was gone. "You might have to lead us out of here," she said to Alie. "I'm all turned around."

"I'm not going back to the Citadel just yet, I don't think." Alie sounded distracted, a line drawing between her brows as she turned in the opposite direction Gabe had gone. Lore peered at their surroundings, getting her bearings again—Alie was headed toward the hallway with all the stained-glass windows of the pantheon, one for each god.

"Where are you going, then?"

A pause before Alie answered, and when she did, there was a hoarse chuckle in her voice, something that could resolve into a laugh or a sob. The same light that gilded Gabe in fire made her ethereal, made her seem not-quite-there, a mist you could walk through. "To pray. Maybe. I'm not sure yet."

Chapter Twenty-Nine

Unsanctioned Mortem users who weren't physically strong enough for the mines on the Burnt Isles were often executed and dissected instead. Many medical discoveries were made this way, including the life-extending powers of poison, though the most interesting discovery the physicians made was, strangely, in the throat. According to records, every Mortem channeler had a small pool of water emit from their mouth in the minutes after death. Early accounts of the deaths of other elemental channelers record the same phenomenon.

–Archived reports from Kettleburgh University, Ratharc

It took Lore a moment to find her way out of the Church—damn whoever had designed it and the Citadel, what did they have against easy navigation?—and once she did, finally spilling through the doors and onto the southern green, the sun was half sunk below the horizon, the sky bisected in swaths of pink and gold.

Will you actually be any help tonight? she asked Nyxara as she trekked through the garden, the lattices of roses and leaf-choked arbors. There'd been hardly any rain, and the sun burned too brightly, leaving the edges of petals curling and brown, the vines rattling dry.

I have only ever wanted to help. Her answer was faint, still bound away by the sliver of sun. *I never wanted this.*

This, meaning the prophecy, Apollius reigning again. *This*, meaning everything that spun from Lore's refusal to die.

Sorry to inconvenience You by not getting murdered, Lore snarled, stomping up to the double Citadel doors.

Don't be, She said. *This has to end, one way or another.*

It wasn't exactly comforting.

The halls were nearly deserted as Lore made her way up to the apartment she shared with Bastian, most courtiers getting in some rest before a night full of parties and debauchery. She wondered if any of them thought it strange that Bastian had removed himself from such things when he became the Sainted King, if they'd expected him to continue on with his frivolity even after he had the crown. Maybe not. Maybe they didn't spend much time thinking of him at all, now that he wasn't their Sun Prince, now that he was Apollius's chosen. Holiness was a cage they'd resigned him to.

She stopped at the bottom of the stairs, feeling aimless. Surely there was something else she could do, something other than wait around for midnight. Briefly, she thought of going down to the holding cells, trying to interrogate Caius and Maxon herself. She wasn't much of a diplomat, but that could work in her favor.

A voice, coming around the corner. Lore ducked into an alcove on instinct, shoving herself into the scant space left between the wall and a statue of a mermaid on a plinth. Bastian had sold many of the art pieces in the Citadel to libraries and universities to fund the citizen payments, but apparently no library or university wanted this one.

"It's strange, is all." A voice she didn't recognize, though that wasn't saying much. Lore hadn't had time to familiarize herself with every minor noble in court. "If I had two obviously high-ranking officials from an enemy Empire in custody, I would be crowing it from the rooftops. It's almost like he doesn't want Jax to know."

"And why would he?" Another masculine voice, lazy and uninterested. "To start a war?"

"War has already started." A loud swallow, the other speaker drinking from either a flask or a wineglass. "All I'm saying is it seems odd to lock them away for a fucking *explosion* and then do nothing. I know we were all surprised by the deathwitch's stunt, but really, does no one else wonder what his plan is? Or if he's just gone mad, like they say old August did at the end?"

Lore stiffened, the plinth digging into her middle.

"What do you think, Amelia?" the voice asked. "Is the King mad, or shortsighted, or just more interested in fucking the poison Queen than ruling?"

The Lady Demonde must have snuck out from beneath the eye of her husband for a bit of respite with people her own age. Despite herself, Lore was a little proud of her.

Amelia's voice came soft. "I think that whatever the King is planning is above us. He knows what he's doing."

"High-handed words from the little churchmouse." The first speaker chuckled. "I thought you'd let go of all that religious nonsense once your parents were out of the picture, but once a churchmouse, always a churchmouse."

Amelia didn't respond. The other two courtiers began speaking of something else, their footsteps fading away. Lore stayed in the cramped corner until she could be sure they were gone, then slid back out into the hall.

Churchmouse. It tugged at her, that her and Amelia's childhood nicknames were so similar. That she'd been used and discarded by religion, too, if in a different way.

Rubbing at her hip, where the mermaid statue had undoubtedly left a bruise, Lore rushed the rest of the way to the apartments, not wanting to risk running into anyone else.

Alexis was the Presque Mort on duty at the top floor. They looked up from cleaning their nails with one of their daggers and arched a golden brow. "Did you run the entire way here?"

"As a matter of fact, I did." Lore straightened her gown, which was now damp from sweat as well as standing water from the bowels of the Church. How queenly of her. "Exercise is important."

"Hope you didn't wear yourself out." A sly smile crossed their face. "Your fiancé has been in his room basically all day. I can only assume he's waiting for you."

Bastian, locked away, battling the god in his head. Lore forced an answering smile. "I'm sure I'll catch a second wind."

Alexis snorted as Lore opened the door and stepped into the apartment.

The hush lay heavy, like a blanket smothering fire, even the burble of the fountain in the center of the solar somehow deadened. Long shadows stretched from the plants clustered by the windows, a trail that tracked the fall of the sun. In her head, Nyxara was silent, but it was an expectant kind of silence, one that wasn't restful.

Lore took the steps up to Bastian's room much more slowly than she'd taken the ones up the turret. She wasn't sure what she'd find at the top.

The spiral staircase at the end of the hall spit her out in Bastian's bedroom, her eyes narrowing to adjust to the dim.

The room was a chaos. A palm was overturned on the floor, spilling dirt across the tiles. The small table was similarly knocked over, like it'd been shoved too hard, and a vase that had been holding a bouquet of roses was now a broken jumble of pottery and petals. A tangle of blankets and pillows was heaped around the footboard of the bed, like they'd been thrashed apart.

And on the bed, curled into a ball beneath the remaining sheet, Bastian.

Quietly, scarce daring to breathe, Lore made her way through the mess to his side. Bastian's face was flushed, his shirt discarded. Scratch marks ran down his temple, livid even in the dusky light. For all that, his expression was peaceful, the slackened ease of a body that had been tense for far too long, like his mouth had held a snarl for hours.

Lightly, she reached out and touched his face.

He woke instantly, starting up from the bed with every muscle held tight, expecting a battle. Lore fought not to flinch, had to keep her hand on his skin through force of will. She didn't want Bastian to see her backing away from him.

"Shit." Bastian saw her, relaxed. He shifted to sit up, wiping at sleep-gummed eyes. "Didn't want you to see me like this," he muttered. "I look like I got tied to the back end of a runaway horse."

"Don't be vain." Even now, clammy and bloodshot as if recovering from a fever, Bastian Arceneaux was still one of the most unfairly beautiful people Lore had ever seen. She pulled her eyes away from him, surveyed the wrecked room instead. "I take it Apollius didn't play nice today."

Her tone was light, but she couldn't disguise the ache in it.

"He didn't," he said softly. "I was able to keep Him... contained... most of the day, but there were times He came forward enough to showcase His displeasure at being locked up." He gestured grandly to the overturned table, the dirt strewn from the broken potted palm. "Pity about the houseplants. That one had just gotten a new leaf."

"I'm sure it will recover." Lore almost said something about calling in Malcolm to fix it, then clamped her teeth around the words. Bastian might be getting better at keeping Apollius subdued inside his head—if wrecking his room could be called subdued—but the god was still present, and she shouldn't mention the other elemental gods awakening, taking vessels of their own.

Wise, Nyxara murmured. *He grew to regret inviting the rest of Us into power.*

The words felt like the introduction to a larger story. But the goddess didn't continue.

There was a wine bottle on the bedside table, miraculously still intact. No glass, but Bastian's lips wore telltale purple stains, harsh as bruises against his sickbed pallor. Doing the same things she did, trying to force his body into dreamless sleep.

Bastian saw her looking. "Overindulgence," he said with a weak laugh. "That's a sin, isn't it? Maybe I should go confess to Gabe."

He said the other man's name like he could use it to draw him here. Like he wanted an excuse to feel it on his tongue. They only made a whole with three parts, and one was always missing.

Lore gingerly sat down on the bed next to him; he scooted over to make room, though not so much that they weren't touching. She didn't mention Gabe. "Are you dreaming, now?"

His hand lifted, rubbed tiredly over his face again. "Just once," he answered. "But it was a long time coming. I'd had flashes of strange dreams every time we channeled together, but I didn't have a coherent one until after the explosion." His tired eyes flicked away. "I was in and out, that day. It was mostly Him, but I was there, still."

You are a wonder. She remembered that whisper, right before she lost consciousness.

Bastian shivered, and she couldn't tell if it was a residual chill from his daylong fight or a memory. "That dream was terrible enough that I didn't want to have another one."

They sat in silence for a moment. Tentatively, Bastian's hand crept into hers.

It pained her to see this man tentative. To see him reduced, his presence made thin by trying to keep hold of his mind when something so powerful was trying to take it over.

And the gesture reminded her of what Apollius said right before He killed Bellegarde. *I love My wife.* Anton and those who followed him clearly didn't want Lore—Nyxara—as part of the equation, here, but it seemed Apollius did.

So how much of this love Bastian professed for her was his own, and how much of it was the god's? How much of the love she returned belonged to her, for him or for Gabe?

You are wholly your own, Nyxara said. An echo, something the goddess had told Lore at the Mortem leak. *But I cannot speak for him.*

Lore bit the inside of her cheek, hard.

Bastian looked out the window at the near-dark. "I should get up," he said, though his voice was thin and brittle and exhausted. "Don't want to waste my few entirely lucid hours." But even as he tried to shift out of bed, he grimaced, his face going paler, making the scratches against his temple stand out in sharp relief.

"No." Her hand on his shoulder, pushing him back. An echo of before, her forcing him to take care of himself, not to run his body or his mind ragged. "Take some time to actually rest. There isn't much you can do at night, anyway."

"I'm the Sainted King." He gave her a tired grin. "I can do whatever I please."

"Not looking like deep-fried death, you can't." She pushed back his sweaty hair. "I try not to play into your constant vanity, but it's probably not a good idea for anyone to see you like this."

He deflated at that, with a sigh and a roll of his eyes. "I suppose not. Don't want to show them how the mighty have fallen."

The idea of anyone seeing him so diminished made dread curl around her stomach, especially after the conversations she'd overheard in the hall. Everything was so precarious, poised on a shatterpoint. There was nothing solid to cling to, and no one could know their weaknesses.

Bastian's hand came to her cheek again, and Lore leaned into his touch despite herself. "Will you stay?"

"Can't." She covered his hand with her own, brought it down to her lap. "I have… things to take care of."

He didn't ask what things. He *wanted* to ask, and knew she couldn't tell, because it had something to do with the god in his head, waiting behind his thoughts while the sun waited behind the horizon.

Bastian nodded, just once, then leaned back into his pillows. "Good luck, then."

Lore nodded back, feeling that infernal prickling at her eyes again. She stood quickly, before the prickling could become something liquid. "Go back to sleep."

"I'll try." But his eyes were already going unfocused, his blinks drawn out.

Lore left before she could start crying again.

Hours later, minutes before midnight, Lore slipped out the door of the apartment.

She expected a guard outside the door, but there was no one in the dark hallway, not Alexis or any other monk. Lore had been armed with a story about attending a party, about the King staying abed because he felt poorly, but apparently she didn't need it.

Well, gift horses and mouths and all that. The fewer people who saw her slipping out, the better. Gabe had probably given an order to keep them away for the night.

The halls were dark and deserted as Lore made her way through them, just as she'd anticipated. Midnight in the Citadel was reserved for parties and trysts, and such things typically took place in one's own chambers rather than out in the walkways.

The few couples and groups she did pass were too preoccupied to notice her weaving through the shadows. It made her think of going to the catacombs again, how Bastian had pretended to kiss her so the bloodcoat patrolling the halls wouldn't think anything of it.

That'd been him. Bastian and Bastian alone, his lips feathering against hers, a moment where their pretend kiss could've become real, when he'd wanted it to.

Gods, wasn't *that* the last thing she should be worried about. Once they got Apollius out of his head—and Nyxara out of hers—then they could wade through which feelings were their own and which were planted there, what they wanted weighed against what the gods did. All three of them.

Not that simple, Nyxara said.

Shut up, Lore replied.

Down the gilded corridors, through the rooms full of art and opulence. Less full than they had been, though Bastian's attempts at leveling the huge wealth gaps had tapered off the more Apollius dug into his brain. Lore scowled as she walked by an icon of the god Himself, His hands dripping garnets. It shouldn't surprise her that the god of life and the day and every-fucking-thing didn't give a shit about people dying in poverty. This was the god who'd spoken to Gerard Arceneaux about obedience and punishment, but never mentioned taking care of the people around you.

Her mood was undeniably sour as she finally pushed through the double doors into the southern green. The Presque Mort on guard just nodded at her, barely looking her direction. Gabe must've told them to expect her; Lore assumed she was probably the only person traipsing through the Citadel in a full-length black cloak in the dead of summer.

Odd that Gabe would order away the guard at her and Bastian's apartment and not here, though.

Lore didn't waste much time thinking on it. She turned right, hurrying over the dusk-dewed grass to the iron fence around the Presque Mort's garden. It was unlocked, and she slipped quietly through the gate, her cloak fluttering behind her.

The moon was full and bright, casting diffuse shadows over the ground. The heat and lack of rain meant that no new flowers had thrived, so most of the garden was still made of burnt husks from the night of the ritual. They spiked into the night air like accusing fingers, oddly sinister in the silvery light.

Her own shadow joined theirs as Lore followed the twisting paths to the greenhouse in the corner. As she passed the well, she kept her eyes straight ahead, refusing to look at it. It was covered, thankfully, the Presque Mort having moved the lid with its small statue of Apollius back into place after discovering that there was no Mortem left to leak. Malcolm said there was a minor eclipse this afternoon; she wondered if any of them had come out here to check.

She pressed her palms against her thighs, hiding the dark-gray star in the center. She hadn't let any Mortem seep out of her since that day, when she broke the stone roses, sent them to dust. Lore didn't necessarily want to think about what it meant that she was so good at containing death's power. That it wasn't even a thought in her mind, most days, as if she was made for this.

In her head, Nyxara kept Her silence.

The stone banks of flowers were streaked with ash and soot, thick with the scent of burning even though the fire was long past. Finally, the greenhouse loomed ahead. A single flickering light shone through the glass walls.

Lore pulled down her hood and stepped inside.

The greenhouse was as full as it had been the last time she was here. Pots of browning herbs, spindly decorative trees too malnourished to flower. Detritus piled up to distract from what waited behind them.

The twigs from the trees picked at her arms as Lore made her way back to that flickering light. It illuminated the space more than it should, stretching farther than was natural.

The power of fire. Hestraon in Gabe's head, not as strongly as Nyxara was in hers or Apollius in Bastian's, but there.

The Priest Exalted was a pillar of shadow in the back of the greenhouse, leaning against the glass wall dressed in Presque Mort black. His eye patch faced her, and he didn't turn her way to show his whole eye as she approached, all his attention fixed on the pitiful creature rooted into the ground.

It'd gotten worse. The roses blooming through Anton were thriving, a gruesome contrast with the rest of the garden. The bloom in the scarred orbital of his left eye had a new bud, brushing up against the runneled skin of his burnt forehead. Thorns had torn through his arms, dried blood in their wake, and more were visible just beneath the skin, pressing outward, ready to rip through at the slightest movement.

"And here comes the goddess." His voice sounded shredded, as if the thorns in his arms were waiting in his throat, too. "Two out of six, coming to visit. To what do I owe the pleasure?" An awful, tearing laugh, ripping out of his ravaged throat. "Six broken, battered cups, when there should only be one. The cycle has begun, now. You can't give back what you've taken, not while He is here. Godhood adapts."

"That seems to be our answer." Gabe's voice was harsh. He still didn't look at her. "There's no way to reverse this."

"Oh, *now* you want to reverse it?" Anton snarled. His mouth was twisted at one side, hooked through by a thorny stem. Blood and saliva dripped to the floor every time he spoke. "I knew this was what would become of you, Gabriel Remaut, son of a traitor. I tried to save you, making you holy, bringing you to a place where you'd never know power other than that of death. And this is how you repay me? Repay *Him*? Fitting that you'd become the avatar of the most traitorous god, after the Buried Goddess Herself."

His one eye rolled in Lore's direction. "Not so buried anymore, is She?"

Nerves tingled at the back of Lore's neck. "What do you mean?"

Anton smiled, or as close as he could get. "Why don't you go find out?"

"This is useless," Gabe said. His voice belied the statement, though. This was painful, and he wanted it done.

Lore was sympathetic, but she couldn't accept that there was nothing for them to do, that fate was a sealed tomb they couldn't break open. She squared her shoulders and glared at the man in the roses and ivy. "There has to be a way to make the gods... make them wait for different vessels. Better ones, more suited. Surely we can send them back to wherever they were before, where they weren't hurting anything."

"You can't *make* a god do anything, girl," Anton said. "You've read my prophecy, yes? I can see it. You read the words Apollius Himself spoke to me, as I breathed the holy smoke of the braziers, as I saw the heavens open and His light shine down." His not-quite-smile widened, making blood sheet from his mouth to the ground. Or maybe it wasn't a smile anymore. Maybe it was a grimace, now. "You read it all."

Something about that didn't read as a full truth. She riffled back through that ritual night, trying to see if there was something she was forgetting, something he might've let slip.

In the back of her head, Nyxara was silent, waiting. This must be one of the things She couldn't talk about.

"So, what?" She crossed her arms and intensified her glare on the former priest. "We just sit back and let the pantheon take us over?"

"Things move in cycles," Anton said, not really an answer. "And there is more than one way to have all the power, everything leaked from the Fount. Though *you*, pretty goddess-girl, are a complication, just as you've always been. He cannot see clearly, with you."

Lore arched a brow. "Are you going to try and get rid of me again? Might be difficult, now that you have roots."

That rasping, tearing laugh. Anton didn't answer.

But Lore's mind had latched onto something, her subconscious churning finally pulling up a helpful memory. That night, with the garden burning around them, Anton said that Apollius had spoken of Lore by name. But there'd been no mention of her in the prophecy they'd read, no mention of any names but the gods.

And there'd been those markings at the bottom of the parchment, the ones Malcolm said he couldn't read…

Lore seized Gabe's hand, tugged him out into the main part of the greenhouse. He didn't resist her pull, though his face was confused when she spun to face him. "We have to go look at the prophecy again."

His brow slashed down. "What good would that do?"

"There has to be part of it we missed. Some new information. We didn't read it all."

She expected to have to argue her point, but Gabe, surprisingly, seemed to take her at her word. He nodded, then looked over his shoulder at Anton. "I don't think he has anything to tell us."

It was a confession, almost. Anton wasn't useful. There was no reason for him to still be here.

Beyond Gabe's shoulder, she saw the former Priest Exalted twitch, more blood falling from his mouth. His eyes shone, unsound in the moonlight. "There's nothing more in that prophecy," he rasped, straining forward. "You read it all. You are doomed."

Lore glanced at Gabe. "That's as good as a confirmation that there's more to it."

Anton snarled, trying to push out of the roses that grew through his body, coming at her like an animal. Despite her deep and abiding hatred for the man, sympathy squeezed her heart.

Gabe looked at his former mentor a moment longer, his mouth flat, the tendons clear and tight in his neck. Then he turned, making his way out of the greenhouse.

"Gabe," Lore murmured. "He isn't…you should…" She couldn't quite bring herself to say the words. *He isn't really living like this. You should take him out of his misery.*

She didn't have to spell it out. Gabe's blue eye closed; his head dipped down, hiding his face from the flooding moonlight. "I can't," he whispered. "I told you. He's…"

And now it was his turn not to say the words, but Lore knew them. The shape of them, at least. He was the only kind of father Gabe had left.

With that, they left the greenhouse, the sounds of Anton snarling and blood pattering on the ground following them out.

Chapter Thirty

The truth is a wound as often as it is a comfort.
—Myroshan proverb

Lore and Gabe slipped through the night like wraiths. The moon, full and brighter than it should be, lit their way as they left the garden and ran through the green. Then into the Church, its hallways hushed with deep darkness, shadows gathering thick in the corners as the corridors narrowed into cloisters.

Gabe made another torch, started down the dark stairs. They knew where to go, now, headed straight to the door that held Anton's prophecy. Lore unlocked it, quicker this time, like the Mortem in the wall recognized her.

Inside, the lectern, the glass dome. She hadn't approached it earlier, but she did now, with the same trepidation as someone sneaking up on a sleeping wolf.

When the irrational fear that the parchment would suddenly grow claws and leap for her subsided, Lore stepped as close as she could, squinting to peer through the glare on the glass from Gabe's torch. The prophecy was written in an ornate, hard-to-decipher script. It was honestly a feat that Malcolm had been able to read it so clearly, even though that part was in Auverrani.

After she muddled her way through the part he'd read again, she came to those strange lines on the bottom of the parchment. Loops and swirls, straight dashes and angular shapes. If she didn't look directly at them, forced her vision to the side so they were only in the corner of her eye, they almost resolved into symbols, but other than that, she couldn't make any sense of them.

Break the glass. I want to see it better.

Nyxara, ending Her silence after nearly an hour. Her voice sounded fainter tonight, and Lore took that as a good sign. If reading the parchment strained the bonds that kept the goddess from speaking clearly about Apollius, it meant they were headed in the right direction.

The glass dome was firmly attached to the lectern beneath it; when Lore pushed, it didn't budge. "Think you could use some of your newfound firepower to get this thing open?"

Gabe's brow rose, but he came to stand by her side, his arms crossed over his chest as he scowled down at the prophecy. "You do realize parchment is flammable?"

"Extremely, yes."

"And that I am fairly new to the whole fire-god thing?"

It was surreal, the way they were able to joke about this. Whatever helped them cope. "I believe in you. It can't be that much harder than turning things into stone with Mortem. Just…" She waved her hand at the glass. "Point fire at the edges and melt it down, or something."

His eye rolled nearly into the back of his head, but Gabe bent to study the place where the glass was fused to the stone, pushing up his long black sleeves. "I haven't tried anything like this," he warned. "I've tried to avoid using it entirely, in fact."

Lore was fairly certain it was too late for that, but she didn't say it.

One blue eye closed. Gabe took a deep breath in through his nose, let it out through his mouth. Gently, he laid his fingers right at the seam of stone and glass.

Nothing, at first. Then a *whoosh.*

She wasn't sure what she'd expected—flames spouting from Gabe's fingertips, maybe. What she saw, instead, were threads of glowing orange, flaring with ember-crackle, seeping along the glass dome's edge.

Earlier, when Alie crooked a finger and called the wind, Lore had paid more attention to what she felt than what she'd seen. Maybe if she'd been more observant, she would've seen other threads, shimmering gossamer-thin as they shaped the air. Like Mortem and Spiritum, but thinner. Less visceral.

A soft sizzling sound, a *pop*, the glass cracking at the onslaught of heat after so long in the underground chill.

Gabe pulled up his hands quickly, closing them to fists. The threads of fire fizzled out.

"Damn." Lore's eyes were wide, her wondering gaze fixed on his fingers.

Gabe flexed his hands back and forth, warily eyeing the now-broken glass and the prophecy beneath it, like he expected the parchment to burst into delayed flames at any moment. "We shouldn't be messing with these powers if we can help it," he said, as if rebuking himself. "We should be doing everything we can to stave them off."

"Hopefully this can tell us how to do that," Lore murmured, reaching carefully through the broken dome to gingerly pick up the parchment. Belatedly, she wished for a pair of Malcolm's manuscript-handling gloves. "Hopefully this will tell us how to make the gods back off for another few centuries."

"Or indefinitely," he murmured.

The pain in his voice sliced at her. Lore's life hadn't left the hollows necessary for easy faith to grow. But Gabe's had. Gabe had made faith his everything, and now they were working against the one thing he'd been taught to anticipate, taught to hope for.

What was left, when your faith burned up? Did it leave the kind of ash that could encourage new growth, or only wasteland?

The prophecy didn't disintegrate in her hands. Tiny glass shards rained to the ground as she pulled the parchment free, glittering in the light of Gabe's torch. Lore held the parchment in front of her eyes and waited for the gibberish scribbles at the bottom to resolve into something she could read.

They didn't.

Am I doing this right? she asked the goddess in her head.

When Nyxara's answer came, it was hushed. *Let Me.*

Only two words, but they swept Lore's nervous system like a poison, too much meaning packed into scant syllables. Let Her come forward. Let Her be in control.

"No." Lore didn't realize she'd said it aloud until Gabe's head swung toward her, blue eye narrowed, his hand on the hilt of the dagger in his chest harness. She pressed her lips together so the rest of the words were only in her mind, not wanting to scare him. *You said You were different. You said You didn't want what Apollius did—*

I don't, Lore. She sounded so weary. *I don't want to take you over. But that script is ancient and I'm the only one of the four of Us who can read it.*

The four of Us. Her, Nyxara, Gabe, and Hestraon, somewhere in Gabe's head. Lore swallowed. *Is Hestraon like You? Does He speak?*

No, Nyxara said, a mourning undercurrent winding through the word. *They all diminished too quickly, when They left.*

And Lore wanted to ask about that, too, but there was a sparking in her head, a twinge of pain. She gritted her teeth against it, and knew that Nyxara was butting up against her bonds, that she wouldn't be able to say anything more.

So she relaxed, or tried to, settling back on her heels, softening the muscles around her tight-closed eyes, her jaw. *How do I do this?*

Just don't fight, Nyxara said, and then the goddess surged forward.

It was, terrifyingly, not an unpleasant sensation. It felt like falling asleep after a long day, like allowing your body to melt into a mattress. Lore's thoughts went fuzzy and blunted, and though she could still see the room—the stone walls, the broken glass, the prophecy in her hands and Gabe behind it, looking at her like he knew something was wrong but couldn't place what—everything was blurry and left trails when it moved, streaking paint or comet burn. It felt a little like channeling Mortem, the flow of her blood slowing, congealing; her skin going cold.

With marked effort, she managed to focus on the parchment before her, the curving lines around the bottom, though her eyes had become the secondary pair in this body. Her vision bifurcated, splitting before coming back together again.

And the symbols on the page resolved.

They weren't words, at least not in any language Lore could read—Nyxara said it was ancient, and Lore was woefully only able to read Auverrani, Caldienan in a pinch. But though the symbols weren't words, she knew what they meant anyway, Nyxara's understanding becoming her own.

Lore is the key, the catalyst, the seed. The one who was needed; the rest were placeholders. The echo of divinity begins in her, then takes root.

The seed of the apocalypse, her mother had called her. The ground from which chaos grew, called by name. And *placeholders*: That had to mean the Night Witch. The others the Buried Watch sent into the obsidian tomb, who came out with something missing. Lesser vessels, not meant for this like she was.

There was more. *Should the other gods come into Their power, the one who desires to live forever must kill Them all again, for true immortality comes only to the one who holds the whole of the Fount. Power is made and unmade in the same way, and those who live lives parallel will be hollowed out.*

A choice must be made among the three who care most. Help will come from the place that was fled. Someone must mend what has been broken.

This coded last part of the prophecy read differently from the first, as if it had been imparted by a different entity. Anton had communed with Apollius; what if something else had slipped through, too? Something that didn't want the Bleeding God's dominion? A remnant of some other consciousness, something that Anton didn't understand as he scribbled these symbols.

Nyxara surged back as quickly as she'd come forward, a tide receding to the sea. Lore gasped as she did, hitting her knees on the hard stone, pulling in lungfuls of cold, stale air.

None of you are safe. Nyxara's voice was afraid, and a fearful god was terrifying. *He wants it all, this time.*

"What do you mean?" Lore asked, defaulting to speaking aloud in her fragile state, but Nyxara didn't answer. It was impossible to tell time down here, but they must be creeping close to dawn, numbing her sense of Nyxara, quieting Her voice.

"Are you talking to Her?" Gabe said the pronoun like a curse. Unfair of him, really. He had a god living in his brain, too.

Lore chose not to comment on his rudeness, wiping at her mouth as she nodded. Now wasn't the time.

"Anything helpful?" he prompted.

"I'm not sure, to be honest." *A choice must be made among the three that care most. Help will come from the place that was fled.*

Someone to fix the broken, but there was so *much* broken.

The parchment was on the floor where Lore had dropped it; Gabe picked it up, gave it a cursory examination, and put it back on the pedestal. It didn't look any worse for wear.

Still, Lore peered at it morosely. "Malcolm will kill us if he finds out we touched that without gloves."

"I think Malcolm is a bit too preoccupied to care." Gabe turned toward the door to the chamber. "Come on. It should be morning soon."

Lore sealed up the chamber again, leaving the mess of the glass dome scattered across the floor. She and Gabe made their way back up the stairs and into the cloisters in silence, moving as quickly as they had before. Weak morning light filtered through the stained-glass windows of the Church proper.

She didn't realize how much she'd wanted some kind of absolution from the prophecy until she didn't get it—Lore had known in abstract that her own ascension had caused everyone else's, that her living had been the gateway that allowed the powers of the gods to find new hosts in her and the people she cared about. The people she kept close, then and now. Lives lived parallel.

Selfish, selfish, selfish.

And who has taught you that is a bad thing? Nyxara sounded almost angry.

Of course it's a bad thing. Lore ground her teeth in her jaw. *Of course it's bad, when it means everyone is going down instead of just me. I'm no great loss.*

Every single person is a great loss, Nyxara snarled in her head. *No one is lesser. Changes on these scales always take more than one person to tip them, even if that person is a god. Don't let Him make His own selfishness someone else's burden to bear.*

Gabe turned down the hall with all the windows depicting the pantheon. The glow through Nyxara's window made the floor in front of it look bruised. Stepping into that purple-black-blue light was soothing on Lore's skin, like shade after sun.

Find another way. A pause, Her next words barely perceptible at all, disintegrating into nothing as night fully gave way to day. *Find Me. Catacombs, Lore.*

Then Nyxara was gone.

Lore and Gabe didn't see anyone as they wound through the uncharacteristically deserted Church. It apparently made Gabe feel like it was safe to talk. "I assume the rest of the prophecy didn't tell you how to stop this." He didn't try to hide his defeat. His shoulders were a crooked line, his hair disheveled in the colored light of the windows.

"Not really." But it had told her something—that bit at the end, about power being made and unmade. About how the one who wanted immortality would try to kill the other gods as they rose.

"It told me you have to leave," Lore said, suddenly sure of herself. "All of you who are showing any sign of…of new power. That prophecy said that if all the gods rose again, whoever wanted true immortality had to kill Them. That has to be Apollius, right?"

"That doesn't make any sense."

"None of this does! We know godhood isn't synonymous with immortality; why else would He return? He's been living in the Shining Realm all these years, or at least living *somewhere*, and now He decides to come back? Why, if not because there was something here He wants?"

"He'd always promised to return." But Gabe looked doubtful. "He's always said He would make His kingdom anew."

"But what does that *mean*, Gabe?" Lore threw up her hands. "What if it's always been about His bid for immortality, and not about the faithful at all? What if it's only ever been about what He wants, and damn everyone else?"

She could feel the truth of it, burning beneath her heart, a seed set there by Nyxara's words and watered by her own certainty. Once, as a child, she'd seen a crocodile down on the beach, sitting with its mouth open in the shallows, still as death. She was smart enough not to get too close, but she sat down on the sand and watched it. Watched as a bird picked its way through the surf in its direction, not noticing the danger because it never moved, because it was part of the landscape, something the bird could write off as normal. Eventually, that bird had hopped in the crocodile's mouth.

And the crocodile had snapped its teeth shut.

It was remarkably, horribly easy to make people accept terrible things if you made them part of the normal landscape. If you designed the world around them so they didn't stick out. People were easy to dupe into thinking that powerful meant benevolent, especially when they had no way out, no recourse but to live beneath something unfair. Reduce their sense of choice—make it seem like they could accept what was, or have nothing—and they'd fall in line.

Because sometimes, finding another way felt impossible.

"Apollius is not good." Why did her lip wobble as she said it? Lore had never thought of herself as religious, never thought of herself as someone who could be deluded into thinking the gods were good. But now, saying it plainly still felt like pulling a bandage off a wound that might not ever heal. "So why keep talking around it? Maybe we should be looking for a way to end Him before He can end us." She took a deep breath. "End Him, before He can make the world in His image. Because if we've learned anything, it's that His image isn't all that great."

Gabe stared at her, shock in his one visible eye. "You can't mean that."

"I can," she murmured. "I do. The gods were human once, Gabe. They have human faults. I won't let one end the people I love. I won't let Him end me."

He turned away from her, fisting a hand in his hair, leaning against the nearest window. It was Hestraon's, Lore noticed, but she didn't bring that up.

A full minute, at least, filled with Gabe's long breaths, ragged and hovering at the edge of sobs. When he spoke, he didn't change position, still leaning against the window. "Did the prophecy say anything else?" he asked, apparently choosing to ignore the fact that Lore had just declared war on his god. "Anything about how we might… might lessen the hold?"

Lore sighed. "It said, *Power is made and unmade in the same way*. I'm too tired to think hard on it right now. We both need sleep, then we'll meet with Alie and Malcolm."

She didn't tell him the very last part. Choices made, help from a place fled, mending the broken. She kept that to herself.

Gabe nodded, his forehead still against the window. Then he started down the hall, not looking at the glass depiction of Hestraon, not looking at her.

They emerged from the doors of the Church and into chaos.

All the Presque Mort they hadn't seen in the halls were here instead, rushing back and forth from the double doors of the Citadel, escorting still-sleepy courtiers from within to wait on the green. All of them looked as confused as Lore felt, murmuring to each other in worried voices.

Gabe grabbed a passing Presque Mort's arm. Alexis. "What happened?"

"Dead body," they answered, face drawn into concerned lines. Their eyes darted to Lore. "Found inside the royal apartments. She was mangled up pretty badly, but they think they can get a positive identification from her husband, if he'll ever stop screaming."

A mangled body, in her and Bastian's rooms. "Do they have a guess who it was, then?"

"Amelia Demonde," Alexis said.

Chapter Thirty-One

I am the only authority. All powers will be held by Me alone, and eternity will give up its secrets.

–The Book of Holy Law, Tract 1004*

The physicians hadn't done anything to make Amelia's body look...well, less mangled. Not that there was much point. The body was laid where it'd been found in Bastian's solar, a smear of lurid red against the pale tiles, away from the prying eyes of courtiers. Amelia's neck yawned open, flaps of skin and sinew folding back to reveal the wet, yellowish gleam of the esophagus. One of her eyes was a bloody mess that Lore didn't want to examine too closely, but it appeared she'd been stabbed there, too. Her nails were broken from scrabbling on the tiles. The Presque Mort had rolled her over so she faced the domed ceiling, but she'd been found on her stomach, one hand stretched out beseechingly.

A pool of water puddled out from Amelia's corpse, shining on the tiles, diffused blood lacing the edges like red ribbons. From

*Part of Apollius's letters from the early Church, never officially recognized as part of the Compendium, but kept in the records of the Priest Exalted.

the angle of her head, though she'd been turned over, it almost looked like it might've come from Amelia's mouth.

Lore had never liked her, and Amelia had made it obvious that she never liked Lore, either. But her throat still constricted, and her chest still felt like it was being squeezed by a giant fist. She still thought of that day at the Demonde estate, when they sat next to each other so neither of them would have to be alone.

Gabe stood behind Lore, very still, his jaw clenched against the grisly scene and one hand hovering near Lore's back, like he wanted to place it there for comfort and couldn't quite make himself.

Part of her wanted him to. But most of her attention was on Bastian.

He stood at the other end of the room, back straight and eyes narrowed, sipping nonchalantly from a china cup as if he wasn't going to let a little thing like a murder interrupt his morning. Gone was the tiredness around his eyes and the pallor in his skin; he looked well rested and alert, regal. He met her gaze, gave her the edge of a sharpened smile, and lifted his cup in her direction like it was a salute.

The sun was high in the sky by now. Bastian wasn't in control anymore; this was Apollius wearing Bastian like a cloak.

And Apollius seemed anything but concerned about the dead woman in His apartment.

A few Presque Mort had stayed in the room, congregating by the walls, occasionally casting worried glances at Gabe as if they wished he would tell them what to do. The guard outside the apartment had been the one to discover Amelia—apparently, he'd been instructed by the King yesterday to come check on Lore at dawn, and had seen the carnage when he'd opened the door.

That bit of news sat uneasily. Lore remembered the mess of Bastian's room, how he'd locked himself in to try to keep Apollius from using him during daylight hours. If he remembered getting out, remembered Apollius breaking through his control, he would've told her.

But he'd given an order that made it clear he knew Lore was planning to sneak out and wanted to catch her in the act. Which meant that Apollius had taken control at some point, and Bastian didn't remember, just like on the trip back from Courdigne.

They were in deep shit.

The attending physician by the body cranked open Amelia's mouth, for reasons unknown to Lore. She flinched back at the cracking sound. Rigor mortis had set in already.

After a cursory look at the inside of Amelia's mouth—what could the reason for that possibly be, it wasn't like there'd be clues to her murder in her teeth—and a murmured word with his assistant, the physician glanced up at Bastian. "Your Majesty, I'm afraid we won't be able to determine official cause of death without performing an autopsy, but—"

"Do you have the tools for such a thing?" Bastian's voice was crisp, as if this were a normal conversation to be having at breakfast time. "With you, I mean."

The physician blinked owlishly behind round spectacles. "I don't know... I mean, I have some tools, but not all—"

"Send your man for them." Bastian gestured to the assistant with his cup. "Make it quick, please. I'd like to have an answer for the grieving widower sooner rather than later. He's relishing the theatrics of it all."

The flippancy of it nearly made Lore flinch. Assistant and physician shared one wide-eyed look, but then the assistant leapt to his feet to comply with the King's wishes.

"The cause of death looks rather straightforward to me." Lore raised her voice enough to carry across the cavernous room. "What with the visible esophagus."

"The bleeding from that particular wound is not heavy enough to have been the cause." The physician stood from the corpse, leaving Amelia's mouth hanging grotesquely open. "The cut didn't hit the artery."

"Still seems like it did enough damage."

"Plenty, yes, but not enough to be the cause of death." He looked down into Amelia's open mouth again. "She died quickly."

There was that, at least.

The gleam of his spectacles went back to Bastian. "Your Majesty, I don't mean to question you..."

"Then don't," Apollius murmured with Bastian's mouth.

The little physician squared his shoulders. "I don't mean to question you, but surely you don't intend for me to perform my autopsy here?"

Apollius was quiet for a moment, sipping from His mug. His eyes burned at Lore from across the room. "My court is rattled," He said. "A murder taking place now, right after the dock explosion, is making tensions run high. I'd rather not stoke them further by carrying a freshly killed body through the Citadel."

The words made sense. The way He said them didn't. Like a challenge, almost, His eyes more gold than brown and never leaving Lore's.

As if He wanted her here for this. Wanted her to see.

"Do the autopsy here," Apollius continued, "and the results do not leave this room."

A swallow worked down the other man's throat. Then he inclined his head. "As you command."

The other Presque Mort in the solar—Alexis and a woman whose name Lore didn't know—exchanged wary glances with each other, and then with Gabe, asking a silent question.

The Priest Exalted firmed his lips, looked at Amelia's body again. Then he jerked his chin toward the door.

Alexis nearly breathed a sigh of relief as they and the woman went to exit.

"Alexis," Apollius called after them.

The Presque Mort turned around, expression carefully nonchalant.

"The orders given you were good," Apollius said, "but next time, you will wait for mine. We must be of an accord, the Church and the crown. Under one rule. Don't you agree?"

Alexis nodded. Then they bowed, stilted and quick. With another quick glance at Gabe, they disappeared out the door.

One more challenge, this one less subtle. Apollius marking Himself as the leader of the Presque Mort, not Gabe.

Lore bit her cheek and tried to keep from nervous fidgeting.

The assistant returned with the tools—scalpels, knives, a saw with serrated teeth that made Lore's bones hurt just to look at. The assistant eyed his employer; the physician gave a nod and a quick jerk of his hands toward the body, a *what am I supposed to do?* kind of gesture that Lore deeply empathized with.

Still looking skeptical, the assistant handed the physician the saw. The man dropped to his knees, lining up the blade over Amelia's chest.

Lore looked away. Once the sounds started, she wanted to plug her ears, too, but couldn't quite make herself, not when Apollius was watching, not when He was clearly doing this for her benefit. She stared at the wall until her vision blurred, trying to tune out the sound of the saw, the snap of ribs and the meaty pull of muscle, the liquid *splat* of interior matter hitting the floor.

When the sounds stopped, she blinked and made her eyes focus again, looking down at Amelia's corpse.

Blood gloved the physician from fingertip to elbow as he set the saw aside, trading it out for a set of gleaming scissors. Those sounds weren't so bad, though the way he brushed bone splinters from his lap before he began made her stomach lurch. Carefully, he cleared out the stringy remains of veins and fat and sinew, opening the cavity of Amelia's chest farther, folding aside her lungs like wings to reveal the gory knot of her heart.

She was a person hours ago, Lore reminded herself. A person

with thoughts and wishes who had people she loved and was loved in return, and even if she wasn't very nice, she didn't deserve this. To be made into a mess of blood and flesh and broken bone, to have her organs examined out here in the open like interesting trinkets. For all Lore's familiarity with death, the savagery still made her head swim.

With a vile squishing noise, the physician grasped Amelia's heart and tugged it from her chest. He held it up in the morning light, incongruously dark against the pale tile and bright-gleaming glass and pattering fountain of Bastian's solar. A drop of blood fell from it and spattered on his spectacles. Another fell to the pool of water around Amelia's head, starbursting from red to pink.

"Hmm," he said, turning the organ over in his bloody hands.

"Something interesting?" Apollius sipped his coffee again.

"Indeed." Apparently, the physician had buried his misgivings in his work; he no longer sounded apprehensive, just filled with curiosity. "The muscles are warped. It's congruent with what happens when the heart spasms, almost, but not exactly." He brought the macabre trophy closer to his eyes. "It looks almost like the heart... beat too much, too quickly. Cycled through too much blood, then stopped abruptly. Perhaps that wasn't the cause of death, just the precursor..."

Lore had stopped hearing him before he trailed off into academic wonderings, stuck on what he'd said before. Channeling Spiritum felt like that: too much air in your lungs. Too much blood in your veins. Too many beats of your heart.

Amelia hadn't been able to channel Spiritum. But if someone manipulated the Spiritum in her body...

Lore's eyes found Apollius's again. He was looking at her, His face arranged in the necessary grave stoicism for a King. But there was a cruel glee in His golden eyes.

"This is interesting," the physician continued, oblivious. He'd set down the heart in a sticky pool on the floor and used the scissors to cut through the muscle of Amelia's lungs. "There's water in here. In the esophagus, too, it looks like." In a move that nearly made Lore gag, he leaned forward so his nose was almost inside the corpse and took a quick breath. "And it smells like salt. At least, the water in the lungs does."

"Interesting, indeed," Apollius murmured around His cup.

The physician dipped his fingers into the pool around Amelia's head, lifted them to his nose. "Not salt water here, though," he said to himself. He held out his hand to his assistant; the other man riffled through the bag he'd brought and pulled out a small cup, handing it over. The physician scooped some of the water on the floor into it, capped the cup carefully, then did the same to the bloody water in Amelia's lungs. "I'd have to test them to be sure, but it appears that the water in her lungs and the water on the floor aren't the same, though the trajectory would make it seem as though she coughed it up."

"A dry drowning," Apollius said. "How could such a thing have happened?"

"I'm not sure," the physician replied, sounding almost excited by the prospect of a medical mystery to solve. "I'll run some tests, surely, ask around to everyone who spent time with the subject prior to last night..."

Apollius wasn't listening. Apollius was still staring right at Lore. The cup in His hand tipped forward, just long enough for her to see what was in it.

Water. Just water.

His fingers twitched, a slight movement that no one else would notice unless they were watching for it. But Lore was, Lore couldn't look away. Not even when the bloody water around Amelia's head started creeping toward her hem.

"It was Apollius."

Lore didn't know why she was keeping her voice down. They were all in the confessional booth, the curtain was closed and so was the door beyond it, shutting the bloodcoat who'd been ordered to accompany her to Gabe's lessons behind it—after Amelia, Apollius had overridden Bastian's orders again, giving Lore another constant guard.

"So now we're accusing a god of murder." Malcolm ran his hand wearily down his face.

"Doesn't seem that far off to me." Alie sat on the bench by the wall, waving her hand in her face to try and generate a breeze. It was cooler inside the Church, but four people in a booth built for two ovened the air. Lore couldn't help thinking that she *could* generate a breeze, very easily, but Alie didn't seem interested in using Lereal's power to keep from sweating. "Nothing in the Compendium ever gave me the impression the gods were kind. There were all sorts of Tracts about destroying your enemies, revenge killings..."

"Point taken," Malcolm said. "I'm not saying He didn't do it, I'm saying that it doesn't change anything. We can't accuse the King—"

"It wasn't Bastian." Lore's voice came a little louder, that time. Her engagement ring cut into the meat of her finger. "It was Apollius, in Bastian's body. He's pushed Bastian out entirely, at least during the day."

A shiver went through Gabe, leaning against the latticed wall that separated the penitent and priest halves of the confessional. She'd glanced at him as they left the apartments. His face was stricken, lost, as if seeing Apollius wearing Bastian's body had grabbed his heart and twisted it.

"I understand." Malcolm seemed like he was getting tired of being contradicted every few words, which Lore supposed was fair. "But I'm saying that if we accuse Apollius, we're accusing

Bastian. Unless you want to explain what's happening to him, to *us*, to the entire Court of the Citadel, and I can't see that going well for anyone."

"For Him, maybe," Alie muttered, capitalization clear in her tone. "But certainly not for us."

"The last thing we need right now is a murderer King," Gabe said quietly. "An empty throne would be as good as a written invitation to Jax."

"You have far more faith in the justice system than I do." Alie scowled. "Arceneaux Kings have gotten away with worse than murder."

Gabe rubbed at the empty socket under his eye patch. "If there was someone we trusted who we could install as regent, someone the court would accept, then we could take Bastian somewhere he couldn't hurt anyone, couldn't hurt himself..."

He trailed off, caught in what he assumed to be futile wishful thinking. But Lore's and Alie's eyes met across the tiny confessional room. A moment, then Alie looked away, chewing on her bottom lip.

"We don't know why Amelia was killed," Malcolm said after a minute of considering silence. "Or why Apollius did it like... like that."

With Spiritum. He'd killed her with Spiritum, manipulating it somehow, then sliced her open as if to hide the evidence. At least from everyone but Lore. He'd made it clear He wanted her to know exactly who had murdered Amelia Demonde, and bloodied the entire damn solar to do it.

"Not just Spiritum." Lore sank down onto the bench beside Alie. "He used water magic, too."

"That's impossible." Malcolm shook his head. "He can only—"

"He did, I promise you. I watched Him do it." Lore crossed her arms against a shudder, thinking of the cold look in His eyes, the way he tipped His cup so she could see the water in it as the bloody pool inched across the floor.

The elemental gods had claimed their new vessels, and all of them were accounted for in this room. All except Caeliar of the sea.

Lives lived parallel.

Lore thought of those memory-dreams, the ones that hadn't returned since she and Nyxara had begun communicating in earnest. A slender figure admonishing her—admonishing Nyxara—for having doubts about Apollius's proposal. Saying *She* would accept, if Nyxara didn't.

Amelia wasn't a friend, but she was someone affected by Lore staying in the Citadel. More than most, even, since Lore had interrupted Amelia's plans to be Bastian's Queen. A congruency to the lives Nyxara and Caeliar had lived before, one chosen and one vying.

"Caeliar," she murmured. "Caeliar came to Amelia. And when Apollius killed her, He took that power."

She expected someone to push back, but apparently they were all inured to strangeness now. Other than a slight ripple of surprise, none of them really reacted.

"If that's the reason He killed Amelia, surely He could've done it in a less ostentatious way." Alie sounded almost insulted. "Why would He make it so public?"

"To cast suspicion on someone else, maybe?" Lore said.

"Maybe," Gabe agreed, though he didn't sound convinced. "Though I can't think of anyone it would behoove Him to frame." A harsh laugh. "Other than me, maybe, but I have a fairly ironclad alibi."

The last thing Bastian would want was to harm Gabe. Lore hoped, fervently, that Bastian could hold on enough to keep that from happening.

She threaded her fingers through her loose hair, tugged at the roots as she leaned over her knees. "Amelia was loyal to Apollius. She wanted Him to be the only god. If she knew she was becoming Caeliar, would she have offered herself to Him? Is that why she was there?"

"There's one way to find out," Alie murmured.

Lore raised a brow in her direction.

Alie shrugged. "You could raise the body and ask."

"I..." Lore was shocked she hadn't thought of it before, this thing she'd been duped into thinking was her purpose in the Citadel in the first place. The idea of it set a spiral of dread in her gut, but it wasn't a bad plan. "I *could* do that."

"Why?" Gabe asked. His face was impassive, but a veritable hurricane brewed in his one eye. "It doesn't matter what led up to her murder, whether she offered herself as a sacrifice or not."

"It matters to me." Lore said it through her teeth. "Because if she didn't sacrifice herself, if this was just a murder, justice has to be done. It's what Bastian would want, and maybe it could be a solution to our problem, if we could get him... sent away."

"You *want* Bastian on the Burnt Isles?" Gabe asked.

"No." She tugged at her hair again. "No, I just want him safe. Safe from what Apollius might make him do next." A hoarse laugh itched at her throat. "And maybe it'd be better if he was there, if war is imminent. He might be safer on the Isles than in the Citadel, once all is said and done."

Gabe kept whatever he wanted to say in the clenched line of his jaw, but the light in his eye softened. He wanted Bastian safe, too.

"Do we know where they took her?" Malcolm asked, after a pause.

"A vault, I'd assume," Alie replied. "The Devereauxs had onc."

But Lore was shaking her head before the other woman finished. "Not anymore. They surrendered it as part of their sentence." She remembered pieces of that day, one in the stretch of fugue-time right after the ritual, right after Bastian became King. Sitting on the silver chair next to his throne, wishing she could hide behind it instead, when she was just his deathwitch instead of his future Queen. When he was himself, mostly, instead of the avatar of a vengeful god.

"One of the city vaults, then?" Malcolm crossed his arms and tapped his fingers apprehensively against his biceps. "It will be difficult to sneak out to see the body, in that case."

"I don't think that's where they're taking her," Gabe rumbled. "I think they're putting her in the catacombs." He looked to Lore. "At least, that's what I gathered from what Bast—what Apollius said."

Lore hadn't paid much attention to what happened after Amelia's impromptu autopsy, as she rushed from the room with her hand over her mouth, rapidly swallowing to keep from further fouling the marble floors. But she did recall Apollius's voice telling the physician to "keep her close."

Now, in the confessional room that was rapidly becoming too humid for comfort, Lore nodded. "That'd make sense, I guess."

"Especially since there's no danger to being buried underground anymore," Malcolm said, with a slanted look at Lore.

"You're welcome, world." She wiggled her fingers listlessly, showing off the gray star in her palms, right where Malcom's and Gabe's candle tattoos were.

Catacombs, Nyxara had murmured into her head, just before night gave way fully into morning. *Find Me.*

It seemed like the goddess would finally be getting what She wanted.

"If we're going to look, we should do it now." Gabe straightened from the wall. "If Apollius told a guard to come look for you at dawn this morning, the chances of you being able to sneak out again tonight are low."

"And what happens when you cause a panic by being gone for hours?" Alie asked. "I doubt that bloodcoat outside will stand there waiting until sundown."

"He will if I give him a distraction," Gabe said.

Alie's pale brow arched. "What kind?"

"This kind." Gabe held out his hand to the velvet curtain covering the confessional. "You should probably move, Malcolm."

He did, squishing onto the bench beside Alie, who elbowed him with a scowl. Gathering orange-red lines, like embers made thread, crackled in the air as Gabe pulled them from the heat in the atmosphere, from the sconce on the wall.

The curtain burst into flames.

"Follow me." Gabe grabbed Lore's arm and turned toward the priest's side of the confessional, wrenching open the wrought-iron lattice. "Back hallways. Malcolm, you take Alie to the Citadel, and Lore and I will head to the catacombs."

"Excellent," Malcolm muttered as he pushed Alie in front of him, coughing on the acrid smoke. "First a murder, then a fire. Truly, I'm having a wonderful day."

Chapter Thirty-Two

A lesson left unlearned is a lodestone. Somehow, you will always return.

–Kadmaran proverb

Once in the back tunnels of the Church, their group split, Malcolm and Alie headed in one direction while Gabe and Lore took the other. She remembered this path, the one that led to the stone garden and the catacombs entrance in the well. As they hurried down the corridor, the faint sounds of shouting echoed from behind the walls. It seemed Gabe's distraction had been discovered.

"You know," Lore said, slightly out of breath from keeping up with his longer stride, "the last time I used my power for a distraction is how I ended up in the Citadel."

Gabe snorted. "You would've ended up here one way or another."

The shouting intensified, some of it seeming to come from inside the back hallways, bouncing off the rock walls. "Hopefully you didn't burn down the entire Church."

"At this point," Gabe growled, "I probably wouldn't mourn too much if I did."

They reached the door; Gabe pushed it open and tugged her out into the morning sunshine, far too cheery for the kind of day it'd been so far. The brown petals of limp flowers rustled as they rushed past, headed for the well with its statue and its descent into darkness.

Lore tried not to think of the last time she'd opened this well with Gabe, tried instead to concentrate on the burn in her muscles as they pushed the small statue of Apollius to the notch in the wall. But the memories were hard to ignore—Bastian's not-kiss, the disappointment of thinking she'd been abandoned by Gabe, only for that disappointment to become devastation when he betrayed them to Anton—

"Lore."

Lost in thought, she hadn't noticed that she'd been staring into the pit of the now-uncovered well, her hands braced on the stone, her unbound hair hanging into the dark. She looked up, met Gabe's eye.

"I'm sorry," he said softly, and she knew it was for all the things she'd just been thinking of. Things he'd been thinking of, too.

She took a deep breath. Couldn't make herself smile, but that was all right. "We were only doing what we thought was best. All of us."

"And getting it mostly wrong," he muttered.

"None of us know the future," she replied, jumping up onto the lip of the well, taking the first few steps down into the shadows. "We just do the best we can with the past and the present and hope they give us a clue."

Gabe followed her, the two of them picking their way carefully down the narrow spiral stairs cut into the side of the well. When he'd gotten far enough down the stairs that his head was level with the wall's lip, he reached over and slowly edged the cover back over the opening, teeth bared in concentration as he tried to keep his balance. He didn't close it all the way, leaving a sliver of light over his head so they could get out easily when they came back up. Risky, but there was nothing to be done about it. Hopefully the fire he'd started in the confessional would keep everyone too busy for a jaunt through the stone garden, especially now that its original purpose was moot.

The gray stars in her palms itched.

At the bottom of the stairs—taken very slowly as their vision adjusted, the last thing they needed was a broken leg—Gabe made another torch, lighting it with more ember-threads that he gathered from the air around them. It took a moment, in the cold and damp of the underground.

"Are you sure you should be using it that much?" Lore asked quietly.

"I'm sure I shouldn't be, actually." The strangely steady light illuminated his grimace. "But we're in deep enough now that it hardly matters, does it?"

"She said that it won't...it won't be the same, for all of you." Telling him about what she'd heard from Nyxara still felt strange, like he'd look at her as an abomination, the same way he had that time he learned of her origins. They'd both changed since then, but she could still see that horrified face in lurid detail. She pushed past the memory. "She said the elemental gods were too diminished. You'll get Their power, feel Their influence, but They won't speak in your head. Won't try to take you over."

Far from being relieved, Gabe's face looked stricken, a swallow working down his throat. "And is She trying to take you over?" he asked quietly. "Like Anton warned?"

"No." Lore shook her head. "No, She doesn't want the same things Apollius does."

But even as she said it, Lore wondered. Nyxara said She didn't want to take Lore over, but something told her that the goddess would if She had to. There'd been a sense of...of relief, when She'd come forward in the room with the prophecy, when Lore surrendered to Her in order to read the symbols. As if She'd relished finally having a body again.

Lore shivered, but managed to make it look like it was from the chill.

Gabe nodded, his shoulders softening. He gestured forward with the torch. "Do you want to lead?"

"That's probably best." Lore took his proffered torch. "I can find my way around down here. I'll know where Amelia is."

Calling up Mortem now was as simple as a thought. Her mental map fell into place behind her eyes, the catacombs like a spiderweb, a tangle of black thread.

The rooms where the army had been kept still held spots of concentrated Mortem, but they were faint, burned-out stars. Amelia's signature would be brighter, since her death was so recent—

Wait.

There, down deep, at the very bottom of the pit of thread. A blazing black knot of Mortem, as there usually was, marking Nyxara's place. But it was fainter than Lore remembered, less vibrant.

And there were no points of white light around it. No signs of life at all.

"Lore?" Gabe's voice, concern edging up to panic.

She couldn't deal with that right now, couldn't waste time wondering about the Buried Watch. About Lilia.

Lore concentrated, turning the mental map over, until she found a burning spot of Mortem close by. "They didn't take her far." Her fingers were numb; she shook them out, but only on one hand, the other holding fast to the torch. "Come on."

Amelia was so close to the entrance that Lore really hadn't needed to use her map at all—if they'd just started forward, they would've found her in minutes. The door to the small room was open, Amelia's body laid out on a dusty plinth. Nothing had been done to her. She still looked like she had in Bastian's apartment, her mouth gaping, esophagus visible through her cut neck, her chest open and missing a heart.

It reminded Lore of statues of Apollius, a thought so repulsive she physically flinched against it.

"They should've done something," she murmured as she stepped into the room, bringing the torch closer to the body. Its light made the violence done to Amelia appear even more awful. "They treated her like trash. Apollius must've wanted her out of His hair as quickly as possible. I bet Demonde doesn't even know where she is."

Behind her, Gabe was quiet, his arms crossed. She turned to him, handed him the torch, sudden anger drawing her face into hard lines. "Do you believe me now? That Apollius can't be good? Apparently Him fucking you over wasn't enough; what about Him doing it to someone else?"

Gabe didn't reply.

Lore turned back to Amelia. Her hands hovered over the woman's corpse, fingers fluttering, as if there was something she could do to change this indignity, something she could fix. In the end, she settled for combing her blond hair back, blood-sticky as it was, arranging it over her shoulders, trying to throw strands across her open neck to cover what lay inside. Seeing Amelia's organs without her permission felt violating.

When she was done, Lore leaned on the plinth, closing her eyes. After a deep breath, she held out her hand again, over Amelia's open chest. She gathered up the other woman's death, braided it around her fingers. Instead of channeling it into the stone of the plinth, Lore tucked it into her own chest, keeping it close and safe, to give back later.

A creak. Amelia sat up. Her flesh stuck to the rock beneath her with congealing blood, making a slight tearing sound as she pulled away. Her face didn't turn to look at Lore, instead staring straight ahead with her one blank, black eye, the other stabbed out.

"Who killed you?" Lore asked, even though they knew. She

made herself watch Amelia, not allowing herself to look away. She'd done this. She remembered Bellegarde's words before Apollius killed him, that Lore's continued life was what made the god so powerful, able to take Bastian over so quickly rather than integrate over time. Her living had made all the other gods rise and find new vessels. Amelia was her victim, too.

"The day," Amelia said through her cracked-open, unmoving jaw. "The day killed me."

An inverse of what the child's corpse had said so long ago, trying to warn Lore of what she was, how she was being used.

Something wet dripped onto her hand, falling from Amelia's open mouth. Clear, watery. Lore lifted her fist and breathed in before she could talk herself out of it. It didn't smell like salt, not like the physician said the water on the floor smelled during the autopsy. This water smelled *fresh*, somehow, which should be an impossibility considering it came from inside a corpse. The scent of open breeze and open sky, a place that should be left untouched.

"Why?" Lore asked, another answer they already knew. But she wanted to hear it all from Amelia. Wanted the other woman to have a chance for truth, even if it was after death.

"Because I was to be a god," Amelia said, more of that incongruously fresh water sheeting over unmoving lips. "Because I had the power of Caeliar, and He would not allow such a thing to stand. That power was to be His."

Lore nodded. "Did you go to Him? Did you offer Him the power back?"

"No," Amelia said, water clinging to her mouth in fat droplets. "I went to kill Nyxara's vessel. She was not meant to be His Queen; it was supposed to be me. But He didn't want Her dead. He wants Her with Him, He wants to be the only god, but still have His wife by His side. He thinks She will give up her power, so He will have all powers and know immortality, and He will share that immortality with Her."

Swallowing hard, Lore closed her fingers, severing the threads and sending Amelia's death back into her body. Slowly, the corpse slumped to the plinth again, black eyes closing, mouth still open.

It all kept coming back to Lore. Every bad thing.

Lore turned and left the chamber, Gabe following close behind. She didn't need her mental map to guide them back to the entrance. They were close enough to see the sliver of daylight from the partially open cover cutting through the dim and dust.

"At least that didn't take long," Gabe grumbled behind her. The torch snuffed out with a hiss; the hairs on Lore's arms stood up with the change of pressure in the atmosphere when he gathered the magic to do it.

"He killed her for me." Lore crossed her arms against a sudden shudder. "How am I supposed to live with that?"

"It's not yours to live with." Gabe's hand on her arm halted her; he made her turn around to face him, limned in firelight and glaring. "Don't hold things that aren't yours."

Lore nodded, as if that were an easy thing to do. As if she didn't hold everything, always, and could never find a place to put it down.

Gabe's hand came up to cup her cheek. So many things could happen while they were alone down here, but neither of them moved, though the space between them thrummed like a plucked string.

"He cares about you, too, you know," Lore murmured, turning her face so her lips brushed his palm. "And I know you care about him."

He didn't deny it, his eye closing, opening again with a softer light. "It doesn't matter," he said. "There's too much there. Too much history."

She didn't argue with him, though it seemed a flimsy excuse, all things considered.

"What about you?" A swallow worked down Gabe's throat. "Who do you care for?"

"Both of you." She closed her eyes. "Can't it be both?"

His breath came shaky.

The vague echoes of shouts filtered through the open entrance ahead of them. The thrumming moment shattered. "Sounds like your distraction is still going strong," Lore said, turning around, breaking contact.

"Good." Gabe spat the word like it was a sharpened arrow he'd been saving. "We have some time, then."

Time. Time to go where Nyxara had wanted her to from the beginning, to follow the pull that led her here that night. When she saw her mother.

The thought terrified her. Lore never wanted to see where the remnants of the Buried Watch had made their home ever again. Not the glittering, mica-flecked walls, the stalactites gleaming in phosphorescent glow, the obsidian hulk of the tomb. Beautiful, in its own strange way, and terrible, and calling to her.

She didn't want to do as the goddess asked. But it was inevitable, she knew that now. It was inevitable, if she wanted any of this to end.

Lore turned away from the well and its spiral stairs before she had the conscious thought to do so.

And with the first step she took, her mind *surged*, the goddess coming forward.

"Lore!" Gabe, calling behind her—she was running, her body acting without her directive, rushing deeper into the dark. "Lore, what are you doing?"

No answer but her pounding feet, rock slicing through the thin slippers that matched her peach-colored dress. Distantly, Lore longed for her old boots. She didn't even know where they were anymore.

Also distantly, she thought about how she should be horrified. She was running deep into the catacombs, toward Nyxara's tomb, and she knew that she wasn't the one directing her movements right now. She could feel the goddess taking hold of things that Lore hadn't given; it was daylight in the world above, but down here was endless night, and it all belonged to Her.

Cursing behind her. Gabe, following, running faster than a man of his bulk should be able to. Another crackling in the air as he lit his torch again, an unwavering flame that Lore didn't need. She could see just fine.

Down they went, spiraling through the warren of the catacombs, so much more chaotic than the halls of the Citadel above. These passages seemed familiar, even after so many years. Smaller than she remembered, from when she ran as a child. When her mother told her to go with love in her eyes, and Lilia said so little with love that it had to be obeyed.

Then: open air, a gentle bluish glow. Lore had never asked what made the moss and mushrooms here emit light; it was an underground cathedral around an obsidian tomb, and things here didn't need to make sense, they just *were*. Nyxara moved backward in her mind, let Lore take over again, let her have control of her own hands, her own feet.

But when Lore skidded to a stop, her legs barely tired and still feeling not quite like her own, it wasn't to marvel at the awful magic of her childhood home.

It was to look at the bones.

The bones, and the open door of the tomb.

Chapter Thirty-Three

The pattern of the world is cycles, things beginning and ending and beginning again.

–Notes from Bran Morinac, Caldienan monk, part of the early Church on the Golden Mount, 165–100 BGF

She focused on the bones first. That felt more logical, more like something she could handle. They were scattered around the vast cavern, fully intact skeletons still in the positions where they'd fallen—some scrambling away from the tomb, others lying in peaceful repose. One trying to climb up the glittering wall.

And Lore knew, with some uncanny sense of the familial, that none of these skeletons were her mother. Lilia wasn't here, killed by the sweep of Mortem that Lore had inadvertently called that day at the docks. Lilia was gone.

Lilia had left her.

Lore didn't fall to her knees. She lowered herself slowly, reverently, like she'd seen penitents do in the South Sanctuary, when the flow of a Ward crowd caught her and it was easier to follow the surge into the Church's holy hush than try to break free. She'd seen the common citizens of Auverraine, the desperate ones, painstakingly take to creaking knees up at the altar, as if something might change in the space between standing and the floor. As if the act might make a god take notice, and care.

That wasn't what Lore wanted. But her body followed that pattern anyway, some instinctual human piece of her wanting something larger and kinder to look down, to make a change, even though she'd learned firsthand that such a thing didn't exist.

"Shit." Gabe skidded to a stop behind her, his one eye wide. "Shit on the Citadel Wall." His gaze skittered back and forth to each individual skeleton, as if he expected them to start moving at any moment. She supposed it wasn't a silly fear; something about being this close to the tomb had held the bones in their proper places even as death ate away everything else. "Lore, I don't understand, what happened?"

"Me." The day of the explosion, when she pulled in all the Mortem left in Nyxara's dead body, to knit it with Spiritum and stop the death above. Here, though, there had been no life to weave it with, no thoughtful braiding of the two. Nothing but a rush of death, magic in flash flood. How it hadn't collapsed the entire cavern and left a trail of destruction in its wake on the surface, Lore didn't know.

Because of Me, Nyxara answered. The goddess did not sound sorry; she was all business. *When you called all the Mortem, the tomb opened, and it rushed out like a leak. I needed you to take it all, to make the connection between us stronger. I directed the power to travel to you through dead matter, but that initial rush—that, I did not temper. I didn't have the time.*

Twenty skeletons. Twenty members of the Buried Watch, still down here, still keeping as much of their holy charge as they could even as the world above forgot them, reviled them. Making sure the goddess didn't rise again.

But She had.

Gabe didn't ask for any further explanation. He hung back at the mouth of the cavern, his torch clutched in his hand like it could be a weapon. She watched him back away from her, just a step, but it was enough. Even imbued with the power of Hestraon, he was afraid of her.

Come. Nyxara, making her stand on staggering legs, urging her forward. Her feet, taking a step though she didn't send the order to the muscles, the bones. *Time is short, Lore, and there are things you must know. If you want to save Bastian, all the rest, come to Me now.*

This time, when she walked, it was under her own direction. Lore strode forward and into the obsidian tomb.

The heavy door slammed shut behind her just as Gabe started to shout.

Lore wasn't listening to him, though. All her attention was captured by the body on the black stone before her.

She was beautiful. Lore had expected Nyxara's body to be overlarge and turned to rock, like the bodies of the elemental gods found all over the continent, a goddess made a monolith. But She was around Lore's size, though a bit thinner and taller, Her hair a lustrous black and long enough to spill over the sides of Her plinth. Her skin was moon-pale, Her eyes closed, Her delicate hands folded across Her chest, around a bouquet of white lilies that showed no sign of decay. Eternal and undying, everything Lore had been told a god should be.

The atmosphere in the tomb hummed. Lore thought of those other people marked with a moon on their hand, sent here in each eclipse, and how they'd come out less than they'd been when they entered. She could feel the tomb trying, tugging at the fabric of herself, wanting to render her into threads it could absorb. To wring out her power and spin it away.

Too late for that. Too late for her.

I tried, with them. Tried to find someone who could hold it all. Still,

Nyxara didn't sound sorry, not for any of it. *But they were always sent back here, to the prison Apollius made for Me, a place to guard Me from My first death. This tomb wound My power out of them, every time, became the holding place for everything I was. But it can't take Me from you. I stayed for so long in the void, waiting and not knowing what for. It was you, all along.*

"Why?" The word tasted like ash.

The goddess was silent for a moment, thinking. *I'm not sure,* She said finally. *But I think it is because we are so similar, Lore. The girl I was, the woman you are. Both looking for somewhere to belong, and never quite finding it.*

All this was too much, a truth too heavy for Lore's heart to carry. She stared at the goddess on the plinth—a woman, just a woman—until Her features blurred. Until they almost looked like her own.

Nyxara's chest on the stone slab slowly rose and fell. Still alive, somehow, down through the centuries. Buried, but living.

You know what to do, Nyxara said in her mind, and Her voice sounded like Lore's own, too, like their throats had fused together and harmonized.

She had to be done running, now. Had to know truths that could only pass to her like this. Lore lifted her hand and placed it delicately on the goddess's brow.

It pulled at her, as if Nyxara were a cliffside and Lore was a river, tugging her over by sheer force of gravity. Lore opened her mouth to scream, but nothing came out.

She drained

to her last

drop

and something new bloomed behind her eyes.

Something like her dreams.

the girl

She sat on the beach and tipped her head back, basking in the sun. It was somehow both brighter and gentler than it was back home on the mainland, a purer light that illuminated more than it should but miraculously didn't burn. The white sand of the beach sparkled as if someone had crushed pearls and sprinkled them here; the blue tide washed up to cover her feet and then moved away, warm as bathwater. The sea was the same color as the sky above, the two of them melting at the horizon line.

"See?" He sat down next to her, grinning. Her best friend, who'd loved her for years, whom she loved, too. Apollius was like sunshine himself, his brown hair burnished copper, his green eyes sparkling. "I told you it was beautiful."

"It feels like magic," she said, and she meant it.

Something strange flickered across his face, there and then gone too quickly for her to parse out its pieces. "Come on." He stood, pulled her up. "The others are up the mountain."

"What's up there?"

He grinned. "The magic."

Calling it a mountain was an overstatement. Or at least it felt like one, with the ease that it could be climbed. Of the seven islands in this archipelago—one that seemed strangely deserted, just like Apollius had told them—this one was the flattest. An expanse of beach changed to an expanse of trees, then became gentle foothills leading to a taller plateau with a flat, wooded top. He'd been so excited to show them, when he returned from his exploration, his months of sailing after his family's death. He'd been so beautiful, his face flushed with discovery as he held Nyxara close, as he told her that she'd have to see it to believe it. That they all would.

It didn't take them long to make their way up the small mountain. It would've taken less time if they hadn't stopped to kiss in a small pool in the foothills, just as blue as the sea, and if that kissing hadn't turned to something more. In the silence of the deserted island, Nyxara was sure that their friends could probably hear her moans on the wind.

The thought of Hestraon hearing made her cheeks color.

When they reached the top of the peak, the other four were waiting. Braxtos was excitedly examining the leaves of a flowering plant Nyxara didn't recognize. Lereal stood on an overlook, their eyes closed, a gentle smile on their face as the wind tugged at their tunic. Caeliar, her long reddish hair burning bright in the sun, was inspecting her nails, apparently unimpressed, her expression sour. She'd definitely heard them. Caeliar held a candle for Apollius, but not in a way that Nyxara really understood. She'd lived a hard life, with parents who cared more about money than their daughter, and she made up for it by trying to attach herself to people she thought could protect her. It wasn't care for Apollius that made her jealous of Nyxara. It was the idea that, somehow, Apollius could keep her safe.

By the edge of the path, Hestraon just stared at them, his lips a thin line.

Nyxara looked away and tightened her grip on Apollius's hand. Never again. It'd been one mistake, one they knew would wreck everything if it came to light. Apollius had been gone for a long time, looking for the answer to the question he'd been asking for years. They'd both acted on fear that he might not return, a want that had simmered unspoken, but it was done now. Done.

Apollius squeezed her hand in return, but didn't waste time. They'd all been friends since they were children; they didn't require ceremony. "Follow me, you lot. If you think this is impressive, wait until you see It."

"See what?" Caeliar asked, arching a brow.

He grinned. "The Fount."

"No." Hestraon shook his head, his dour look perking into a grin despite himself as he tore his gaze from Nyxara. "There's no possible way you *actually* found It. I thought you just wanted us to see the island?"

"I guess you'll have to come look for yourself." Apollius started off into the trees. It was uncanny, the forest on either side of them, how it dropped into open air where the plateau ended. One more otherworldly thing about this place, one more way it seemed outside of regular rules. Nyxara supposed that if one *were* to find the Fount, it'd be in a place like this.

The trees broke, opening up into a clearing. Crumbling stone columns held up the remains of a roof, the cracks in the rock filled in with moss and a profusion of blooming flowers. The ruined structure looked similar to the plazas built in every city, all housing a small fountain of their own, homage paid to the thing that had created their world.

But the fountain in the center of this ruined plaza was both finer and simpler than any Nyxara had ever seen. The pale stone gleamed with seams of gold, as if woven through with sun rays. A series of tiny carvings ringed the lip. A sun, a moon, a leaf, the swirl of a wind gust, the crest of a wave. A small jet of water burbled in the fountain's center. She couldn't see where it came from; there didn't appear to be any mechanism within the fountain that would propel the water upward. And the water around it wasn't disturbed, remaining flat and shining as a mirror.

Her ears rang as she drew closer, almost resolving into song—

A hand on her arm. Hestraon. He tugged her back to his side, away from the fountain, looking troubled.

"That's It?" Braxtos didn't sound convinced.

"Sure is." Apollius eyed the fountain before them like one might watch an oncoming army, with a sort of grim excitement. "The source of the world. The essence of everything. All here."

They stared at It, the six of them, awe stilling their tongues.

"How can you be sure?" Hestraon, ever the skeptic, who'd dropped Nyxara's arm like it burned him. "I mean, yes, it's a fountain on an island, but how do you know it's *the* fountain on *the* island?"

"I asked It a question," Apollius said. "And It knew the answer."

Hestraon's eyes slid to Nyxara's, understanding a rope drawn taut between them. The three of them had known one another the longest, the best. They both knew what kind of question Apollius would ask the Fount, the reason he was searching for It in the first place.

"Well?" Lereal widened blue eyes, their ethereal face curious. "What was the question?"

"What happens after you die," Apollius said, still staring at the Fount. That strange look had come back over his face, the darkness Nyxara had caught a glimpse of down on the beach. Part of her was surprised that he'd give up the question that had long pulled at his heart so easily, but this place felt like one that wouldn't tolerate untruth. Like any question asked here would get the correct answer, even if it wasn't one you could understand at first.

"Care to share what It said, then?" Caeliar twisted a strand of hair around her finger, trying to look bored, though her eyes were keen.

The shadow stayed on Apollius's face, his green eyes narrowing at the golden fountain he'd brought them to, the supposed source of all power the earth was made from. He snorted half a laugh. "I said It knew the answer," he said. "Not that It told me. It said I wasn't ready. That no one living should know what happens before their turn."

Braxtos crossed his arms. “So you’re back at the beginning, then. Found the Fount, but It’s useless.”

“Not useless.” Apollius stepped forward, tugging Nyxara along with him. She didn’t really want to get any closer to the Fount, or whatever It was, but his grip on her hand didn’t give her much choice. Hestraon stepped forward, too, his hand rising toward her before he made it fall back to his side.

Her jaw set tight as a prison lock. Both of them did this, all the time. Acted like they knew best, like she was something that needed protecting, something fragile. As if her own mind were a mystery to her, and both of them knew it better than she ever could.

It was exhausting, sometimes. She knew herself just fine.

“The Fount wouldn’t give me Its answers,” Apollius said, turning to face the friends he’d brought here, the ones he’d chosen to share this with. “But It has them. Somewhere inside. And we can find them.”

It took a moment for his words to sink in, for them to understand what exactly he was suggesting. Lereal realized first. They shook their head. “You want us to go *in* there?”

“Not go in,” Apollius said. “We drink from It. Take part of It into ourselves.” He glared at the flat surface of the water, his reflection beaming the anger back at him. “Then It won’t be able to hide things from us.”

Lereal tugged nervously at the ends of their golden hair. “Sorry, Apollius, but I really don’t want to do that.”

No one seemed particularly enthused by the idea. Braxtos and Hestraon hung back at the edge of the ruined plaza, casting wary glances between them. Caeliar frowned at Apollius like she thought she hadn’t heard him correctly.

But Nyxara stared only at the Fount. She thought of power, of being someone that wouldn’t be underestimated, someone that no one would think they needed to protect. Protection was just control, in the end. A leash held by a benevolent hand was still a leash.

She shook free of Apollius's grip.

He glanced at her, brow furrowed, before looking back at Lereal. "Do you know the way home, Lereal?"

Not a threat. Not yet. But the potential hung there, and it could alchemize at any moment.

Braxtos didn't let it. He always said things in plain language. "You're saying if we don't drink, you won't show us the way home."

"Technically, you said it." Apollius smiled, though his eyes stayed narrowed and flinty.

"Why?" Caeliar crossed her arms and canted her hips, though the posture didn't dim the avid look in her eyes. "You want the answer, *you* drink."

"I tried that already," Apollius said quickly. But there was a tic in his neck, a strain in his jaw. "It needs more than just me."

Hestraon stared at him, then Nyxara. They knew he was lying, at least partially. But what was there to say?

"I hate you sometimes," Hestraon said to Apollius, and it didn't sound like he was joking. Odd, how easily hate and love could fade into each other, passion in fluid forms.

Another not-quite-smile from Apollius, then he gestured at the Fount. "I'll go first, take another drink. Show you there's nothing to be afraid of. And you'll come after me."

And there was no question that they would, no matter how uneasy the five of them looked. Apollius had been the leader of their small group for so long; none of them really thought to gainsay him. There was something about his presence, like it held more weight than anyone else, like he took up all the air in a room. Since he'd returned from his journey, telling them all he'd finally found the Fount, that personal gravity had only grown heavier.

Apollius stepped up to the golden ledge. There was no chalice—he reached in with his hands, cupping them in the glass-clear water, disturbing the placid shine. The ripples expanded, reached the sides, kept going like a tide, as if the Fount had its own rhythms. As if a cycle started here was unending.

Water streamed from Apollius's hands as he lifted them, shining in his palms. He closed his eyes. "You will give me what I need," he murmured, almost a threat. "I will know all the answers."

And that sounded so good, to have something that couldn't lie to you. To know the secrets of the world, so it could never take you off guard.

Nyxara ran up to Apollius's side as he lifted his hands to his mouth. She pressed her face near his, and opened her lips, and drank at the same time he did.

He startled, but just for a moment. Then he pressed closer to her, and she lifted her hands, too, so the water wouldn't escape, and they both drank deep. It felt like they were even closer than they had been moments before, when he was inside her, his mouth on her own. This felt like they were two sides of the same coin, the sun and the moon, the light and the dark.

A rumble through the ground. The faintest sound of something cracking.

"One more," Apollius murmured to her, tipping the rest of the water toward her mouth even as it streamed through his fingers. "Take one more."

And she did. Two sips, singing through her like lightning.

Apollius's wet hands came to either side of Nyxara's face, cradling it like she was something precious. "I will never be apart from you," he said, the waters of the Fount streaming from his mouth. "You will be mine forever, and you will never speak against me, never share my secrets or betray me. You will never try to leave me, ever."

A faint line drew between Nyxara's brows. The words twisted around her mind like serpents, like shackles.

Another crack. She looked to the Fount. Faint hairline fractures slithered between two of the small carvings. The sun and the moon.

Another rumble through the ground, a gentle earthquake. It never resolved into anything larger, but something about the atmosphere—*broke*, became a little less stable, knocked slightly off its axis.

Apollius sat down, hard, his hands falling away from her, staring into nothing. "I know," he said, and she couldn't tell if it was in despair or exultation. "I *know*."

And Nyxara's vision spangled.

The water of the Fount spun her out into composite parts, sliced her to trailing ribbons. She had no sense of her body, no sense of anything, all her awareness flung far and made diffuse.

The world was reduced, too, simmered to its most basic components, surrounding her in a miasma of matter and magic. Shreds of power, of worlds that had come before this one, worlds that might come after. The soul of the earth, gathered here, boiling and mutating and renewing itself all the time.

Here, reduced, all her previous ideas about herself were sloughed away, replaced by a shining certainty with no room for such rudimentary emotions as shame, jealousy, hope. The sad girl who clung to anything that gave her warmth, even if it burned. The woman who wasn't afraid of the dark. The person who loved a man obsessed with finding a way out of death, when she herself thought, sometimes, how nice it sounded. How peaceful and quiet.

Something that represented all those things flowed past her in the miasmic sea the Fount had made of the world. Something that felt like maybe it could be *hers*.

She didn't think. She reached out and grabbed that thread of magic, of power, and she didn't let go, and it didn't struggle.

The thread twisted into her, gathering up the far-flung pieces she'd become. Her being reconstituted around it, the Fount allowing her to take part of Itself and lay claim.

Do you have a question, too? Not a voice, not anything she could understand. Something speaking into her mind, reordering itself into language so it could communicate. **Is that why you grip such a thing and try to make it yours? You want power, like him?**

"Yes," Nyxara replied, feeling as if she spoke, though in this state she wasn't sure she even had a mouth. Power was what she wanted, wasn't it? To be unassailable. Sovereign, and her own.

At least you are honest, the Fount said. **What is your question, then?**

"Will he have some peace now?" She saw once again that flash of darkness on Apollius's face. "Will you finally tell him what happens after someone dies?"

His father, his mother, his siblings. All massacred in a senseless killing, a border squabble between minor lords. He'd been obsessed with knowing ever since, after seeing how easily death came for you, how it slipped up like a lover and smothered you out in seconds, on a day that seemed like any other.

No one had a concept of anything coming after; when you were gone, you were gone. Apollius didn't accept that. Apollius wanted the world to bend around him, he wanted to know its secrets, and change them if they weren't what he wanted.

We told him he could not know while he was human, the Fount said. **So now he takes in power that can house itself in no human. And he will know.**

"No human?" Nyxara asked, but not with any kind of surprise.

You take it, too, the Fount replied. **All of you, hungry for something more. This power will make you more than human, but even not-human things come to an end. Do you understand?**

"Yes." And she did, even as her body restructured itself into what she would become. Darkness and moonglow, the peace of long rest. Not human, but still mortal, because death was the unshakable caveat to life, and there was no true escape.

You will go, one day, the Fount said. **But this power gives you two lives, two deaths. One for the human you were, one for the god you've become. The power will always find a new vessel, and until your second death, you will be tied to it, unable to rest. Do you understand?**

"Yes." But she didn't, not really. Who could?

Then become.

For a brief moment, for an eternity, she knew the answers Apollius had been looking for. Death opened itself to her, its new Queen, and she saw all the way through to its ending.

But then it was gone, locked away deep inside her.

And then she knew nothing.

the goddess

"What can I do to make you happy?"

The refrain could be pleading, had it come from anyone else's mouth. But from Apollius, it would always sound like an order.

Nyxara didn't answer. She had a few times before—told him that it would make her happy if she could leave this island, told him it'd make her happy if he'd told them the truth of what would happen when they drank from the Fount. Though that part wasn't exactly fair, which he'd wasted no time in pointing out. He hadn't forced them. They'd drunk of their own free will. She doubted it would've worked, if they hadn't.

Doubted the Fount would've made them all gods. Would've trapped them all here on this island as it rapidly decayed, the power they'd stripped from the soul of the world tipping it off balance.

They should've known that day, when the edge of the Fount broke, three pieces bearing carvings splintering from the whole. A sun, a moon, another piece with the leaf and wave and wind gust. They'd left them where they'd fallen.

She didn't answer Apollius. She kept quiet and dangled her feet from the rocky overlook, staring out at the blue-on-blue horizon. The trees had thinned since they'd taken from the Fount, some fallen ill, others growing in stilted, unnatural shapes, as if the island sickened from the essence the six of them had taken. It cleared the view enough for Nyxara to see straight down to the shoreline.

Boats were arriving. Small ones, but full of people who'd heard of the Fount, of the gods on the mountain. It'd been a strange thing, when they were discovered, what felt both like years and like days after they'd drunk from the Fount. Time had no meaning here.

At least, it hadn't until the sailors came. They'd washed up on the shore one night, tossed here by an unseasonably tempestuous ocean. Caeliar still didn't have the trick of smoothing the waters, making them follow their proper order. She and Nyxara worked together for the tides, and those were off, too. They held the reins of the world, but didn't know how to ride.

Apollius healed the sailors. Braxtos and Hestraon repaired the ship. And Lereal sent it home with a gust of wind—one of the first they'd managed to send in the right direction, rather than stirring up a storm.

The pilgrims came soon after.

Often, they just came to pray, but some of them stayed, built huts along the southern-facing shore. Nyxara and the others didn't like it, and didn't have much to do with the people who came, but Apollius did. He'd heal them, let them cry at his feet in gratitude. He'd go walk among the huts of the ones who stayed, gathering followers, letting them sing songs composed in his honor. When some would leave, he would raise one hand and watch as their boats faded into the horizon.

Nyxara was always filled with near-painful jealousy when she watched the human penitents leave.

She didn't go down among the pilgrims often. Just as well. The powers the Fount had given her were not the kind they'd want to see. None of them needed night to fall faster, or the moon to wax or wane out of season.

None of them needed her to raise a dead body.

She'd only done that once, one of the first times a boat full of people had come to the island, after the sailors. It'd been a child. That was why she tried. A child who'd taken sick and passed before he and his mother could make it here for healing.

But either Nyxara did something wrong, or raising people back to their fullness was a power beyond her own, because the child had been a horror, black-eyed and with an unhinged jaw, and the mother had screamed at her to undo it, undo it, it was worse.

She didn't interact much with the people who came after that.

"Nyxara." Her name sounded like a prayer. The thought was uncomfortable, given the trajectory of her earlier thoughts; she shook it off. Apollius lowered himself to sit beside her. A moment, a deep breath. "I've told you I'm sorry. I didn't know what the Fount would do—"

"But you knew it would do something," she murmured. "You knew it would do something, and you didn't want to be alone with whatever it did, so you dragged us into it, too. Why did you do that? Why could you never just learn to face your own consequences?"

They kept discussing this, over and over, long after she probably should've just accepted it. They were gods; they had penitents. She'd come to see Apollius at the Fount more than once—the ruined plaza now new-built and gleaming, thanks to human hands, the broken pieces picked up and set in places of honor—and seen him poring over a manuscript with one person or another, offering advice. They always stopped when she approached.

This was what he'd wanted. In a slanted way, at least. Divinity was the price he paid for his answers. It'd been unfair of him to make the rest of them pay for it, too. To use their love and twist it into chains.

He was silent for a moment. Then: "You never did well on your own, either, beloved."

Her eyes pressed closed.

She hadn't meant to tell him. It'd been one of those intimate moments when things just slipped out, a few days—she wasn't sure how many—after they'd all drunk from the Fount. Seeing the world spun out like that, and raw with new power, made

Nyxara think that truth was what they should want from one another, that it couldn't hurt them. The new power within them made it so they could tell when one of them lied, anyway. So she'd told Apollius about the nights with Hestraon while he was traveling, how they'd comforted each other, how she thought she might love him like she did Apollius.

It hadn't gone well. They might be gods now, but Apollius still had a jealous streak.

"Hypocrite," Nyxara said calmly, leaning back so the breeze off the sea threaded through her hair. "As if you haven't slept with all of us, at one point or another."

Truth. Especially since they'd been here, trapped on the island as it slowly decayed. Wasn't like there was much else to do, since everyone but Apollius tried to avoid the pilgrims.

"It's not the same," Apollius said. "You told me you loved him like you love me. What am I supposed to do with that, Nyxara? How am I supposed to feel, when you're the one I love most of all?"

"You have plenty of people to love you now," she said, watching the pilgrims disembark down on the beach. "Why does my love matter?"

His eyes glittered, an otherworldly gold at the edges of the green. "Because it was mine first."

You will always be mine, he'd said when they drank from the Fount together. At the time, it had only bothered her a bit, enough to make her frown. Now it felt like poison, and she could feel the subtle bonds he'd laid around her mind closing in more often than not.

She felt him get up, felt the air move as he reached for her, a crackle of heat. Nyxara opened her eyes and looked at the hand he extended curiously.

"I don't want to fight," Apollius said. Something was in his other hand; he kept twisting it nervously. "I made you something."

And what else was she going to do? She didn't want to fight, either. Not if this was all there was. Two lives and two deaths on an island slowly breaking down, with people foolish enough to worship them.

She took his hand.

He led her to a grove.

The trees here looked so much healthier than any of the others on the island, growing straight and tall with no signs of suppurating rot. Nyxara could tell they weren't exactly natural. Too uniform, the colors too vivid. Not like the old growth and wildness that had been here before they drank from the Fount, but an imitation of it, as if made by someone who hadn't really seen a forest before.

But she loved it anyway.

She pressed a hand to the bark, looked up into the lattice of green. The branches grew close, like a wall, like a sanctuary. Somewhere she could hide from what she'd become. Beyond, the blue of the sky, gleaming and endless.

"Braxtos grew it," Apollius said. "I told him to."

Another reminder of the patterns they'd all fallen into, taking orders from Apollius, letting him default into their leader. Nyxara pressed her hand harder against the rough bark. Braxtos had taken to directing his new power better than the rest of them. Though the island was still slowly dying, he managed some flowers in spring, some new trees in summer, colorful leaves in fall. Of the six of them, he was the only one who could still measure time.

"No one but us can come here," Apollius reassured her. "Just the gods. No people. This is sacred to us."

And it did feel a little bit sacred, having somewhere private. Somewhere no one would look at her and see a terrifying goddess.

She knew they looked different. Years had bled the surprise of differences out of them, for the most part, made the figures they saw now seem as familiar as who they'd been before. But she saw the way the penitents looked at them, mingled awe and horror. Her fingers sharpened to dark claws. Iridescent scales wreathed Caeliar's arms, and the whites of Hestraon's eyes glowed ember-orange. Apollius's skin shone as if sunlight ran in his veins, nearly as golden as the Fount itself.

"Braxtos helped make this, too." Apollius held out the hand that had been twisting nervously at his side. "He pulled the stone from the earth. Hestraon forged it. I didn't tell him what it was for, but I don't think I needed to. He knew."

Nyxara looked at his hand.

A ring.

She laughed. That was her first instinct. A ring, such a human and pedestrian thing, when they'd passed all that at his insistence?

A stormy look crossed his face, and when he spoke, it was with the tone of an order. "Marry me."

No. There was no court to marry them here, not like there was back home, no King's official to set them before their friends and kin and declare them bonded—but she didn't want it, not now, even if it was only symbolic. Before the Fount, she would have married him in a heartbeat, but now she was something different. Something stronger.

Something fighting against the way they'd all fallen in line for him.

But Nyxara didn't say all that. Instead, she said, "Give me time."

And surprisingly, he did.

She spent most of that time in the grove. The others would come sometimes, too, but it was her space, and they knew it. Lereal would pass through on their way to the cliffs, where they said they could hear the wind speak. They'd tell Nyxara about their experiments with Caeliar—how she would go to sleep, and Lereal would follow the patterns of her breath into her dreams, watch them, sometimes manipulate them with Caeliar's consent. "It's interesting," they said, twisting their nearly translucent hands together, "but it also scares me, a little. What if someone else could learn? What might they do?"

"You don't have to worry about that," Nyxara would reassure them, lying on her back and staring up at the cloudless sky. "No one else has power like you."

"It isn't my power that makes it work, I don't think." Lereal absently braided their hair, their eyes far away. The slender ivory of their bones shone through the glasslike skin of their hands, fading back to white sun-touched flesh right before the elbow. "It works with any power. They all come from the same source, so anyone who holds any magic from the Fount can walk through the dreams of someone else who also does." They dropped their braid. "I'll have to experiment more. Take notes."

Nyxara envied those of her friends who could find some sort of purpose in their godhood, who wanted to understand the power they held. She mostly wanted to forget it.

Braxtos came by sometimes to check on the trees, to see how his handiwork held up. The trees greened when he was near, unfurling toward him. The tiny leaves blooming from his nailbeds and the corners of his eyes did the same, reaching farther, curling from him like lace. "Maybe I can do this for the whole island," he'd say, but even when he tried, the changes didn't stay. Rot ate away at the greenery, wet and stinking, every day a little worse.

Caeliar hardly ever came to the grove. When she did, she argued with Nyxara, told her that she was being ridiculous by not taking Apollius's offer. She thought that if Nyxara gave him what he wanted, his love might make him work harder to find an escape from the island.

She didn't understand that Apollius didn't really love, not anymore. He just owned.

So Caeliar mostly stayed down by the sea on the northern shore, prodding at the waves, convinced she could find a way off the island. Every time she walked into the tide, her whole body seized, pain contorting her muscles and her heart beating so fast it was nearly visible. She'd fall back on the sand, defeated. The same thing happened to all of them, when they tried to leave, but she was the only one who kept trying over and over. The penitents had learned to steer clear of Caeliar, to avoid the northern shore entirely. They collected driftwood from the southern beach only, building their houses, their tall buildings carved with their six names.

When Hestraon came to the grove, he didn't say anything, not usually. He just sat with Nyxara, quiet.

He was with her the day Braxtos ran up to the grove, grass rippling over the ground and then dying instantly where his feet landed. "She got into the tide this time," he said, wide-eyed, not out of breath despite running all the way here from the shore. "Come see."

The changes in their bodies made them move differently, faster and liquid, almost like the water in the Fount. Nyxara and Hestraon followed Braxtos down the mountain, weaving around huts and cathedrals, the boatbuilders hard at work on the vessels that they sent out from the island, bringing word to the world of the new gods that had risen to take the place of the Fount. The three of them ignored it, even as work stopped in their wake, as every human knelt and pressed their faces to the ground.

Caeliar was on the beach, staring at the ocean as if it had personally insulted her. Her feet were planted firmly in the foam, her hands clenched by her sides. Lereal stood a few yards back, arms crossed, worrying at their nearly invisible nails with their teeth. Apollius was nowhere to be seen.

At the sound of their approach, Caeliar turned around, her eyes flinty. "Watch," she said, no preamble. She stepped forward, into the sea.

It parted for her, the water forming small walls on either side, her bare feet making their way over shell and coral as if this were softest carpet. Nyxara had seen her do this often enough that she knew the exact place where she'd stop—just beyond a barnacle-covered rock a few feet past the shoreline.

Caeliar reached it. Kept going.

The walls of water grew higher as she moved forward, a determined gait into the depths. Nyxara knew that if nothing stopped her, she'd walk all the way back to the continent like this, crossing the seafloor as if it were a ballroom.

But then Caeliar froze. Her whole body stood straight, too straight, then cramped to the side, as if some giant fist had closed around her, crumpled her like paper. A strangled scream wrenched from her throat, but it was closer to rage than pain.

Everyone else's eyes stayed on their friend in the sea, but something brushed across the back of Nyxara's neck, some awareness. She turned.

Apollius, right where gravel became sand, where the line of decaying trees began. His hand was outstretched, fingers crooking in the air, pointed right at Caeliar. Manipulating the life within her, seizing the threads of it in his fist, weaving them into a cage.

He met Nyxara's eyes. He didn't look away.

That night, she met Hestraon in the grove. They kissed, they slid together, heat and skin and sweat, and afterward they lay looking up at the sky, at the moon hanging like a jewel in the dark.

"We can leave," she murmured. "He's the one keeping us here."

He sighed, as if he was disappointed, but not surprised. "But why?"

"Because he never learned to be alone." Just saying that much against him was enough to make the edges of her mind ache, a phantom pulling at her temples. His bonds, stretched to their limits.

"He isn't alone. He has the whole world to worship him now." Hestraon looked at her, the moon shining in his eyes. He'd made a fire in the center of the grove, and the flames stood tall and still as stone. "Maybe you can convince him to let the rest of us go, now that he has that. Maybe he'll let you go, too."

Nyxara knew that wasn't true. He'd never let her go. But maybe there was hope for the others.

So she rose and held out her hand to Hestraon. He took it. They went to find Apollius.

He was in the plaza, sitting at the edge of the Fount, staring into its mirror-like surface. The penitents had made this place a palace, had brought him cloth-of-gold and sumptuous embroidery to wear, but the robe he wore now was simple linen, hanging off his shoulder, and he wore nothing beneath.

She didn't speak when she went to him, though she could tell by his sharp intake of breath that he smelled Hestraon on her. She kissed him, and pushed aside his robe.

Behind her, Hestraon pulled her own robe from her body, baring her for the other man. He bent to kiss her shoulder, and Apollius's hand that wasn't in Nyxara's hair tangled in Hestraon's, instead, pushing his head down, making him kiss all along her collarbone, her neck. Apollius sat back, and Nyxara stepped forward, Hestraon's hands on her waist—

No. This is mine.

Later, when Hestraon had gone and it was only Apollius and Nyxara lying by the Fount, he pushed up on his elbow. "Did you finally get him out of your system?"

"Did you?" she countered.

His hand was in her hair. It tightened, almost enough to be painful.

"It won't happen again," she said, both an answer and not. She threw her leg over him, pinned him to the ground. He was hard again; she slipped him inside, clenched down hard. "I'll marry you, Apollius."

He rolled his hips even as he glared. "I sense a bargain."

Nyxara swallowed, fighting against a moan despite herself. "I'll marry you," she repeated, "if you let the others go."

The snarl was back, twisting his face. He'd been handsome before; now, he was so beautiful it was terrifying, gold phosphorescence running beneath his skin, making him shine like a man-shaped sun. "I can make that deal," he said, thrusting into her again, harder. "As long as you're with me, near the source, the power will be, too. We need each other, Nyxara, we always have." His thrusts slowed, now, became something that felt like he actually loved her and didn't just want to possess her. "As long as you're here, I don't need the rest."

He rocked upward, and she gasped at the sky, breaking apart around him, same as always.

But she married him, and he still didn't lift whatever it was that he'd done to keep the others on the island. They still contorted in pain when they tried to step off the shore.

"You made me a promise!" she screamed at him in the plaza of the fountain, one generations of penitents had built into a palace with driftwood and the trunks of trees they could fell before the rot attacked them. The seasons were off balance—it was autumn, but rain lashed at the roof like it was the pits of spring. Once, she'd thought the longer all of them held power, the better at it they would be, but the opposite was proving true. The reins had long slipped from their hands; the world was a runaway.

"I am the god of life and the day," Apollius said, holding her wrists so she couldn't strike at him. "I am beholden to no one."

She left the plaza. She threw the ring off the cliff. It glinted golden as it fell.

gone

The day they decided to escape seemed like any other in their long string of uncountable days.

Hestraon gathered the others down at the northern beach. Nyxara had told him to wait until the moon was high. She'd distract him, then. That was when they could go without Apollius stopping them.

"What about you?" he'd asked, and she hadn't answered.

Now, watching the moon fade into the sky as it went from cornflower to indigo, she felt something like peace. As close as a being like her could get, at least.

In her hand she gripped a torch, one Hestraon had lit for her, the flame tall and unwavering. They stayed that way even as they ate her grove, consuming the trees in a wave of fire-glow. She stood in the center and breathed deep of the smoke, watched it twist through the slowly darkening sky.

Shouts from below. The penitents had seen; they'd hurry to save the sacred grove. Nyxara stepped out of the ring of burning trees and started to the Fount.

"What's happening?" Apollius asked as she approached. He'd just sent off another boat that morning, a group of men with a bound manuscript he'd helped to edit. He looked tired.

"One of the cathedrals caught fire." She said it flippantly, sauntering toward him, slipping her robe off her shoulders. "I thought we could take advantage of your followers being distracted. You're hard to find alone these days."

And though there was still a flinty light in his eyes, he let her come to him. Let her kiss him, let her lay him down beside the Fount.

As Nyxara rocked above him, she watched the moon, heat coiling in her middle as he gripped her hips, as he gasped her name.

She did love him. Still. Even after everything.

"Why do you need us?" She hadn't meant to ask, hadn't meant for the words in her mind to trip off her tongue. But being with him like this had always brought out truth, even when she didn't want it to.

He tucked her hair back from her face. "I only need you."

It wasn't the comfort she thought it would be.

"Why do you ask?" he asked, rolling his hips, making her bite her lip.

She didn't answer.

Apollius stopped. "Why, Nyxara?"

And they'd never been very good at lying to each other, had they?

With a curse, he shoved her off him and leapt up, running out of their driftwood palace, down the ruined hills in that strange, quick way they all had. The grove burned against the sky, the distant shouts echoing ghostly as penitents tried to put it out.

All her friends were gone when she got to the shore. Even the sea had fallen back into its rhythm. They'd rushed off through the things they held dominion over, using them to escape—Lereal on the wind, Caeliar through the water, Hestraon through the crackling heat in the air just waiting to become fire, Braxtos through the earth. They were gone, safe, away, no longer imprisoned.

Nyxara laughed. Her mouth unhinged, and she cackled, filling the air with her joy, and it didn't stop until Apollius's hand cracked across her face.

He glowered down at her with an unsound smile. "You think they escaped?" he murmured. "You think any of you can escape from me, the god of life? *I own you*, Nyxara. I own you all. They won't last a week away from me. They'll fade, die their first death, and all that power will be mine until they find a vessel for their second life, to die their second death." He leaned close. "And I'll find them when that happens, beloved. I will find them *quickly*."

She slapped him back, but that wasn't good enough. Her dark-clawed hands raked for his face, wanting to draw divine blood. "Then why did you say you'd let them go?" she screamed.

"You knew it wasn't true." He caught her hands, gentle again. "I didn't lie to you, beloved, I just let you think what you wanted to. But you knew we couldn't separate. We aren't things that can live apart, now. We're all pieces of the same source, and as long as we contain it, we have to stay together." He cupped her face. "You're the key, Nyxara. You drank with me, you drank twice just like I did, and took a greater portion of power. We are tied for eternity, you and I."

"So you'll never let me go." She'd known that, but to hear it felt like a dagger.

"Never." He said it like an endearment.

"We didn't want this." She tried to shove away, but Apollius held her tight. "None of us wanted this!"

"You will." Both hands held the sides of her head, craning her neck so he could see her eyes. "Nyxara, I promise you, you will. I know things you don't. I'm finding a way to save you." He paused. "I only ever want to protect you, beloved."

Protection. A cage, a leash, control by a more palatable name.

Rage, eclipsing everything, rising up in her until it crowded out rational thought, crowded out fear. She jerked backward, reaching for her own throat with her claws.

Golden light shackled around her wrists. It burned; she cried out.

"No, beloved," Apollius murmured. "You won't get away from it like that." He smoothed back her hair. "I should've just brought you. Left the others. If I'd known, I would have. You and I could've been the only gods."

"I never wanted to be a god."

A thoughtful look drew his brows together. "I see," he murmured. "That might make it easier. Maybe I could grant you this."

But the way he said it didn't make her think he'd changed his mind about letting her go. He'd only reconsidered the cage he wanted to keep her in.

He hauled her back toward the broken Fount, moving as a man would, not the liquid quickness power lent them. Nyxara tried to fight, twisting in his grip, but he dragged her along, up the mountain, across the rock. They passed knots of penitents, some of those who'd been there for years building their monasteries, their huts and cloisters. She screamed at them to help her. They pretended not to hear. The sacred grove was ash.

When they reached the Fount, Apollius finally let go of her. She stumbled, curled up on the stone. Her back pressed against the place where the carvings had broken from the lip of the Fount.

"Is their power back here, now?" Apollius snarled, gripping the golden lip of the Fount with white knuckles. "Now that they've left me? Or do I have to wait for their first deaths?"

No. From above and beneath and behind, rumbling the ground, a sound that could crack the sky. **It doesn't work that way. The power will trickle back here, eventually, but it will take eons. We cannot hold it all, not while broken.**

Apollius reached out and struck at the surface of the water, making it ripple. "And when it finally comes back to You, will You tell me how to achieve what I want? Have I danced prettily enough? Gained the worship You truly wanted?"

Immortality is an impossibility, the Fount said. **We told you this.**

"I don't accept it!"

Accept it or not, it is the truth. You have two deaths, one more than you did before.

And that's when Nyxara decided to take one from him. She reached up, clawed hands gouging into his chest—

"Lore!"

Chapter Thirty-Four

If you sin, make it count.

–Ratharcan proverb

She didn't know where she was. Who she was. Her head ached, her body hurting from things it hadn't actually done, crying out against all the memories that had been poured into it.

"Lore!" That word again. Her name. Someone was pulling on her hand. "Lore, we have to go, the tomb is collapsing!"

Her limbs wouldn't obey her directions, her vision was blurry. But the voice was right. Chunks of black stone rained from the ceiling, the reflective walls cracking. In front of her, a woman on a plinth, beautiful and still.

As Lore watched, the beautiful body rotted, moving through years of decomposition in moments. Her face sank in, the flesh decayed, became a skull, became dust. The bouquet of lilies in Her pale hands grew soggy and rotten, their matter mingling with the body's.

Nyxara's first death, finally.

Whoever was tugging on her hand swore in a voice that was becoming more familiar, pulling at the weave of her memories, putting them back to rights. Her body was hoisted into the air, hung over a broad shoulder.

The owner of the broad shoulder—Gabe, it was Gabe, not Hestraon but Gabe—muscled out of the door that he'd miraculously forced open. As soon as he did, the ceiling fell, shaking the cavern as the tomb shattered in on itself.

The shock wave sent them sprawling, Lore pitching forward out of Gabe's grip. Something clattered, hitting the side of her head—bones. She'd tripped right into a skeleton, shattering it out of articulation, making it nothing more than a mass of yellowed ivory.

No time to be horrified, to let loose the scream caged in her throat. Lore pushed her way through the now-broken skeleton and got to her feet, just in time to avoid a falling rock that absolutely would've caved her own skull in.

She kicked aside a spine that nearly tripped her, felt a moment of crushing guilt for it. Then she and Gabe ran out of the cavern, up the corridors, slipping on the packed dirt and slick stone that made up the catacombs. Dust and soil shook down from the ceiling, and Lore stopped, turning to see where the last hall opened up into the cathedral of the Buried Goddess, the place she'd been born.

A falling rock blocked it from her view. Just as well. Now wasn't the time to get sentimental.

Gabe grabbed her arm and hauled her forward. The closer they got to the surface, the less the ground rumbled. "Is the whole thing going to collapse?" she asked, out of breath.

"I don't think so," he said grimly, "but I'd rather not be down here to find out."

Through the corridors, swinging wide around corners, until that sliver of light shone up ahead from the well. It'd dimmed down to dusk.

Nyxara? Lore murmured tentatively into the darkness of her own head. *Are You there?*

No words, but the impression of a nod. She was there. Exhausted, but there.

The goddess's memories battered at Lore's insides as she climbed up the well, following Gabe's back in an echo of the way she'd once followed Bastian up these same stairs. The girl Nyxara had been, who loved Apollius enough to follow Him into ruin. The goddess She became, who ripped out His heart.

That must've been His first death, if the Fount gave everyone in the pantheon two. Bodily death, and now His power lived in Bastian. Nyxara had found a way to send out Her consciousness, though Her body was technically still alive in the tomb—but now She'd had her first death, too, and Lore knew, somehow, that it meant She would be even stronger inside her head.

Two deaths, and now both Apollius and Nyxara had experienced one. It was an answer for how to expel Them from the world, but Lore shied away from it. It was an answer she didn't want.

And there was another answer there, too. Apollius hadn't wanted Nyxara to leave, because His power would diminish if She did. Power is made and unmade through the same means, like the prophecy said.

Gabe reached the top of the stairs and heaved the cover aside, opening the well into a fast-falling twilight. No one was in the stone garden as he reached his hand down and helped Lore out, then turned to pull the cover back on and push the small statue of Apollius as close to its center as he could manage.

When he was done, he sat down on one of the wrought-iron benches by the path. His one blue eye watched her avidly, worry-brightened. "Are you all right?"

Lore made a noncommittal noise and sat down next to him. "Honestly, I'm not sure yet. What happened?"

His brow arched over his eye patch, like he should really be the one asking the question, but he answered her anyway. "You went into the tomb, and the door closed nearly as soon as you did. There's no damn latch on the thing, so I was trying to haul it open." He held up a hand with a rueful smile. The nails were broken. It was the same hand missing the tip of his index finger, the one he'd lost when he reached for her at the Mortem leak so long ago.

Guilt scoured her throat. Lore took his hand and laced her fingers with his.

He was quiet a moment, looking at their hands on her lap, before continuing. "The door cracked on its own, and everything started shaking, and I went in to get you."

Her brow furrowed. "How long was I in there?"

"Five minutes. Maybe less." He knocked the back of his hand against her thigh, but didn't unclasp their fingers. "Your turn."

She pulled in a breath, pushed it out in a huff. "I saw Nyxara's memories. Of Her time on the Golden Mount. How They all became gods."

Gabe froze. She thought about how that would sound to someone faithful, or someone who used to be. She'd seen the rise of the religion this whole world followed, and it was such an ugly, human thing.

So she knew what his next question would be. "Did you see the Godsfall?"

No. She hadn't. She'd seen how the elemental gods left, heard Apollius say that They wouldn't last long without Him—and that had been true, hadn't it? They'd finally escaped the island only to all die slowly, their corpses grown monstrous and stony, leaking the power They'd drunk from the Fount.

Power that had leaked into her friends, now. Second life.

"I saw its beginning," she said, thinking of Nyxara's claws ripping into Apollius's chest. "But that was it."

Gabe's fingers stiffened in hers. He disentangled his hand. "Figures," he muttered. "Figures She wouldn't show you the things we really need."

"She would have." Lore knew this. Nyxara had been cut off, the tomb beginning to collapse before She could pour the rest of her memories into Lore's head, show her all the things She couldn't talk about. It must have something to do with the way She was bound to Apollius—those vows He'd spoken when They both drank from the Fount. So had Apollius stopped Her, somehow? Known what was happening?

The thought pricked nerves down her spine.

With a sigh, Gabe sat back on the bench, reaching up to rub beneath his eye patch. "So did She tell you anything useful, then? Anything in all those memories that can help us get the gods out of our heads?"

There was one easy answer, but it wasn't something either of them could bear. Wasn't something Lore would even consider.

A piece of another possible solution turned itself over in her mind, the seed of a plan. But Gabe would stop that one, too. Infuriating, beautiful, lonely man; he wouldn't bear losing either of them.

So Lore lied. "I'll let you know when I figure it out."

Gabe nodded. Then he stood from the bench. "Getting late. We should probably sleep while we can, seeing as we keep finding things to do in the wee hours."

His face seemed blurred in her vision. In Nyxara's memories, Hestraon hadn't looked like Gabe, but when Lore tried to recall them now, his face was all she could see. His face above her in that grove, a pleasurable strain, his eyes closing and then opening again like he didn't want to miss a moment of seeing her like that, didn't want to waste any of it. The brief glimpses of his face Nyxara had allowed her to see in the memory of Him and Her and Apollius together, before She'd broken it off, kept it for Herself.

So how much of the want Lore had felt for Gabe had really been hers? How much of it had been the goddess choosing her as a vessel, even as Hestraon's power chose him, drawing them into a caring they had no real ownership over?

She thought of Apollius wearing Bastian like a costume. Of Nyxara essentially doing the same thing to her, albeit kindlier.

Bastian had told her something like that, once. About how she didn't recognize when she was being used, as long as it was done kindly.

Apparently, not much had changed.

Moonlight glinted in Gabe's one eye, was swallowed by the leather of the patch where his other should be. Light and dark, bisecting his face, making him two things at once. He stepped closer to her, his scent of Church incense flooding her breath. "Lore?"

"This is mine," she said.

And she kissed him.

It was different from the kiss they'd shared on that long-ago night in their shared turret apartment, unreal and ethereal and informed only by heat, by what their bodies wanted from each other. This was deliberate, this was decided, and Lore molded herself to every muscled curve of him, melted them together as much as she could.

Being Nyxara's avatar had to mean that there was some deep-seated kinship here, some piece of her that mirrored a piece in the Buried Goddess, and surely that meant the love she felt could belong to both of them, couldn't it? She loved Gabe, Nyxara loved Hestraon. She loved Bastian, and, despite Herself, Nyxara loved Apollius. It was all too much to hold, but Lore wouldn't let go of it. Any of it.

Gabe's mouth opened hungrily over hers, his tongue flickering at her lip. She gasped him in, let her own tongue slide against his, the imitation of something they both wanted. His hardness pushed against her stomach, and she wanted to reach for it, but that would be cruel. She didn't have time to give him that. Not right now.

There were things she had to do.

Still, when he feathered kisses over her shoulders, her neck, her collarbone, she held him close. And when his teeth and lips and tongue loved a bruise into the skin just below her ear, she pushed into him, let him do it, found pleasure in the ache.

One more deep kiss, and Lore thought she'd have to be the one to break it off, but she wasn't. Gabe stepped back, shaking his head. "We can't," he murmured.

Once again, she was reminded of that night and how it ended, and a wry smile picked up her kiss-swollen lips. "The more things change, the more they stay the same."

His brow furrowed. Then he laughed.

After a moment, she joined him.

They cackled in the stone garden, the rocky petals throwing back the echoes. Gabe bent at the waist, like the muscles in his stomach hurt; Lore wiped at her streaming eyes. As their hysterics subsided, Gabe wrapped his arms around her, resting his chin on top of her head. Lore hugged his waist, burrowing her face into his shoulder.

"Are you wiping snot on me?"

"It's better if you don't know."

They stood in silence, then, once all the laughter had petered out completely. Another lingering moment, the two of them pressed together, then they broke apart. Gabe didn't kiss her forehead—that was Bastian's tenderness—but he caressed her face, his thumb running over her cheek and then down her jaw. "I'll walk you back."

There were things to do, first. Things she had to gather before she went. Lore had two items of business to take care of, and he would stop them both. "I'll be fine. You go get some sleep."

Lore expected him to resist leaving her here alone. But Gabe nodded. With a gentle squeeze of her hand, he faded into the dark, headed back into the Church.

She waited until she couldn't hear his footsteps anymore. Then Lore went to the greenhouse to complete her first errand.

The scent of roses and blood was thick in the humid air. Lore breathed shallowly through her mouth as she searched the shelves of dusty gardening equipment, but that just made her tongue taste coppery, which wasn't much improvement.

Once she found what she was looking for, she entered the back room.

Anton wasn't sleeping. She didn't know if that was a thing he could do anymore. But his remaining eye was closed, his head tilted upward to the skylight, washing out the rusty stains of blood into shades of black and white and gray.

"Moon's out," Lore said. "I don't think you're going to be hearing anything else from your god until morning."

A dry, scraping laugh. "You won't let me see morning."

Slowly, Anton lowered his head. A brace of thorns in his neck caught on skin and pushed through, a slow, violent bloom. "So She read the rest," he murmured. "I don't know what it was that guided my hand, for that last part of the prophecy. It wasn't Apollius. Something older. Something evil."

Lore didn't buy that. The lines of good and evil had been crossed and tangled so many times, they were impossible to unravel now.

"I couldn't read what it made me write," Anton continued. "But the anger of my god told me it was something that shouldn't be. So I hid it. It should never have been found, never have been written. Apollius Himself should have destroyed it by now."

Bastian, trying his hardest to cage the god in his head. Maybe Apollius had tried to go destroy the prophecy, so she wouldn't know about powers made and unmade. Maybe Bastian had kept Him from it.

Infuriating, beautiful, lonely man.

"One more way you've ruined things by living," Anton said, but he sounded tired. As if Lore's continued existence had gone from catastrophe to annoyance. Pain laced his voice; Lore supposed living like this would make everything else pale in comparison.

She thought of Gabe as she raised the garden shears, as she positioned the blades on either side of Anton's neck. How he couldn't bring himself to do this. Both because it was Anton, and because he still so desperately wanted to be good.

Lore was past that.

Anton didn't say anything. Didn't struggle. He stood up a little straighter, or tried to, still tangled in all those roses. "Send me on to the Shining Realm then, deathwitch. Free me from the world you're making."

"I hope you find the world you deserve," Lore said.

Then she snapped the shears closed.

It took more than once. The shears were dull.

When it was over—she blanked out her mind as it was happening, trying not to hear the wet-crunch sound of his throat breaking, the splinter of bone—Anton's head was on the floor, surrounded by rose blooms that had been caught in the shears' teeth. Lore didn't look at his head as she bent and picked up one of the roses.

It was pointless. She knew that even as she left the greenhouse, walked back over to the now-closed well. Her mother wasn't down there. If she'd been in the catacombs at all, she'd probably been killed in the aftermath of Nyxara's death.

Still. Lore shoved the cover of the well off, just enough to reveal a fissure of darkness, and dropped the rose through the crack. "Help me, Mama," she whispered. "I have to leave."

Then she turned on her heel and left the garden.

Chapter Thirty-Five

Until the road leads you back and the wind pulls you closer.

–Malfouran goodbye

Lore stood at the base of the spiral staircase that led to Bastian's room and breathed deep.

She shouldn't be here. Her bag was packed, the second of her two errands. Her cloak was on, her hands were scrubbed of Anton's blood; she was ready. It was night, so Bastian should be Bastian, but the gods were getting stronger, and there was no way to be sure. Even if he was himself, he wouldn't want to let her leave. Even if she explained, he'd just try to talk her out of it, maybe even lock her in her room, or the holding cells with the Kirytheans. It wouldn't necessarily be out of character.

Her hand twisted on the small bit of cloth in her pocket. She'd prepared for that.

She had to go away, as far as she could. Caldien, even Ratharc, maybe. Farther, if she could get there. Mortem no longer tied her to the city, to Nyxara's body; she could go wherever she pleased.

And maybe, once she was gone, the hold Apollius had on

Bastian—the hold the gods had over her friends—would lessen. Go away entirely, even.

It all hinged on her. On the fact that she'd lived. Apollius had obviously been waiting to take Bastian over, but hadn't done it until he had part of Lore's power. In Nyxara's memories, they'd drunk from the Fount at the same time, tied themselves together. Her mother called her the seed of the apocalypse, Anton and August had lured her into the Citadel to be close to Bastian so her power could sharpen his own. *Apollius's* own.

So if she was gone, maybe it'd go away.

It was a less brutal solution than the two that had originally presented themselves. Killing Bastian, which she dismissed as soon as she thought it. Not only because she personally couldn't bear it, but because Auverraine couldn't, either.

The other obvious option was finishing the job Anton had started that night. But the thought was only in her head for a heartbeat before Lore dismissed it. She'd fought for a life, gods dammit. Like hell would she throw it away.

Even if it meant she had to live the rest of it far away from everyone she cared about.

Mouth set in a determined line, she mounted the stairs.

Bastian wasn't asleep. He stood at the window, his dark hair tousled, his eyes bright when he turned to watch her approach. That stopped her until she got a good look at them—tired and dark and his own. The ditch of night still kept Apollius buried in his head. That was something.

He turned from the window. Even in the dark, his eyes went to the place beneath her ear, the mark Gabe's kiss left. Tentatively, he reached up, brushed his fingers over it. "You smell like him," he breathed. "Church incense."

Lore said nothing. Her pulse quickened under his touch.

Bastian's hand dropped. "You're leaving." It wasn't a question. He wore no shirt, bare-skinned in moonlight, so there was nothing to hide the feather of the tendon in his neck, reined-in anger.

"I have to."

The muscles in his shoulders bunched. "I order you not to."

"Good try."

"I'm still your fucking King." He grabbed her arms, his fingers digging into her flesh. They were warm, so warm, and he still smelled like that expensive cologne she'd never been able to place.

"I have to," she repeated. Her hand wanted his skin; she allowed herself to lay her palm on his shoulder. "If I go, His hold on you will weaken. Power is made and broken in the same way. Your magic increased because I was here, it will diminish if I go."

He shook his head before she'd finished speaking. "There has to be a different way. It's not safe for you to leave, Lore, not with the Empire sinking in their claws, not when everyone knows who and what you are."

"It's not safe for me here, either." Her hand on his shoulder flexed, just a little, just enough to dig in her nails. Bastian's breathing quickened, and she was reminded, for just a moment, of when they were in the arbor. When he'd begged her to tell him exactly what to do, wanting her to take charge.

She couldn't think of that now. "Apollius killed Amelia, Bastian."

His eyes closed. A swallow worked down his throat. "No, He didn't."

Her brows drew together.

When Bastian's eyes opened, there was a fierce light in them. Just as terrifying as Apollius's, but all his own. "I did. He wasn't in control when it happened. *I* was."

Her hand fell away from him. He caught it, cradled it in his own. "She was trying to kill you," he said, looking at her fingers instead of her face, telling her everything the corpse already had. "She came here, saw me. The sun was still shining; she thought I was Him."

She let him keep holding her hand. She had no desire to pull away, even now, and that horrified her a bit.

"She had a knife," he continued, head still tilted down, his hair hiding his eyes. "And when she saw me, she expected me to be... proud. Happy." He shook his head. "She said she had been trained to be my Queen, *His* Queen. That she understood how I'd been led astray, how Nyxara was trying to bewitch me again as I'd been before, but she would take care of it."

Amelia in the hallway, sneering at her, thinking she'd taken something away. The marriage with Demonde was supposed to be a sham, then, cover so no one would know the Devereauxs were plotting to install their eldest daughter as Queen.

But then all their plans had been dashed, Lore living when she wasn't supposed to, Bastian sending everyone who'd conspired to make him King to the Burnt Isles. They'd married her off quick, keeping her safe, keeping her in the Citadel. Amelia probably thought it was only a matter of time, that she just had to be patient until Apollius took over from Bastian fully and cast Lore out.

"I didn't think," Bastian murmured. His voice had gotten smaller and smaller as he spoke, and now it was barely a whisper. "I used Spiritum. Sent it to her heart. Made it beat so hard it stopped." He finally looked up, now, meeting her eyes. She expected to see regret in them, but there was none. "He came forward, then. Slashed her throat open, stabbed her eye. For no reason, she was already dead. Just because He could." He shuddered. "Apollius took her power. Caeliar was inside Amelia the way He's inside me. I don't know what that means."

But Apollius did. Apollius knew that if Caeliar had awakened, Braxtos and Hestraon and Lereal had, too. Maybe He knew who they were, even, and was just biding His time.

But if Lore left, they'd fade away, hopefully. Her stain on their world would be gone, the magnetism of her magic would let them go. The Law of Opposites reversed.

"So you don't have to leave," Bastian said, like he'd read her mind and wanted a counterargument. He pressed his forehead against hers and brought her hands back up to his shoulders, where they'd been before. He arched his fingers over hers and pressed her nails into his skin, wanting that pain, that pressure. "I told you I would make you safe, Lore. I made you Queen. You *will* stay here."

"Not Queen yet." She kept her voice quiet, but she dug her nails in harder, like she knew he wanted. "And you can't order me."

His eyes flicked up, fixed on hers, dark and liquid with heat. "But you can order me."

They'd slipped into something else, no longer talking just about her leaving, though that was still hanging here. Now they also talked of the fire building between them, the way his eyes glazed when she pressed her nails in just a little bit more, dimpling his sun-bronzed skin, the way he caught his bottom lip between his teeth.

She was mesmerized by the change in him, that she was the one bringing it about. Bastian was so in charge of himself all the time, dominating whatever room he walked into; should it really be a surprise that sometimes, when he felt safe, he wanted to lay that down? That she was the one he felt that kind of safety with, she who knew what was happening to him more intimately than anyone else ever could?

"You can," he murmured into the humid air between them, the little space they'd left. "Order me, Lore. Please."

Her breath hitched; her nails dug in harder. "Why?"

"Because then it's you." His voice was hoarse. "Because if I want you to order me, and you do, I know it's not Apollius and Nyxara. It's us. He would never." He swallowed again. "I want to be able to at least pretend you love me like I love you. That you still would, even without the gods in our heads. That you—"

She cut him off with a kiss.

He melted into her, his arms coming up around her body, holding her close. Lore threaded her hand through his hair, tugged lightly; Bastian arched with a sigh, his teeth grazing her lip. "Order me," he said against her mouth. "Tell me what you want. Show me."

Lore had taken charge in such matters with other people before, but then, it'd been to make sure she got what she needed, not because she'd been asked. It threw her, just for a second, but she tried to turn off her churning thoughts, let instinct take over.

A moment's terror, that trusting instinct would let Nyxara come forward, Her presence in Lore's mind strengthened by Her first death. But the goddess didn't stir. The goddess stayed gone. Some things should only belong to one mind.

She pulled back from Bastian, her hand still tangled in his hair, using it to turn him to face the canopied bed. "Go."

He went, sinking down to sit on the edge of the mussed mattress, sheets and pillows spilled over the floor. His hardness jutted a clear outline against the thin pants he wore to sleep; he palmed it, his eyes burning on hers, his mouth slightly agape, like he couldn't believe she was doing this, just as he asked, that she was letting him have this.

Lore pulled off her gown, left it in a heap on the floor. The thin chemise she wore underneath stirred around her feet as she walked toward him, the peaks of her breasts standing out against the gossamer, making her shiver. She waved a hand at him. "Off. All of it."

And he obeyed that, too, like he'd been waiting years for her to give the order. Lore's eyes widened when she saw him bared for the first time, his skin sun-bronzed and desire-flushed, and she didn't realize she'd sunk to her knees in front of him until she felt the cool hardwood pressing into her legs.

His eyes were hazy on hers, his hand coming up to cup her cheek. "Beautiful," he murmured, like he'd plucked the word from her mind.

But she reached up and took his hand, put it firmly down on the bed. "You don't touch me until I tell you to," she said, not letting herself think too hard, being driven only by want, his and hers. She picked up his heavy length, working her fingers up and then down. His eyes closed, his head tossed back, his breath a strain in his throat. "You sit there, and you let me do what I want."

"Yes." He murmured it to the canopy above them, bathed in moonlight, the shadows of it playing down the column of his neck, outlining every muscle and every scar, all bared for her to see. "Whatever you want."

Lore took him in her mouth.

This wasn't something she particularly enjoyed, usually. But for whatever reason, she wanted it with Bastian, wanted him here, panting beneath her lips, his hands fisted in the bedclothes because he was trying so hard to follow her orders, to not touch her until she gave the word. He tasted like musk and salt, and she hummed an appreciative noise as she pulled him farther into her mouth, flicking her tongue. Her hands were on his thighs, sliding around to his back, making her breasts brush against the edge of the bed; that was *good*, and elicited another pleased sound from her, vibrating in her throat.

"*Gods*, Lore." Bastian sounded like he was being strangled; a look at his fists on the bed showed that he was the one doing the strangling, at least to the sheets. "If you keep that up, this will be over before it started, and I'll need at least half an hour to recover."

"Can't have that," she murmured against him, pulling away slowly, standing between his legs at the edge of the bed. He reached for her, remembered her orders, grabbed the sheets again, staring up at her as if awed.

She picked up his hand and put it on her breast, tender and peaked through her thin chemise. "Touch me." Her voice was hoarse, too, her breath catching in her throat as he followed her direction. "You know, you remember—"

He did, his fingers closing in a pinch; she gasped, arching against him, her hips swaying forward in desperate search of friction. Bastian made a low noise, nearly a growl, and pulled her toward him with a hand on her backside. His fingers continued their work on one breast while his mouth started on the other, making a slick mess of the thin fabric, gently biting her through it, swirling his tongue.

And gods, she was getting close already, it'd been so long, she'd wanted him so long. Lore took his hand away from her nipple, pushed it toward the apex of her thighs instead, her hips still moving in anticipation of his touch. Bastian took the direction with another low sound, going over the chemise instead of under it. A slow draw of his finger against the place that longed for it, enough pressure to drive her higher, not enough to send her over.

"Bastian." His name came out shaky, not the order they both wanted; she thrust her hips at him. "Please."

"Aren't you the one giving the orders?" He smiled against her, with another slow, torturous drag of his finger. "Be specific."

And of course he would turn this around like that; of course Bastian Arceneaux would be able to flip the tables on her and leave her a quivering mess when she was supposed to be in charge. Lore fisted her hand in his hair and pulled him away, glaring down at his amused, glazed eyes. "Touch me with your finger the way you plan to touch me later," she ordered, breathless. "Please, Bastian, please—"

Her last words broke off as his hand delved under her chemise, finally, his finger into her, finally. She rocked against his hand, the heel of it hitting exactly where she needed, and it didn't take long for her to come apart, breaking into stars and darkness, her head thrown back and every muscle in her body going tense and then shuddering, shuddering.

Bastian flipped her onto her back on the bed, her chemise rucked up over her hips. "Not waiting for orders on this one," he said, pulling her still-limp thighs apart. "Wanted it too much to wait." And then his mouth was on her and her head was spinning, again, her body coiling for another release.

It came right on the heels of the first one, and when Lore went to sit up and pull him over her, Bastian's hand went hard against her pelvis, holding her down, making sparks fly behind her eyes again. "Not yet," he murmured against the crease of her knee, kissing down the length of her leg and then back up again. "Tastes too good." Then he was back at her center, coiling her up again, and this time when Lore shattered, she screamed.

But she was ready to take control again, knew how she wanted this next part to go. "Behind," she said breathlessly, turning on the bed, getting on hands and knees.

He did as she asked, caressing the small of her back. "You sure you want it like this?"

She did. Nyxara's memories were still too close to scrub completely from her mind, and in those memories, at least, it hadn't been like this. It'd happened before, she was sure, but not in an instance she'd seen in the goddess's head. She wanted this to be just them, a memory that couldn't be interposed over any others, something that belonged to her and Bastian alone. "I'm the one giving orders, aren't I?"

He chuckled, ran his hands over her ribs before settling behind her. Then the push, the gasp, the give, and he was inside her, warm and close.

They stayed like that a moment, both breathing hard. Then Bastian moved, sitting on his knees, and pulled her up, keeping them connected, so she almost sat in his lap. He kissed her shoulder, his hand rising to gently span the front of her neck, not squeezing, just there. His other hand went to the bundle of nerves between her legs. His finger brushed across it; she made a strained, pleasing sound.

"There we go," Bastian growled, and then he started to move, his hips slowly pressing up at her.

She matched his rhythm, clenching down as he pushed up, as his finger circled just where she needed it, his other hand mimicking the motion on her breast. "Do you know how much I've thought about this?" he murmured into her hair. "Do you know how many times I've gripped myself and pretended it was you? I haven't had anyone else since you came to this damn Citadel, Lore. You're all I can think about, all I want, it's driven me fucking *mad*."

He was on the other side of where Gabe had kissed her, where his touch had left a pleasurable bruise. Bastian's teeth gently bit the skin beneath her opposite ear, asking.

She pushed back into him.

His growl vibrated against her neck as he mouthed at her, making his own mark, a mirror to the one Gabe left.

Everything blurred as Lore moved until the only thing she could feel was him, and then she came apart and he followed behind, hiding his shout in her hair.

They slid apart, fell to the side. Bastian gathered her close, his arms around her waist, his chest against her back. Neither of them spoke.

Lore didn't realize she was crying until she felt the tear slide down her cheek, land on the pillow.

But Bastian must have noticed, because he pushed up on his elbow, gently cleared away the track with his thumb. He still said nothing—what was there to say?—but he bent down, and he kissed her, soft and asking for nothing.

And they lay like that for a bit, sweat drying. They'd made a mess, but the bed was big enough that they just rolled away from it, a problem to be dealt with later.

"We should sleep," Bastian said finally around a yawn, as if he was halfway there already.

Lore squeezed her eyes shut, snuggled farther back into him. She waited, listening to his breaths until they evened out, until his grip around her slackened.

Then, careful not to disturb him, she climbed out of bed.

Her gown still lay in a crumpled heap; Lore leaned down and dug through the fabric until she found her pocket. The cloth was still inside, still smelling faintly of chemicals.

Chloroform. The smell was almost nostalgic, reminding her of Gabe and the first time she'd seen him in the alley after she'd raised Horse, of all the things that had conspired to bring her here.

And now she was getting out.

She hadn't planned to sleep with Bastian. She'd planned to use this, knock him out for long enough that he wouldn't know she was gone until she was *long* gone, make it difficult for him—or Apollius—to follow her.

She'd lost valuable time, but she didn't regret it. Not one thing.

Slowly, Lore crept to Bastian. He slept curled on his side, like she was still there, and it put a painful twinge in her chest.

Lore lowered her hand with the cloth scrap until it covered his face. He didn't stir, just breathed in deep, letting it out on a contented sigh.

Holding her breath, afraid it would come out in a sob if she didn't, Lore crumpled the cloth in her fist and got dressed, hurriedly, her thighs still sticky. Then she rushed down to her room, got her bag, and went out the door, leaving the Citadel behind.

Chapter Thirty-Six

True predators don't sleep, they only wait. Be wary.
–Advice from a Caldienan hunter, written in a letter archived at Farramark University

It was easier to get out of the Citadel than it should've been. Lore supposed that made sense—the Presque Mort were still preoccupied with the fire that Gabe had set in the Church, and she guessed the bloodcoats were, too. The halls were nearly deserted, the usual guard outside of their apartments nowhere to be found.

They hadn't been there the night Amelia was murdered, either, Lore remembered. Though now that she knew why she was killed, she wondered if that was on purpose. Maybe Amelia had bribed the bloodcoat to leave.

The thought made Lore shudder, but she stayed her course, winding through opulent hallways toward the green that led to the North Sanctuary and the storm drain Bastian had led them through so long ago. If there was a single good thing about all this, it was that she knew Bastian could take care of himself, now. The guards outside his apartment had long been to keep her in rather than to keep anyone out. Apollius wouldn't let anything happen to him.

Lore pressed her forearm against her mouth until she was sure the pained sound in her throat wouldn't make it past her teeth.

The door to the northern green opened soundlessly. There was a guard here, something Lore found herself absurdly thankful for, even though it could throw a wrench in her plans. She wore a cloak, the hood tugged up over her head, but her departure didn't seem to catch the guard's interest. Two courtiers were kissing next to a bush by the door, and all his attention was on them.

Quickly, she made her way over the cobblestone paths, into the manicured forest. It reminded her of the one in her mind, the one in Nyxara's memories, and she tried to think of anything else as she hurried through it, to the Church wall and the storm drain.

Lore wondered if the goddess had seen everything that had just happened with Bastian, or if She'd somehow turned Herself away completely. She hadn't felt Nyxara in her mind the whole time, so she could only assume the goddess at least tried. *You can come back*, she said into the darkness of her head. *It's done.*

It never is, Nyxara replied. *Even if you never see him again, it will never feel done.*

Well, wasn't that comforting.

The Buried Goddess said nothing about the plan Lore was currently executing, getting the fuck out of Auverraine in the hope her absence would lessen the gods' hold, but Lore could feel Her relief. This was the right path, then. This was the way to fix it.

As much as it could be fixed.

Because, in the end, all Lore was doing was running away. She was good at that, both physically and mentally, simply ignoring anything unpleasant, removing herself from it as much as possible. Yes, maybe the gods would lose their footholds in her friends' minds when Lore was gone, the same way her presence had awoken Bastian's power, but Apollius wouldn't be beaten. He'd simply be postponed, put off. He'd chosen Bastian as His heir, as His vessel, and if that plan was disrupted, maybe things would return to normal. Apollius would go back to wherever He'd waited for Bastian, and the world would right itself, for a while. Maybe even longer than Lore would live, taking the goddess with her, giving Nyxara Her second death.

But Apollius would come back. Someday, He would come back, choose a new vessel from the Arceneaux line, and then He wouldn't even have Nyxara to try to temper Him. Just Himself, and a world at His mercy, and no one with His wife in their head to try to stop Him.

Any input from You on all this would be grand, Lore snapped at Nyxara as she barreled through the trees.

I have nothing to add, Nyxara replied. *You summed it up rather succinctly.*

Lore made a frustrated sound.

The grate over the drain was locked, and unlike Bastian, Lore didn't carry a lockpick in her boot, or anywhere else, seeing as she didn't even have boots anymore. But Mortem lived in iron—she stretched out her hands and twisted the threads, warping the metal until it fell from the drain with a clang. Cursing, Lore glanced around, but it didn't appear anyone was close enough to hear.

She glanced down at her hands. Her palms were nearly covered in corpse-gray, the dead color expanded from her time watching Nyxara's memories, and it was starting to inch up her fingers. Very attractive.

The water was just as disgusting as always; Lore sighed as she jumped down into it, holding her bag above her head in a futile attempt to keep *some* clean clothes. She slogged to the other end, climbed up onto the ledge—much more difficult on your own, without a Prince or a monk to help you out—and channeled the Mortem in the grate again, twisting it off its hinges and sending it splashing into the water below.

When she climbed out of the culvert, shaking her skirt in a vain attempt to dry it, the street on the other side was nearly deserted. Fine by her. Lore shouldered her bag again and started walking, noticing as she did that parts of the road seemed in much better repair than she remembered. Wooden struts and piles of rock stood in some corners, ongoing construction that had finished for the day. Bastian, doing good things. Trying, still, even as a god who didn't care slowly took him over.

She swallowed the thorny feeling in her throat.

Tickets for voyages out of the harbor were sold from a derelict booth nearest the north dock, before you got to the abandoned warehouses beyond, one of which was Val and Mari's headquarters. Lore wasn't sure whether she should expect someone to be on duty in the middle of the night, so it was a pleasant surprise to see the light on. She kept her hood up as she walked to the open window, and briefly considered trying to alter her voice, but decided that would draw more attention than it would defer. "When's the soonest ship to Ratharc?"

Good choice, Nyxara murmured in her head. *You want to stay far away from the Isles.*

The grizzled woman in the window lifted a gray brow, but didn't look up from the battered novel in her hands. "Who's asking?"

"Someone who would like to sail to Ratharc," Lore said through gritted teeth. At least her choice of destination was goddess approved.

The woman closed the novel with a huff, leaned back in her chair. "As of about four hours ago, all commercial ships out of the harbor have been canceled until further notice," she said, sounding like the fact was a particular pain in her ass. "You want to get to Ratharc, you'll have to get your own ship, and good luck finding a crew for it. No one wants to sail out with the Kirytheans on the waves like flies on shit."

"Is that why there are no commercial voyages?" Lore thought she was doing an admirable job of sounding calm, when all her organs seemed to have dropped toward her toes. "Because of the Kirytheans?"

"There's no commercial voyages because the King in the Citadel said there shouldn't be." The woman cracked open her book again, apparently deciding that Lore wouldn't be a better distraction. "Not sure why I'm still here, to be honest. But until my employer says he ain't gonna pay me for sitting here without selling tickets, here I will damn well stay. Beats my room at the Foghorn and Fiddle." And she turned back to her book, Lore dismissed.

Her legs felt like sandbags as Lore trudged away from the ticket booth and out toward the rows of warehouses. Apollius must've felt Nyxara's first death in the catacombs, known what it meant. Known that Lore had found Her body, that Lore was taking Her memories and would learn that getting away might lessen His hold on Bastian. He'd trapped her here.

Going overland, her only possible destination was Caldien, if she wanted to stay out of the Empire. And it'd take weeks to get there, even by carriage, and she'd be so easy to track…

Her body followed a familiar path without her mind telling it to, trudging through streets she knew, the wind off the sea a welcome balm to the humidity in her cloak. She peeled back her hood and let the breeze dry the sweat in her hair. Sweat from Bastian, from everything they'd done. Her eyes blinked closed, and she saw him, naked and heavy-lidded and awe-filled on the end of the bed, fisting his hands in the sheets, gilded silver in moonlight.

She stopped in front of Val and Mari's warehouse, because where else was she going to go?

The special knock, the one they'd taught her. A moment, and the door opened, but the figure behind it wasn't one of Lore's mothers.

It was Michal.

It took him a moment to recognize her, for all that they'd lived together for the better part of a year, for all that he'd seen her raise Horse in the Ward square, that day her whole life spun off its axis and landed her in the Citadel. When he did, his eyes flew wide. "Lore?"

But she was already bolting, already turning away, she'd known this was a mistake—

His hand on her arm, gentle. "Lore, are you all right?"

And she most certainly was not, perhaps hadn't ever been, and Lore was sobbing, then, sinking to the ground like she had in Courdigne, gods when had she become this person? She'd gone twenty-four years without being someone who cried, someone who *blubbered*, and now she crumpled under the slightest pressure, all the scaffolding that held her up brittle as Mortem-fed rock.

None of this pressure could be called slight, Nyxara murmured in her head. *Have some grace for yourself.*

That echoed something she'd told Gabe, once, and just made her cry harder.

Michal's hand on her shoulder, his worried voice calling back into the warehouse. The flutter of a faded scarf, the scent of the thick lotion Mari used on her hands to keep them from getting dry while she did paperwork, the clink of sea-glass beads and the roughness of a work shirt Val had owned for as long as Lore had known her.

Even through her tears, Lore expected their questions, expected worry and urgent requests for explanations. But none of those expected things happened. Just Val's hands on her face, Mari's on her shoulder. "Come on, mouse, let's get inside."

They led her to a made-up cot, and she lay down, and they pulled the covers up over her head. Against all odds, Lore slept.

"I don't think it's a stretch to say that whatever happened has something to do with the commercial ships suddenly being scuppered."

Val's voice, tilted low, like she didn't want to wake someone. Lore assumed she was the someone.

"We don't know that." Mari, on the quick windup to irritated. "There's no sense in borrowing trouble."

"Seems more like trouble showed up on our doorstep," Michal said ruefully.

Lore frowned under the blanket. Since when had Michal been part of Val's crew? Why was he here, acting like he had more right to be than she did?

"Something must've happened at the Citadel." Mari, again. "Something with her new fiancé." She sounded sympathetic. Lore wished it was just romantic problems that had brought her back to her mothers' door.

"Her new fiancé, the fucking Sainted King," Michal said, with a rueful snort.

"And that is why I think it has something to do with the ships, and not just some lovers' quarrel," Val said. "Gods know Lore has never let those get to her head like this before."

If Michal had something to add to that, he kept it to himself.

A scuffle of papers as Val gathered them up—they must've been going over monthly figures before they'd veered off into discussing Lore. "The King froze all sea travel, and then Lore shows up. Those two things have to be connected."

"You're right." Lore pulled the covers off her head, sitting up and rubbing at her tear-and-sleep gummed eyes. "They are."

Val didn't seem surprised at all by her sudden waking; she simply gestured to Lore with an *I told you so* expression. Mari looked worried; Michal looked mortified, as if embarrassed to be caught talking about Lore at all.

She narrowed her eyes at him, then looked to her mothers. "Since when does he work for you?"

"Since we got a contract," Mari said, coming to sit on the end of Lore's cot. She smoothed her hand over Lore's tangled waves. "More people than you'd think have tried to get on with us since then."

"The joy of not having to watch for bloodcoats," Val said, sitting on Lore's other side. "At least, not as closely. Now, you were saying?"

She didn't tell them everything. She didn't think she could, it was too much—the goddess in her head, the god in Bastian's, the threat of an apocalypse that she could only defer by getting as far away as possible. But Lore told them enough, embroidering the frayed edges so they didn't stand out. Told them that she needed to leave the country, that things would go badly if she didn't.

It was clear what that made them think, in the sidelong looks Val and Mari slid to each other, in the way Michal's arms crossed tightly across his chest. "I *will* beat him up again," he said, recalling that day on the docks, a boxing match that showed Bastian exactly who she was. "I've done it before."

"It's not like that. He hasn't hurt me." Bastian hadn't; every hurt had been Apollius. "I just…if I don't leave, something bad will happen."

Another look between Mari and Val, this one considering. "Mouse," Mari said quietly, "would this have something to do with your…with how…"

"Your Mortem problem?" Val said, doing away with niceties. She grabbed Lore's hand, looked at the gray skin of her palms, frowned. "Or do you still have one? It seems that the rest of the city doesn't."

"I still have one." Lore curled her hand closed, snorted. "I have all the Mortem problems, in fact."

Val nodded. "I wondered if you had anything to do with that."

Her heart twisted, the worry that she'd somehow ruined her mothers' business as well as everything else coming in a long-deferred rush. "How has that affected things here?"

Mari waved a dismissive hand. "Honestly, not much. Poison

works on the Mortem within a body; people still use it for pain, for a high. You just have to take a bit more now, is all."

Well, there was one less thing to worry about.

"I'd like to return to the question of something bad happening if you don't leave." Val was never one to be put off track. "We need a little more explanation than that, mouse."

Lore sank her head into her hands, tried to find a way to put all this into simple words.

Good luck, Nyxara said, Her voice faint. Lore glanced at the one skylight set into the ceiling; dawn blushed the clouds. She wondered how long she'd slept, after stumbling here and having a breakdown on the stoop in the middle of the night.

"I don't know how to explain," she said finally, quietly. "I just need you to trust me. Please."

A quick look between Val and Mari, one she remembered well. Mari nodded, sighed. "What do you need?"

Relief hit her so hard it felt like a punch. "I need to get out of Auverraine. Go somewhere that isn't controlled by the Empire. If there's no ships, it looks like my only choice is Caldien."

"Hold on." Michal held up a hand. "You need to get to *Caldien*? That's at least two weeks' journey, and only if you get a fast carriage. The cost alone—"

"Not helping, Michal," Val said.

Michal closed his mouth and tightened his arms over his chest again.

"But he's right." Mari furrowed her brow. "Going overland to Caldien would take forever, and cost a fortune. The fortune part you could probably spare—the dress you're wearing is worth a small one—but it seems like time is of the essence."

She was so thankful for them, Val and Mari, who never wasted time trying to place blame or demand answers. There would be time for that later, they knew; they only wanted to make sure Lore had what she needed. She loved them so much it hurt.

"Thankfully, there are no restrictions on privately owned vessels, at least not yet," Mari continued. "We own a small one. It'd be enough to get you to Caldien, and if you stayed close to the coast, you wouldn't have to worry about Kirythean ships."

"Too bad I can't sail," Lore murmured.

"I can," Michal said with a sigh.

Her eyes jerked up, met his. "You would..."

He shrugged. "You obviously need help," he said. "Seems selfish not to provide it, when I have the means."

Lore chewed the inside of her cheek. "Thank you, Michal."

He huffed a laugh. "Consider it reimbursement for all those times you got me out of paying rent."

Mari nodded, the matter seemingly closed. "Michal will take you to Caldien in the morning, then, and you write to us from there. Tell us what you can, when you can."

"You're being remarkably calm about this," Lore murmured.

Val shrugged, standing up to toss an arm over her wife's shoulders. "We always knew things would be complicated with you, mouse. We've been prepared." She gave Lore a crooked grin. "Keeps us young."

With that, Val and Mari adjourned themselves to the office, speaking in low voices of the ship and where it was docked, of how secretive they'd need to be to get it going and who they could send to make sure it was in traveling shape. The door closed behind them, and then Michal and Lore were left alone, neither of them wanting to make eye contact.

Michal broke the awkward silence. Strange; Lore was used to being the one who had to do that. "So he wasn't cruel to you?"

"No." If she tried to talk about it more, she'd start crying again, and she was frankly tired of crying. Lore crossed her legs on the bed, knotted her hands together. Her engagement ring cut into her fingers; she hadn't taken it off before she left.

"You know you could tell me, if he was."

"He wasn't, Michal. This has nothing to do with him. It has to do with me." Part truth, part lie.

"Well." He blew out his breath in a huff. "That's good, at least."

She twisted her ring.

After a moment, Michal came and gingerly sat down beside her, as if expecting her to push him away. She didn't, scooting over instead, making room.

Michal shifted, making the whole tiny cot creak. "I assume you're expecting me to offer to stay with you in Caldien," he said. "And you're trying to find a polite way to say you don't want that. But you don't have to worry about it." He slid his eyes her way. "I'm over you."

Lore snorted, loud and un-lady-like. "Fantastic news, thank you."

"Thought it might help."

The silence didn't feel so brittle, after that. Lore sighed, rubbing at her temples. "Sorry to pull you into my bullshit, yet again."

Michal shrugged. "At least it's always interesting bullshit." He glanced at her again, thoughtful. "I hope you can find some rest soon, Lore. I hope that you can find something simple. You deserve simple, I think."

Tears threatened at her eyes again, thinking of Bastian, thinking of Gabe, of how it could never really be simple. She forced her mouth into a smile.

A knock at the door, not the coded one that meant it was Val's crew, but the rhythmic banging of someone demanding entry.

Lore stood as the door to the office opened, Val's face pale as she stared at the door. "Bloodcoats," she snarled, ducking back through the threshold, coming out with her pistol. "Lore, you and Michal go—"

"Lore!" Her name, shouted from beyond the door, in a familiar feminine voice. Alie's voice. "Lore, it's us!"

"Put that away!" Lore rushed across the room to the door and wrenched it open. On the other side stood Gabe, Malcolm, and

Alie, all dressed for traveling, all looking like they hadn't slept the night before.

"I thought you'd be here." Gabe didn't say it like triumph, though. He said it like he wished he had been wrong. "Please tell me you're trying to leave the country."

She nodded, her brow deeply furrowed. "It looks like you are, too."

"Seemed like a good idea, now that we know for sure Apollius is just fine with murder." Heedless of the fact that he'd almost been shot by a poison runner, Malcolm walked through the door, putting down his satchel. "Too bad there are no damn ships."

"Hold on." Val had blessedly holstered her pistol, but she still didn't look pleased by the sudden intrusion, even if her eyes did narrow in recognition on Gabe's face. "What's this about Apollius and murder?"

Gabe sighed, closing his one eye. "The Sainted King is…at least, we think…"

So much for trying to give easy explanations. "Bastian is possessed by Apollius," Lore said. "And that isn't a good thing."

Val's mouth hung open. Mari's, too. Still seated on the cot, Michal looked like a soft breeze would knock him over.

"You know what?" Val waved her hand, as if erasing a board so it was clear to try again. "I don't really want to know. I assume this means the three of you need a ship to Caldien, too?"

"No, they don't." Lore turned to her friends, brows drawn low. "If I leave, the gods will get out of your heads. I'm the catalyst. You can't come with me, or the power will keep growing."

They all three stared at her with varying expressions of incredulity. Alie leaned around Lore's shoulder, speaking to Val. "A ship would be wonderful, thank you."

With a sharp nod, Val went back into the office, cursing under her breath. Mari gave Lore an arch look, the same she would give her when she was a teenager and on the cusp of trouble, and followed her wife inside.

But Lore wasn't done. "You can't—"

"No, *you* can't." Alie poked her hard in the shoulder. "You aren't fucking off to Caldien or anywhere else by yourself, Lore. If your theory is true, and your distance makes Apollius leave Bastian's head, that's great. But we aren't taking chances." Her voice softened. "Not with ourselves, and not with you."

It'd be pointless to argue. Lore sighed. "Fine. So I assume He knows about you?" She looked anxiously to Gabe. "He knows what all of you are?"

"We aren't sure," Alie answered. She sat on one of the cots, arms crossed. "But He was... not exactly reasonable, once He realized you were gone, a couple hours ago. And what happened with Amelia made us all decide that it's probably best if we're not here."

"It feels like a coward's way out," Malcolm said softly, looking at the floor, "but I'm not sure what else we can do. I have contacts in Caldien, at the university. They have close ties with the Prime Minister. If we can get an audience with him and explain what's happening, we may be able to get some help."

Some help. A fight. Another war on Auverraine's doorstep, closing them in. But... "How exactly do you think we can explain this?"

Malcolm rubbed at the bridge of his nose. "We'll work that out when we get there."

Lore's jaw clenched. "And the Kirytheans? What are they doing?"

"Nothing, as far as I know," Alie said. "No one is greatly concerned with them; you leaving is all they want to talk about. Some are putting it together with Amelia's murder, and some think it might have to do with the boat explosion." Her green eyes were sympathetic. "The most prevalent rumor right now is that you killed her because you caught her and Bastian together, and he's railing to get you back so you can face justice."

Lore barked a laugh. "I guess that's better than thinking I'm an explosives-happy traitor."

It shouldn't surprise her that the situation had twisted like that, the pieces almost truth. She sat down heavily next to Alie and thought of the actual murder she'd committed. It wasn't likely anyone would discover it for a while, if Gabe was here.

She should tell him. Soon. But not right now.

The clearing of a throat; Michal stood at the edge of the group. He looked extremely out of his element, but also like he'd rather die than admit that. "Well," he said, "I'm Michal, and I guess I'll be captaining your boat in a couple hours. The good news is that I've beat up Bastian Arceneaux at the boxing ring on more than one occasion, so I'm confident I could do it again if necessary. The bad news is that I doubt I could beat up a god."

Chapter Thirty-Seven

> The ways of gods will always overcome the ways of men. Do not attempt to understand that which is not for you to know.
>
> –The Book of Holy Law, Tract 864

Two of Val's crew came by the warehouse—Alie, Malcolm, Gabe, and Lore hid in the back to avoid questions—and got instructions on where the ship was hidden and what needed to be done before it could sail the hundred-plus miles to the Caldienan coast. Mari gave them the rundown. It all sounded like gibberish to Lore, rigging and portside and lots of hoisting. Michal, thankfully, seemed to know what he was doing, so there was one thing going right.

Lore almost wished he didn't, that she'd have to dedicate a large part of her mind to worrying about running aground or sinking or whatever else one had to worry about on an ocean voyage. It'd give her something to think about other than Bastian, other than the fact that they were all leaving him here alone.

Just like the gods had done to Apollius, so long ago.

Bastian wasn't the only thought she was trying to avoid. Seeing Val and Mari made her think of Lilia, of the rose she'd thrown down the well. She'd thought she had no hope that help would come from her birth mother, if she was even still alive. But that wasn't quite true, apparently, because the fact that no help had come, that she was being let down once again, felt like a hole in her stomach.

When the crew was gone and they no longer had to hide, there was nothing more to do than sit. Sit, and wait. It wasn't a state that their anxious minds were conducive to, so Alie pulled out a pack of cards and tried to teach Lore some complicated game that neither of them had the attention necessary to play, while Gabe paced, and Malcolm and Michal sat on one of the far cots, talking animatedly.

Alie arched a brow in their direction. "Seems like Malcolm will have plenty of distraction on our trip."

Lore glanced back over her shoulder to where Michal was ogling Malcolm's scarred arms. "I'll have to tell Michal about that celibacy vow, even though I'm fairly sure Gabe is the only one who takes it seriously."

"More like you'll have to warn him about Malcolm's endless enthusiasm for discussing old-ass books." Alie dealt another hand. Lore was pretty sure she was winning, but truly had no idea.

Val herded them all behind the boxes again an hour later, when the crew members came back to report that the ship was...well, shipshape. And moments after that, they were leaving.

Mari pulled Lore into a fierce hug, the sea-glass beads at the ends of her braids clinking musically. "Write to us," she murmured. "And if you can't do that, we'll come to you."

Lore's arms tightened around her mother. "Can you not just come now?" Being here always made her revert to her younger self, when fear had always meant trying to keep her mothers close. She hated that she was having to think of that now, wanting to keep them safe from Bastian—from Apollius—but the thought of them staying in Auverraine set cold dread into her middle like a leech on a wound.

"We can't just leave, mouse," Mari replied, pulling back to put her warm hands on Lore's cheeks. "People are counting on us here. And it would look suspicious, for us to leave right after you do."

He would come to question them. Lore knew it, and she knew Apollius's modes of questioning would not be kind. "Please, Mari. He'll know I came to you. He'll—"

"He'll ask us where you went. We'll say we don't know." She shrugged, a hard light glinting in her eyes. "That's the only answer the Sainted King will get, god in his brain or no."

"I don't want you to get hurt," Lore whispered, tears burning at the backs of her eyes.

Mari gently pushed her hair behind her ear. "That's half of what love is, mouse," she murmured. "Learning to live with fear. Deciding it's worth it."

Lore hugged her again.

Warmth at her back—Val, closing them both in her corded arms. "Love you," she said, her voice the gruff tone that said she was feeling far more emotions than she wanted to show. "Write us. We're coming there when we can, either way."

"Once we tie up all the loose ends here," Mari agreed, reaching up to lightly tug on her wife's braid.

"You concentrate on staying safe," Val continued. "Don't worry about us."

"You know I will." The words came out mangled from where Lore's face was pressed against Mari's shoulder. She nudged back at Val. "Leave off, Ma, I can't breathe."

She so rarely referred to either of them by anything other than their names, even though they were her parents in every way that counted. Val hesitated a moment, then hugged her harder. "What's that? Couldn't understand you."

Lore made a garbled sound, and all three of them were laughing, then, shaking from being pressed together. Finally, Val let go, straightening Lore's gown and her cloak. "Gods dead and dying, this dress is far too nice for you to be wearing it down here."

Lore grimaced. "I'll sell it as soon as I get to Caldien. I miss wearing boots."

Behind them, Alie watched, her lower lip between her teeth. As Lore broke away from her mothers, she thought of Alie's own, and of Bellegarde, left rotting in Courdigne. She went over to her friend and wrapped her arms around her, half expecting the other woman to seize up and stand stiff, but Alie returned the embrace, pulling in a long, deep breath through her nose.

"We'll be all right," Lore murmured.

Alie just nodded.

They trooped out into the morning, thin fingers of pink streaking the sky. Lore studied the approaching dawn with nerves writhing in her gut. Last night, she'd left the Citadel with no problem, and the lack of guards busting down the door to Val and Mari's warehouse meant that Bastian hadn't given them the word—Alie said that he was already awake, already knew she'd left. Apollius was in control. Surely, Bastian knew where she'd gone. It all came down to whether he could hide that information in his head, seal it up somewhere Apollius couldn't find.

Or maybe Bastian himself would give the order, no godly influence needed. Afraid to be left alone, afraid to let her go, even if it was the only thing that could save him.

Lore fell behind the others as she thought, mist swirling over her slippered feet. They were stained from trekking through the storm drain last night; part of Lore expected to be struck down with some hideous storm-drain disease before they even reached Caldien. Wouldn't *that* be an anticlimactic second death for Nyxara.

Alie fell into step beside her, letting the others pull farther ahead, following the cobblestone road down to one of the smaller docks where merchants kept their galleys. "I've never been on a sea voyage," Alie said, clearly trying to shine a positive light on things. "Or to Caldien. Or to a university." She snorted. "So this should be full of new experiences for me. I've never really been farther from the Citadel than some noble's house on summer progress."

Strange, that even wealth could be a cage. A gilded prison rather than a squalid one.

"I've never been, either," Lore said. "I've never been outside of Dellaire, until we went to the farmlands. Mortem wouldn't let me."

"But it will now," Alie murmured, eyeing Lore's hands. The gray skin of her palms showed when her arms swung. It seemed like it covered a larger area of her skin than it had before, like it was spreading ever since Nyxara died her first death.

Lore's instinct was to close her hands to fists, but she fought against it. "It will now," she agreed.

They walked in silence for a moment. Until it was broken by a gunshot.

Cold spread through Lore's body. It took a moment for her to realize it was because a bullet had ripped through her middle.

"Oh," she said, almost annoyed, then dropped.

Her knees barked against the cobblestones, her breath coming in a long gasp. The bag she'd quickly packed last night before going to Bastian spilled out over the street, shimmering gowns not fit for traveling, things she'd shoved into her pack without thinking. The glimmer of them caught her eye, expanded, became nearly all she could see, the only thing her brain would latch onto.

Shouting. Running feet. "You weren't supposed to shoot her, you fucking idiot, he wants her back! If she dies he'll have you drawn and quartered!"

Lore looked down.

Blood on her stomach. An echo from the past. She would laugh, if she could gather up the breath for it.

Breath. Life. Spiritum.

Next to her, Alie screamed, but then she was pulled away, the bloodcoats suddenly flooding the street from where they'd hidden in warehouses, taking anyone prisoner they could reach. Lore couldn't pay attention to that right now. Instead, she closed her eyes, forcing herself to focus past the cold-burning pain. Winding in golden threads around her fingers, concentrating them over the gunshot wound in her stomach, almost exactly where August had stabbed her months ago.

It was harder to heal, this time. The bullet was savage in a way the knife wasn't, a contradictory truth—one was so much more personal, but the distance of the other lent it violence. Her insides were mangled around the thing's trajectory, and it was still lodged in her, caught somewhere between organ and rib. Repairing it took so much more effort than healing her stab wound had, and it fucking *hurt*, the bullet drawing slowly out of the bloody cavity, sucking at muscle and flesh.

The chaos around her faded to background noise; she had to concentrate to see what was happening, quite a feat when she was also trying to reverse a gunshot.

Bloodcoats held Alie as she shrieked, the sound of it echoing through the empty morning. A guard had clapped irons around her hands, fighting against the gusts of harsh wind she summoned with twitching fingers. Farther down the road, Malcolm and Gabe fought off other guards, but not just with daggers, and not in the subtle way Alie did. Their hands were outflung—thin blades of grass surged forward where Malcolm pointed, surprisingly strong, latching around polished boots. Fire torrented from Gabe's hands, catching on red coats, the smell of burning meat and hair billowing into the seaside air, chased by hoarse screams.

Well. If Apollius hadn't known that the other gods had found vessels, He would now.

"Idiots," Lore mumbled, the blood in her mouth slopping over her numb lips, her chin. They had to leave. Had to *go*.

The dock was visible down the gentle hill of the road. Mari and Michal had sprinted to the ship, doing...something...with ropes and hooks, which Lore assumed was supposed to make a ship ready to sail. They *had* to sail. Gabe and Malcolm and Alie had to be on that ship. If they weren't, it was a death sentence.

Her breath came more steadily as her insides knit back together. The bloodcoats had left her mostly alone, as if afraid to touch her now that she'd been shot, afraid to somehow be implicated in her death.

Death. Her other power.

Lore stood up. Her legs were shaky, and her too-fine dress was soaked in blood. Down the hill, Gabe caught her eye, attuned to her movements even now. He shouted something, but it was lost in the boom of more gunfire, the shouts of burning men as he hurled flame. Some had caught on the warehouses; more than one was ablaze, billowing thick smoke. Alie's shrieks echoed as the bloodcoats hauled her back up the street.

But Lore just watched Gabe, his face a grimace, limned in firelight that stood out so strangely against the pale glow of dawn.

"You have to go!" She flung out her hands along with her shout, indicating the ship—Mari and Michal were doing more things with ropes, and Val was standing at the gangplank, firing her pistol at any bloodcoat who came near. She was a hell of a shot, and at least three crimson-coated bodies sprawled at the edge of the sea. "You have to be on that ship! I can take care of Alie!"

An empty promise, possibly. But she had some measure of influence over Apollius, something He wanted. Surely she could bargain for her friend's life. The god was a malleable being, able to change His mind—she could do something. She had to.

But even if she could save one of them, Lore didn't think she could save them all.

Gabe shouted something back, probably some martyr-like sentiment about how he wasn't going to leave her. But Lore was prepared for that.

She stretched out her hands. She tugged at the Mortem in the cobblestones.

They exploded.

She'd directed it with careful precision; the only stones that blew into pieces were around the bloodcoats, sending them falling back, rending bloody gouges in more than one head as shrapnel flew. A piece of flying rock clipped Lore's shoulder; she healed it without a second thought, twisting a golden thread of Spiritum around her finger, channeling it through her.

The erupting street forced Malcolm and Gabe back, closer to the ships. Lore raised her hands, grabbed Mortem, made another row of rock blast apart, forcing them back farther. She'd do this all the way to the docks if she had to.

Finally, Gabe seemed to get the picture, to realize that he was of no use to anyone if he was dead. And he would be, if he kept this up—he might have Hestraon's power to manipulate fire, but the bloodcoats had *guns*, and all it took was one bullet to find its mark. With a wrench of his jaw that looked like a pained, helpless scream, Gabe turned and ran toward the ship, dragging Malcolm behind him. Val started cranking up the gangplank before they were off it, sending them tipping onto the deck in a tangle of singed monk. She kept firing into the crowd of bloodcoats, though most of them were turning around, now, headed in Lore's direction. She was the thing they wanted most. She was what they'd come for.

What He wanted.

The ship pulled away from the dock, ropes falling into the sea as if Mari and Michal hadn't quite finished their preparations, setting sail prematurely to get ahead of whatever storm would follow. And there would be one. Of that, Lore had no doubt.

But it looked like Val and Mari were going, too, headed to relative safety in Caldien. That was good.

The bloodcoats surrounded her. She didn't pay attention as they shackled her wrists, as they looked askance at the blood on her gown, the place where a bullet hole should be. She just watched that ship get steadily smaller on the horizon.

Chapter Thirty-Eight

You cannot run from My justice.
–The Book of Holy Law, Tract 190

Part of her thought that the bloodcoats would be secretive as they brought her back into the Citadel. That they'd remove her shackles, let her put on a dress that wasn't stiff with her own blood. But they did no such thing. They marched Lore and Alie from the docks and through the streets while the citizens of Dellaire looked on, whispers rising in their wake. The hemlock Queen, the deathwitch Queen, the murderer, maybe the traitor.

She'd forgotten they'd pinned that on her, forgotten how fast rumors traveled in the Court of the Citadel. How fast they made it beyond the walls.

Next to her, Alie hung limp in another bloodcoat's grip, a strand of pale hair falling to curl against her cheek. Somehow, she still looked ethereal, even with Lore's blood streaking her sky-blue skirt, bruises blooming on her arms. She kept quiet, staring straight ahead, fear lending an animal gleam to her dark-green eyes.

There had to be enough of Bastian left to make sure nothing

happened to Alie. Enough to spare her life even though she was the avatar of Lereal.

Surely, there was some of Bastian left.

The gates of the Citadel cranked open. The bloodcoats marched them through.

Courtiers gathered along the pathways into the Citadel proper, murmuring behind their hands, eyeing Lore with open disgust. It was no surprise when the first one spit at her. It dripped down Lore's cheek. She didn't react. She stared straight ahead, not giving them any more ammunition. Disquiet and violence hung in the air, thick as the humidity, just waiting for an opening. As bad as this was, it could always get worse. Lore could at least be sure that Apollius wasn't going to publicly beat her to death. Mostly.

Alie got none of the same treatment, thank all the gods. The looks she received from the crowd were almost…reverent. Awed, curious.

The other woman turned her eyes to Lore. *They know*, Alie's face said, naked fear. *Somehow, they know who I am.*

At first, Lore thought of Lereal, of the god-power lurking in Alie's head, in her fingers. But there was another facet to her identity, something Lore had forgotten. Something that might save her.

Alie was August's daughter. An Arceneaux.

Surely, *surely*, Bastian wouldn't let Apollius kill her.

The doors to the throne room were open. More courtiers lined the iron-barred floor, gathered near the walls, silent and staring and brewing in their hate. On the throne, the Sainted King, his knees thrown wide to take up all the space, his elbow on the arm, cheek propped against his fist. His sun-rayed crown rose over his head, the garnets sparking in the light through the solarium window.

The pose was all Bastian. But the eyes were all Apollius.

The bloodcoats deposited Lore and Alie in the center of the

room, one of the iron bars crossing the floor snaking beneath their feet. Lore's shackles clanked. Alie's fingers worked back and forth, as if she might call the wind again, before thinking better of it.

Apollius shifted on the throne, steepling Bastian's fingers together, looking down at them like one would look at children who needed correcting. His mouth twisted to the side, and Lore remembered that mouth, its heat, the things it would say. She squeezed her eyes shut.

When Apollius finally spoke, it wasn't to her. "I'm glad to find you safe," he murmured, the words directed to Alie. "Sister."

A collective intake of breath in the throne room, so deep and so simultaneous that Lore was surprised there was air left afterward.

"I was so worried when you were kidnapped by the Priest Exalted and head librarian," Apollius continued, his voice firm, spinning the story they would hold as truth. "They would have succeeded, had we not moved so quickly. An attempt was made by my betrothed to slow me down, but thank all the gods, it was unsuccessful." His eyes, far more gold than brown, turned to Lore, a wicked smile curling the edge of His lip. "The next time she tries such a thing, she should be more . . . submissive."

More whispers from the court, shocked. The way the Sainted King spoke sounded like He planned to keep his poison Queen alive, keep her *around*, surely that couldn't be right? Not after she'd killed Amelia Demonde in a fit of jealousy? Not after she may have planted an explosive in that ship?

But Lore wasn't thinking about that. She was thinking about that word, *submissive*, what it meant. He'd seen, He'd torn through Bastian's memories and relived their last night together, something that was supposed to be only theirs. She'd known He would, that He would be strong enough to break through Bastian's defenses eventually. Still, it made her furious. Made her want to weep.

She fought through that, focusing instead on what it meant that He was telling lies for Alie, telling the court she was an Arceneaux. That meant He wouldn't kill her, right?

Or it meant that Apollius was so far ahead in this game that it was pointless to try keeping up.

Apollius gave her a slow, heated look, as if wanting Lore to break, wanting her to cry. When it became clear she wouldn't, He turned back to Alie. "My father treated your mother horribly. For that, I am sorry. But I wish to raise you to your proper place, Alienor. To give you all that should've been yours as a member of the Arceneaux family, one of Apollius's chosen." A smirk flickered at His mouth. "To that end, I have brokered a betrothal for you. A much better one than you had previously, I think we will both agree."

"I don't want a betrothal," Alie said. "I don't want to be an Arceneaux."

"An argument I've heard before," Apollius murmured, eyes flashing. "You'll get used to it." He raised His hand and His voice, addressing the room rather than just the two of them. "Alienor Arceneaux, may I present your betrothed—Jax Aronicus, Emperor of Kirythea."

Silence. The Court of the Citadel held its breath.

A figure stepped up onto the dais with Bastian. A figure it took Lore a minute to place, here in the sunny throne room, when the last time she'd seen him had been in the shadows of the holding cells.

Caius.

Caius was Jax.

Pieces snapped together like setting bone. Why the Kirytheans had been so content to languish in prison. Why Bastian—Apollius—had never introduced them to Gabe, for fear he might recognize the man who had killed his father. Why the Empire hadn't taken the arrest of their diplomats as an act of war. All a plan, from the beginning.

Which meant Apollius had been taking over Bastian for

longer than Lore knew. Longer than he knew to tell her, in those snatches of lucidity, when he was still himself. Bastian couldn't keep things from Apollius, but the god kept plenty from him.

An entire conspiracy had spun out without Bastian knowing. A start to the world Apollius wanted.

A globe-spanning Holy Kingdom, starting here.

Alie stared at the Emperor, openmouthed. "No," she whispered, hoarse. Then, louder. "No, I will *not*."

Apollius sat back in his throne. "Jax and I have been discussing peace." His voice reached every ear in the room, dangling that word above them like a carrot on a proverbial stick. "Our conclusion has been that it makes the most sense to unite. To become one ruling kingdom, bringing the entire continent beneath one crown. *My* crown."

First the continent, then the world. How had He gotten the Kirytheans to turn over their Empire?

Or had this been the point of the Empire all along? Making a kingdom for a god they knew would return?

Jax was looking at Alie, his face unreadable. But at Apollius's pronouncement, he turned, inclined his head deeply toward the throne. Far more deeply than one royal to another.

More like a man to his god.

"To do this," Apollius continued, acknowledging Jax's bow with a nod, "we must unite our families. We cannot ask of the continent what we cannot do ourselves."

No mention of Alie's power. No mention of the god in her mind. It should reassure Lore, maybe, make her think that Apollius wouldn't chase Gabe and Malcolm, maybe He didn't know Alie had Lereal's share from the Fount.

But it didn't. It just made her wonder how much worse His plan for all of them must be.

"Bastian." Alie's voice was thin. A tremble started in her still-bound hands. "Bastian, please."

Apollius looked at her through Bastian's eyes. He didn't say anything, but He gave her a tiny smile, a tiny shake of His head. There was no Bastian, not anymore.

Nausea clawed at Lore's throat.

Moving slowly, like Alie was an animal he didn't want to startle, Jax stepped off the dais. "I will do my best to be a good husband to you, Alienor." Gingerly, he took her trembling hand, closed it in his own. "Our union will bring about the union of the Enean continent, and then the world."

Alie didn't say anything. Her cheeks were blanched beneath her freckles.

"Now that one betrothal is made," Apollius said, finally standing, "another ends."

Lore closed her eyes again, not wanting to see Him walk forward, not wanting to watch Him use Bastian's body like a puppet. Murmurs rose around her, sickly pleased. *Here* was the justice they were after. Finally, an end to the hemlock Queen, this pretender who should never have been allowed among them.

She didn't open her eyes even as she felt Him take her hand, felt Him adjust the engagement ring on her finger. "Showtime, beloved," He murmured, so close she could feel His lips brush the shell of her ear.

"I'm not your beloved," Lore murmured back, her nails clawing into His hand. It reminded her of last night, and her heart lurched even as her eyes opened, glaring at one of the golden frescoes on the wall instead of looking at Him. "She's not, either. And She's not here."

"She's always here." His hand came to her cheek, forced her to turn toward His face. Bastian's face, but changed, the angles sharper, all traces of joy gone. No one who didn't love him would notice. Just her and Gabe.

"She's always in your head," Apollius continued, still whispering. "And now that She's had Her first death, Her hold on you will be even stronger." His grip tightened. "Did you like that, Lore? Seeing us fuck in Her memories? Seemed only fair that I look in on yours, too."

She snarled wordlessly, but Apollius was leaning back, gesturing toward the throne again. "Alexis, if you please? Just the bare-bones vows will do." He grinned, pitching His voice to carry. "I know you all expected a sentencing. For my betrothed to be sent to the Burnt Isles for the murder of Amelia Demonde. But I've received word from Farramark, where pieces of the ship that exploded those weeks past have been tested. Amelia Demonde was responsible."

Shocked gasps from the crowd. One from Lore, too. What game was He playing now?

Apollius held her eyes, smiled. "Lore discovered Amelia's guilt before the rest of us, using her power," He said, "and meted out justice. We should thank her, not punish her. And that is why I'm making her my Queen. Today."

Lore didn't buckle. Her knees stayed locked and firm, her hands didn't tremble in her shackles. But she did hiss in a breath, sharp, and the silence of the room made it echo.

The god seemed almost disappointed that He hadn't gotten more of a reaction. He gave her one long look, His eyes glittering, then waved Alexis forward.

Alexis, for their part, looked completely out of their element. They wore white robes, hiding their Presque Mort black—Lore almost expected to see the Bleeding God's Heart pendant hanging from their neck, a hastily made appointment now that one Priest Exalted was gone, but it wasn't there. Gabe must still have it. Gabe must still officially hold the office, though surely that couldn't last long.

The Compendium was open in Alexis's hands. They met Lore's eyes, then glanced at the blood on the front of her gown, looking confused and almost guilty. Their hands moved like they might shut the holy book, might refuse.

But Lore gave them a sharp shake of her head. She couldn't have anyone falling on a sword for her, not now.

A shaky sigh, then Alexis began, reading from the Book of Mortal Law. "And should any two people wish to be joined in the sight of Apollius, they should seek to cleave together like the night and the day..."

Lore didn't really listen. Lore stared at the solarium window above the throne as she was wed to the Sainted King in irons and a bloody dress, stared at the sun shining down on them, too hot and too bright. When she became the Queen of Auverraine, she didn't even hear the applause.

When Apollius kissed her, she just closed her eyes.

Apollius took her to the North Sanctuary.

Lore was still drifting in her mind, still hanging on to only the barest tether of her thoughts. It kept her from panicking, kept her distant enough to try to look at her situation objectively. She only clocked the direction they were going as a small relief, since she'd assumed Apollius would lead her to Bastian's bedchamber, the same place she'd slept with him the night before.

No. Don't think of that. Don't think of him.

No courtiers followed them, no merry band of celebrants to ring in their new marriage. Her shackles had been taken off at some point, at least.

"Don't get any ideas, wife," Apollius said as He walked her quickly down the path and into the double doors of the North Sanctuary. "Remember that I can channel Mortem, too. I don't want to stick you in stone while I wait for you to come around, but I will if I have to."

She hadn't gotten any ideas. His trap had been laid over centuries, and any attempt she'd made to wrestle free of it had only tangled her further.

The sanctuary was empty. The pews had been polished to a high shine, the braziers bordering the platform lit and filled with fragrant incense. Red rose petals lined the aisle, and two glasses of wine waited on the lectern. He'd decorated the sanctuary the same way someone would decorate a bridal suite.

Her stomach twisted.

Apollius kept His iron grip on her arm, steering them down the petal-strewn aisle. When they reached the lectern, He took a glass of wine, held the other out for her.

She looked Him in the eye as she poured it on the floor.

With a sigh, Apollius put His glass back down on the lectern, took off the sun-rayed crown and set it on one of the pews. He reached for her; she backed up, her slippers squishing in the sticky mess she'd made of the carpet. With a lift of His brow, He let His hand drop. "This doesn't have to be a battle, Lore. You love Bastian, don't you? Planned to marry him? Essentially, nothing has changed."

"Yes, it fucking has." She tried to work up some spit in her throat, swallow enough to make her voice sound less scratchy, less weak. "You aren't him. You... You stole him!"

That arched brow lifted farther, that familiar smile curling higher. Apollius tapped a finger against His temple. "He's still in here," He murmured. "And if you play nice, maybe I'll let him out occasionally. I don't mind the two of you having some time together. It was fun to watch."

Lore's shriek of rage wasn't much, just a thin ribbon of furious sound. Her fingers thrust out, twisted, called up a storm of Mortem like black thread from the ground.

But Apollius anticipated that; gold flared around His hands, and He slashed through the threads, cutting them loose. Mortem and Spiritum might be held by them both, now, but one could still cancel out the other.

"Let's not start with all that," Apollius said smoothly, stepping over the puddle of wine. Lore backed up again, and again, until her back hit the stained-glass window. It cast His face in rainbow colors, made Him glow. "You know you can't match Me in power, Lore. Or rather, you can, and that's the problem. We are perfectly, evenly matched. A fitting pair."

He was right in front of her, now, caging her against His body—Bastian's body—and the window, one hand coming up to rest beside her head. Like in the alley, after the first time Bastian brought her to a boxing match, snarling down at her because he thought she was a spy for his father. It made all this so much worse, how familiar it was, how she knew every line of his form pressed against her and knew it wasn't *him*.

Apollius's other hand rose, cupping her cheek. He searched her eyes. "All four of us could find a way to live with one another, Lore."

"You're building an *Empire*," she snarled. "You're wrecking the whole damn world, because You want to live forever, and You want the entire earth at Your disposal when You do. I will never find a way to live with that."

"You say it like it's a bad thing," Apollius said, drawing His thumb down her cheek. "Who says a Holy Kingdom has to be bad? All of us united, together."

"Empires don't work like that," Lore said, trying to turn her head so she didn't have to look at Him. He tightened His grip on her chin. "Empires flatten everything they touch."

"Think what you want." Clearly, Apollius didn't give a shit about her opinions on Empire. "We both know you aren't a political mind. Your concern is for Bastian, and for your friends that left you here."

Lore tensed, wondering how far the ship had gotten by now.

"Even Gabriel left you," Apollius murmured. "I heard he put up a fight first, though. A fight with fire. Interesting."

She sagged.

"I'll let you say goodbye, when I bring them back," Apollius continued. "Before I kill him. As thorough a goodbye as you want." He grinned. "There are other ways to get back the power that is rightfully mine. If the others play nice, we'll use less violent methods. But Hestraon... Him, I want dead."

So He knew. He knew, and He had a plan.

"Maybe I'll let Bastian out for that." He moved closer, so His lips brushed her temple. "Both the killing, and the goodbye. He cares for him, too. It will be like old times—"

Lore brought up her knee, driving it into His groin. Apollius growled but didn't loosen His hold on her—a god's pain tolerance was too damn high. Lore's head slammed back into the glass, hard enough to make stars swim behind her eyelids.

"You're just the same," He snarled. "Just the same as Her. Willing to sacrifice everything for Them, when I could give you so much more." His golden eyes stared down into hers, searching, His lip lifting to bare His teeth. "Are You in there, beloved? Hiding from Me, still?"

A hoarse, painful laugh wrenched from Lore's throat. "She doesn't want to talk to You."

"We'll see." He gripped her chin harder, brought His lips closer. "Let's leave questions of Empire and our reawakened friends alone, for the moment. It's our wedding day, after all. We should talk about us."

She tried to squirm out of His grip, but He held her as surely as those shackles had, pinned her to the window.

"If I live forever," He said, tracing a finger down the line of her jaw, "that means Bastian does, too. Shouldn't you want that, if you really love him?" His head cocked to the side. "Or is that love really yours? Is it just echoes of Nyxara and Me?"

"It's not," she said, craning her head so she whispered in His ear, "because Nyxara doesn't love You. Not anymore." She laughed, dry and rasping. "She *hates* You, Apollius. She wants You gone even more than I do."

The god growled again, one hand tightening on her chin, the other grasping at her hair and wrenching her head to the side. It hurt, and Lore cried out, and maybe this would be Nyxara's second death—

The pressure of His body was gone in a rush; Lore nearly fell, sliding down the window before she got strength in her knees again. Apollius stood away from her, in that puddle of spilled wine, head hanging forward so His hair hid His face, breaths panting in and out.

Then He looked up.

Not Apollius.

Bastian.

He looked horrified, his eyes wide and bruised beneath, lips gone pale. Lore lurched toward him, but he held up a hand, backing away from her. "Don't." His voice was ravaged, like he'd spent hours screaming. "Don't come close, Lore, I can't— He's too—"

Then he was gone, eyes bleeding from brown to gold. He shook His shoulders, like Bastian was a cold breeze. "That was probably a good thing," He said, almost to Himself. "Can't go killing You now that I finally have You back. That'd be a waste. You just make Me so *angry*, Nyxara."

Apollius turned, making His way back up the petal-lined aisle to the door. "We'll speak at nightfall," He said. "It might be somewhat more difficult to keep My hold, but I want to hear from My wife."

The door closed softly behind Him.

Chapter Thirty-Nine

What do they call a prison with particularly good food?

Marriage.

–Overheard in a Kirythean tavern

Lore slept at some point. Curled up on one of the pews, a pillow meant for penitent knees tucked beneath her head. It didn't do much as far as comfort went, but she was exhausted, and she was asleep almost as soon as her body went horizontal.

She'd expected a dream, once sleep finally came. But this one wasn't what she expected, not one of those that played out Nyxara's memories. At least, not in the same way. This dream was of magic, of twisting black and golden lines, of shadow and white light. The shadow expanded, expanded, and then the white light snapped back at the last possible moment. It reminded her of the docks, where she'd saved everyone, put their lives and their deaths back where they belonged, even if the alchemizing from Spiritum to Mortem had already begun.

It was strange, she thought in that between space that wasn't quite sleep, wasn't quite waking. She'd always thought true resurrection beyond the scope of her power. And it was, in a technical sense. The only reason she'd been able to bring those people back that day was because she'd stepped outside of time; the second when life changed to death stretched and expanded and made something she could grip. True death reverting back to true life.

Seemed like something she should remember.

When she woke, neck aching, Nyxara was in her mind again, a dark presence at the back of her thoughts. But it wasn't the easy carriage Lore had grown used to. This was a flare of white-hot pain, like her brain was trying to claw its way out of her skull, bonds stretched to breaking. She cried out, barely sound with her dry throat, clapped her hands over her ears as if that could do anything.

You have to kill Him. Nyxara's voice, grating, every word a fight. Straining against the bond Apollius had put on Her when They drank from the Fount.

But Lore was already shaking her head, as if the goddess could see, a negation of both the pain and Her order. "I won't. I can't."

The Buried Goddess didn't try to convince her. The pain snapped back as soon as it had come, as if She couldn't risk more.

Lore looked at the window. Golden sunlight still filtered through the stained-glass depiction of Apollius, His chest a hole, His bloody hands outstretched. She'd been just between them, when Apollius in Bastian's body had trapped her. Talk about metaphors.

But she didn't spend much time thinking about that, because she was too caught up in the fact that it was still light outside. Still light, though that light was falling fast, and yet Nyxara had spoken.

"You can talk in the day, now," Lore murmured.

Something like a sigh from the recesses of her mind. *You gave Me My first death.* She said it like it was a gift. *My essence in you is stronger, now.*

"Fat lot of good it does us."

Nyxara snorted. It was an extremely disconcerting thing to hear coming from inside your own head.

"Did I lie to Him?" Lore asked after a moment, her eyes still fixed on the window. "When I said You hated Him?"

A stretch of silence. *I don't know*, the Buried Goddess said.

Lore pulled her knees up and crossed her legs on the pew, dropping her head back to look at the high ceiling, the dark crossbeams, the diamond-dripping chandelier. "Godhood is a scam, if it can't even bring you certainty."

Another snort.

Slowly, the light faded down to dusk, deeper into dark. Lore didn't know how much time had passed before the door opened.

She whipped around, expecting Apollius, hoping that maybe Bastian would be a bit closer to the surface now that night had fallen. But it wasn't him.

It was Jax.

The Emperor of Kirythea was dressed unassumingly, in dark breeches and a crimson tunic, the collar embroidered with a pattern of golden laurel leaves. He had no sword or dagger, but a short spear was strapped to his back, and the sharp tip assured it would be just as effective. He stopped in front of Lore, his hands clasped behind him, his brow furrowed. He didn't speak.

There'd been a predatory ease to Jax before, when he was pretending to be a diplomat. A studied slickness, as if he was fashioning himself after other courtiers. That was gone, now. The true Jax was stolid and serious, a slight look of concern in even his neutral expression. It was attractive, or would be, if the sight of him didn't make Lore want to individually pull out his teeth.

Lore sighed. "Can I help you? Or did you just come to stare?"

"He told me you would be intractable," Jax murmured in perfect, unaccented Auverrani, as if he'd been practicing for his time in the Citadel. "Of all the vessels She'd attempted to take, He told me you would be the most difficult to deal with, and that was why it was imperative that you not be allowed to live beyond the ritual." A sigh. "If only that had happened. I think He learned to like that you're difficult, after you managed to survive."

"Who told you what I am?" But she knew.

"Apollius, of course." Jax gave her a look that said he doubted she was capable of tying her boots on her own. "You think your former Priest Exalted is the only person the Bleeding God has ever appeared to?"

It'd honestly never occurred to her that He would appear to anyone else, but there was no reason for her to think that. Everyone on the continent—the world, as far as she knew—worshipped Apollius, though some did it differently from others. It made sense that He would grant visions to many of His followers.

Especially the heirs of Empires that He wanted to claim.

Jax followed the trajectory of her thoughts across her face, sneered. "The Auverrani are so arrogant. Thinking that because He chose your country as the resting place of His wife, you are higher in His favor." His shoulders tensed, as if the hands clasped behind him had turned to fists. "Giving you Nyxara was a curse, not a blessing."

"You're telling me," Lore murmured.

But Jax clearly had many feelings on this subject, and wouldn't be deterred from airing them. "She was only meant to rise long enough to grant Apollius Her power, but His Arceneaux vessel had to go and fuck it up." He shook his head. "I offered myself. But I, who killed my father so I could take his Empire and make it the start of the Holy Kingdom, wasn't what He wanted. He chose Bastian Arceneaux, and would not be swayed."

"Probably because Bastian is better looking."

She meant it as a flippant barb, but Jax grinned. He'd stood still before her this whole time, but now he advanced a step, and she pressed her back into the pew. "You care for His vessel," Jax said quietly. "That is yet another complication. You've made Apollius care for you."

Ice pricked down Lore's spine. "He only cares about Nyxara. He doesn't give a shit about me."

"It'd be easier if that were true," Jax murmured. "But He's started to care for the both of you. And if He can't have one, He'll have the other."

The ice in her spine spread to her organs, slow-rising dread.

Lore swallowed. "So is that why you tried to blow up the ship with us on it? Apollius wasn't acting the way you wanted Him to?"

The Emperor looked horrified that she would even suggest such a thing. "That was not us. It was Amelia Demonde, as He said, trying to kill *you*."

"Bullshit. Amelia wouldn't have known a bomb from her ass, how in the myriad hells would she have been able to plant one on a heavily guarded ship?"

"She was Caeliar's avatar. The ship was in the ocean. She didn't need a bomb."

Her teeth snapped closed on another retort. If Amelia had known enough about her power to blow up a ship, she'd been aware that she was Caeliar's avatar for a while. She thought of August and his ideas about transubstantiation, substituting one vessel for another. Maybe Amelia thought that by killing Lore, she could take Nyxara's power, become the avatar of the Buried Goddess instead. Become the one other member of the pantheon that Apollius wanted to live.

Amelia crying in the garden, saying everything was fucked up. She'd been going through nearly the exact same thing Lore was. It made her chest ache to think of all the ways that maybe, in different circumstances, they could have helped each other.

"Fine." Lore shook her head. "So Amelia blew up the ships, but clearly you're here with some ulterior motive. Why did Apollius hide you from everyone?"

"An Emperor can't simply stroll into enemy territory," Jax scoffed. "Especially when there's some who might recognize him."

"Gabe," Lore murmured.

A gleam came to Jax's dark eyes. In the dim light of the sanctuary, illuminated only by a handful of sconces and the glowing braziers, he looked fiendish. "He seems to have done well for himself. As well as a traitor can, with one eye."

"He's not a completely insane religious fanatic who thinks the whole world should be under his rule, so yeah, he's doing better than you are."

"Not under my rule," Jax corrected, though he didn't touch the *religious fanatic* part. "I am only His priest, His right hand. Apollius is the one true god, the one true King." He sighed. "Apollius was able to push aside His vessel for nearly all of our planning. Arceneaux knew nothing of our true purpose, my true identity. But even without that knowledge, he was insistent that we be kept away from Gabriel."

Trying to protect him. Bastian hadn't known Caius was Jax, but he'd still wanted the Kirytheans far from Gabe, not wanting him hurt by the constant reminder of his father. The only time they'd been in the same room was that one First Day service, and Lore recalled the brief look of relief that had flickered on Bastian's face when Gabe left early.

"Was the plan always to marry Alie to you?" Lore asked. "Has Bastian always known she was his half sister?"

Bastian's name made Jax's lip curl, but he nodded. "He's always suspected, yes, but never planned to make the information public. Not unless Alie wanted him to, once she found out. But Apollius thought it could be useful."

Apollius, who moved humans around like pawns on a board.

"If you hurt her..." Lore didn't know how to finish the threat. Saying she would kill him felt too tame.

But Jax looked nearly as horrified as he had at the accusation that he'd blown up the ship. "I would never hurt my wife."

She could still feel the ache in her scalp from where Apollius had pulled her hair, a twinge in her neck from Him bending it to the side. If Jax refused to hurt Alie, it put him on a higher road than his god.

Her head lolled back again, her eyes finding the shadowed ceiling, weariness suddenly weighing out all her care. "Why are you here, Jax? I don't think Apollius will want company on our wedding night."

"I'm merely here to support," he answered.

Lore's eyes narrowed at the ceiling. That must mean Apollius thought He needed support...because Bastian had broken through, earlier, had fought free of the god's hold for just a moment.

Her hands drew to fists on her lap. Hope was such a small thing, just a flutter beneath her breastbone, but it was there and she would take it.

In her head, Nyxara was silent and still.

Jax's eyes flickered to the back of the room, where the door was slowly beginning to creak open. "In fact, here comes your husband now."

Lore whipped around.

Apollius, still. The dim light hid the details of His face, but the way He moved was nothing like Bastian: all angular and precise, none of Bastian's casual nonchalance.

Jax bowed as Apollius drew closer; the god waved His hand. There was something in that movement that caught Lore's eye, shifting that tiny flutter of hope into a spark.

A tremble in His fingers.

"Holy One," Jax said, looking slightly concerned, "are You sure it must be tonight? If he's causing problems—"

"Shut up, Jax."

And Jax did. It was almost funny, seeing the feared leader of the Kirythean Empire so subservient. Looking so worried.

The spark became an ember.

Apollius turned to Lore. And yes, there, even in the flickering light, she could see the war playing out on His face. Bastian, shoved deep inside his own mind, fighting his way to the surface. Giving it everything he had to come back to her.

Nyxara had said to kill him. She'd balked against bonds and incredible pain to do it, to bring Lore that instruction. But as long as there was even a little bit of Bastian left, she couldn't. She couldn't.

It took the god a moment to speak, like He had to center Himself first. He closed Bastian's eyes, opened them again. "Nyxara. It's time that we talked."

Chapter Forty

We have learned that death is not a concrete thing, but something that can be manipulated.

—Notes from Hakim Belcar, Malfouran naturalist, 3 AGF

Lore considered telling Him that Nyxara wasn't here, that She was taking a rest, that She had no interest in talking to Him. But the goddess was stirring at the back of her mind, a churn of darkness cut with moonlight, and Lore knew She wouldn't stand for that. It'd been centuries since They had actually spoken to each other, as face-to-face as They could get, and it was long past due.

Please, Nyxara said in Lore's head. *Let me.*

And Lore knew what she was asking. And she let it happen.

Like before, when she'd allowed the goddess to come forward to read the ancient script at the bottom of Anton's prophecy, it almost felt like a relief. Like fishing a stone out of your shoe that you hadn't even known was there, like soothing a muscle that had ached for so long you almost forgot about it. Lore was still present in her mind, still able to hear and see, but everything had the odd resonance of a voice heard underwater, and everything looked like comet-trails, like streaked ink.

But when He touched Her cheek, Lore felt it.

Nyxara in Lore's body stiffened at the feeling of His palm, scarred with an eclipse. His touches could go from gentle to gouging so quickly.

"My love," He murmured in Bastian's voice. "I've missed you so much."

You have a funny way of showing it, Lore said. But it was all in thoughts and feelings, and didn't come out of her mouth, not while Nyxara had control.

The goddess said nothing, just heaved a shaky sigh.

Apollius stepped closer, His other hand cradling Nyxara's neck, the same neck He'd so brutally twisted just hours before. "I know You still love Me," He murmured. "You wouldn't have done it if You didn't."

Done what? Lore asked.

Another shaking sigh, Her answer coming in mind rather than voice. *My memories. I didn't get far enough before the tomb collapsed. I can't speak of them, I could only show them, and there is more you must know...*

The goddess trailed off as Apollius's finger traced Her lips—Lore's lips—His eyes fluttering closed, His breath deepening. Lore wanted to shout, wanted to rail at Nyxara that She had to find a way to show Lore the rest of the memories, but it would be pointless. Nyxara was caught in Apollius's thrall, again. Just like She had been on that island no one should've ever found, eons and eons ago. Just a girl who loved someone and was naively surprised to find that love returned, even if darkened, even if hurting.

His forehead tilted against Hers—Bastian's against Lore's—and He breathed in deep, like He could draw Her into His lungs, trap Her there. "And because You still love Me," He said, His hands tightening to a bruising grip, "I'm going to give You one more chance."

If Lore had been in control of her lungs, she would've gasped against the sudden pain. But she wasn't in charge, and Nyxara just gritted Her teeth, as if She was used to this.

"Be the Sainted Queen," Apollius murmured. His voice was still so soft, even as His fingers dug in painfully. "Be Mine, forever, like You promised." He lifted Her hand, the one He'd crushed, and kissed it. Soothing the hurt He caused. "This world was made to serve Us."

"But it wasn't," She breathed, contradicting Him even as She leaned in closer, all the things She loved and hated wrapped up in one being. "It was here before Us. The world, the Fount. They don't serve Us."

"They do." Tightening, again, and She bit Her lip. "I will make them."

"You will pull at the earth's foundations and rip them apart." Nyxara dropped Her eyes, looking at Her hand. At the ring She'd been given, so long ago, the one Apollius had somehow found again and put on this mortal finger. The human She was trapped inside, who loved the human Apollius had taken over. Too much, too much. "You will unravel the very thing You are supposed to rule in search of an eternity You cannot touch."

"I can touch it. We can. With You by my side, Our power held together, Us and *only* Us. Death cannot touch Us when We become something beyond it."

"I know death," Nyxara said. "It cannot be conquered. Only delayed. And I've helped You do that, Apollius. More than I should."

They stood locked together, a posture that could've been passion or pain. It was both. "Give me Your answer," Apollius said finally. "Say it plain. Will You stand with Me, beloved? Or make Me an enemy?"

Lore wanted to scream, locked inside her own head, but all she could do was shout into the darkness. *He doesn't love You, Nyxara! He wants to own You! It's not the same thing!*

I know, Nyxara sighed into her mind. *But they can live together, sometimes.*

With Lore's mouth, She gave Her answer. "No, Apollius," She whispered. "I won't."

Even with the strange, muddled vision that being a passenger in her own head gave her, Lore could still see the sneer cross Apollius's face. "Well, then," He said. "What use are You to Me?"

His hand reared back, and curse Her, but Nyxara faded away, unable to face a blow from a god, leaving Lore in control again, screaming forward to take over as Apollius's hand arced down—

The god snapped sideways just as His hand was about to crack against Lore's face, the blow falling against a wooden pew instead of flesh with an audible crunch of bone. Apollius growled, low in His throat. Jax started forward, but the god threw out His other hand, halting him.

"You'll pay for that, boy," Apollius gritted out. But it was faint, even as His hand began to heal, the bones righting themselves and snapping back into place. He looked up, dark hair falling back from His face.

And the face was Bastian, Bastian looking out of his own eyes.

"Lore." All he could get out was her name. "Lore, I—"

Gone again. Apollius, shaking out his now-healed hand, trailing gold in the dark sanctuary air. "I should've expected that answer," He said, stepping toward Lore again. She tried to back away; her knees hit the pew, making her sit down heavily on the hard wood. "But I wanted to give Her one last chance, you see. For old times' sake." The same hand that had made to slap her caressed her cheek, now, almost unbearably warm. "She really did love Me. Like I said. She might've hated Me, but She loved Me, too."

"What did She do?" Lore asked. "When You said She wouldn't have done it if She didn't love You, what was *it*?"

But Apollius wasn't interested in Nyxara's memories, in old history. There was a light of determination in His eyes, a god on a mission. "Here's what's going to happen, Lore," he said, relishing her name on His tongue. "It's quite simple, really. Pretty much what should've happened the night of the eclipse, with one very important exception. You are going to give me Nyxara's power. Then you are going to be my Queen." He smiled, and it looked like Bastian's, the one he'd give her when he was particularly pleased with himself. "You get to live. Isn't that what you damned the whole world for?"

It was the only thing she'd wanted, the refrain that had run through her head constantly the night of the ritual. Her life, her own, paltry and ragged thing though it was.

Don't let him make His own selfishness someone else's burden to bear.

Lore didn't know if the words were a memory, or Nyxara murmuring them again into her head.

"I didn't damn the world," Lore said. "That was all You."

"I'm sure you wish that were true." Apollius still grinned, but there was a flicker in His eyes. Not fear, but wariness. "I would've had the others' powers if Nyxara hadn't risen in you. But when you chose to live, the others followed. You caused the elemental magics to go out from the Fount again, to tip the balance of the world."

"None of that is my doing." Lore stood from the pew, glaring up at Him. "You chose this path, because You're terrified of dying. Terrified of facing the hell You've undoubtedly made for Yourself. Because that's what this is about, right? If the Shining Realm exists, You can't go there."

It still wasn't quite fear in His eyes, but it was closer. Like she'd brushed up to a truth, but not landed on it fully.

"You've made Your own choices, Apollius," Lore said. "But You could never live alone with them. Not then, and not now."

She thought He might try to strike her again, saw the twitch of His hand. But it stayed by His side. Bastian, in there, fighting.

You have to kill Him, Lore. More pain in her head, but it felt secondary, now, faced with a terrible and furious god and the ultimatum He was giving her. *You have to, you have to begin the end.*

But Bastian.

"Living is preferable to dying, alone or not." Apollius tipped a finger beneath her chin. "I'm sure you'd agree. And this is the choice you have, though it's not much of one: Give Me Nyxara's power, and live. Or die, and I'll take it anyway." He touched her lips, feather-soft. "She knows how to give it to Me."

Lore was frozen, there on his fingertip, desperately looking for a solution, for a way out of this that didn't lead to death for one or both of them. She didn't think she could kill Apollius, even if she made herself forget about Bastian locked inside—Jax was right here, spear in hand. If she tried to channel death, the god could just sever the threads; His aura shone so bright with Spiritum that Lore could nearly see it, even without trying.

Apollius caressed her hair, twisting one brown-gold strand around His finger. His thumb brushed along her jawline, and He looked in her eyes.

And He let Bastian come forward, just a little.

The god was still in control, at least of the body. Every one of Bastian's muscles was held tight and tense, nearly vibrating with the effort of keeping still. But the eyes were all him, all her Bastian, and they were terrified.

"Lore." Their voices came from the same throat, but his sounded so different from Apollius's, raw and hoarse as if he'd been screaming. "You have to do it."

A flicker of a self-satisfied smile across the mouth that Apollius still controlled, so incongruous with those terror-stricken eyes. Sure that Bastian was telling Lore she had to take the deal, she had to give up Nyxara's power and live at Apollius's side.

But Lore didn't think that was what Bastian meant.

"You have to," he said again, words that didn't match the pleased curve of his mouth, an awful composite of god and man. "For me."

For him. The real him, trapped in his own body, watching a god wear it to do awful things. To bring down war on all who would oppose Him, to tear the world apart.

Lore closed her eyes. When she opened them, Bastian was gone, Apollius fully in his place.

There was no way to know if he was gone for good. Maybe he could keep fighting his way to the surface, over and over, snatches of moments when he was in control. But what kind of life was that? Was it enough of one, if she loved him?

She held life and death in her hands, braided them together, wove them into tapestries of her will. There had to be a way to have both, to thread the strands through the same needle. She thought of the docks, of that dream on the pew. The moment when life and death were one and the same, both real and both present, a forked road where either turn could be taken.

In her head, Nyxara was silent, silent.

"I'll do it," she murmured, and it was an answer to all of them at once.

He'd said Nyxara would know how to give Her power back, and Lore's acquiescence gave Her enough control to do it. Something flooded Lore's mouth. Water, seeping from her pores to coat her tongue, her teeth. It was cool, tasted sweet, reminded her somehow of a pool at night, still and quiet and reflecting the moon.

Nyxara's drink of the Fount. Lore had said she would give it up, and she was Nyxara, now, in every way that mattered. She looked down at her hands.

Slowly, the skin of her fingers turned to stone, creeping down to her gray palms, beneath the gold-and-silver band of her engagement ring. So this was what happened to the others. They renounced Their power, *really* renounced it, denied every part of Themselves that had ever secretly thrilled to plucking the strings of the world. Their swallow of the Fount had poured out of Them, and taken their human pieces with it.

Mortem crept in. Lore felt it all around her, in the rocks and wood and glass of the North Sanctuary and the larger Church it was part of, the walls it made around the Citadel, keeping nobles and commoners forever separate. Those blessed and those cursed. The holy and the damned.

It stretched for her stone fingers, those strands of death. It curled around them like a lover. And the death within her rose to meet it, her life slowly alchemizing, light to dark and dead.

"Quickly." Apollius cradled her head, acted like she was something so precious, now. A replacement for the goddess who'd spurned Him. Something new to own. "Give it to Me, Lore. Then I'll have all of it, not just the dregs that make it back to the broken Fount. I'll stop the stone and make your living flesh undying."

She knew how to give power up. It felt like all she knew.

Lore didn't fight when His lips came down on hers, let Him hold her as if there could ever be anything between them. Because there was something between her and the body He'd taken, between her and the man she knew was still in there, somewhere.

Lore kept the swallow of the Fount in her mouth, didn't let Him drink it out, not yet. She expected His frustration when she pulled back, water still pooling in the bottom of her jaw as stone crept up her wrists. It should choke her, that water, but it didn't, as if her whole body had become a chalice just for its use.

But Apollius just looked down at her with something like awe. It took Him off guard enough for Bastian to surge forward, just a bit, his eyes tired and resigned and with that same tiny ember of hope.

She'd been able to channel Mortem before Nyxara was in her head. The eclipse ritual had given her the ability to channel Spiritum. Surely she could hold on to those, even if she managed to get rid of Nyxara? Just for a moment. Just long enough for this to work, just long enough to linger in death's antechamber.

"I love you," Lore said around all that sweet, crystalline water. "This is us. This is mine."

And Lore swallowed.

At the same time, she yanked on the threads of Mortem she'd gathered in her hand.

The Church crumbled around them.

Every stone in the Church flew apart, those heavy beams falling from the ceiling, the diamond chandelier breaking with an oddly beautiful tinkling sound. Jax bellowed from where he'd been waiting, pelting for the doors, getting out right before a beam fell in front of the entrance and blocked the way. Another beam fell between Lore and Apollius, knocking them in opposite directions.

Flying shrapnel struck Lore in the temple, and her world went black, but she didn't lose consciousness. She'd learned how to hold on to it in an iron-knuckled grip, and Nyxara's power, the drink of the Fount that Lore had briefly given up before taking it back again, made it easy to do what she had the day of the explosion on the docks.

Sidestep out of time. Drop into that place where life and death were stars she could watch burn out.

Or relight.

But she had to wait. Wait until both of their sparks were almost extinguished, until almost all the gleaming white light of Spiritum had evanesced into the black cloud of Mortem. Until a second death she could bring them back from—both herself, and Bastian, while hopefully leaving Nyxara and Apollius behind.

If she could time it right. If she could kill them both long enough for the sparks of the gods to blink out, then bring them back as only themselves. If she could hold on to power that tightly.

She could see him. Bastian, Apollius. One body, outlined in so much light it was hard to look at, even like this. Starbursts streaked from him, a comet, life leaving and death taking over. Apollius was able to heal Himself, but this much onslaught at once was too much for Him to handle, too many places for death to creep into the mortal body He'd taken. He tried, she could see it, strands of Spiritum reeled back into the whole, but there was always another one arcing out, always another fatal wound.

Her own change from Spiritum to Mortem was happening much more quickly. Vaguely, she felt the fall and crush of rock, hitting her body, beating out life piece by sharp-edged piece. But it was distant; there was no pain, not here. The shore of time, soft and liquid-like. The place before eternity.

This was what Nyxara wanted. What Bastian wanted. A death, Her second, Apollius's second, Bastian's only. But Lore held life and death both, Lore could thread that needle. Could free Nyxara and Apollius from their second, bodiless lives, and knit both her body and Bastian's back together around the space the gods left.

She had to believe she could do it.

But she had to be careful. Had to stay *here*, in the moment when one thing became another, had to ignore the currents tugging at her and willing her to move on.

Her light faded, faded. Became a flickering thing, a candle wick in the seconds after being blown out, bright threads of Spiritum stretching far-flung into the darkness. And Bastian's was close, too, both of them barely hanging on, death a creeping spiderweb growing ever closer.

And then here was the moment. The split second when lives blinked into death, when a body was both. Lore paused it, there on the shore, this last heartbeat when her head emptied of everything but herself, but she could still hold the dregs of her power. She was dead, and so was Bastian, and the gods had no life to cling to.

Nyxara was gone. There was a blankness at the back of Lore's thoughts, as if She'd made a burrow in her mind that would always be empty. But there was no trace of the goddess. She had faded away. Dead and gone, surely, finally.

I hope... but Lore didn't know how to finish that. She didn't know what she hoped for the Buried Goddess, whose two lives had each been cruel. Maybe the hope itself was enough.

If Nyxara was gone, surely Apollius was, too. They'd died, she and Bastian, anyone who looked at them now would say so. It's what Nyxara wanted her to do, to kill Bastian and thus kill Apollius, so it had to work for Lore, too, right?

It was hard to hold on, now, both to the magic and to herself. The currents had her, they wanted to pull her away, and even though her whole life had been defined by a reckless determination to keep living it, Lore almost wanted to let them. See where they would take her, what this atrium would open into. She could feel it gaping next to her, an open maw of dark, of things no one could understand until they fully crossed the threshold. Eternity, waiting, just like she'd felt on the docks.

She wondered if this was what other people saw when they gained the ability to channel Mortem. She wondered so many things, and maybe there were answers she could find, if she let this moment go. If she relinquished these threads, chose the path at this crossroads that led to restful dark.

But she couldn't leave Bastian and Gabriel. The two halves of her heart needed her here.

It took monumental effort for Lore to reach out, to grasp the thin, straggling strands of Spiritum still clinging to her body and Bastian's, the exploding stars of themselves. She grasped them, twisted. Channeled it through her, in this last frozen second when she could, and sent it toward Bastian.

Spiritum coalesced back into Bastian's still form. Dim, but there, and no longer leaking out. He was alive. Alive and alone, dead for just a moment, just enough to banish Apollius.

Now for her.

It was harder to grasp your own life in your hands than someone else's. Lore grabbed at the trailing threads of Spiritum as she stepped back into reality, off time's shore, winding them around weak hands, letting them breach her skin again. She felt herself heal, Mortem receding, but gods, it was worse. The dark and the currents and the gaping star-hollow that was the gate to everything after drained away, leaving her in dust and unimaginable, crushing pain.

Lore expected the awareness of Mortem and Spiritum to fade. She'd killed herself, killed Bastian, and banished the gods; shouldn't They take Their power with Them? But she could still sense the threads, could reach out and touch them if she wanted.

She heard a groan from Bastian's vague direction, and didn't have the presence of mind to stop herself from weeping, loudly, nothing like dignity left. Because he was alive. He was free.

Right?

The clatter of footfalls outside, shouting. "The King and Queen are in there! We have to go see if they survived!"

"Of course they did." Jax's voice, imperious. "The Sainted King is blessed by Apollius Himself."

Blessed might be a stretch.

Lore's eyes flew wide open. But she'd done it, four deaths in two bodies—

No. Sorrowful. *Death cannot be cheated, Lore. Not with us. It only counts if it lasts.*

Lore's sob turned into a scream, loud and long and rage-filled, choking on dust and debris. Outside, someone shouted that they heard her, that it must mean they were alive, but Lore wasn't paying attention. She screamed until everything went dark.

Epilogue

Gabe

He woke to waves.

Not surprising. They'd been on the damn ship for what felt like weeks, though surely that couldn't be right. Gabe had never sailed before—his life before the Presque Mort hadn't required it and his life after hadn't had time—and he found that keeping track of things like how many days had passed wasn't an easy thing to do when all you had was sea and sky. He'd tried counting the times he slept, at first, but since there was nothing else to fucking *do*, he found himself sleeping far more often than night fell.

Perhaps it was unfair to say there was nothing to do. There was plenty to do, really, but he didn't know how to do any of it. Val, Mari, and Michal seemed to be holding things down just fine, since the galley was so small. Michal was often distracted by Malcolm, the two of them sitting close by the railing and murmuring together over things that Gabe never overheard, but he pulled the ropes when the ropes needed pulling and hoisted the things that needed hoisting. Val steered, her pale-green eyes narrowed at the horizon like it had personally wronged her, and Mari kept up with whatever else a ship needed to keep skipping over the water. Gabe helped, when she let him. It wasn't terribly often. Everyone wanted to keep to themselves.

Gabe both did and didn't. When he kept to himself, with nothing to distract him, all he could do was think about the people he'd left behind.

Alie. Lore. Bastian.

Alie, screaming as she was hauled away. Lore, bleeding out again, an awful echo of that awful night two months ago, and once again he could do nothing, nothing. Bastian, who he hated and loved in equal measure, who was being taken over completely by the god Gabe had been taught to worship. That was what he'd been thinking about, in that moment, when Lore was bleeding and Alie was screaming and bloodcoats were pouring from the alleyways. That at least he could see them. He could say goodbye. And he'd never have that chance with Bastian. Never have the chance to tell him about all the conflicting feelings he had, never have a chance to touch his face with tenderness instead of anger.

Then there was fire. It'd come on him like a wave, quicker and more powerfully than Mortem ever had, because this was his. It belonged to him and the god in his head, the one that blessedly didn't speak to him like Apollius did to Bastian, or Nyxara to Lore. The one who was just an alien ember in the back of his mind, telling him to burn.

So that's what he did. He stretched out his hands, and he burned.

But they'd gotten Alie and Lore anyway.

Gabe stood, planting his forearms on the rail of the galley, the wind ruffling his hair. It needed a trim, and he looked up as he pushed it back.

Then he squinted.

Land.

"I think…" He trailed off, his voice too quiet in the sough of waves, tried again louder. "Is that Caldien?"

Malcolm looked up. A weary smile broke over his face. "Should be."

"It is." Words from Val were rare, and the sound of her voice made them all turn her direction. The old poison runner didn't look at any of them, her eyes trained on the horizon. "We'll be there by tomorrow. Then it's another three days' ride inland to Farramark, if that's where your friends are."

"Friends might be an overstatement," Malcolm murmured. "Colleagues, more like it."

"As long as they have somewhere for us to sleep while we plan." Gabe glared at the oncoming coast. "If Apollius wants a war, we'll fucking bring Him one."

Lore

She woke to waves.

Waves, and an unholy stink, like dozens of unwashed bodies all pressed together. When her eyes opened, the sky above was clear, deep indigo scattered with stars that faded near the glow of the full moon.

Gods, her head ached.

Slowly, Lore sat up.

It stank like dozens of unwashed bodies because she was, in fact, packed in with dozens of unwashed bodies. They crowded the floor of wherever she'd found herself, all asleep, shifting and snoring and a whole host of other unpleasant bodily functions happening beneath the glow of the moon, right up to a splintered, salt-stained wooden railing.

Beyond that, ocean.

"The Queen finally graces us with her conscious presence."

She turned too quickly, creaking her aching neck. "Fuck," Lore muttered, clapping her scarred hand to the muscle.

"Very queenly indeed." The speaker crouched behind her, a man with eyes that had gone mostly cataract and teeth that had gone mostly rotten. His breath was no improvement on the stink. "Wed and then wasted," he said, shaking his head. "Ol' Sainted Arse only kept ya long enough to make sure you were still alive after that collapse, then he sent you on your merry way. Hell of a thing." His hand rose, caught a strand of her hair. "Bet you'll be popular, once we reach the Isles. Bet you'll find yourself a whole new court—"

Lore was long past being frightened by how easily she could call Mortem, now. It flowed to her easily as water downhill, black threads arcing out from the dead wood of the ship, the tattered cloth of the man's shirt. She channeled it quickly through herself as she reached out her hand.

Delicately, she wove just enough Mortem around his unwelcome fingers to turn the tips of them to stone.

With a garbled sound, the man sat back, staring at what she'd done. "They were right, then," he said, tucking his hand close. "You're a deathwitch. I'd heard the rumors, even in the Isles, but I didn't actually believe it."

"It's true." Lore pushed herself up from the hard deck. "And when I'm sure you'll remember, I might even fix those fingers for you."

Wincing, she lurched over to the railing, leaning over to try to catch a breath of fresh air. Her deep gasps ran the risk of becoming something panicked, but she forced herself to calm, gulping in salt spray, letting it lash against her face.

A prison ship. Headed to the Burnt Isles.

And Bastian had sent her here.

For a moment, she wondered if maybe that part wasn't true. Maybe Jax had given the order, only pretending it was from Bastian. But that wouldn't make things better; that would mean Bastian was still unconscious.

Or still inhabited by Apollius.

Her last few moments of lucidity after she pulled down the Church filtered back into her mind. The familiar voice in her head.

Slowly, Lore turned over her palm.

Still gray as a corpse.

And something else, less important, but still making her stomach sink. Her ring was gone. Apollius must have taken it back before putting her on the prison ship.

"I do not want this," she hissed because it felt necessary to let the world know it. "I do not want Mortem. I do not want to be an avatar of Nyxara. I never did."

The waves lapped against the side of the ship. The sky listened.

She closed her eyes. Probed at that place in the back of her head, the place she'd thought was empty. *You're still here, aren't You?*

A pause, reluctant. *Yes.*

"Fuck." This time, Lore said it loudly enough that a few of her fellow prisoners stirred around her feet. "Fuck!"

The mad hemlock Queen, talking to herself in the moonlight.

You're going to the Burnt Isles, close to the Fount. Nyxara sounded weary. *You will still feed His power, there. Near to its source.*

Lore pushed her teeth painfully together, keeping the rest of the conversation silent. *What did I do wrong? You told me to kill Him, and I killed us both!*

You died, yes. Technically. But you never crossed the threshold. You took it back. Death does not accept half measures, Lore. A sigh deep in her head. *He still has two deaths, and must feel them both.*

Lore's fingers tightened on the railing, the old wood creaking beneath the force of her grip. *What do you mean, He still has two deaths?*

Silence, long enough for her to know the answer even though Nyxara's vows meant She couldn't say it outright. They were of a kind, Lore and the Buried Goddess. Both trying to find loopholes. Both grasping at half measures.

Lore stared forward as the prow of the prison ship pushed through dark water. As the fog and ash of the Burnt Isles closed around the deck, surrounding her in the scent of smoke.

"You did the same thing," she whispered, speaking aloud rather than just in her mind. "You tried to save him. His body is still here, somewhere. Still living."

Nothing from the goddess in her head but a long, shuddering sigh.

Bastian

He woke to waves.

Being trapped in his own body while Apollius took it over was like slowly drowning in a golden ocean. Occasionally, he would surface, sometimes even enough to briefly take control, to speak with his own mouth, move his own limbs. Usually, it was only enough to see out of his eyes, to see exactly what the god was doing while he wore Bastian like a costume.

He could do without that, really.

So he saw that Lore was alive. Saw her wounds mended, though there would be a scar on her temple like a sunburst where something had hit her; it only made her beauty fiercer, belied her softness. Lore wasn't soft, but she looked it, all gentle and curved. He loved that.

But he also saw his own hand sign the order that sent her to the Burnt Isles. He railed, screamed, clawed for the surface, but control kept slipping out of his grasp.

It grew more slippery all the time.

Quiet, boy. Apollius's voice wasn't really a voice, not here—it was a vibration in the golden current, reverberating in every pocket of space. *You're done.*

And he would be, if he didn't have them to think about. Lore, who he'd do anything for, even though she'd never quite need him like he needed her. And Gabe, who he'd done his best to shield from the god in his head, who'd been caught in the crossfire anyway. Two people he loved, two people he could so easily doom.

The golden current closed over him again.

Below

The bloom was withered. It lay in the dark, petals bedraggled, the red color nearly drained away. Not that it could be seen in the dark, anyway. Not by anyone who didn't have eyes grown used to dimness.

She stared at the flower, lips pressed together. She'd left this place, unable to face what she'd done, who she'd been. But something had drawn her back, the knowledge that she was needed. She was asked for.

She picked up the rose her daughter had thrown down the well.

Then she began to plan.

ACKNOWLEDGMENTS

Middle books in trilogies are weird. This one tried to kill me at least five times. Thanks to my agent, Whitney Ross, for staving it off the first time, and to my editor, Brit Hvide, for saving me the other four. My books wouldn't exist without your help and insight, and I'm forever grateful.

Thanks as always to the entire Orbit team, particularly Ellen Wright—the books don't do the thing without you.

To the Pod, you're my safe place.

To Sarah, Ashley, Chels, Stephanie, Jensie, Elizabeth, Nicole, and Leah—I love you all endlessly.

And to Caleb and our kids—you're my people, and I love you more than words can say.

Lastly, to the readers. I can never thank you enough for championing my work, for reaching out and telling me what it means to you, and for allowing me to do this job. You're the reason any of this happens. I can't wait to keep making stories for you.